Also by JJ Spain

Three Days in Daytona

It Started in Laughlin

LAST NIGHT IN STURGIS

A MIKE SALAS NOVEL

LAST NIGHT IN STURGIS

A MIKE SALAS NOVEL

J J SPAIN

HMS PRESS

HMS Press
PO Box 2
Valentine, NE 69201

MikeSalasNovels.com
1-402-322-9197
jeffreyaspain@gmail.com

Printed in the USA

Ordering Information:
Quantity sales. Special discounts are available on quantity purchases by corporations, associations, and others. For details, contact the publisher at the address above.

Library of Congress Control Number: 2022923355
ISBN-13:   979-8-9872733-0-2   [Paperback Edition]
               979-8-9872733-3-3   [Digital Edition]

Disclaimer:

This is a work of fiction. Names, characters, businesses, places, events and incidents are either the products of the author's imagination or used in a fictitious manner. Any resemblance to actual persons, living or dead, or actual events is purely coincidental.

I have tried to recreate events and locales from my memories of them. In order to maintain their anonymity, in some instances I have changed the names of individuals and places, I may have changed some identifying characteristics and details such as physical properties, occupations and places of residence.

SALAS

They met at Walgreens off Creighton Avenue, the one a mile east of the Fort Wayne Police Department.

Salas noticed her when she walked in through the sliding glass doors. Everyone noticed her. She wasn't loud like making a lot of noise—but very loud physically. Blond, bouffant hair, eighties-style wavy bangs swept back on her forehead. Lavish lips, red lip smackers. Of course, the attention-getters were her boobs: two cymbals in the high-school band, large, no bra, stuffed into a Jerry Garcia T-shirt. Salas was sure the shirt was a large, but it fit like a small. Ten pounds of sugar in a five-pound sack. Short shorts, muscular quads, maybe a high-school volleyball player in the day, black stiletto heels. Fortyish, thought Salas, old enough to know better, young enough to keep trying. Lose twenty pounds, and she could be a model. If Salas lost twenty pounds, well... he would still be Salas.

Salas forgot why he was in the store. Deodorant? Razor? Now it didn't matter.

He tucked his white V-neck T-shirt into his Wranglers, followed her to aisle eight—bath products, hair gels, creams, shampoo, conditioner—and inched along in her direction. At the last section, before the vitamins, she stopped and grabbed a small bottle. Salas looked over her shoulder; reading the highlighted words, "Warming Gel." (Yes! Someone was watching over him!)

"Looks fun," Salas said with a smile, revealing pearly-white caps.

She looked at Salas, first, directly into his eyes, then trailing up and down slowly, from boots to bald head. She liked bald guys. Her eyes met his. "One would hope," she said. She was also smiling.

"Any way I can be of service, miss, please let me know. We at CVS aim to please," Salas said, returning the body inspection but focusing on her eyes. It was more difficult than he'd thought.

"We're at Walgreens, sweetie," Blondie said, her tongue stretched out. She gave a slow lick of her lips. Salas's knees buckled.

"My apologies miss. You have me a bit distracted. I'm a big Grateful Dead fan." Salas reached out and moved a few strands of hair from her cheek to behind her ear.

"I'm Angelina." She held out her hand as if to shake.

Salas took her outstretched hand, turned it, bent slowly, and lightly kissed the back of her wrist. He stood up again, made deep eye contact, and said, "I'm Brad. Nice to meet you, Angelina."

Angelina smiled. "Brad and Angelina! How perfect."

Twenty minutes later, they were in the Fort Wayne Super 8. Twenty-two minutes later, he was out of his boots and jeans, wearing only the white T-shirt. Two hours later, he was back at work. Forty-eight hours later, they were at the Fort Wayne Motel 6. Sex, rest, repeat.

This pattern continued over the next few weeks. Three times per week, two hours per trip, times four weeks equaled twenty-four hours of pure sex. No talking, just down to business, and she still thought his name was Brad.

Today they broke their motel routine, and thank goodness, thought Salas. At nearly $250 a week for hotel rooms, the sex was breaking him. He could have taken Angelina to his place, but it was a shithole, and he knew this relationship, if that's what this was, would flame out soon. She didn't know his real name, so why let her know where he lived?

She had texted "Brad" at eleven-thirty: "My place at 1:00! 440 Industrial, 2nd floor."

Salas arrived at twelve forty-five to scout out the area, a little advance reconnaissance.

He parked a block south, in front of an Ace Hardware—no sense in letting her know the make and model of his car.

The neighborhood was primarily commercial. Parts and supply stores, a Lowe's, a cement plant, an HVAC, a manufacturer of engine parts, and a welding shop that fixed trailers.

Salas walked the block north and found the building marked "440 Industrial." It was a standard commercial-grade-looking building. The exterior featured grayish metal siding, a double-door entryway into Dan

Davis General Contracting, and no windows in the front. The sign on the door said, CLOSED.

Walking to the north side, he turned the corner on 5th and found an entry door with steps leading upstairs. The door was unlocked. He climbed the seventeen steps to the second floor; he had a habit of counting steps. The stairway was barren: no handrail, no windows. A single light bulb hung from the ceiling next to the door at the top of the steps. He knocked lightly, the door sneaking open with each rap. Salas stepped in.

"I'm in the kitchen!" Angelina called out.

The apartment was clean: no clutter, no clothes or empty beer cans on the furniture. Hardwood floors, a small living room showcasing a Pheasants Forever print above the leather couch: two pheasants taking flight in corn stubble, a yellow lab on their tails.

Salas walked into the next room, a small kitchen with a wooden table, and there she was. Like the Indiana August weather, it was hot and so was she. He couldn't wait to unleash her bosom and enjoy. Like the previous twelve times, talking wasn't on the table, but soon Angelina was. Salas hoped the solid oak table really was solid oak.

Angelina wasted no time either. Salas had a barrel chest and massive arms. She pulled his T-shirt over his head. Salas, in his early fifties, could stand to lose some weight, hit the gym more, slow down on the drinking, maybe eat a salad every once in a while, but now wasn't the time for self-reflection.

As much as he loved Angelina's bosom, she loved his arms. A former college light-heavyweight wrestler at Nebraska, Salas was still built like one, cauliflower ear and all.

Down to his gray Fruit of the Loom boxer briefs and sporting a major erection, Salas stood to drop his final piece of clothing. Angelina was bare chested, her skirt pulled up and thong panties lying on the floor. They froze when someone yelled up the steps, "Ange, you home?"

"You have a boyfriend?" Salas whispered.

"Husband."

"Shit, please don't tell me it's Dan Davis Construction," Salas said a little louder.

"Shhh, yes, that's our business!" Angelina rushed to get her shirt.

"Are you shitting me? You brought me to work?" Salas was looking for his pants, his shirt, his boots, his boonie hat. The guy coming up the stairs was on number fifteen if he had the count correct.

"He was supposed to be across town!" Angelina was putting her shirt on.

Dan Davis walked in, baseball hat turned backward, a pencil behind his ear, the eraser facing Salas. Salas had his clothes in his hand, his erection facing the man.

"Ange, what the hell? Who is this son-of-a-bitch? What the hell? Angelina?" Dan Davis stammered.

"Honey, it isn't what it looks like," Angelina said in her defense.

"Sir, I had no idea she was married. I sincerely apologize. I'll just get my stuff and let you two talk it out," Salas said softly, clutching his clothes, his manhood standing at attention.

"You stay right the fuck there!" Dan Davis pointed at Salas. "I'm gonna knock the shit out of you. I'll fuck you up for the rest of your Godforsaken life!" Davis, standing taller than Salas and quite a bit heavier, had Salas's attention.

"I understand, sir, but there's no reason to fight. We didn't do anything. It's my bad. I said I'm sorry. I'll just be leaving now." Salas was quickly trying to exit stage right.

"You ain't goin' nowhere till I'm done with you, you asshole!" Dan Davis screamed as he started across the kitchen floor.

"I don't want to fight you. I just want to leave. Now let me be." Salas was very calm, considering.

"Fuck that! I'm going to kick your ass!" Dan Davis yelled, charging Salas, his arms straight out, like he was going for a standing chokehold.

Salas crossed his right arm over, bent his knees to lower himself—keeping his back straight—and neatly ducked under the outstretched arms of Dan Davis. Wrestling 101, the duck under. Salas kept close to Davis and put him in a bear hug. Wrestling 201, the bear hug. Salas's chest was to Davis's back, with both of Davis's arms trapped under Salas's.

Salas lifted Davis off the floor. "Now, I said I don't want to fight," he repeated in a calm, yet threatening voice.

"Let me go! You let me go, you asshole. Is that…is that…you? You've got a fucking boner?! I can feel it on my ass! What the hell is wrong with you, man? You're fighting me with a boner!" Dan Davis was not at all comfortable in his current position.

"It's medicated, bro. It has a mind of its own." Again, Salas remained calm.

"Uuuuggghhhh!" Dan Davis was squirming and kicking, trying to head-butt Salas with the back of his skull.

Now redressed, minus the thong—she couldn't find it—Angelina stepped in and said calmly, softly, "Brad, please let him go. Dan, honey, I'm sorry. We didn't do anything—this was a mistake. You and I can work this out. Now, Brad is going to let you go. He'll leave, and we can talk. Okay, honey?"

"Okay, okay, just fuckin' let me go," Dan Davis pleaded. "And you, you…*Brad*, get the hell out of here. Now!" Dan Davis finally quit struggling.

Salas unleashed the bear hug he'd used to hold Dan, backed away, and again picked up his clothes, boots, and hat.

Dan Davis looked at Salas, who was still high and hard. "You son of a bitch!" he screamed, lunging at Salas.

Trying to tackle Salas, Dan Davis came in low like a linebacker. Salas faced him head on and again lowered his body, twisting slightly to the right, and put Dan Davis into a monster headlock. Salas cranked Dan Davis's head and neck hard, up and back—Salas the cowboy at the National Finals Rodeo, Dan Davis the steer. Davis let out a howl.

"Now, again, Dan, you need to relax. I can really hurt you right now, so just relax and I'll leave." Still, Salas remained calm, trying to defuse the man.

Dan Davis, still in a headlock, tried to answer Salas, his words coming out jumbled and gargled as he struggled to breathe, "You pussy! You need Viagra to get a hard-on."

"Now, I'm being nice, Dan." Salas squeezed a little tighter. "Let's not get personal." He was started to enjoy this headlock.

"Guess when you're old and bald, your pecker's the first to go!" Davis said.

"Well, you know what the commercial says: 'For an erection lasting more than four hours, call Angelina.'" Salas said it, but knew that he shouldn't have.

Dan Davis was furious. He would have been red regardless of the headlock. His face just mere inches away from another guy's erection, the erection that was trying to screw his wife. Dan Davis started to reach forward, moving his hand off Salas's forearms and extending it to Salas's manhood.

"Don't do it. *Do not* do that!" Salas no longer had a calm voice.

Humiliated, saddened, and embarrassed, Dan Davis went to grab Salas's dick.

Salas lifted and dropped Dan Davis to the floor.

Dan Davis cried out in agony.

"Told you not to do that," Salas said.

Angelina rushed to her husband's side. She knelt beside him, stroking his hair, kissing his cheek, her boobs in his face. "It'll be okay, honey. I called the police. They'll be here any minute."

"Are you shitting me?" Salas murmured. He buttoned up his Wranglers and slipped on his white T-shirt. He left the socks and went down the steps, stopped at the bottom, pulled on his Tony Lamas, and walked into the warm Indiana sunshine. He tugged his boonie hat down, got it snug, and slowly headed to his car.

Salas was standing in front of his dark-blue Ford Taurus when a black-and-white Mercury sedan pulled up. FORT WAYNE POLICE was painted on the door, with WE PROTECT AND SERVE decaled on the running board.

"Mike!" the police officer on the passenger side of the car called out to Salas. "What are you doing here? They call in a detective for a domestic dispute?"

"Don't know what you're talking about, man," Salas said, lifting the brim of his hat. "Just here for the hardware." He pointed to the Ace Hardware store.

"Oh, okay. We're checking out a marital issue at Dan Davis Construction," the cop said.

"Need some help? I have the time," offered Salas.

"No, we got it. See you at the station. Thanks!" The cop at the wheel parked the police car in front of Salas's. Both officers exited the sedan and headed over to Dan Davis Construction.

Salas watched them turn the corner as he got in his Ford and drove off.

ALBERT

The plan was to ride as far as Omaha, Nebraska, on day one. Spend the night and hit the road the next day.

Albert loved to ride. He had purchased the '02 Harley-Davidson Road King five years ago with the help of his mother. Well, his mother actually bought him the Harley. It was blue and silver, with original factory pipes and a factory seat. He didn't get any of the customized add-ons Harley is known for. He had 93,000 miles on the bike.

Albert rode year-round. On bad wintry days, his mother gave him a ride to the school where he worked, but for the most part, he rode every day.

The Harley cruised best at sixty-five miles an hour. At seventy and over, it burned a little oil. When he rode it below sixty, he felt he needed to downshift. Albert liked back roads when he traveled, no interstates. Something about riding with a semi-trailer tire right next to his head at seventy-five miles an hour gave him nightmares, so it was always back roads.

The trip from Auburn, Indiana, to Sturgis, South Dakota, was around 1,100 miles, about 1,300 when riding off the interstate. Riding looks easy to a lot of folks, but the long distances are physically taxing.

At five foot six, Albert struggled to hold the bike up at stoplights—had to be on his tippy toes—and then it was a precarious balancing act. Harley could lower bikes to accommodate shorter riders, but Albert couldn't afford to have that done. Being an avid weightlifter helped a little. Though he never entered any powerlifting competitions, his personal bests would have placed him in the top five at the Indiana powerlifting championships last fall. More than once since he'd gotten the Harley, he'd had to dead-lift the bike off its side—once while riding home in a snowstorm and another time after his foot slipped on some oil when he was stopped at a traffic light.

Albert gathered his tent, sleeping bag, roll-up mattress, and folding chair and strapped them to the Road King. All were bungee corded tight on the backseat and on the rear bags. The saddlebags held his rain gear, extra clothes, a towel, toiletries, and shaving kit. Albert was traveling light: only one extra pair of pants for the week, four T-shirts, his leather jacket, and a couple changes of underwear. He could wear them inside out to double up.

Albert had ten days; Friday and Saturday to get there, Sunday through Thursday to be at Sturgis, home by late Saturday of the next week, rest on Sunday and back to work early Monday morning.

This was his fifth road trip to Sturgis; the big vacation he budgeted for all year. Albert always used his earned vacation days for trips on his Harley. It was an expensive trip, which was why he camped out and saved his money year-round. It was $250 just for the camping spot, but that fee included tickets to the concerts every night. Once there, he ate very little because the food was so expensive. Drinking wasn't an option, though he did pack his own bottle of Jack Daniels, along with some beef jerky and breakfast bars that he had collected or stolen from work. Being the night janitor at a school gave Albert access to the left overs.

This year was promising to be the biggest year in the history of the annual Sturgis Motorcycle Rally. Last year was kind of slow, with an attendance of around 350,000. This year, for the rally's seventy-fifth anniversary, the organizers had estimated an attendance of about a million. Albert couldn't figure out how they could estimate the number of attendees or who sat and counted them.

He had come across Sturgis by accident. Actually, Sturgis was the only thing he'd ever thanked his father for. Albert was eight or nine when his father took the family on vacation to Mount Rushmore in Rapid City, South Dakota: just Mother, Father, and Albert packed into the two-door Chevy Monte Carlo. Father was a chain smoker, three or four packs of Pall Malls a day. Albert would lie on the floor of the backseat with a blanket over his face to get away from the smoke. Whenever he'd ask Father to open the window, he'd always yell back, "Makes too much damn noise. Quit your bellyaching."

Twenty hours in the car. The family drove straight through, with Father smoking even more to stay awake. They didn't call ahead for a hotel. "It's the first week in August," Father had said. "Who the hell goes to South Dakota anyways?"

When they drove through Sioux Falls, Mother commented on the number of motorcycles on the highway and challenged Albert to count the bikes they passed.

From Sioux Falls to Murdo, South Dakota, Albert counted more than 350 bikes. When they stopped for fuel in Murdo, he counted 112 motorcycles at the gas station. He loved them all: shiny two-wheelers, some with windshields some without, all colors. He especially loved the ones with flames on the gas tanks. Father hated them all.

Father, all five foot three of him, would yell at the bikers from the car, with his windows rolled up, but at the gas pumps he didn't say a word—he just cussed them out under his breath. He didn't like that they took up all the room on the road, that they traveled in groups and were hard to pass. He hated that the bikes were so loud and that the bikers wore leather and looked like thugs. Father said they were all crooks and gang bangers and did drugs.

They arrived in Rapid City at five in the afternoon. They stopped at the Foothills Inn, then the Ramada, then the Best Western—all no vacancies.

Father was livid. Why the hell were all these damn bikers there? It was South Dakota, for God's sake. People who live in South Dakota don't want to be in South Dakota, so why was everyone here? Father yelled at the traffic, yelled at mother, yelled at Albert.

The family slept in the car that night, in a Walmart parking lot. At least Father had rolled down the window. It was a hot, muggy night, and no one slept very well. Albert remembered washing up in the restroom of Walmart and peeing next to the car at night. That was fun.

The next day, the family drove to Mount Rushmore by Keystone, South Dakota. Albert was excited to see what he had read about in school. On the way there, Mother quizzed him on the people whose faces were carved into the rock. Abe Lincoln, Teddy Roosevelt, Thomas Jefferson, and George Washington. Father—well, all he could do was cuss about the traffic.

Bikers were everywhere. As Father drove up a really steep hill, he had to slow down time after time as bikers stopped on the shoulder, parked their bikes, and took pictures.

Finally, as they neared the entrance to the national monument, they realized the line was hundreds of bikes long. Father was honking his horn while bikers flipped him off and hollered at him. Deciding to bypass the line, he pulled out and sped forward. He then turned on his right blinker and tried to cut in by the entrance.

A state patrolman pulled Father over. He took him to his patrol car and talked to him for what seemed like an hour as they sat in the smoldering heat. The officer brought father back to the car. Father looked so small compared to the patrolman, his head barely to the officer's shoulder.

Father got into the Monte Carlo, and then they drove off down the hill. He was cussing the officer for the white piece of paper he had in his hand. Father tossed the paper on the floor and said he was never going to pay the fine and wasn't ever coming back to this shitty state. They never got to see Mount Rushmore and never got to take any pictures.

Leaving Mount Rushmore, they went down steep highways to Hill City. The landscape was gorgeous, with green trees and green grass and curvy roads. Albert watched the bikers in front of the car lean into curves, the tailpipes of the bikes just missing the asphalt.

Bikers with ladies on the backseat, all dressed in leather—leather boots, leather jackets, leather chaps—bandanas, and dark sunglasses. They all looked like they were having so much fun. Albert told his parents that they should get a motorcycle. Mother said it was a great idea, and Father told Albert to shut up. He said everyone on motorcycles dies in a fiery crash, and it was stupid to even think of it.

Father stopped for gas at a Mobil station that was crowded with bikers. He sat in the car with Mother and Albert, waiting in line. Albert waved through the window at all the bikers getting gas and parking their bikes; the bikers waved back and smiled. Father grew more impatient, smoking, cussing, and yelling out the window for them to move their damn bikes so he could get gas. Most of the bikers paid him no attention. Father honked his horn as a burly biker finished filling his tank and started to walk into the station, leaving his bike parked in front of the gas pump. "Move that damn thing so I can get gas!" Father yelled.

The biker smiled, went back to his bike, and rolled it out of the way. He approached the passenger side of the car and told Albert's mother through the window, "Sorry, ma'am. I should have moved it first." The biker reached through the window and handed Albert a black bandana with yellow flames and said, "Here you go, little fella."

Father got out of the driver's side and yelled across the hood of the car, "Damn right you should have, you big asshole! All of you are assholes!"

It got really quiet—like all the bikers shut off their engines at once. The big biker had on black boots, jeans with a tear at the knee, a black T-shirt, a black leather vest, and a black bandana, like a pirate would wear. No sleeves on the shirt, just these huge hairy arms covered with black tattoos. The biker looked left and right, hung his head down, and walked toward Father. "Do you have a problem, sir?" he said.

"Just tired of your shit," Father replied.

"You're not a nice person," the biker said.

"Yeah, well, you can kiss my ass. Get out of my way!" Father yelled up at the biker.

The big man reached out with both arms, grabbed Father by the throat, picked him up, and walked with the man's feet dangling in the air over to the trash can. The biker lifted him even higher off the ground and placed him in the receptacle feetfirst and said, "This is where you belong."

The biker then headed back to the Monte Carlo, looked into the window, and said, "Sorry, ma'am. Sorry that you and your fine son to have to live with that man." And he walked away.

Father scrambled out of the trash can, as bottles, cans, and wrappers fell onto the pavement, and ran to the car. He got into the driver's seat, turned the ignition key, and drove off. They headed south to Custer, South Dakota, and drove back to Indiana. Albert's mother tried to talk to father but he backhanded her across the face and told her to shut the f-up. No one spoke the entire way.

Now, as Albert rode his Harley, he remembered the biker's face, so calm and steady as he picked Father up by the throat and put him in his place.

After the family vacation to South Dakota, Father became even more verbally abusive toward his wife and son. It was then that Albert knew that someday he had to become a biker. And ever since he was little, he dreamed of putting Father in his place forever.

KEVIN AND MATT

ustin, Minnesota, was the home of SPAM (3.8 cans of SPAM are eaten per second in the USA), the Land of 10,000 Lakes, and the home of Kevin Buckles.

"Matty!" yelled Kevin. "Yougotyourbagspacked? Youreadytoroll?" Kevin spoke very fast, running his words together. He was always in a hurry, stopping only to sleep for five hours or less a day.

When everyone in high school was playing football, wrestling, or chasing girls, Kevin was working. At five foot four, he was too small for football, even too light to wrestle, and too shy for girls. He learned how to weld in junior high; by high school he was working on cars and creating and manufacturing parts for trailers, feed wagons, farm implements, and heavy machinery. By the time college rolled around, Kevin was making six figures manufacturing parts for a combine company.

When most young men were finding a wife and having kids, Kevin sold a trailer hitch he had designed to a national manufacturer, and became an extremely wealthy twenty-eight-year-old.

He took that money and purchased a hundred housing rental units from Austin to Worthington. Now, in his mid-forties, as the hundred units each averaged $1,000 a month in rental income, he, as he liked to say, "made a good living."

In 2014, Kevin made the trip to Sturgis riding a Ducati. A crotch rocket capable of speeds well over 180 miles an hour. Kevin was disappointed—the Sturgis biker crowd, well, they just weren't into a Ducati. No compliments; no one asked how fast it would go, or how fast he had ridden it. He felt like an outsider who wasn't welcome or part of the crowd. It didn't help that he wore bright-red leather pants, a red jacket, and a red helmet with a black facemask. One guy actually said, "You look like a douche."

Plus, he stayed in downtown Rapid City. It was busy, but it wasn't Sturgis. The historic Hotel Alex Johnson might have housed dignitaries and former presidents, but bikers stayed at the campgrounds in Sturgis: The Chip, Glencoe, the Broken Spoke. Kevin vowed to visit them all.

In 2015, he would start with the Buffalo Chip Campground. This year would be different for Kevin and for his nephew, Matt.

To start, Kevin went to his local Harley dealer and purchased the best, most expensive bike they had—a 2015 Ultra Classic Screamin' Eagle package—and then added extra chrome and engine enhancements. He was the ultimate customer for a salesman working on commission.

The Ultra, with its 110-CVO twin-cooled, twin-cam engine, was the result of Harley-Davidson's Rushmore project. Kevin didn't know what the Rushmore project was, but he liked the sound of it. What pleased him the most was the 3-D touch-screen GPS system, heated seats, Typhoon Maroon paint, and the four six-hundred-watt, bi-amped, three-way speakers.

Kevin then got into the RV market and purchased a 2015 Chariot Freightliner Coronado. The forty-five-foot RV offered 360 square feet of living space and was powered by a 515-horsepower Detroit diesel. With a thirty-foot trailer in tow, and his RV and trailer all in Harley black and orange, he definitely stood out as he drove down the highway.

Matt, at 26 years old, was his favorite and only nephew. He was also the opposite of Kevin. At six feet tall, 220 pounds, he was all-state in football, state champion in wrestling, and got all the girls. Matt had spent a few years wrestling at the University of Minnesota under Jay Robinson, but injuries eventually left him back at home in Austin.

Kevin hired Matt to work in his shop, help take care of the rental properties, and train Kevin in exercise, weightlifting, and self-defense. Matt was overpaid and underworked, but both Matt and Kevin understood this.

"Matt! I'm going to Skip's to get some booze. Be back in an hour. Get your bike ready!" Kevin yelled, with an emphasis on "getting ready." Matt moved at his own pace, which was slow and deliberate—again, the exact opposite of Kevin.

A dive bar that also offered package liquor, Skip's was about thirty minutes from Kevin's acreage. Skip and Kevin were high-school buddies from the late '80s, and Kevin was actually an investor in the bar. When times were tough for Skip, Kevin had bought the building and rented it back to Skip at a much lower monthly payment than Skip's mortgage payment. Kevin was an investor, a friend and he also dated Skip's waitress Gloria.

"Skip! Stella, please!" Kevin announced as he entered the bar. It was 11:00 a.m. on a Saturday, and the bar was empty except for one patron, his head down, a glass in hand. "Hope you're having a wonderful day!" Kevin said to the guy at the bar, his voice high-pitched and piercing.

Skip delivered the beer in a Stella challis, filled to the brim. "Got your order ready, Kevin. That's a lot of booze! You just missed Gloria. She will be back for the late shift."

"Yep, headed to Sturgis. I'll give her a call later," Kevin said, just as the beer hit his lips. "Gonna be a riot. Can't wait to get there!" His voice sounded like the cackle of a chicken. "We are gonna partayyy!"

The patron at the end of the bar, with bed head hair, a shirt and blue jeans in dire need of a washing, raised his head. "You know, this was a nice peaceful bar until you came in," he said. "Why don't you shut the fuck up?"

"Relax, my friend. No need to get upset. Hey, buy this man a drink for me, Skip."

"I ain't your friend, and I don't want no drink from some short, little sawed-off pissant like you," the man said.

"Goodness, are we having a bad day?" Kevin said in a singsongy, mocking tone. "Does someone need a hug?" He laughed at that one—a long, loud laugh like Woody Woodpecker's: "Hahahahaha, hahahahaha, hahahahaha, hehhhhh."

"Relax, sir. I don't want any trouble. Let me buy you the drink," Skip intervened, as he stood in front of the patron.

"Shut up," the man said, as he stood and walked over to Kevin, who was standing now as well.

The man reached out as if he were going to stick his finger in Kevin's nose. Kevin grabbed the man's hand and wrist and twisted it back and up, bending the elbow, locking the wrist, and locking the elbow at severe right angles. The man bent over in pain, trying to relieve the pressure of the wrist and arm lock. Kevin was now behind the man, twisting the wrist and elbow lock upward. The man screamed in pain while tapping his right shoulder.

Skip stood motionless.

"Now I can break your wrist, sir. By your unkempt appearance, I take it you're not a surgeon or a violinist, but perhaps you still value your right wrist." Kevin spoke as slowly as Skip had ever heard him speak.

"Uuuggghhh," the man groaned, trying to stand straight to rid himself of the pain.

"To break or not to break…that is my question to you," Kevin said.

"Don't break it! Sorry…I'm sorry. Let me go," the guy pleaded.

"You may leave." Kevin released the lock as Skip came around the bar with a bat.

The man was rubbing his wrist, tears in his eyes. He laid a ten-dollar bill on the bar and left, not looking back.

Kevin turned to Skip and said, "Well that was awkward." Skip shrugged his shoulders and went back behind the bar.

Kevin loaded his order into his Lexus. Thirty minutes later, he was back home.

Matt helped him load the beer and booze into the RV. Kevin had enough of both for thirty people for five days, much more than what he, Matt, and Matt's buddy, Jerico, who was meeting up with them on the way to the rally, could consume themselves.

Kevin peered into the trailer. It was customized with a motorcycle lift and stocked with every tool imaginable, as well as all kinds of parts, oil, and can after can of cleaning supplies: leather cleaners and protectants, windshield Rain-X, tire cleaners, stove cleaners, Windex, various sprays, solvents, and wax and bug removers.

He rechecked the straps holding down the bike as well as the straps anchoring the golf cart. Kevin had read that golf carts were a necessity at the campgrounds, as you usually had to park far away from the action. Plus, when you're drunk, a golf cart is much easier to drive than a motorcycle.

"Matty, you're not going to trailer your bike?" Kevin asked. "You're not going to ride in the RV with me?"

"Uncle Kevin, it's a motorcycle rally," Matt said, shaking his head, "not a trailer rally. I'm riding!"

"**S**alas!" Captain Thomas Green yelled from his office to the floor of cubicles, computers, officers, and detectives. "My office. Now!"

Salas knew this was coming. He was hoping that since it was Saturday, Green wouldn't be in the office. He didn't know how to prepare. Just deny, deny, deny. It worked for Clinton.

He entered the captain's office as Green was walking out. "Sit," he told Salas. Green turned right and headed into the break room. He didn't offer to get Salas coffee or water.

Salas didn't sit. He wasn't a dog and didn't like the order. Instead, he walked around the captain's office. Though he'd been in here several times, he'd never been in here alone. A large oak desk, the size of a casket, sat in the center of the room, facing away from the window. The desk was covered with papers, folders, and files. A traditional green banker's lamp sat at the corner of the desk, and an oak office chair sat behind it.

Behind the captain's chair, a wall of windows overlooked the city park. Against the opposite side, a leather couch stood against another wall of windows, which looked over the station's third-floor cubicles. Two leather straight-back chairs were facing the captain's desk. Salas figured this was where he was supposed to sit.

The north wall of Captain Green's office was covered in pictures. Larry Bird in an Indiana State University uniform. Larry Bird in a Boston Celtics uniform, autographed. Larry Bird in a suit and tie with the Indiana Pacers, autographed. Larry Bird with Captain Green at some black-tie event. Larry Bird and Captain Green on a golf course. Larry Bird and Green on a different golf course in different plaid pants and different golf shirts. Salas used his detective skills to determine Captain Green had a man crush on Larry Bird.

Salas thought of his own office at the station. A cubicle with a view of the captain's office above. The north wall of his cubicle, which was shorter than Salas, had one picture on it: his daughter Samantha. Sami posing on the steps of her dorm at Notre Dame, freshman year. She was a junior now and living in an apartment.

Salas needed a new picture. Maybe he'd get Sami to autograph it. He smiled as he thought of her. She was the best thing to happen to him and the best thing he and his ex-wife Deb ever did together. Did he cheat on her first or did she on him? Didn't matter; they were now friends, and they both loved Sami.

Back to Green.

Captain Green walked in and shut the door with a little more force than Salas thought necessary. Salas remained standing, while Green sat down at his desk, holding a cup of coffee that looked more like hot chocolate than coffee.

Tom Green in his early fifties, was tall, maybe six foot six, thus the basketball fetish. If you were tall and couldn't play basketball, well, then you were just tall. Green was straight out of *GQ*. Full head of hair that never moved, even in the strongest Indiana winds, parted left to right. He had to go to the barber—forget that; to a *stylist*—every week. Salas shaved his own head daily.

Green's clothes were pressed and crisp like his hair. His pencil neck made it easy for him to wear a tie. When Salas wore a tie, it looked like he was strangling himself or was in a neck brace. Green's shoes looked brand new: heavy leather, straps across the tops neatly clasped in a silver buckle, which matched the buckle on his belt, which was the same silver as his watch. Green always made a point of looking at his watch. Probably expensive and wanted you to know. Salas had a Timex from Shopko.

"Damn it, Salas! I know it was you. What the hell were you thinking, Detective Boner?" That was Green's attempt at humor.

"Don't know what you're talking about, Tom," Salas said softly, looking Green in the eyes. After ten years of working together they shared a common thread, they didn't like each other.

"You're on thin ice here, Salas. You know, you shouldn't even be a detective. You should be a beat cop, on the street. I'm encouraging this guy to file charges against you." Green returned Salas's stare.

"Still don't know what you're talking about." Salas said, his eyebrows raised.

Green glanced at a file then looked back up at Salas. "Don't bullshit me. Dan Davis said it was a big bald guy with barbwire tattoos on both biceps."

"All of us bald guys look alike, Tom, and who doesn't have a tattoo these days?"

"Okay. He said the guy also had a tattoo of a chain down his wrist with a cross at the end of it. How's that for a positive ID?" Green said, pointing to Salas's wrist.

"These are rosary beads, Tom, and there are two crosses, not one. Tell me, are we looking for a Caucasian, African American, Native American, Asian, Hispanic? What does your report say?" Salas countered, leaning forward to look at the report.

Green flipped through the pages before going back to page one, then did it again. "It doesn't say."

Salas smiled. "Goodness, Captain. We don't even know where to start."

"I'm bringing Davis in when he gets out of the hospital. He'll positively ID you, and then you're screwed, Salas. Done, out of here." Green forced a smile back. "Now the good news. We have a dead body at the Sunset RV Park and Campground off 79. Go and detect, Detective. And…the body's been stuffed into the holding tank of a port-a-potty. Sounds shitty, doesn't it?" Green said with a bigger smile than before.

"One more thing," he said as he stood. He went to the door and shouted, "Ronnie, get in here!" A skinny guy with floppy hair entered. "Salas, meet Ronnie. Ronnie, meet Salas." Green was looking at files, not at the two men. "You have a partner now, Salas. Ronnie, your job is to watch Salas's every move and report back to me on everyone and anyone he talks to. Watch, listen, and learn, Ronnie."

Ronnie reached out his hand. Salas ignored it and walked closer to Green.

"What's this? A watchdog? Your own internal tattletale? I don't need this shit, hell, what is he 20 years old?" Salas vented.

"Then quit, Salas. Leave your resignation papers on my desk. Now go." Green turned and sat down.

"Is he even a cop? Has he ever been in a squad car or walked the streets?" Salas continued.

"Part of the mayor's Millennial Innovation Incentive Salas. Get over it." Green still wasn't looking up from his desk. "Each department gets a millennial for advance placement. And Ronnie just got placed with you."

Salas and Ronnie walked out the door. Salas shut it with a little more force than necessary.

Ronnie held out his hand once again. "I'm Ron, Ron Higginbotham. This is my first day on the job, Detective Salas. Just out of the Fort Wayne academy."

"Congrats. Go find your desk and get it arranged and do desk stuff." Salas grabbed his shoulder harness, weapon, and badge on a chain lanyard and started for the door.

"But I'm supposed to follow you, Detective Salas!"

"Hey, Salas," another bald officer in a police uniform called out. "Having a shitty day?"

"Are you shitting me, Salas?" the officer by the copier said. "A DB in a shitter?"

"Shit rolls downhill, Salas," another detective said with a smile.

"Salas, you look like shit, buddy. You going to be okay?" commented the cop behind the cage.

"Oh, you guys are just hilarious," Salas said dryly. "Is that all you got? What? No 'Shit happens'? Or 'Don't take that shit.'"

Salas left the station with Ronnie in his shadow. Salas got into the Ford and made Ronnie knock on the window three times before he hit the "unlock" button. Ronnie slid in and buckled up quickly. He looked at Salas and said, "Thank you for letting me in the car, Detective Salas."

"Call me Mike or call me Salas." Salas started the car, backed out, and headed west to Sunset RV Park and Campground.

As they drove, Ronnie took out a brown leather-bound notebook with a magnetic clasp to close it. He opened it and began to write.

"What you go there? Your journal?" asked Salas.

"Kind of, Detective Salas. Captain Green told met take notes. I looked at several notebooks at Barnes & Noble and liked this one the best. A simple stenographer's notepad would have worked, but this leather makes it look more professional."

"What kind of notes does Green want you to take?"

"He said to record wherever you went, whatever you said, whomever you spoke to. And any dirty words, dirty jokes, off-color remarks, or offensive language."

"Are you shitting me!"

"No, sir, I am not." Ronnie said as he was taking notes.

"So, Ronnie, you're a snitch. And don't write that shit down!"

"No, I'm just doing what I was told to do."

"Let me see your notebook, please."

Ronnie handed it over. Salas grabbed it with his right hand.

Salas laid the book on his lap and pushed down on the driver's-side window button. The window responded. Salas picked up the book, waved it at Ronnie, then tossed it out the window.

"Hey, that was my new notebook!" Ronnie yelled, reaching for Salas's window.

"Look, Ronnie, if you're my going to be partner, then get this: we don't snitch on each other; we don't hold back from each other. I got your back; you got mine. I'll defend you against anything unless you break the law, do drugs, do a hooker, or take a bribe. Then I'll bust you myself. Got it?"

"I don't do drugs. I've never had a sip of alcohol. I'd never do a hooker, and I don't take bribes."

"Then we're good. Got it?"

Ronnie nodded. "Got it."

ALBERT

The plan was Omaha by Friday night, but the plan wasn't going as planned. Albert had gotten off work from his night shift later than he wanted and had ridden only about thirty miles from Auburn, Indiana, to Fort Wayne. It was nearly eleven in the morning when he decided to stop and grab a sandwich at Subway for lunch. He hadn't eaten last night or this morning, and his belly was crying out to him. He was only five foot six but a muscular 165 pounds, and after an intense chest-and-arm workout this morning, he needed fuel for his body.

It was at Subway that he changed his plan.

Albert stopped his Harley, pulled forward, then backed his bike into a parking slot in front of the sandwich shop.

Across the parking lot, a family was getting out of an old Holiday Rambler RV. Albert noticed they'd parked the RV so that it took up six parking spaces. The lot wasn't that full, though, so it wasn't really a big deal.

The father was the first one out. He opened the door, bent over, and slid out the three steps that were tucked under the RV. Then he turned and walked away. The mother was next. There was no handrail, so she went down the steps slowly, with no helping hand from her husband. Then came a little boy, maybe six or seven years old, with bright-red hair. The boy was looking up, not at the steps. He took one step, and then his foot slid forward. He crashed down hard on his bottom, on the RV floor, then rolled down the three steps to the asphalt and started to cry.

The boy's mother was right there to help, holding her son while inspecting his arm for cuts and scratches. The father returned, jerked the boy from his mother, looked at his arm, and said, "You're fine. Quit crying like a baby." And then he pushed him away.

"My arm doesn't hurt, Daddy," the boy countered. "My bottom does."

"I'll give you a reason for your bottom to hurt," the man yelled as he spanked the little redhead on the butt, one hard smack. "Pay attention. I've told you and told you to watch those steps."

The man walked past Albert, who was still straddling his Harley. He was about the same height as Albert. As he walked past him, he said, "What are you looking at?" then entered the Subway.

Albert waited for the little boy and his mother to walk by. The boy was still teary eyed. Albert smiled at the kid, who buried his face in his mom's belly.

He followed them into the Subway. The father already had ordered and was sitting down. "You didn't wait for us?" his wife said, giving him a dirty look.

Albert used the restroom first. He calmed down somewhat, but he knew what he had to do tonight. This meant he would be late getting to Sturgis, but he didn't care; he had to put Father in his place. Albert came out of the restroom and headed outside; Father was already in the RV, the motor running. Mother and son had their Subway plastic bags and were hurrying to the RV.

Albert put on his helmet, fired up his Harley, let Father get about one minute ahead of him, then followed the RV down the highway. He would stop where they stopped. A Holiday Rambler with Wisconsin plates was easy to follow. Albert never had to go over fifty-five miles an hour to keep up.

Father pulled into Sunset RV and Campground twenty minutes later. The campground advertised a pool, game room, laundry facilities, electric hookups, sanitation dumps, and fresh water. Albert was hoping Mother would take the little boy swimming.

Albert stayed back as Father checked the RV in. He watched from the entrance as Father drove the RV toward the rear of the campground, and then he lost sight of the Rambler.

Albert paid the twenty-dollar camp fee with his Visa card. He had a $1,000 limit and wanted to keep the cash he had for Sturgis. No one in Sturgis would take a credit card—it was all cash. Albert rode his bike quietly through the campground, not revving up the motor to show off the Harley rumble. He went in the opposite direction of the Rambler.

He rode past several cars, campers, and RVs with license plates from as far away as New York, Maine, and Florida. Most of the vehicles were RVs, but a few tents were popped up.

Near the back entrance of the campground, he found a shade tree and parked his bike. The tent spot was perfect for an early-morning getaway from the campground.

Given the change in plans, he'd most likely have to get to Sioux Falls on Saturday, an eight-hundred-mile ride. Setting up the tent was easy, as he had practiced it several times in his own yard before he'd left. Albert didn't want to look stupid at the campground in Sturgis. He unrolled his sleeping bag and sat placed the folding chair by the tent, in the shade.

The receptionist had told him there was a snack shack in the middle of the campground that sold hamburgers, hot dogs, soda, and water. Albert walked to the shack in his Harley boots, steel-toed, not the best for walking long distances but great for the ride, and he always had his leather jacket on no matter the heat.

Albert took the long way to the snack shack, looking for the Rambler. He heard it before he saw it—rather, he heard Father before he saw the RV. Father was yelling at his son again. This time the boy seemed to have done something wrong with the lawn chair.

"I told you to put the chair in the bag it came in," the man hollered. "Where's the bag? Look at me—where's the bag? See this chair? It's ruined because you forgot to put it in the bag. When I pulled it out of the storage bin, the leg was bent! This is all your fault."

Albert was so glad he'd broken away from his plan. This was like destiny. He would put Father in his place once and for all. Right now, though, he had to leave before he lost control. The mother was holding her son again.

Father screamed at her, "And no swimming for him! He broke the chair...he sits in the chair."

Albert was going to enjoy this.

The snack shack was better than the receptionist had led him to believe, plus the food was less expensive than it was at Subway. A grilled hamburger, chips, and a cup of water was $3.50. At Sturgis, $3.50 would get you just a bottle of water.

The afternoon dragged on. Albert studied the map, planning tomorrow's stops for fuel and food. With the sun setting, he knew his time was coming. He used the cover of darkness, along with his black jeans and black leather jacket, to blend into the evening and scout the campground.

Father's Holiday Rambler RV was aged and weather-beaten. Pockmarks from a prior hailstorm marred the side with the entry door. The rear of the Rambler looked as if it had been backed into several posts or trees. The bumper was dented in three spots, and the fiberglass had a stab wound above one of the rear taillights, perhaps from a tree branch or the tailgate of a pickup.

Father had set up camp with an awning over a picnic table that was provided by the campground. The awning, torn at the base, flapped in the gentle wind. A Weber kettle grill, with smoke curling up through the vents, stood next to the table.

Albert made several trips around the RV park. Bystanders, perhaps, thought he was just a camper getting his exercise, but he was looking for a place to put Father. He liked the bathhouse best. Inside the men's shower building were five stalls, each with a wooden door. He could place the body there, shut the door, lock it from the inside, and climb over the top. Outside the shower house was a line of five port-a-potties, green units with white tops. That might work, but the shower house would be best.

In the darkness, Albert waited patiently, watching and waiting.

Around midnight, Father came out of the RV. He picked up the folding chairs and placed them under the front RV bumper. Then he picked up a few pieces of trash, lit a cigarette, paused, inhaled deeply, left the cigarette between his lips, and rolled up the awning. Father then did what Albert was hoping for; he walked toward the shower house. He wasn't carrying a towel, so he probably wasn't going to take a shower. His white T-shirt was visible from several feet away, the ember of his cigarette glowing.

Father stopped in front of the first port-a-potty and took one last drag from the cigarette. He threw the butt on the ground, stepped on it with a twist, and entered the green cubicle.

Albert quickly walked to the entrance of the portable unit, looked around, and saw no one. With his right hand, he reached into the left chest pocket of his leather jacket and pulled out an ice pick. The pick was eight inches long, with a T-bar handle, and fit comfortably in his hand. He spun the pick in his palm and rubbed the shaft of the pick with his fingers.

Albert heard Father peeing into the holding tank of the unit and then zipping his pants. A few moments later, the man opened the door saw Albert's figure in the darkness. "Excuse me," Father said as he took the lone step down from the port-a-potty to the ground. Albert stepped forward, meeting the downward step of Father, and jammed the point of the pick upward, penetrating the man's throat just below the jaw and driving it upward with all his force. The impact of the initial thrust of the pick lifted Father up and off his feet, slamming him back into the port-a-potty.

Blood streamed down the pick and down Albert's arm inside his leather jacket. Albert's right fist was against Father's throat, the point of the pick driven upward through his brain and hitting the inside of his skull. It was a clean kill, Father didn't even have time to talk, much less scream.

Father was small in stature, with narrow shoulders. Albert was able to stuff the man's head into the holding tank then force his shoulders through the seat. From there it was easy to cram the rest of his body into the toilet recess.

Albert yearned to see Father covered in the shit and piss of the port-a-potty, but it was too dark inside. He stepped out of the unit and looked left and right—no sign of anyone who might have heard the scuffle. He turned and shut the door of the unit, then used his pick to flip the inside handle of the unit down, locking the door and showing a red label that read, "Occupied." Albert pulled out his cell phone camera mode and took a picture of the 5 port-a-potties. The flash startled him, he looked left and right for any signs of movement. All clear.

It was quiet, with just the traffic noise echoing from the interstate. Albert walked calmly to his tent, unzipped the screen, crawled inside, and fell asleep in seconds with the blood of Father inside his jacket, down his arm, and covering his chest.

He was a restless sleeper, and tonight was no different. After putting Father in his place, Albert thought he would be able to sleep. But the nightmare returned. The one in which Father put Albert in his place. Father grabbing Albert by the arm, dragging him to the bedroom closet, and tossing Albert inside like a pillow. His arms hurt from being grabbed and twisted. Albert heard the closet door being slammed shut, and he twitched in his sleep. He tossed and turned in his tent, trying to open the door, but it was locked, and then he heard his mother crying. Parents yelling and screaming, the sound of someone getting slapped, and then Mother so quiet. Trapped in the darkness for hours, Albert was terrified to close his eyes. A glimpse of light through the bottom of the door, and then Father opening the door. Albert was so excited to see light and see his mother. But Father, seeing Albert had peed in the closet, yelled, "You pissed your pants again, you little bastard." He slapped Albert hard on the right cheek then the left cheek, his ring drawing blood. Albert, even now in his sleep, rubbed the scar on his left cheek.

He awoke well before his cell phone alarm could ring. It was just before 6:00 a.m. He had everything packed and strapped to his Harley by 6:10. He glanced over at the shower house and port-a-potties; all was quiet. He peed by the side of his bike as he tried to locate the Holiday Rambler RV. He knew mother and son were still fast asleep and would thank him one day.

Albert then pushed his Harley through the rear exit gate of Sunset RV Park and Campground. About twenty yards to the highway, he swung his right leg over, turned the ignition on with his barrel key, then hit the start switch. The Harley roared to life, and he was on the highway by 6:12. His next stop would be for fuel in Plymouth, Indiana.

"Why? We're broke, that's why," Jessica said, stuffing her clothes into a duffel bag.

"Jess, this isn't modeling. You want to be a model, not a stripper." Her boyfriend, Jimmy, was in his late twenties, with hair that looked like he'd just gotten out of bed.

"This isn't stripping. I'll be tending bar, a waitress. The agency says I can make ten thousand or more in just a week," Jessica countered.

"From the looks of the clothes you're packing, you're going to be a street whore," Jimmy yelled back.

"Why don't you just go back to your video games and let me pack?" Jessica said tersely.

"What's that supposed to mean?"

"All you do is play those stupid games. When was the last time you worked a full day?" Jessica asked, standing up straight and glaring at him.

"I'm in sales. I can call my own hours," Jimmy said, his head down. He was talking more to the floor than to Jessica.

"Well, your mom might buy that line, but you haven't sold anything for a month, and you haven't even been off the couch for two weeks." Jessica's voice was hot. "If you're a salesman, shouldn't you be out trying to sell something?"

Jimmy shrugged. "It's a slow time. Everyone's buying computers online now."

"Whatever" was all Jessica could muster.

"Whatever! Whatever! I hate *whatever*!" Jimmy was yelling now.

Jessica let out a long sigh. "Look, Jimmy. This isn't working out. When I get back in a week, I want you and your stuff out of here. Go live with your mom and sleep on her couch. Eat her food and let her do your laundry."

"I love you Jess. I want us to get married." His tone had gone from whining to yelling to begging.

"Married?" she said, shaking her head in disbelief. "That's not going to happen." She lifted her duffel bag and headed to the door. "We've been together over a year, and all you've done for me is get me into debt. You've never even talked about marriage, and now that I'm kicking you out, you want to commit? Not happening."

"Come on, Jessica. Don't go. I forbid you to go!" Jimmy screamed.

"Get out, Jimmy. Get your stuff and go back to your mommy. I'm tired of filling in for her," Jessica said coldly.

"Yeah, well, when you get to Sturgis, all they'll want is to screw you. It's your vagina. Good luck." Jimmy shut the door as Jessica walked out.

"You're an ass!" she yelled back.

Jessica walked down the steps to a waiting Ford Fusion with "Sturgis or Bust" painted on the rear passenger window.

St. Louis to Sturgis was an eight-hundred-mile drive. In the front seat was Ann, the driver and owner of the Fusion, and her friend Shelly, both natives of St. Louis. Summer would share the backseat with Jessica; both of them from across the river in Illinois.

"Well, that looked like a romantic good-bye scene," Ann said.

"He'd better be gone when I get back, but I bet he'll be sitting there on the couch with a rose or something," Jessica said. "He's an ass. He just won't change."

"They never do!" Ann and Shelly said in unison.

"All I want is a guy who'll take care of me. Is that too much to ask?"

"They never will." Again, in unison.

All four girls had visions of being supermodels, being on the cover of *Vogue*, traveling to exotic locales, and marrying their own Tom Brady. They were all beautiful young ladies in their mid-twenties and represented by All-American Models Talent Agency. Each had enjoyed some success. Shelly had been featured in some regional jobs for Target's ladies' apparel; Ann had appeared in a few ads for a small chain of auto parts stores; Jessica had appeared in several bridal magazines (which only made Jimmy's proposal more of an insult); and Summer had done a couple of local TV commercials but was hoping to get into local news and weather broadcasting.

Most of their work consisted of gigs like this Sturgis bartending thing. The agency said it would help with exposure and look good on their résumés, just like the other events they'd done: the home-and-garden trade show at the TD Ameritrade building, a state Republican political convention, and several other small-time meet-and-greets where older men wanted to flirt with young women. The tips were good and the hours poor, with no benefits and no covered expenses. The modeling career thus far was more a bartending gig, they could all mix a great drink. This time, however, the agency had guaranteed each girl $5,000 for this trip and even fronted them $500 for gas. So off to Sturgis, for a few days of limited fame and fortune.

The girls thought the online pictures of the campground, the Buffalo Chip, looked fun. They were promised a luxurious cabin at the Chip, within walking distance of all the action. The building appeared to be a small log cabin on the peaceful prairie. The concert lineup was impressive; the girls were especially looking forward to seeing Godsmack and Lynyrd Skynyrd.

None of them had ever been to South Dakota, much less Mount Rushmore. Summer had printed the map and directions from MapQuest, as she didn't know how to get the GPS on her phone to work. Jessica had the trip detailed on her phone's google map.

All four girls wanted to visit Mount Rushmore before they came back to St. Louis. Ann had mentioned that Reptile Gardens in Rapid City looked fun, and Shelly had read where there was a cave where gravity didn't work—or maybe it was fire or electricity; she couldn't remember.

By their calculations, they would arrive in Sturgis Saturday afternoon, early enough to get acquainted with the campground, meet the management, and maybe relax by the pool or even go shopping. Summer's boyfriend, Tony, wanted a Sturgis shirt. Summer hoped they'd see a T-shirt shop somewhere in town; after all, Sturgis's population was only 6,500; there probably wasn't a whole lot to do there. Ann plugged her iPod into the Ford Fusion, cranked up some Guns N' Roses, and they hit the road.

Matt texted his buddy Jerry: "Meet us at Wall Drug Saturday at 4:00."

"Will do," he replied.

Matt and Jerry were friends from college. Matt had wrestled at the University of Minnesota, and Jerry had played two years of football there—a redshirt year on the scout team and one year on the bench, his Achilles' heel torn and his career over. At five foot ten and 210 pounds, he still looked like he could still play; he just couldn't run.

After ball was over, so was school. Jerry only had gone to college, even high school really, to play football. Not that he'd ever had dreams of playing professional football—he just loved to compete. With football out of his life, he got his CDL and started trucking. He hauled cattle, grain, potatoes, rock, salt, hay, and lately, with his HAZMAT endorsement, fuel.

Jerry owned his own truck and rented different trailers. He had a dispatcher and was on the road five out of seven days a week. The decal on his truck read, JERRY COBURN COMPANY. He wasn't the best at enunciation; he was good at the first syllable but lost energy after that, so…well, he mumbled. When he picked up the phone and said, "Jerry Coburn," it came out as "Jerry's cooo" or "Jerico." Thus, the name stuck.

Everyone called him Jerico. Even his girlfriends, Laurie, Whitney, and Jenny, called him Jerico. Now, none of these girls knew about each other; only he did. Life on the road led to girls on the road, each in the major towns he drove through. The Peterbilt truck with its extended cab was his love shack on wheels.

Jerico lived in the small town of O'Neill, the Irish capital of Nebraska, located conveniently between I-90 in South Dakota and I-80 in Nebraska. For his 340-mile trip to Sturgis, he'd ride west to Valentine, Nebraska; north on 83 to White River, South Dakota; west on 44 to Interior; north through the Badlands to Wall, South Dakota then I-90 to Sturgis.

He could have met Matt and Kevin near Chamberlain or Murdo, but he had a lady he was working on in Interior. So, Jerico chose to meet up with them in Wall instead.

The black-and-white Big Dog Pitbull motorcycle that Jerico owned was a sweet ride, with fenders styled after lightning bolts. The large back tire and narrow front end accentuated his broad shoulders when he rode. Although Big Dog was no longer in business, the S&S motor was easy to work on. Jerico had jetted the carb and burned a high-octane AV fuel when cruising around town. When he laid on the throttle, flames spat out from the Vance & Hines street sweepers. Jerico once rode the Pitbull at over 130 miles an hour with tach to spare—too fast to ride with that light of a front end.

The T-bag fit tightly on the rear sissy bar; his saddlebags were filled with T-shirts, shorts, rain gear, bandanas, and a large bottle of hand sanitizer (Jerico had a sanitizer fetish and washed his hands more often than a surgeon). His leather jacket was rolled up and bungee-corded on the front handlebars as he hit the highway.

Stops for fuel in Valentine and White River had him in Interior at noon. Jerico parked the bike at the Horseshoe Bar under the big red-and-white tent. Every year at this time, the owner of the bar set up the tent to provide shade for bikers cutting through South Dakota on Highway 44 to the rally. Cruising through the Badlands was a favorite ride for many bikers.

The Badlands were just that: bad land. The scenery looked like photos from the 1960 lunar landing. White stone, no grass, no trees, no water, no animals.

A Brahma bull was tied up next to the Horseshoe Bar sign, which featured a cowboy in a red-and-white-striped shirt; a dirty, bent, white cowboy hat; and jeans tucked into over-the-calf boots. Five dollars for a picture with the bull. You could sit on him or stand beside him—no matter, still the same price. Jerico said no to the picture with the bull, sanitized his hands, and headed into the bar.

There were two bars in Interior, population ninety-four. Up from the 2000 census figure of seventy-seven. The bar smelled of stale beer;

the carpet looked like someone—everyone—peed on it; and the walls were covered with a dense fog from years of smoke accumulation.

Behind the counter was the woman Jerico had come to see: Julia, a blond petite thing in black yoga pants and a black T-shirt that read, "Good Girls Go to Heaven…Bad Girls Go to Badlands." The yoga pants left little to the imagination; they hugged her form perfectly, and Jerico loved to stare. Her pale skin in contrast to Jerico's olive complexion.

"Hey, sweet thing." Julia smiled at Jerico. "Driving your big rig through town?" Jerico had first met Julia through trucking—hauling rock from Rapid City to Winner, a construction run—a month ago. Since then he had stopped in twice; once she was here, and the other time he missed her.

"On my bike today, Julia. Sturgis for the week. Ride with me," Jerry said, smiling.

"Tempting, Big Rig. Very tempting!" She leaned forward on the bar, her breasts on her forearms, pushing them upward through her shirt and pushing up Jerico's blood pressure. She loved to flirt and was good at it.

"What can I get you?" she asked, placing her hand on his.

"All I want is a girl like you," Jerico said softly.

Julia loved his soft voice, having to lean in to hear him. She whispered, "There's only one me."

"Good, 'cuz you're the only one I want," Jerry whispered back.

Julia gave him a Coors Light. "This Silver Bullet will have to do for now!" She walked off, stopped, looked back and smiled, then went to the other end of the bar to wait on other bikers. They continued their flirting repertoire as she juggled several patrons at once, flirting with them all but always coming back to Jerry when she had a slow moment.

Two buffalo burgers later and another Coors Light and Jerico waved her over.

"Gotta run, beautiful. I'll be back later this week. Here's my number." Jerry handed her his cell number on a napkin. "Call me sometime."

"How will you know it's me?" Julia asked, she liked his broad shoulders and flat belly.

"You're the only girl I've given my number to," Jerico said.

As he opened the bar door, sunshine shot through.

The Saturday-afternoon crime scene was pretty simple. An outhouse, a dead body, and an RV with a terrified wife and little boy.

Salas and Ronnie drove up and walked over to the wife and child, who were sitting at the picnic table near the Rambler. Mrs. Kenneth Hart, Nancy, repeated her story to Salas. She had awakened at 7:04 a.m., per the clock on the microwave. Ken wasn't in the RV or outside at the camp. Nancy made coffee, brought out the cooking equipment, and was waiting for her husband to return from wherever he had gone, to light the grill.

At 8:00 a.m., Andy, the little boy, came out of the RV. Nancy took Andy and herself to the shower house. He showered in the men's, she in the women's, and they returned to the RV by 8:35, per her cell phone. Still no sign of Ken.

Nancy and Andy had cereal and juice then walked around the campground to the main office, the laundry facility, the pool area, and the snack shack. No Ken. She admitted she was worried at ten but said Ken was a runner, and she thought maybe he'd gone for a jog. Nancy checked the RV; his running shoes were in his bag, as were his wallet, money, and ID. At ten-thirty she called the police.

Two Fort Wayne officers arrived within a few minutes; it was a slow Saturday. The officers called the local hospitals, an urgent care facility, a couple nearby bars, and even a massage parlor. No one had seen a five-foot-three white male, approximately 135 pounds, between the hours of midnight and 10:00 a.m. There had been no reports of accidents, hitchhikers, or transients. The two officers did a sweep of the Sunset RV Park and Campground, talking to nearby campers and the owner of the campground, they found nothing and heard even less.

The case broke at 11:54 a.m. with the arrival of Grady Sanitation. The sanitation truck was a straight flatbed with a Ford E4500 engine.

Perched on the flatbed were two large off-white plastic tanks. The first tank had a six-inch-diameter, two-hundred-foot-long hose coiled around the tank. The second tank, a little smaller, was attached to a portable sprayer that was attached to the flatbed with two large orange straps that could ratchet tightly. A Briggs & Stratton motor/pump also was anchored to the flatbed. The green cab of truck advertised, GRADY SANITATION: WHERE A FLUSH BEATS A FULL HOUSE.

The driver parked the truck in front of the five port-a-potties. At the last unit on the right, he knocked but got no response. He yelled, knocked again, and tried to open the door, but it was locked. He was determined; he yelled and knocked repeatedly. Finally, he slid the blade of his pocketknife into the crack of the door and flipped up the locking mechanism; this obviously wasn't his first sanitation rodeo. He grabbed the two-hundred-foot hose, stuffed the end into the holding tank, went back to the Briggs & Stratton, hit "on," and the pumping began.

Within minutes, the pumping came to a halt, the engine whining; the pumping was either complete or the hose was clogged. The Grady employee went back to the portable outhouse, reached in with his elbow-length plastic yellow gloves to grab the end of the hose, and started screaming. The two Fort Wayne police officers, following the screams, then solved the case of the missing Mr. Hart. His pale face in the blue water stared up at them from the bottom of the holding tank.

Salas and Ronnie watched the crime-scene technician work the port-a-potty. "Reimers," Salas called out, "what are you doing?"

Reimers, the tech, had his kit, a large black briefcase—more like a tool kit—spread on the ground in front of the port-a-potty. Also on the ground were his sport coat and tie, which obviously weren't needed for the upcoming activity. Reimers, like the Grady employee, was wearing elbow-length gloves, the thin white latex type. He also had on a yellow jumpsuit over his street clothes.

Reimers was inside the outhouse, trying to get the body out of the holding tank. The door of the outhouse, however, kept hitting him in the rear, and the Grady employee had run over to help. Reimers and Grady were both sweating profusely.

"Hey, Detective. It's gotta be a hundred degrees in that sauna of a bathroom!" Reimers said. "We're trying to remove the body from the tank. I can't figure out how he got in there."

After slipping on a pair of latex gloves, Salas walked over to the port-a-potty and lifted the door up and twisted it. The door popped off its hinges, and he set it on the ground. "Excuse me," he said, nudging the Grady employee and Reimers to the side. He reached up with the butt of his palm and slammed it into the unit's ceiling. The roof was anchored by eight notches, thick plastic grooves that slid into the side-wall latches. Eight pops with his fist and the roof was on the ground. The side walls then swayed back and forth, easily lifting up and off the thick plastic base. Salas handed each section to the Grady employee, who laid them on the ground with the rest of the outhouse's plastic parts.

"There you go, Reimers. That should make things easier," Salas said.

"Thanks, Detective. I never thought of taking it apart."

The Grady employee shrugged. "Me neither."

"Now how do we get the body out?" Reimers stated more than asked.

Reimers went to the tank, bent over, saw how it was also attached to the plastic base, and decided to tip the tank to its side to snap it off the plastic base. Why? Salas too was curious.

As the tank landed on its side with a thud, the blue antiseptic and deodorizer liquid mixed with piss, shit, and toilet paper rushed out of the tank to the ground…and onto Reimers shoes, his kit, his coat and his tie.

"Well, that's one way to empty the tank," Salas said with a laugh.

The Grady employee came forward with a handsaw. "Let's cut the top off," he said, and started to saw from the side of the tank.

After about thirty strokes, Salas interrupted him. "Why not just expand the current opening instead of cutting off the entire top?"

The Grady employee shrugged again. "Never thought of that."

Ten minutes later, Kenneth Hart's body was on the ground. It was easy enough for Salas to see the hole in the man's neck; blood and blue liquid were oozing out of the wound.

"Looks like he was murdered" was Ronnie's input.

"You don't think he committed suicide or cramped up while swimming and drowned?" Salas said dryly.

Ronnie confirmed with the campground owner that more than two hundred guests had registered the previous night. Another fifty had paid cash, and he didn't always register those, he admitted. Passes were good for five days, so there could have been more than five hundred people with access, not including vendors, maintenance workers, friends, and visitors. Many of those people were now on the road, on vacation, and impossible to track. The campground had no security system and no fencing, so basically any one could have entered the premises and made the kill.

By three o'clock, they had no witnesses, no weapon, no clues, no motive, more than five hundred possible suspects, a traumatized wife, and a fatherless little boy.

Salas's fellow officers were right: this was a shitty job.

Deuce was sitting on his Harley, his ashen gray hair pulled back in a ponytail; he was waiting for RJ by the front gate. RJ's Harley was parked next to Deuce, freshly washed and filled with gas.

This was RJ's first free step in five years. He had spent his late forties and early fifties in lockup at the US Penitentiary, Administrative Maximum Facility, in Florence, Colorado—aka the Alcatraz of the Rockies. This was RJ's second stint in prison—eight years total behind bars. He swore there wouldn't be a third trip.

RJ never understood why he was in a maximum-security prison; he wasn't like the rest of the inmates. The federal judge, however, felt RJ was a threat to society, called him a terrorist, and sent him to Florence. So over the past five years, he was neighbors with the Boston marathon bomber, Dzhokar Tsarnaev; shoe bomber Richard Reid; and a 9/11 terrorist.

RJ never saw any of them, and if he did, he wouldn't have recognized them anyway. He was just one of a handful who wasn't a lifer at Florence. Oh, he was a lifer but not a prison lifer. RJ was a member of a gang. Thus, the judge's decision to be politically correct and place a bike gang member with other terrorists.

When RJ was a teenager, his parents were killed in an auto accident outside Greeley, Colorado, and he spent three years of high school with his grandparents. For graduation, they told him congrats and to move out. Grandma and Grandpa were long dead now; he had missed their funerals years ago while incarcerated, the first time.

In his early twenties, RJ had gone from job to job, city to city. His skill set was limited; he wasn't good with numbers and had no gift for mechanics, but he could fix almost everything on his Harley. He was too quiet and reserved for sales, lacked the discipline for a nine-to-five job, and probably should have joined the marines. He'd spent some time as a roughneck in the oil fields near Casper, Wyoming, and then as a truck driver for Crete Carriers in Lincoln, Nebraska, until they found out that he had forged his CDL. In Denver, RJ had loaded furniture at a warehouse but then quit to be a bouncer at a strip club—now *that* he was good at. And there, at the Players' Club, was where the Sons had chosen RJ; he didn't decide on the Sons himself.

At the beginning of any fight, RJ did his job and escorted the gentlemen out the door of the Players' Club. He was six foot three and a solid 220 pounds, so people moved when he guided them. Once outside, he usually called the police and headed back inside to do his work.

On one particular night, however, he stayed outside. RJ didn't like the match-up: a young guy, maybe twenty-six, RJ's age, had started a fight with a guy in his mid-forties. The older guy was out of shape—fat, really—and wearing a Sons of Silence leather vest that hadn't been buttoned in years. A typical bar fight, with pushing and shoving, lots of threats, and the old guy looking around for backup. The young guy popped a left jab—a really good one, RJ thought, like a real boxer—and snapped the old guy's head back. A couple of crisp body shots bent the old dude over, and after a right hook to the temple, he was out before he hit the pavement. Fight over, or so you would think.

The young guy's buddy, another twenty-something, then got tough and stepped in and kicked the unconscious old guy in the side not once but three times—all solid kicks to the ribs. The old guy wasn't feeling anything, as he was out cold, but he'd be very sore for a couple of months after. RJ didn't think—he just reacted—as he stepped in. He faced the kicker and landed a punch to guy's right eye that dropped him like a bad habit. The first guy yelled, "Hey, that was a cheap shot!" and squared off with RJ, whose arms were up, as if the referee had just said, "Are you ready to rumble!"

RJ faced the guy and did a leg kick that any UFC fighter would have appreciated, striking the guy on his lead leg. The guy's knee buckled, his anterior cruciate ligament ripped in two and his medial collateral ligament stretched and torn. The guy bent over, grabbing his knee and howling in pain. RJ did his own left jab and caught the guy in the eye, dropping him back on his butt. "You want me to do to you what you did to that old man?" RJ said, standing over him.

"No, please," the guy begged as three Denver police cruisers pulled up.

Locals versus the Sons of Silence was how it went in court.

Biker gangs don't fare well in that legal arena.

The old man with the Sons of Silence vest, well, he wasn't found after the fight when the cruisers pulled up, seems like his backup showed up and got him out of there. RJ was tagged a Son as he had fought with the guy who was wearing the Sons of Silence vest on. RJ was charged with assault on the two local boys. One with a fractured eye socket, the other with a black eye and blown knee. RJ was found with a knife on him, which didn't help. A knife he had confiscated from a strip club patron earlier in the evening. It didn't matter; RJ was railroaded and in jail within a month. Ten years for assault with a deadly weapon. The judge was hard on gang-related activity.

On his first day in the Colorado State Penitentiary prison yard, RJ was approached by group of skinheads, with swastikas tattooed on their necks and the back of their hands. Expecting the worse, he clenched his fists, but they merely informed him that he was protected; anything he needed, he would get.

Later that week, a group of Latinos approached RJ with the same message; he was protected. No explanations, just word from the two groups in charge that RJ was good, no worries.

He served three years of his ten-year sentence. A high-priced attorney he'd never met got him out early on good behavior. RJ was assigned a parole officer with strict orders to stay away from the Sons of Silence.

The day he left the Colorado State Penitentiary, like today, leaving federal lockup, Deuce was sitting on his Harley waiting for him, with an extra Harley by his side. RJ thought Deuce looked a lot thinner; at least the vest was buttoned, without extenders.

The night of the fight, Deuce disappeared but never forgot. The day Deuce met him at the penitentiary, RJ became a Son, no initiation, no trial period. RJ was now Deuce's protector.

RJ was awarded a black leather vest with the Sons' motto *"Donec Mors Non Separat"*—Latin for "Until Death Separates Us" stitched onto it.

Seems Deuce was an original one percenter and had stood next to Dude Richardson when the club was founded in the mid-sixties. Even the best lose their edge, though; Deuce had gone to the strip club early and alone, waiting for others to join him. As in any bar, wearing your colors was an invitation for trouble. The young, stupid, wannabes always were there to challenge you, and standing alone made you a target.

Deuce knew RJ had saved his life that night. Something he taught RJ and what he'd never forget was that you always pay back. RJ now had a family and a respected position within that family.

The second time RJ went to prison, it was also because he was protecting Deuce. Of all things, it happened during a Toys for Tots bike run in Denver. More than three hundred bikers—on all makes and models, though mostly Harleys—were lined up and had paid their twenty-dollar fee to ride fifty miles through metro Denver to raise money for the organization. The event culminated with burgers and beer in the Foothills Harley parking lot.

RJ, Deuce, and three other Sons had made the ride for several years and donated more than the twenty dollars a head, in addition to bringing saddlebags full of toys.

After the burgers and beer, twenty plus riders entered the local pub for additional adult beverages, RJ and Deuce included. The pub was empty except for the twenty bikers, who spread out and enjoyed the air conditioning and the Rockies on TV. Everything was going fine, but there's always one in every bar. Deuce blamed himself; he knew better than go into a bar with just two guys but thought, *Who's gonna pick a fight after a Toys for Tots charity ride?*

And of course, it's always the biggest guy in the state who wants to challenge your colors. This guy looked like Ed "Too Tall" Jones from the Dallas Cowboys. Tall, dark, and hostile. Too Tall got close enough and spoke loud enough for Deuce and RJ to hear him. "Yeah, they think they're fucking tough, wearing their colors. Real American badasses. Paid their entry fee with drug money, probably stole the toys they gave today."

Deuce and RJ made no response. Like a bee or a wasp, they can sting, but leave them alone, don't pay attention to them, and they usually go away.

"They should get fucking jobs like the rest of us!" was the limit of Too Tall's repertoire.

Still no response from RJ and Deuce. They watched the Rockies and ordered another beer.

Too Tall stepped closer behind the two Sons. *"Donec mars non separat,"* he pronounced, reading the back of their vests. "What's that mean? Pig Latin for 'I slept with my sister'?" He laughed loudly as several of the other bikers left the pub.

RJ tensed, the veins on his neck pulsating and went to turn, but Deuce held his arm down.

The large man stepped to the side and pushed Deuce hard against the shoulder, knocking him off the barstool to the floor. RJ reacted with force. A swift strike upward, and RJ crushed the tall man's larynx and windpipe. The man grabbed his throat and dropped to his knees, where RJ met him with a right and a left. The fight was over as the Too Tall collapsed on the barroom floor, blood streaming out of his nose, mouth, and ears.

A minute later, RJ looked up as an armed SWAT team rushed into the bar, knocking anyone inside down and on to the floor. The bartender had called the police when the big guy had first sounded off; SWAT was there within ten minutes. More than a dozen police officers surrounded the bar. Deuce and RJ were arrested, the only two arrests out of the twelve bikers. Too Tall was taken to the hospital and thankfully not to the morgue.

Deuce was released within hours; surprisingly he had a very clean record, with no arrests, and a strong military history. As for RJ, this was his second arrest, and he was still on probation. He had been ordered to stay away from the Sons and again was carrying a concealed weapon, this time a Glock 9mm pistol. No permit to purchase, no permit to carry, and the gun was stolen. Ten years in federal lockup, off in five for good behavior.

So here Deuce was again, waiting for RJ, like a father waiting for his prodigal son. A proud father sitting on his Harley, with RJ's '98 black Fat Boy at his side.

RJ hugged Deuce then swung his leg over the saddle. It felt good. "You look skinny, Deuce."

"Thanks. You need a haircut or a ponytail. You look like Jesus—well, a muscular Jesus. You've been lifting."

"Yeah, had some spare time on my hands."

"Let's ride."

It was Saturday, 1:00 pm.

Five hundred miles to Sturgis.

ALBERT

The ride to Omaha went faster than he'd expected. Albert did divert from his usual routine and rode the interstate for several hours. Cruising at a constant speed and making few stops got him past Omaha at five o'clock, so he pushed forward the last three hours to Sioux Falls, off I-29.

The ride was refreshing but also nerve-wracking. Albert was exhilarated for the first hundred miles, reliving putting Father in that shithole and relishing the feeling of the pick penetrating Father's brain and the dull thud of the pick hitting the skull. He could still feel the tug as he pulled the pick out. How the pick wanted to stay put, forever lodged in Father's brain. The warmth of the blood running down his arm on to his chest, how sticky it felt; the smell; the whites of Father's eyes shining in the moonlight.

The farther he rode, the more he started to panic. Albert was wondering if anyone saw him, if the police were looking for him. Every state patrol car that passed him made his heart beat faster. He dare not speed and rode at a constant seventy-three miles an hour.

By eight o'clock, Albert was tired and hungry. Nearly fourteen hours on the road, his longest ride ever. He pulled into a McDonald's and got a couple of one-dollar burgers and several cups of water, his first food of the day. After he gobbled down the meal, he found a KOA a few miles down the road where he would camp for the evening.

Per his calculations, if he left by seven in the morning he would be in Sturgis by two, set up camp, and hit the concert, the crowds, and the hunt. At Sturgis there were races, mountain climbs, vendors, special rides, and parties. You could find drugs or Jesus—depended on what you were looking for—but this year it was the hunt.

When Albert arrived at the Sioux Falls KOA, it was packed. At the reception office, the attendant said, "Tents only. We're full!"

Albert looked back behind him as if he had a trailer or was leading a caravan of RVs and said, "Okay."

He paid in cash then rode to the back of the campground, around the north side. Once again, he looked for a tent space by the exit. He didn't need a tree for shade or a spot near the restroom, although he did need a shower and to get rid of a bloody shirt. Albert still had on the T-shirt from the night before, it felt good to sleep in it, crusted with blood and stuck to his chest; he hated to get rid of it.

Sioux Falls would be a quick in and out. All Albert wanted and needed was sleep. The restless five hours on Friday night and the fourteen-hour ride had taken a toll on his body and mind. He looked forward to climbing into his sleeping bag and wanted a night under the stars—no tent tonight, just a bedroll on the ground.

It was always two or three things that would set Albert off: a high-pitched, demanding voice; an annoying laugh; or anytime someone was being belittled or picked on. Tonight, as he walked to the shower house, Albert heard two of the three.

He felt he was a lot like the biker who had put Father in the trash can all those years ago: quiet, controlled, strong, and apologetic to others. As he walked to the showers, he heard a man yelling at someone named Kelly. The man was saying something about a credit card and not notifying the company of their trip. "You stupid, bitch, why don't you do what I tell you!" Albert could feel her embarrassment and pain.

As he walked around the side of the RV, a Dune Seeker bumper-hitch toy hauler, Albert saw Kelly, her head hung low and sporting what Albert thought were the purple stains of a four- or five-day-old black eye. "I'm sorry, Ray," Kelly said, but Ray pushed her out of the way and went inside the trailer. Kelly saw Albert, lowered her head again, and sat down at the table, head in her hands. Albert felt sorry for her as she sat there at the picnic table. She had the campsite adorned with red Solo-cup lights hanging from the awning, along with two lawn chairs side by side on top of a piece of Astroturf, facing the setting sun.

Inside the shower house, Albert enjoyed the hot water and massaged his lower back, contemplating his next move. He'd never made kills two days in a row. That alone excited him, and the thought of putting that asshole Ray in his place made him want to leave the shower and pick him in front of the entire campground—in fact, they'd probably cheer him.

Albert dried himself off with paper towels supplied by the campground, saving his towel for the rally. He quickly dressed, then stuffed his bloody T-shirt into the garbage can underneath layers of dirty paper towels, empty toothpaste tubes, and shampoo bottles.

No plan…Albert was just walking to the RV to check the layout and the people.

It was just after ten, dark enough to blend in. The campers next to Ray and Kelly were in their RVs. No one was sitting by a fire; most likely no one wanted to be near Ray.

Albert remembered his first kill, it was the first year he had his bike: Auburn, Indiana, his hometown. He had stopped for a few minutes, in an alley, parking his Harley behind a red Dodge Ram pickup. He got off the bike and walked to a dumpster to toss out some trash that was in his saddlebags. While he was at the dumpster, the owner of the Dodge, a short guy with a loud mouth, came out of a building. "Hey, dumbass," he said. "Move that scooter."

"Okay, just throwing out some trash," Albert said.

"Move it now, dipshit, or I'll run the fucker over!" the man yelled, standing by the Dodge with the door open.

Albert said nothing as he went back to his bike, opened the rear saddlebag, and removed a Phillips screwdriver. He turned and walked up to the guy. Without a warning, threat, or sound, he drove the screwdriver under the man's chin, upward, lodging it inside the man's skull. The guy never knew what hit him; his eyes were wide open as Albert put him in the driver's seat of the truck, yanked out the screwdriver, then locked, and slammed the door of the Dodge.

Albert returned the screwdriver to his saddlebag, started the engine, and slowly rode away. There was no news of the murder in the Auburn paper for nearly three days. The body had been found by the city garbage haulers, as the alley was blocked and they had to move the pickup.

Tonight was similar: no plan, just a pick and the desire to get rid of the menace.

This guy, Ray, was a little bigger than he liked—bigger than Father but just like him in every other way. Albert walked up to the RV. Ray was sitting in the dark, in a lawn chair, smoking a cigarette, the ember of the menthol glowing. The lights were off inside the RV, and rock music played on the outdoor speakers of the toy hauler: "Sweet Home Alabama." Albert would see Lynyrd Skynyrd play in Sturgis. That made him smile.

"What do you want, dickweed?" was Ray's greeting.

"Wonder if you could help me. Could you check this out, please?" Albert said softly, heading to the back of the RV.

"What?" Ray stood, cigarette hanging from his lips.

As Ray came forward, Albert turned and thrust the ice pick up and through Ray's flesh, just under his jaw to the back of his skull. Albert looked Ray in the eye as the pick took out his life. No sounds, no screams, no grunts. Ray's was life gone, with Albert to thank for it.

Albert laid Ray on the ground, rolled the body up with the piece of Astroturf, and placed it under the camper, between the rear wheel and the leveler. Quietly, he placed the two folding lawn chairs and their covers on top of Ray's green turf. As Albert left, no lights came on in the RV, nor did he see any lights or movement at any of the neighboring RVs. He snapped a quick picture, this time being sure the flash was off. Just a picture of the RV, a picture of his summer vacation.

Back at his campsite, Albert rolled out his sleeping bag, lay down, and again slept restlessly, with visions of his father jumping in and out of his dreams. Tonight, it was when Father was training their new puppy, a gift from Grandma, a little brown lab Albert had named Harley. Father screamed at the dog and yanked on the leash, trying to get Harley to come to his name. Father always screamed at Harley and yanked the leash. Harley tried to run away, scared. Father yelled, "Harley!" and yanked. The force of the puppy going south and Father yanking north broke Harley's neck; the puppy died in Albert's arms.

At dawn, Albert awoke crying. He rolled up his sleeping bag and strapped it to his motorcycle. He put the bike in neutral, walked it through the exit to the street, started the engine; and slowly rode off.

Albert hoped Kelly would be happy. He didn't look back.

S alas had nothing. Here he was working on a Sunday, trying to figure out why some random guy in a random RV park was randomly killed while on vacation and, of all things, was stuffed in a shitter. Salas had no clues, no weapon, and a crime scene that had piss and shit all over it. The outhouse had plenty of fingerprints, enough that Salas said, "Forget it."

What they did know: the dead body was a thirty-seven-year-old white male, five foot three, 135 pounds, name of Kenneth Hart, father of one son named Andy, married to Nancy. No priors, not even a speeding ticket. Worked for FedEx in Cleveland for the past ten years; per human resources, he was well liked but known for his hot temper. Death was due to a sharp penetrating wound, entry approximately two inches from mid-mandible, a quarter inch in diameter. The wound was approximately eight inches in length. The weapon went through the esophagus and trachea, penetrating midbrain. Death was most likely instantaneous. The weapon could have been a screwdriver, a long nail, or an ice pick, something without serrated edges. The wife was not a suspect.

"Detective Salas?"

"I'm busy, Ronnie. It's Sunday. Go home and play with your kids," Salas said, his feet on his desk as he reviewed the file in his hands.

"Oh, I don't have children, Detective Salas. I'm not married, and well, I'm not really seeing anyone at this time. You know, I did just get my own place, a one-bedroom apartment on 5th Street. You know where that is, Detective Salas?"

"Ronnie?" Salas looked up at him.

"Yes, Detective Salas?"

"Shut up. And call me Mike or Salas." Salas went back to his file.

"Oh, yes. I forgot. Detective Salas?" Ronnie asked again.

"I'm busy, Ronnie. I want to get this report to Captain Green for the morning meeting, and I have no clues, no suspects, no motive, and no weapon. Just a DB in a shitter." Salas was impatient.

"But Detective Salas?" Ronnie tapped him on the toe of his shoe.

"What, Ronnie? You've got thirty seconds," Salas replied, taking his feet off the desk and grabbing another file.

"Well, they—they being the Sioux Falls Police Department—found a dead body, a DB, under an RV in a campground this morning," Ronnie stated, looking at Salas.

"Ronnie," Salas said, "my advice: your next vacation, do not stay at a campground."

"I agree, Detective Salas. Actually, I'm not a fan of camping. I'm not really an outdoors guy. I prefer major hotel chains—you know, ones that offer predictable rooms and service. I don't like surprises when I travel. I'm actually a gold member with Choice Hotels. I prefer Comfort Inns; they have excellent breakfast. Last month I stayed at a very nice Comfort Inn in Grand Rapids, Michigan. Have you ever been to their art week?"

"Ten, seconds, Ronnie."

"Oh, yes, ten seconds. Well, the dead body, DB…cause of death was a puncture wound under the mandible, through the esophagus and trachea, and into the brain. Medical examiner stated the most likely weapon was a screwdriver or ice pick." Ronnie finished and looked at his watch.

"Are you shitting me?" Salas stood.

"Yes, sir. I mean, uh, no, Detective Salas, I'm not shitting you." Ronnie backed away.

Salas went to Ronnie's desk, read through the report on the computer monitor, and read it again. Detectives in Sioux Falls with same dead ends as Fort Wayne. The big difference was that the body there wasn't in a port-a-potty but wrapped in a green rug and placed under an RV. No witnesses, no weapon, no motive, no clues. Wife went to sleep, woke up, and discovered the husband was gone. A couple of hours later, she saw the Astroturf under the RV and dragged it out. The report stated that the wife showed obvious signs of physical abuse. She was their primary suspect.

Salas turned to Ronnie, who was dressed in brown-and-off-brown plaid pants, black slip-on shoes, and white socks. His pants were at least two inches too short. If Ronnie weighed 140 pounds, he was all wet. At nearly six feet tall, he could look Salas in the eye. He had a sunken chest and most likely never had completed a push-up. His white polo shirt had coffee stains on the belly, mustard on the shoulder, and an alligator on the left breast. Ronnie was wiping his nose with the back of his hand when Salas said, "What do you think?"

"Me?" asked Ronnie.

"Yes, you. Related or unrelated?"

"Definitely related, Detective Salas," Ronnie said with conviction. "And as per the last page of the report"—he turned the computer monitor toward himself and hit the "page down" key twice—"the investigating detective found a bloody shirt in the campground's shower house. They're testing it to see if the blood is a match."

"Really," Salas said under his breath. "What's our next step, Ronnie?" He was looking at Ronnie's computer again.

"Well, I'd like to check a few things. If this guy has killed two people in two days, most likely he's killed before. Obviously with success, since he isn't in jail. My thought is to look for any other cases where people were killed with a screwdriver or ice pick."

"I like it, Ronnie. Tell you what, check out campgrounds in the following states for unsolved murders by ice pick or screwdriver: Indiana, South Dakota, Illinois, Michigan, Iowa, Missouri, Nebraska, Ohio, and Wisconsin." Salas was writing this down on paper.

"Yes, Detective Salas. It won't take long." Ronnie settled back into his office chair, adjusted his computer, and started typing.

"Call me Mike or…whatever."

Salas looked at his watch. It was three o'clock, Sunday. The weekend was over.

K evin pulled the RV off I-90 onto the first exit into Murdo, South Dakota. Matt followed and went straight to the gas pump for fuel. The RV held more than a hundred gallons of diesel, and at ten miles per gallon, he could nearly make it to Sturgis and back without filling up.

Parking the RV and trailer was no easy task; the fifty-foot-long RV plus the trailer took up eighty feet of space. Kevin found a spot along a side street with straight in and out access. He locked up the RV and walked the block to the café next to the gas station.

After a buffalo burger, fries, apple pie, and Diet Dr Pepper, both men decided to tour the Pioneer Auto Museum. During their stop, they took a few pictures of what was touted as Elvis's motorcycle, a car that was a replica of the General Lee from *The Dukes of Hazzard*, and of the waitress—all were sweet.

After they were back on I-90, their next stop was Wall, South Dakota, to hook up with Jerico. Kevin had never been to Wall, but the endless array of billboards advertising the place made it seem like the vacation Mecca of the Midwest.

The traffic was intense and would've been bad enough on a good road; however, the South Dakota Department of Transportation had decided to make it even more of a challenge. Bridgework drew all traffic from two lanes to one and from eighty mph to thirty-five mph for a stretch of more than thirty miles.

The Sturgis rally was the state's biggest annual moneymaker, so why they were doing road construction during this time was beyond comprehension.

Kevin drove by two accidents, one with an ambulance and a medevac. Two bikers were in a ditch, along with a pickup and a horse trailer that most likely took the ditch to miss the bikers. The trailer was empty.

Matt was content to follow the RV, which wasn't only blocking the wind but also taking care of the mass of grasshoppers that seemed to take over the highway; he had a welt on his left cheek from a grasshopper collision earlier that day.

Wall South, Dakota, isn't a big town, but more than two million people visit Wall Drug every year; after all, they advertise water for five cents. Wall Drug opened in 1931, the 5-cent water was free then, an attraction in the Dirty Thirties and the Great Depression.

As Kevin drove into Wall, he realized his first mistake. One million of its two million annual visitors seemed to be there on this particular Saturday; thankfully he didn't need fuel. He slowly pulled the RV to a remote side street and parked in front of two private residences (which he'd soon find out was his second mistake).

Kevin walked up the street to the gas station where Matt had stopped for fuel. Matt was just getting to the pump after a ten-minute wait in line. The station was so packed with bikers that Kevin couldn't see the pavement, the curb, or even the gas station windows. The noise was deafening: the roar of the bikes, the yelling of the bikers, the grinding of gears, the barking of dogs.

Matt filled the tank and parked the Harley, backing it into a spot at the curb of the gas station. He used his barrel key to lock the handlebars in the left-turn position, locked the gas cap, then locked the padlocks on each saddlebag.

Kevin was texting Jerico, who was waiting for them inside Wall Drug.

Committing to tour Wall Drug was mistake number three. The line to enter the drugstore was thirty to forty people deep and consisted of bikers and, well, more bikers. If they'd been taking a cover charge, the place still would have been packed. Standing in line in ninety-five-degree heat and eighty-five percent humidity, with the western sun boiling down on and no wind, was like doing hot yoga without the stretching. Kevin and Matt stood there and sweated.

When they finally made it through the throng, they found Jerico just inside the entrance. Jerico was washing his hands with a three-ounce bottle of Purell.

The air conditioning inside Wall Drug was finally cooling them off. The three men greeted each other with hugs, after which Matt and Jerico faked takedowns, haymakers, and punches to the belly. They hadn't seen each other in a couple of years but were picking up where they'd left off.

They walked the length of the store; they never did find the five cent water or the free doughnuts for veterans, but they did get a picture of Matt and Jerico side by side with a mechanical T. rex.

Kevin kept true to his picture album and asked the prettiest waitress for a group picture. He then convinced two biker babes—ladies in their early forties, sporting bandanas, tank tops, and butt-less chaps—to pose with Jerico and Matt. Jerico got a cell-phone number from the brunette and a promise to meet at the Chip.

When they left the store, Matt and Jerico headed to their bikes and told Kevin they'd meet him at the second Wall exit off I-90. Kevin walked over to the residential street, where he realized his mistake number two. The side street that he had pulled the RV and trailer onto was a dead end, thus he would now have to back the eighty-foot unit up the incline and make a sharp right turn into a narrow alley lined by trees, bushes, and a storage shed.

The other option was to back up the way he had come in, about a one-mile trip up a hill that was lined with cars, motorcycles, and two pickups with horse trailers. This route required backing all the way up to the gas station before he could possibly turn and go forward. Kevin opted for option one, the alley. Why? Well, there was no one there to watch. Option two had a gallery that would best the Masters crowd.

Now Kevin had the most sophisticated trailer package imaginable, complete with cameras and a flat-screen built into the dash that showed distance and objects on all sides. He fired up the 8.9-liter 350 HP Cummings diesel and started the backup process. It was easy going at first, as the diesel backed the trailer up and Kevin started the right turn down the narrow alley.

Down the alley was where the confusion started. The trailer was nearly as wide as the alley, with the trees and bushes scraping the aluminum siding and obscuring the view of his backup cameras. Kevin got out and crawled his way through the dense trees and bushes only to find the next five feet would have him backing into the metal storage shed. His only hope was to go forward and try a sharp turn.

Back in the RV, he looked right and left. No one was in their yards, and he couldn't see anyone peering through their windows. He put the diesel in low, cranked the steering wheel hard to the left, and pulled forward. The RV's left tire jumped the curb onto the sidewalk but still turned left. Kevin was turning hard, and he knew he was going to go onto the grass. When the right front wheel hit the curb, the steering wheel jumped out of his hands, and the entire RV went forward another five feet. Now both tires were in someone's front yard.

"The hell with it!" he yelled, then floored the gas pedal and slammed it into second, driving the RV over the yard, through the side bushes, and onto the street.

A mile later, he was at the exit. Matt and Jerico were waiting with their hands out, as if to say, "Where the heck have you been?"

Back on I-90, they had forty-four miles to Rapid City, another twenty-five to Sturgis, then ten to the Chip. As Kevin drove the RV, he kept a close look in his side mirrors, watching out for the two boys following him. He rarely changed lanes and was very proactive and defensive with his driving. Better to be safe than sorry on the road, he figured.

Kevin enjoyed the wide-open view the RV gave him and appreciated the name "Black Hills" as the hills came into clearer focus. The pine trees lining the hills against the western sky did make the hills look black—one long black horizon.

He thought the motorcycle traffic in Murdo and Wall was heavy, but compared to I-90 from Rapid City to Sturgis, it was nothing. Traffic slowed east of Rapid City, near the new Cabela's, to the Locust Street exit, to less than fifty-five miles an hour.

From Locust past Rushmore Mall, cars and bikes were traveling at around forty-five miles an hour. And from there to the Deadwood Avenue exit—the Rapid City Harley-Davidson exit—traffic was moving at less than thirty-five, with the right lane, the exit lane, at a complete standstill.

Once he got past Deadwood Avenue, traffic got back to as high as sixty, but it was bumper-to-bumper and tire-to-tire the last fifteen miles before the first Sturgis exit.

A month ago—or really anytime, besides the first few weeks of August—Sturgis was a quiet, peaceful ranching and farming community of 6,627 people. The Black Hills lay to the south, running almost to the large cattle ranches and farms of Nebraska, with the vast empty lands of Wyoming to the west; and cattle and fertile alfalfa fields in North Dakota. Every year the rally nearly doubled the population of South Dakota; this was especially the case during its seventy-fifth anniversary.

The transformation of the city of Sturgis to a motorcycle-rally venue always began a couple of weeks before the rally. Local stores changed their facades, from flower shop to tattoo parlor, from lumberyard to bar, from bar to bar and grill. Vendor's tents lined Lazelle Street from the west exit to the east exit. Some bars were open all year, though most were seasonal. Houses were rented; yards became camping spaces; many people owned homes in Sturgis just for the rally; and home garages became gathering spaces for friends and family.

A town where just a few weeks ago kids rode their bikes to school and neighbors left their houses unlocked, became a lockdown area where more than $300,000 worth of bikes would be stolen; three hundred people would be arrested for DUIs; and 110 drug arrests would occur—not to mention a dozen fatalities, hundreds of accidents and injuries, and several concealed-weapon violations.

Driving the RV through Sturgis was grueling for Kevin. He just wanted to set up camp and have a cold beer. The drive from the first Sturgis exit to the turn at Lazelle and Highway 34 to the Chip took more than an hour. When they arrived in town, Jerico and Matt shut down their bikes, straddled the seats, and walked their motorcycles the mile to Lazelle, all the while breathing the diesel from Kevin's RV. The South Dakota sun and idling V-twins under their asses were melting the boys.

The right turn at Lazelle was tricky, as the RV took up nearly three lanes in the turn, this time with no grass to drive on. Kevin was thankful to the bikers in the westbound lanes for moving aside, as if they had a choice.

When they finally arrived at the Chip, the check-in process was relatively easy: thirty minutes waiting in line, the RV searched for alcohol, and an escort to their designated campsite.

Kevin had enough beer and whiskey to open his own bar, all neatly packed under the floorboard beneath the king-size bed. Online chat rooms had forewarned him about the alcohol ban, so he had the RV customized with a secret storage space.

A blonde, blue-eyed teenage girl with a Sturgis High School State Wrestling Champions T-shirt and a dirt-smudged face from the road dust, guided Kevin and the boys through a maze of campers, tents, RVs, trailers, and cars to their concrete slab. When the young lady left, Kevin arranged the RV and trailer to take up two spots, forming a northwest wall to block the wind. Their campsite would directly face a group of two hundred or so campers. Several of them stared as the enormous RV and trailer nearly blocked out the sun. Kevin hooked up the electrical, cranked up the RV's air conditioner, and yelled orders to the boys to set up camp.

A twenty-four-by-twenty-four-foot brown-and-black indoor/outdoor carpet was first to be tacked into the ground. The RV spot came with a picnic table, which the boys placed on one end of the carpet. A large folding table was brought from the undercarriage storage space; a three-foot-tall fan was connected to keep the camping area cool; and Matt drove a steel pole into the ground at each end of the campsite to hang the bug lights. The electric awning offered shade, and LED mood lights were strewn from the awning and along the camping perimeter.

Telling Jerico to forget the Purell and get to work, Kevin gave his buddy firm orders regarding how to raise the thirty-foot-tall flag post at the side of the RV and also instructed him on how to unfold and hang the American flag. Within minutes, Old Glory was waving in the strong northern breeze.

Next was the outdoor TV, connected to DISH Network. The indoor stereo was cranked to 98.6 FM classic rock, with the outdoor speakers feeding the campsite and tenters. The grill was a slide-out with a direct connect to propane. A dozen lawn chairs were set up around the carpet, with coolers of beer placed under the RV by the rear wheels, out of the sun.

Kevin gave the order to unload the trailer. Jerico lowered the ramp while Kevin backed the golf cart out and parked it next to the road, between the tenters and the campsite. Matt backed out Kevin's Harley, and both Matt and Jerico pushed the bike to park it next to Jerico's Big Dog. Kevin's ride clearly outshone the bikes of the two guys who had actually ridden theirs to Sturgis.

Inside the trailer was a mechanic's paradise. Kevin pointed out the cleaning materials, which he expected Matt and Jerico to use on their bikes, as well as the tool cabinet, parts department, extra gas, oil, and fluids. The trailer was also air-conditioned, and as Kevin pointed out, offered two additional beds that came down from the ceiling like bunk beds.

Inside the RV, Kevin triggered the three bump-outs, which drastically increased the size of the living quarters. He claimed the back king-size bed, and the RV also had a restroom with a shower and a bath, along with granite counter tops, and a full-length mirror. Both Jerico and Matt had queen-size bump-out beds in the living room, giving everyone easy access through the entire RV. They didn't unfold the kitchen table; they'd only need that if it rained and they had to eat inside. The ceramic tile floor was heated, though Kevin doubted they would need that.

The dark Cherrywood custom cabinets now held basic liquor staples like Jack, Fireball, several kinds of tequila, and Ketel One. Most of the hard liquor (especially the Jameson) would stay under the bed, in case there were any additional Gestapo-type inspections.

The standard-size fridge held eggs, juice, some fruit, seltzer water, club soda, Pepsi, Diet Pepsi, and enough Gatorade to last a month. The pantry was stocked like a minimart with breakfast bars, chips, and crackers, and the freezer with bacon, T-bone steaks, rib eyes, New York steaks, and more than fifty pounds of chicken drummies, thighs, and wings.

They also had four coolers of beer, three coolers of ice, and a cooler of bottled water. Kevin set up the Keurig coffee maker with French vanilla, mountain roast, and hazelnut options.

By 9:00 p.m., the camp met inspection. Kevin ordered Matt and Jerico to the center of the campsite and awarded each with a cold

Heineken and a shot of Fireball. They toasted each beer and each shot, and then Kevin threw the steaks on the grill.

After dinner, Kevin told the boys to take the golf cart to the main stage while he cleaned up camp. Plus, Kevin wanted to call his girlfriend Gloria.

Jerico and Matt were off on the golf cart; Jerico felt he was far too drunk to ride his bike but felt driving a golf cart was okay. They drove about a hundred yards when Matt had a great idea: if he stood on the back of the cart, where the golf clubs would go, and Jerico floored the gas pedal, they could pop a wheelie. Matt, the rocket scientist of the two, was right about this, although it was just the 220 pounds of Matt that made the front wheels go in the air rather than the actual physics of speed times force.

After four or five wheelies and cheers from the crowd, they slowed down and picked up two girls who were walking to the main stage, then a couple more and a couple more, until twelve people were hanging on the golf cart, and it was going about five miles an hour. Fortunately, the golf cart's gas engine was the little engine that could and made it to the entrance. After they all got off, Jerico took the key, and they went to the first bar, where three of the riders had Jäger shots while waiting for the boys.

It was Saturday11:05 p.m. t their first night at Sturgis.

ALBERT

The ride from Sioux Falls to Sturgis went fast. Albert went slightly south and hit Highway 44 through South Dakota. He liked getting off the interstate. He was so excited over his last kill. That man needed killing, and he was sure everyone at the campground was happy about. He wished he could go back and get his hand shaken and have Kelly tell him, "Thank you, Albert."

On Highway 44, he rode through Lennox and Parker and got fuel in Corsica. Bike traffic was busy, even on the off roads; he thought the interstate would be even busier. He stopped at Lake Francis Case and the Missouri River. He took some pictures with his cell phone, pictures he knew his mother would like. He only had about 50 percent of his battery left and wondered where or if he'd ever get the phone charged again. Albert shut off the phone and placed it in his saddlebag.

His next fuel stop was in Winner South Dakota; he could have ridden farther, but had to pee. He bought a sandwich at the Little Feller gas station then rode to White River, where he took a right at the junction and then the first left to stay on 44.

Albert's next stop was in Wanblee, and he definitely had to stop this time since he was nearly out of fuel. The pump was pay-before-you-pump. This was the first station where he had stopped where there weren't several bikers. Wanblee was a reservation town—Pine Ridge Indian Reservation. The people inside the station, all Native Americans, were pleasant and smiled at Albert when he walked in to pay.

On the ride from Wanblee to Interior, he jumped in behind a white-and-silver Big Dog bike. The rider had a huge back, and the rear tire was the widest he'd ever seen on a motorcyle. The street sweepers on the bike were loud, so Albert backed off fifty yards or so to escape the noise. He'd never heard a bike that loud before. They rode the forty miles to Interior at near eighty mph, with Albert struggling to ride that fast. The Big Dog turned left at Interior then quickly turned right into a bar with a huge white-and-red tent. Albert rode on but thought about stopping to see the large bull in front of the tent.

He rode through the Badlands, long lonely stretches of rural highway, with the haze of heat waving off the asphalt. Traffic was sparse, with nothing coming toward him, although a few bikes popped up on the horizon several miles ahead. His mind drifted to junior high. Back then, he went through an awkward stage, like most adolescents. Acne-faced, uncoordinated, clumsy, hormonal—and he had a crush on the neighbor girl. One day, Albert was talking to Rebecca over the chain link fence that separated the two backyards. Blushing, he shuffled his feet, thankful Rebecca was a talker.

Father came home from work, pulling into the driveway, the Chevy stopping in front of the two teens. "Well, hello, Al-bert! This your lady friend? Be sure not to cum in your pants like you pee in your bed." Father laughed to himself. Crushed, Albert ran inside the house and to his room and shut the door. He heard Father laughing in the kitchen.

Tears streamed down his face as he rode past Caputa and into Rapid City.

Albert stopped again for fuel in Rapid, checked his atlas, and decided to continue on to Highway 234 and Nemo Road. He was now in the Black Hills. The roads were narrower, with thirty-five-mile-an-hour curves. The number of bikes on the road picked up past Interior, with Rapid City getting busier. This road to Nemo was the busiest yet.

Eventually he fell into a group of twenty-five to thirty bikers. He was last in line and tried to count them as he rode. After a few miles on the road to Nemo, he had another five to eight bikes behind him. Albert loved riding in large groups like this in alternate formation; it made him feel like he was in a biker gang.

The road to Nemo turned into Vanocker Canyon Road, which was full of twists and turns. The biker gang rode into Sturgis under I-90 at the first Sturgis exit, and then they slowed from thirty-five to forty-five miles an hour to a dead stop. It took longer to go the next mile than it took to ride there from Rapid City.

Albert held his clutch for what seemed like an hour; traffic was barely moving. Sweat poured off his head from the heat from the sun and the heat from the engine; his leather jacket was like a personal sauna. Bikers were in front of him, in back of him, and on the both sides. And Albert was with them all; he was a biker.

As the group approached the Highway 34 turn, the guy next to him yelled, "Put that bike in neutral, bro. You're going to burn out your clutch!" Albert nodded in thanks and did as told. He didn't know what burning out his clutch meant but would look it up on the Internet when he got home.

After he turned right, it was an easier ride the last few miles. He stopped at the Full Throttle Saloon, parked his bike, and walked around the world's largest biker bar. Back home, Albert always watched the reality show based on the bar. He didn't like the owner, Michael, on the show and wondered why he had those stupid-looking dreadlocks. Michael's girlfriend, though, she was very pretty, but Mother thought she dressed slutty and was only after Michael for his money. "Why else would a pretty girl like that be with him?" Mother had said.

There were so many bikers at the bar that it was shoulder-to-shoulder. Men were drinking beer, talking loudly, and flirting with the waitresses. Albert thought all the girls were so pretty, and one day he'd get a girlfriend just like one of these girls because he was a biker. But he'd never bring his girl here; all the bikers would hit on her.

Albert left the Throttle, went east on 34, and rode into the Buffalo Chip. He paid with his Visa card, and again the registration lady told him, "No campers or RVs. We're full. Tents only."

Albert looked behind him then looked back at the lady and said, "I don't have a camper. I just have a tent."

"Good. Put your tent anywhere you see other tents. No tents by RVs, no tents by campers, *capiche*?" said the lady.

Albert tilted his head and looked at her.

"Understand?" she said.

"Yes, tents by tents. I understand." Albert signed the credit card slip and left the office. He got on his bike and entered the Chip.

Albert had pitched his tent, placed the rain fly on top, and secured the guy-wires. Next, he laid out his mattress pad and unrolled his sleeping bag. After he unfolded and set up his camp chair, his campsite was ready—it took all of five minutes. Albert faced the tent to the south to avoid the north wind. He then unloaded his saddlebags and arranged his clothes and breakfast bars inside the tent. The spot he had chosen had a slight downhill lean to it, so when he placed his camp chair out to face the sun, it too tilted downhill. After trying several spots, he found the most level part of his campsite was next to his Harley and facing the road.

As he sat in his chair, the approaching RV and trailer weren't hard to miss. The owner of the RV angled his unit back and forth to take up what looked like two spaces. Maybe he'd paid for both; Albert didn't care.

What Albert noticed most and gawked at were the two younger men who were with the loudmouthed little guy who drove the RV. They were huge. Albert thought they both could have been linebackers for the Colts.

He was surprised at how the little guy barked orders at them and how they obeyed. The biggest guy—he thought they'd called him Matt—had enormous arms and thighs. The other guy, Jerry—at least that's what he thought his name was—was nearly as big and had a slight limp when he walked. Albert wanted to be as big as they were. He loved to lift and could tell both these guys were weightlifters. Maybe he would talk to them about their weightlifting routines and get some pointers. Albert had gotten his routine from a magazine a couple of years ago. He worked his chest and back on Mondays and Thursdays, shoulders and arms on Tuesdays and Fridays, and legs on Wednesdays. Saturdays, he jogged. Sundays, he rested, but every day he did sit-ups and crunches. Albert could bench-press more than three hundred pounds, pretty good for a guy who only weighed 165. He could squat four hundred pounds and dead-lift 425. He dreamed of becoming a pro bodybuilder, the next Franco Colombu.

The linebacker named Matt had hammered in a long steel post with two or three swings of a sledgehammer; he made it look easy. Albert wondered if those two really did play pro ball.

Listening to the little RV guy give orders with his high-pitched voice and ungodly annoying cackle of a laugh convinced Albert that this was the one. This was destiny—he was in Sturgis, and it was his destiny that the guy in the RV straight across from his tent would be Father. It was destiny that this was the seventy-fifth year of the rally and destiny that it was the largest biker rally ever. The biggest crowd, the baddest people, the two huge football players with Father. This was it; the hunt was over. With the two football monsters next to Father, Albert would have to plan carefully, look for the right opportunity, and always be prepared to take advantage of any given moment.

Albert's first decision: where to put Father? The shower house? A dumpster? He loved the port-a-potty kill; perhaps he'd kill this guy in that huge RV and stuff him in the RV's bathroom. Albert didn't know if all RVs had a bathroom and wondered how he could get inside to find out. The kill might go down tonight. On the other hand, he would love to tell him, "Today you live, but tomorrow I'll most likely kill you." Like in that one movie with the pirate, André the Giant, and the man with six fingers.

"Tomorrow I'll most likely kill you," Albert said softly, then repeated, "Tomorrow I'll most likely kill you." He smiled as the three men touched their glasses in a toast.

Albert sat in his lawn chair, alone, facing the little guy's RV. He sat and watched as the three men drank and drank, toasted again and again, sang along to several songs, and pissed behind the RV.

He was surprised when the two linebackers jumped onto the golf cart and rode away, leaving the little guy alone at the RV. Albert sat patiently, watching and looking for the two weightlifters to return. He thought about going up to the campsite, introducing himself, and asking the little guy to show him the inside of his RV, then ice-picking the asshole and stuffing him in the toilet. Resisting the urge, Albert sat and waited; he knew the big guys would return. He knew if he went over there now, he'd be caught, so he sat and waited. And waited.

The boys didn't come back anytime soon, but eventually two guys rode up and pitched a tent next to his.

When Albert saw that the two men were wearing Sons of Silence vests, his heart raced. He was camping next to the Sons! He told himself he would take their picture in the morning, maybe see what it would take for him to join the gang. He wondered if he should tell them about his kills; they would love that, he thought.

Albert sat in his lawn chair, stealing glimpses of Father, the little annoying man in the RV, and staring at the two gang members. The old man pitched the tent and lay down while the big hairy one with the barrel chest tried to work on his Harley. Albert thought he should go help, but then the little guy from the RV walked over and beat him to it, which pissed Albert off. They talked for a minute or two, and soon the big guy pushed his Harley into the RV guy's enormous trailer.

When the little guy turned on the trailer's interior lights, Albert was amazed at the tools and the hoist; the trailer was bigger than his living room at home and a lot nicer.

Albert watched the Son work on his Harley while the little guy put a couple more steaks on the grill. They were both drinking beer. Albert thought he should go over and join them, be a part of the conversation, and maybe they would offer him a beer too, but he just sat there and watched. He couldn't hear the conversation, but he heard Father's squeaky, annoying voice and laugh. Albert knew he'd take care of the little man and put him in his place, but tonight wasn't the night. He crawled into his tent to go to sleep.

Be patient, he thought. Tomorrow I'll most likely kill you.

The ladies were driving straight through to Sturgis, taking turns sleeping and driving. Ann drove to Kansas City, Missouri; Jessica from Kansas City to Omaha; and Summer the early-morning shift, through Sioux City, Iowa, to Sioux Falls, South Dakota.

They had five hours left. The girls were on schedule when they stopped for breakfast at Perkins off I-29 in Sioux Falls.

The restaurant was packed with bikers, and the parking lot was full of pickups pulling campers, fifth-wheel toy haulers, and a few RVs. When the four girls entered Perkins, all heads turned. Everyone in the place stopped talking and eating when they saw them. Several wives slapped their men on the shoulder, and one lady told her husband to shut his mouth as his jaw had dropped when they walked in. Another man said, "Those can't be real," while another whispered, "They must be hookers."

As the girls were being seated in the back room against the wall, Summer stopped in the restroom to freshen up. All eyes were on them as they walked through the restaurant. Jessica ordered a pot of coffee—no sleeping from here to Sturgis.

A young man sitting across from them got up from his table of three guys. The man was dressed in leather chaps, black leather boots, a black leather jacket, and a leather bandana. "Good morning, ladies" was his opening line as he proceeded to sit in the empty chair saved for Summer. "We'd like you ladies to join us for breakfast."

"Sorry, sweetie." Ann spoke up first. "You only have a table for four."

"Tell you what, a couple of us can sit here, and a couple of you can sit over there." He pointed at his friends, all of whom wore wide grins.

"Are you a real biker?" Jessica asked.

"Sure am, beautiful," the young man replied, his chest puffed out.

"Well, then, you must have just bought new leathers. All your gear looks like you just got it out of the box," Jessica replied, and all three girls laughed hysterically.

The guy got up and rejoined his buddies, who were also laughing.

Summer came out of the restroom. She had watered down her hair and pulled her hair back in a ponytail. The mini shower she had taken had gotten water all over her white tank top. It was a wet T-shirt breakfast at Perkins.

A hush settled over the entire restaurant as Summer walked through the crowd. Spotting her friends, she smiled and hurried to their table. The increase in speed correlated well with the movement of her breasts. No bra, just a T-shirt—just a wet T-shirt—and the water must have been slightly chilled.

Summer sat down at the table, grabbed a menu, and asked the others what they were getting. She had no clue as to the scene she'd just made.

The girls ordered their food, drank two pots of coffee, and discussed their outfits, their boyfriends, the weather, and how nice everyone was at Perkins.

Several guys walked by and said hello to the girls. An older gentleman approached their waitress and said, "I'll take their bill." He then turned to the girls and said, "Young ladies, I take it you're going to Sturgis. Have a great time and thank you for coming to Perkins." He walked away to the cash register.

"Was that the manager?" Summer asked.

"I don't think so. He had a Harley shirt on," Jessica said.

"People in South Dakota are so nice," Shelly added.

As they walked to the car, they were greeted with whistles, stares, and offers to ride on Harleys. The ladies held firm, smiled, and politely said, "No, thanks."

Ann told the girls, "This'll be nothing compared to what we'll get in Sturgis. Remember, always smile and wink and wink and smile. We're going there for the tips and the cash, not to land a husband or a boyfriend! Agreed?"

The four girls made a pact. No relationships. Just work.

Aside from a delay near Murdo, South Dakota—some kind of accident—the drive to Sturgis was smooth going. They pulled off I-90 at the first Sturgis exit at 11:00 a.m.; they had gained an hour near Kadoka. The traffic off of the exit was backed up for a mile out.

As they drove down the two-lane road to Lazelle and Highway 34, biker after biker rode up next to them, whistled, yelled, and asked them to roll down their windows. The girls obliged at first, advertising that they were working at the Buffalo Chip, but the ninety-five-degree South Dakota sun quickly changed their minds—they decided it was smarter to keep the windows up and the air conditioning on.

Ann was driving as they pulled into the Chip. The girls got out and went to the main administration building and checked in with security. The receptionist gave them a map of the campground, a list of the bars and their locations, the names of the barbacks assigned to each bar, as well as directions to their cabin.

A campground security guard, Bobby, escorted the ladies on his Honda Trail 90 to their cabin; his bright yellow security shirt was easy to follow.

Their vision of a log cabin against the background of rolling hills and a sunset on the prairie was soon forgotten. The cabin, more of a utility or storage shed, was one of fifty in five rows of ten. Bobby unlocked the cabin door, turned on the window air-conditioning unit, and gave each girl a key.

Bobby reminded them that they each had a secure lockbox in the admin building to store their tips, and anytime they wanted, he was there to give them a ride.

"On that little thing?" Jessica asked, pointing at the Trail 90.

"No, we have golf carts too," he said, his mouth agape as he stared at Jessica's chest. "Here's my cell number and the number to security. Call anytime and we'll come get you. It's about a mile walk to the main stage." Bobby didn't look any of the girls in the eye; he just stared at their chests.

The "spacious" cabin, as promised by the modeling agency, was crammed with four twin beds—two beds on each side of the cabin, pushed together end to end. There was maybe two feet of walking space between the beds, along with a mini fridge against the wall. There were four hooks on the back door, and the ceiling consisted of the rafters. There was no insulation, and the walls were just the four-by-twos. The door had a lock, but you could see daylight through the open spaces at the top, the bottom, and on both sides. A fine layer of dust covered all the beds. Camelot, it was not.

Each girl claimed a bed, a door hook, and their own personal rafter. They hung their clothes and towels, and arranged their shoes under their beds. They were told to report to their assigned bar at two o'clock. No time to lounge by the pool, no time to shop, no time to eat.

Summer dressed in butt-less leather chaps with pink panties that said "Pink" on the butt. She wore a pink swimsuit top that was perhaps a size or two too small for her. Her belly ring was a three-inch-long gold chain that went nearly to the top of her panties and the buckle on her leather chaps. She also wore black, leather, spiked heels, which were impossible to walk in and would soon be off while she was working. Summer had several random tattoos, including the Tasmanian Devil on her left foot, a four-leaf clover on her inner thigh, and a silhouette of her sister on her left shoulder.

Ann wore fishnet stockings under a red-and-black plaid schoolgirl miniskirt. Her white blouse was tied in the front, above her belly button, with the sleeves rolled up to the elbows. She wore blacked-rimmed glasses, even though she didn't need them; they just matched the outfit. Her brunette hair was tied back in a ponytail with a red-and-black plaid ribbon. Her shoes were more practical than Summer's: black flats with Dr. Scholl's inserts for extra padding.

Shelly went for the devilish look. She had on a bright-red swimsuit, thong and all. There wasn't a whole lot of material on her; she might as well have been naked. She made up for the thong with a trident as a tail. The trident was secured to her thong by a light fish line. On her head she wore devil's horns, bright-red bobby-pinned into her hair. Shelly was the only one of the three with a tramp stamp on her lower back, some kind of barbwire in wings. Her shoulders were covered in tats as well, small birds flying and huge angel wings on her back.

Jessica wore a black bikini top and bottom, along with black mouse ears pinned in her hair. Her short black leather vest went just below her breasts. "*Semper Fi*" was embroidered on the back of the vest. Her nose was painted black, and she had etched three whiskers on each cheek.

Each girl had a bucket to house their tips, along with their purse. Their room keys and cell phones were inside their purses. They each entered security's phone number as a contact in their phones, as well as Bobby's number, even though they all agreed Bobby was kind of freaking them out.

Their call to security was answered, and a ride was there within five minutes. One cart for four girls and the driver. This time it wasn't Bobby, but a tall guy named Jake. When he opened the cabin door, he had to duck to enter. His body blocked out the sun. Jake was proud to tell them that he played football at Chadron State College, was on the "O" line, and he and three of his buddies would be in charge of security tonight. He gave each girl his cell phone number—his personal number, as he said, as if he had a business number too. As he dropped each girl off at their assigned bar, he asked for their cell numbers, but no one volunteered.

Jessica was amazed at how busy the bar at the entrance was and how well the bikers tipped. Beers were four dollars; most paid with a five-dollar bill, which meant a one-dollar tip for opening a beer. The more she smiled and winked, the better the tip. "Please come back!" she told them all. "Don't forget me!"

If they paid with a ten-dollar bill, she gave back six ones, and then the tip was usually two dollars. If they paid with a twenty, she gave back a ten-dollar bill and six ones; again, the tip was usually two dollars. Jack and Coke was the mixed drink of choice at six dollars, double Jack at eight dollars. She always offered the double Jack—nine out of ten took her up on it, thus another two-dollar tip. She was opening beers and mixing drinks at a sprinter's pace, with no time to check her phone, her tips, her hair or take a drink or go pee. This pace went on all afternoon and increased as the sun went down.

The bar Jessica was stationed at was on the second floor. A winding metal staircase at each end was constantly packed with guys going up or down.

Rock music was playing, and she would sing along with some songs, touch a guy's hand a little too long when giving change, smile, and wink some more. Jessica also called each patron by a different name—big shooter, bad boy, honey, handsome, brown eyes, blue eyes, sweetie, darling—always being sure not to use the same name too close to the last, making each guy feel special.

By sundown she had some regulars, with bikers easily spending $100 over the past few hours at five and six dollars a time. As the night wore on, some guys were buying a beer for four dollars and tipping her six dollars off a ten-dollar bill. One old guy gave her a twenty and told her to keep the change. She'd ask for those guys' names and was amazing at remembering them when they came back up. Twice she emptied her bucket, folded the cash, wrapped it with a rubber band, and stuffed it into her purse. The emptier the bucket, the more the guys tipped.

If it slowed, which it rarely did, Jessica would ask men to pose with her for a picture. She'd grab some guy, usually the oldest one in her vicinity, and yell, "Take a picture with me, please?" Her lower lip would be pouty, and the cameras and cell phones would come out in force. Jessica's beautiful white smile and outfit brought a number of takers, all of whom handed her a five- or ten-dollar bill for the chance to get a picture with her so they could send it to their buddies.

At 1:00 a.m., the band on the Wolfman Jack main stage bid their farewells, waved, and left. The crowd, getting one for the road, swamped her again for about thirty minutes. When it started to die down, she could actually see the floor of the bar. She also noticed she had some special friends. Two younger guys, more her age, kept asking her to party with them when she got off work.

"We've got a camper, lots of booze, and a little weed. Come with us!" the guys kept offering.

"Not tonight, sweetie. I'm exhausted!" Jessica kept replying. Unrelenting, they offered her back massages, foot massages, a hot shower, and a warm bed.

Another guy, in his mid-forties and wearing a wedding ring, asked her to elope with him.

To the side of her bar was a tall guy with long hair, dark eyes, and a beard. Jessica noticed that he didn't drink and hadn't bought a beverage from her all night, but he was there for hours just watching her, the bar, and the people. She thought he was odd but harmless.

At 2:00 a.m., security guards gently guided everyone to the exits and down the winding steps. The two "party boys" had moved on, most likely to the next girl looking for booze, weed, and a massage.

The guy with the wedding ring was handed down the steps from security guard to security guard; he was far too drunk to maneuver the steps by himself. Jessica wondered how or if he'd ever get to his campsite. Tall, dark, and eerie was gone. Jessica hadn't seen him leave.

Jake, the security guard and football player at Chadron State College, as he boldly announced again, was there to take Jessica to her cabin. He drove the golf cart; it didn't have any headlights, but he carried a large Maglite that showed the way.

The drive to the cabin was slow, with crowds of people, empty beer cans, and bottles lining the road. Once they were through the main gate, the crowd eased up somewhat, though it was sporadic. Drunken bikers stumbled along, arm in arm, some singing, some cussing, some fighting, all loud.

Jake had done one thing well, Jessica thought: he had brought her a blanket, so she could cover up, which made for less people noticing her.

A few minutes later, he pulled up to the cabin. Ann was already there, standing in the open door, wearing a bathrobe and a towel on her head.

"Hey, Jess! Was that an unreal night or what?" Ann proclaimed as Jessica got off the cart and handed Jake the blanket.

"It was crazy!" Jessica replied.

Jake was pulling away when he spotted a tall guy with a beard enter the light of the cabin. The bearded guy stormed forward, grabbed Jessica by the waist, and was trying to force himself and Jessica into the cabin. Both girls screamed; Jessica was kicking and punching the man. Jake stopped the cart and ran to the door, where the tall man let go of Jessica and met Jake with a hard right to his chin. Jake dropped to the dirt.

Jessica and Ann rushed inside the cabin, slammed the door, and locked it. The bearded guy raised his knee to his chest and kicked the door, which easily flew open. Jessica screamed while Ann jumped onto the bed.

As the bearded man entered the cabin, someone came up behind him and put him in a bear lock. The bearded guy was lifted off the ground, his feet dangling in the air. Jessica saw a bald man with huge arms take the bearded guy to the road and swing him to the side, the guy's feet going above the bald man's head. The bald man then drove the bearded guy face-first into the dirt. Another guy was right there, just as big as the bald guy, and the two of them pummeled the bearded man with punches and kicks.

Jake had recovered and called for more security. Within minutes, five golf carts and ten security guards had arrived. The tall bearded man lay motionless on the ground. Jessica went inside the cabin, shut the door and wept, Ann's arm around her.

Security had the bearded man belly down on the ground. They took his arms behind his back and tied his wrists together with zip ties. Jake, a red bruise on his cheek, bent the bearded man's legs at the knees, used plastic ties to secure his ankles together, and secured his ankles to his wrists. After proclaiming the bearded man was "hogtied," Jake swiftly kicked him in the ribs.

The bald man who had thrown the bearded guy to the ground went to the window of the cabin and looked in. He gently tapped on the window. When Jessica looked up, she saw the bald man, with his red beard, dimples, and blue eyes.

"Are you okay?" he said.

Jessica smiled. "Yes, thank you so much. Please come back and see me tomorrow."

"I'm Matt," the bald guy said. He smiled too, pearly whites. He looked smitten. He turned and walked away.

Jerico went to the same window. He and Ann made eye contact, and they both smiled. Ann's hair had fallen out of the towel and was spilling over her shoulders.

She winked at Jerico and wetted her lips with her tongue.

It was 3:00 a.m., Sunday morning.

They bypassed Nebraska. Deuce had never ridden a Harley with a helmet, and he wasn't going to start now. Nebraska's helmet law probably cost the state a million dollars a year in lost revenue and taxes just from people avoiding the state on their way to Sturgis.

Off I-25 to Cheyenne, they hit Highway 85 through Wyoming to Newcastle. From there they reached the Black Hills and rode 14-A to Lead, South Dakota, elevation 5,280 feet.

It was cold at eleven at night, with temperatures at that altitude dropping to near freezing. Lead is popular for its Terry Peak Ski Area, and both men expected snow at any turn. Shirtless, dressed only in a vest and jeans—fighting rain, with no windshields, and no fairings— they rode fast.

Deuce and RJ dropped another thousand feet elevation by the time they hit Deadwood. In a town with a population of less than two thousand, there were at least five thousand bikes lining Main Street and the rail station.

The last twelve miles from Deadwood to Sturgis off 14-A consisted of thirty-five-mph hairpin turns and state patrolmen at every straightaway. Deuce and RJ hit the turns fast, leaning into the curves and seeing who could get their tailpipes to hit the asphalt without laying the bike on its side. Deuce went first, no sparks. RJ passed him and laid into the next turn with sparks flying off his pipes. They both yelled and cheered as Deuce rode up next to RJ for a high-five.

They rolled into Sturgis Saturday night at eleven-thirty, about two hours later than planned. RJ's Fat Boy was leaking oil. Deuce blamed himself; the Fat Boy had sat for a long time without being started. The first couple of years RJ was in the pen, Deuce rode RJ's bike about once a month, but as time passed, he forgot.

Deuce had the Fat Boy delivered the day RJ was released, without thinking to get it serviced or inspected. He just figured that since it had cranked right up, it would ride.

After 135 miles, they stopped to stretch and get gas. As they filled their tanks, oil was quickly accumulating under the engine of RJ's bike.

"Rocker gasket," RJ said. "Probably dried out over time. Easy fix. Let me get some oil, and we can make it into Sturgis, grab a gasket, and we'll be good."

"My bad," Deuce said.

Once in Sturgis, Deuce took a right into J&P Cycles. After parking their Harleys, Deuce made a call on his flip phone, and within ten minutes J&P was open for business.

RJ picked out two different gaskets, a couple of quarts of Harley-Davidson 20W50 oil, and went to pay.

Deuce said AMSOIL or Lucas 20W50 were the same, but the man at the register said, "Don't worry Deuce. The AMSOIL's on the house."

Deuce handed the man a fifty-dollar bill. "This is for you," he said. "Have fun. I don't forget."

RJ and Deuce left through the front door, got on their Harleys, and headed east. They rode through Sturgis on Highway 34, slow and easy. At every stoplight, they saw four or five guys wearing gray polo shirts with "Sturgis PD" on the back—radios on their shoulders and 9mm Glocks in their holsters.

Deuce and RJ hit the Chip at the perfect time: no lines, no escorts.

They paid $250 cash for a tent space. It was supposed to be $500, but Deuce told the registration lady that his buddy had just gotten out of the military, and she gave him a free pass.

They rode the zigzag of trails and paths then found a tent spot next to the road and across from a huge RV and trailer. After they parked their bikes, Deuce pitched the tent while RJ worked on his bike.

Deuce was exhausted. His leg and back were killing him, and he wanted to lie down.

RJ was wired. This was his first free night in five years. He didn't want to sleep and looked forward to working on his Harley.

Deuce lay down inside the tent, telling RJ he was having back spasms.

RJ was trying to hold the flashlight in his mouth and work on the rocker box. He thought he should have chosen a tool kit from J&P, especially since it probably would have been free.

What a contrast it was between Lead and the Chip. He had gone from freezing rain in Lead to ninety degrees at the Chip. RJ took off his vest and was shirtless while working on his Harley, while Deuce, shirtless as well, was trying to stretch out his lower back inside the tent.

RJ was struggling. He wanted to run, yell, get laid, drink, sleep, do anything without bars in his face.

Fixing the rocker-box gasket was proving harder than he'd thought. For one, it was dark, and he couldn't see shit; two, he was hungry; and three, he'd give anything for a beer.

Deuce was in pain, moaning and groaning, while RJ was just enjoying being free.

"Hey, you need some help?" a voice called out from behind him.

"Yeah, I'm leaking oil and want to ride in the morning, but I can't see shit. Would you hold this flashlight for me?" RJ said without looking at who was talking to him.

"I've got a trailer. Well, a garage, like…with all sorts of lights and tools and stuff. Bring your bike over here, and we can work on it."

"Thanks," RJ said.

The two men introduced themselves and shook hands.

RJ lifted the bike upright and used his right toe to flip the kickstand under the Harley. He pushed the bike to the trailer, his back lowered, his legs back, in a d-line position.

"What's the problem?" Kevin asked as he lowered the trailer ramp, hit the light switch, and turned up the AC.

"Rocker gasket, easy fix. I have the gasket and some oil. Just need tools and some light," RJ said, pushing the Fat Boy up the ramp.

Kevin tried to help on the left side, but RJ did all the work.

"Hoist is there. Lock it in, and raise it up. Easier to work on, plenty of lights," Kevin said as he went to the tool cart. "Take your pick."

Deuce walked into the trailer. "Nice shop," he said, looking at the tools, the hoist, the parts.

"Thanks. Use it as if it were your own. Glad I can help," Kevin said, then took a swig of his beer.

"I'm going for food," Deuce said, walking up to the trailer. "What you want?" He was looking at RJ.

"Anything, man. You call it," RJ said.

"You aren't gonna get good food after midnight, and yougottamilewalktogetthere," Kevin said, running his words together as usual. "I got food. You guys work on the Harley. I'll cook."

Kevin, went to the rear tire cooler, opened it, and brought out two Busch Lights. "Here, enjoy. I'll start the grill."

Both men hesitated. "Nice rig, and thanks for the beer," Deuce finally said as he took a long pull from the long neck.

"First beer in five years," RJ said as he put the beer to his lips.

"Whoa, whoa!" yelled Kevin. "You ain't going off the wagon on my beer. If you've been clean and sober for five years, I'm going to keep you that way!" He grabbed the beer from RJ.

RJ laughed. "I was in prison, not AA." He took the beer from Kevin and emptied it in one long drink.

Kevin shook his head. "You guys are just fucking with me. Fix your Harley, and let me fix you some food, assholes." He smiled as he fired up the grill.

Twenty minutes later, RJ's Harley had a new rocker gasket and was parked in front of his tent. Deuce and RJ were sitting at Kevin's picnic table, enjoying their fifth Busch Light and second shot of Jack, swapping biker stories, and smelling the aroma of two T-bones.

"Here you go, gentlemen. Medium rare and some potato salad. Another beer?" asked Kevin.

"That'd be great. My thanks," Deuce replied.

RJ got up, went across the road to his tent, put on a Harley T-shirt and his vest, then walked back to the RV as the James Gang's "Funk #49" played on the radio. He sat down at the picnic table as Kevin emerged from the RV, a couple of beers in hand.

"Let me tell you boys, my favorite places to ride…Whoa, whoa, whoa fucking whoa…shut the front door. RJ quit fucking with me. It ain't wise to steal a vest from the Sons, man. They'll mess you up when they find you," Kevin announced. He was looking east and west, north and south, his head on a swivel, as if the vest police were coming to get him.

"This is *my* vest. Relax," RJ said, exchanging a look with Deuce.

"Yeah, we're good. No worries," Deuce said, a grimace on his face as he arched his back. He thought the beer and the shots were helping his back and leg pain.

"Wow. I've never met a gang member before," Kevin said bluntly.

"We ain't a gang. We're a club," RJ said. "Anyway, thanks for the hoist, the beer, and the food. We appreciate it."

"Gotta ask," Kevin said. "What does RJ stand for? Robert Joseph?"

"No," RJ said.

"Randall Jeffrey?"

"No."

"Richard Ja—"

"No," RJ interrupted. "Just R and J."

"Just R, like the letter R?" Kevin asked.

"Yeah, and just J like the letter J," RJ said flatly.

"Would've never got that one. How about you, Deuce. What does Deuce stand for?"

Deuce held up two fingers, like the Hook 'em Horns from University of Texas.

Kevin nodded. "Oh, Deuce just means two. Got it."

The men sat in silence, maybe ten seconds. Kevin had to talk again.

"So, RJ, you married?" he asked.

"Nope."

"Any kids?" Another Kevin question.

"I got a daughter, haven't seen her in years. I hear she's a good kid." RJ said, draining another beer.

"You, Deuce? Married?" Kevin asked.

Deuce held up the Hook 'em Horns sign again.

"Two wives or two ex-wives?" Kevin asked with a smile

"Exes." Deuce smiled as well.

"Kids?" Kevin directed another question to Deuce.

Deuce held up the Hook 'em Horns sign again.

"Shoulda figured two," Kevin said.

"I'm done. Gotta lie down," Deuce said. "Thanks again, Kevin." Deuce stood slowly, dragging his right leg behind him, both hands on his lower back.

"Me too," RJ added, "but I'm sleeping under the stars. You get the tent tonight, Deuce. Thanks again, Kevin."

The two men crossed the road and vanished into the darkness.

Kevin cleaned up the campsite, scrubbed the grill, went into the RV and shut off the outdoor music. He checked his phone. No missed calls or texts from Gloria.

It was just after 2:00 a.m.

Once again, Albert slept in fits. Recurring dreams, with his father's face, his father's voice ringing in his ears. He tossed and turned in the small tent. His eyes were closed tightly, his arms wrapped around himself like a blanket.

Mother was his protector, his security. Albert would run to her when Father came home from work; he was afraid to be alone with his own dad. Father was always upset when he entered the house, yelling about his boss, his dinner, the TV, the Colts, the Reds, his wife, and Albert.

In the dream, his recollection of the past, Father came home, went into the living room, and stepped on some of Albert's toys, LEGOs. Albert had been building a castle, his imagination running free with knights and dragons. As boys do, Albert went from the land of building castles in the living room to drawing dragons at the kitchen table while his mother prepared dinner. Albert liked to be within his mother's watchful eye, and Mother wanted Albert where she could see him.

Albert heard Father enter the house then heard him mutter, "Damn it!"

Father yelled for Albert.

When Albert came around the corner of the kitchen to the living room, Father grabbed him by both arms, lifted him off the ground, and shook him. "Put these damn things away!" he screamed. "Why do you have so many of them anyway? I work too hard to waste all my money on this shit."

Father threw Albert to the floor; his neck was already hurting from Father shaking him. His arms bore red impressions of Father's fingers.

Mother ran in from the kitchen, a kitchen towel in her hands.

Mother and Albert both went to their knees on the living-room carpet. They hurried to gather the LEGOs and put them in the blue plastic bucket they came in.

But they were too slow. Father kicked the bucket from Mother's hands, sending LEGOs flying across the room. Mother was still on her knees and screamed when Father backhanded her, sending her facedown onto the carpet. Albert wasn't spared; he too was slapped, which sent him hard against the wall then flat on the floor. He covered his head with both hands, hiding his face in the shag carpet.

"I'm so sick of this shit!" Father yelled.

Trying desperately to intervene, Mother reached for Albert as Father once again slapped her across the face.

Father picked Albert up by the back of his jeans and belt, his head and arms dragging on the floor, his body in a V with his legs dangling in the air. He carried the boy to the second floor, his head and arms banging against each step. At the top of the stairs, Father turned past the master bedroom into Albert's room, went to the closet, opened the door, and tossed him inside.

Father slammed the door to the closet and told Albert to stay there until he came back, and not to piss in the closet.

Now Albert lay still in his tent, his heart racing, his eyes fluttering under closed lids.

Inside the closet, he lay as still as he could. He felt he had sat there for hours in the cold, dark closet—too scared to move, too scared to breathe, tears rolling down his cheeks.

Albert couldn't hold it any longer; he had to go to the restroom and knew he couldn't pee in the closet or Father would beat him again. Another time, when he was locked in the closet, he had wet himself and gotten urine all over the floor. That night Father had beaten him with a belt; the welts on his back and bottom hurt for days. He remembered how, after that beating, Mother had rubbed his back and bottom with vitamin E oil and sang him to sleep.

Albert tried the closet doorknob; it wasn't locked. As slowly and quietly as he could, he walked to his bedroom door, which also was open. He looked both ways and didn't see anyone. He was crouching low, bent at the waist, on his tiptoes.

He listened; he heard groaning from Mother's room. He stepped into the hallway then tiptoed his way down the hall. He had to cross the entrance to his parents' room to get to the bathroom.

Albert stopped at the door to their room; it was open. He saw Mother, her dress hiked up over her bottom. She was bent over the bed, her face on the mattress. Father was behind her. His pants were off, and he was jamming himself into her over and over. Father was groaning. Mother turned her head and saw Albert; she was crying. Father saw her turn her head, but he didn't look toward Albert. He just stopped and slapped her hard on the side of her head then spanked her bottom again.

Albert continued to the bathroom, did what he needed to do, but didn't flush. He didn't want Father to know he had left the closet.

Again, he silently tiptoed back. When he reached his parents' bedroom door, he didn't hear any groaning and again looked into the room.

Mother was standing at the front of the bed, straightening her dress and wiping tears off her cheeks.

Father didn't see Albert; he was putting on his pants. He was bent over, his white buttocks in the air. For some reason that made Albert want to laugh.

Albert hurried to his closet, quietly shut the door, and sat there waiting.

Within minutes, Father opened the door and saw that the floor was dry. "Good boy!" he said. "You didn't piss yourself for once."

Albert started to stand, but Father slammed the door on him and told him to stay there for the night until he learned how to pick up his damn toys.

Albert abruptly sat up in his tent. He woke up when the two linebackers came back to the RV; they were drunk and talking loudly. He scooted to the front of the tent and peered out. The guy he thought was called Jerry had his arm around Matt. "That was the best damn sweep and pile driver I've ever seen," Jerry told him. "You crushed him!"

"Yeah, he was out cold when he hit the ground," Matt said. "I actually thought I might have broken his neck. Guess we didn't need to keep hitting him."

"The hell we didn't!" countered Jerry. "We hit him 'cuz he was a total ass. He was going to rape that girl. We should still be beating him. I hope he hurts for a month and gets raped in prison, see how he likes it."

"Did you see her, the girl he grabbed? She's beautiful." Matt eyes were wide.

"She is, and so's her friend!" Jerry chimed in as he was putting some type of gel on his hands.

"I gotta meet her. She has to be a waitress here at the Chip. Why else would security drop her off? I have to find her tomorrow," Matt said.

"Her friend is gorgeous. I'm going to find her too. She was into me. I could tell."

They both stepped behind the RV. Albert figured they went there to pee.

When they came back around, Jerry again put the gel on his hands, and then the little mouthy guy came out and stood on the steps of the RV.

"Would you guys shut the fuckup!" the little guy said. Albert could hear him plainly. "Some of us are trying to sleep. Oh, man, you're not going to believe who I met."

The three men entered the RV and shut the door. The interior lights of the RV stayed on for another ten to fifteen minutes.

Albert figured they were still talking about the girls. He wished he had been there to see what had happened, and he wished he knew what a sweep and pile driver were.

He lay in his tent and looked out the zippered screen door. "He sounds so much like Father," he whispered, and then he sobbed into his sleeping bag and fell asleep.

Day two at Sturgis didn't officially start for the boys until after 1:00 p.m. Kevin was up by nine, as he didn't drink much and wasn't hungover. Still, they didn't fall asleep until after 4:00 a.m. Awake, Kevin stayed in the back room of the RV to let the boys sleep in.

He got online and checked the local news. A couple of accidents had claimed three lives the first day of the rally. There'd also been several arrests, some drunk-driving and reckless-driving violations, and basic stupidity.

Kevin was able to check on his home and shop back in Minnesota through the mounted security cameras he had installed. All the cameras and video surveillance streamed through his computer, so he had 24/7/365 access. He watched his shop foreman, Steve, enter the business on Sunday morning, clean up, and arrange tools. *He shouldn't be there on a Sunday*, Kevin thought. *He needs a raise.* When he got home, he would address both issues.

On his computer, Kevin was also able to pull up five of his most expensive rental properties. He didn't put security cameras inside the homes—his attorney had told him not to—but he did have cameras facing the outside of the units. The camera behind Skip's bar showed am empty alley way, Skip's Dodge Durango parked by the dumpsters. Skip lived in the apartment above the bar so his SUV was nearly always there.

Kevin hand his index finger on the log-off button when the rear door of Skip's bar opened. Skip walked out into the morning sun. He was naked above the waist wearing only his boxers. Skip was holding the hand of Gloria, his waitress and Kevin's supposed girlfriend. The couple stopped by the door of the Durago, they embraced. Both of Skip's hands were on Gloria's rear-end. They kissed for a long time. Skip went to break away and Gloria pulled him back into her arms. The kissing continued.

Kevin grabbed his cell phone, he dialed Gloria. On the computer screen he watched his girlfriend turn away from Skip. Skip was now holding her with his chest to her back as she pulled a cell phone from her purse. Skip was kissing her neck. Kevin could see Gloria looking at the cell phone, ignoring it and placing it back in her purse. She didn't take his call.

Laying on the bed, Kevin was furious. He felt betrayed by his girlfriend and his best friend. He had gotten Gloria the job with Skip. They both rented property from him. He thought of emailing the video to Skip or maybe having one of his welders rough Skip up and advise him to keep his dick in his pants. Kevin needed to think this over. Either way Skip and Gloria's rent were going to be increased.

Kevin walked through the RV, Matt and Jerico were still out cold, snoring in unison. Jerico was lying on his back, mouth open, and had his headphones on. Matt was snoring louder than Jerico, even while lying on his side. His cell phone was playing white noise beside him.

Kevin was impressed with how dark the RV was for eleven in the morning. The curtains and window coverings were very effective at keeping out the sunlight. He turned on the outdoor stereo system, grabbed a couple of Gatorades from the fridge, and headed outside.

The Chip was busy and loud, the roar of bikes a constant thunder.

Kevin looked for Deuce and RJ, but their bikes were gone.

Most of the tenters were outside their tents, on their bikes, or at the main area of campground where the food and bars were. Kevin couldn't imagine being inside a tent when the temperature was in the nineties with no breeze.

Suddenly a loud explosion came out of nowhere—a boom and several cracks from the northeast side of the Chip. Kevin would later find out that the campground had a shooting gallery where you could shoot a cannon, a tank, a howitzer, and AKs.

He walked around the RV, inspecting and taking mental notes of rock chips, tire pressure, the levelers, even bug marks. He reached in his pants pocket, removed a ring of keys, found the right one, and opened a side compartment of the RV. He took out a milk crate of cleaning supplies, grabbed a bottle of Poorboy's bug and tar cleaner and a new rag from a bound roll of white rags, and went to work on cleaning the

RV's bug splatters. At five foot four, he couldn't reach the higher spots on the RV and quickly finished his work.

Next, he went to the golf cart. It was covered in dust, and the seats and floor were sticky from spilled beer. Kevin figured the boys must have been giving rides last night. Kevin switched from bug cleaner to Armor All wipes and went to work. He was just finishing as Jerico and Matt came out of the RV, squinting in the midday sun.

Both boys were shirtless, in their underwear, they sat down at the picnic table.

"'Morning, boys!" yelled Kevin, putting the bug spray and cleaning materials back in the storage bin of the RV. "Damn, boys! It's one o'clock! Can't say you drank all day if you don't have a beer before noon!"

"Don't want no beer," Jerico mumbled as he disinfected his hands with his Purell. They all felt Jerico spoke better after a couple of beers. He mumbled when he spoke, so they usually only got the first couple of words of every sentence.

"Me neither. I need water," Matt said, his head in his hands.

"I ain't your mama. Get it yourself." Kevin grinned. "But…I will make you lunch!"

Matt got up, went into the RV, and came out with four bottles of water. He handed two to Jerico.

"You guys hit it hard last night. Fights and girls! A great first night." Kevin proclaimed as he started the grill. "Bacon and eggs on the way. How 'bout some toast too?"

"Sounds good," Jerico said. "Any aspirin?"

"Who's playing tonight? What band?" Matt asked.

"Thirty-Eight Special, should be packed. Aspirin's in the bathroom," Kevin said.

"Good," said Matt.

"Good," said Jerico.

They cracked open their first beers at five, after showers and a nap. Even though they were at a motorcycle rally, they didn't start their bikes today. Kevin had yet to ride at all.

Kevin had more than twenty pounds of chicken on the grill, all chopped into cubes, no bones. Matt and Jerico had brought out the beer coolers, and bottles of Jim, Jack, and Stoli, water, club soda, and Diet Pepsi were on the table. The party was on.

Kevin invited Deuce, RJ, some neighboring RV'ers, and a few tenters who just happened to be female. Soon nearly thirty people were standing in front of the RV, talking, drinking, and eating. Having two Sons of Silence there helped draw in the crowd. Although Deuce and RJ did pose for a few pictures, they both were camera shy.

RJ was hanging out with a particularly good-looking redhead, while Deuce was in obvious back pain and was hitting the Jack pretty hard.

At six-thirty, Kevin brought out the beads. As with Mardi Gras, you show your boobs, you get some beads, a free beer, and your picture taken. The beads and the beer attracted an even larger crowd; Kevin was busy snapping pictures on his iPhone and logging them into his boob album.

RJ helped himself to a dozen beaded necklaces and went straight to his redhead. Soon her top was off, his vest was on her, and her hand was in RJ's. They were snuggling like high-school kids.

By eight they were all pretty drunk, and the grilled chicken was all gone. Many had already said thanks and were wandering to the main stage when Kevin announced the bar was closed. Matt and Jerico slid the coolers under the RV, stashed the hard alcohol inside, and packed the chairs into storage. The camp was locked down by eight fifteen.

Kevin told Deuce to keep the bottle of Jack that he had his fist wrapped around, as if Deuce were going to give it up. Deuce gave Kevin the Hook 'em Horns sign and stumbled back to his tent.

RJ and the redhead were gone with no good-byes.

The golf-cart ride was the same as Saturday's, except Kevin kept yelling at them to lay off the wheelies. By the time they arrived at the main gate to park the cart, Matt was driving, with Jerico and Kevin surrounded by four women and three guys. Ten people on a cart. Kevin thought next year he would bring a four-wheeler, maybe one of those Raptors.

He decided the first stop would be to get the boys a couple of slices of pizza. Something heavy to help absorb the alcohol. While Kevin stood in line, Matt and Jerico checked out the bar nearest to the food court, which offered no sign of the girls from last night. From the food court, they each went their separate ways, Jerico and Matt to find the girls, Kevin to find a place to watch 38 Special.

A hundred thousand people had been expected at the Chip, and Kevin thought that was an understatement. The endless flow of people moving east to west and west to east was mind numbing. People coming, going, getting beer, or getting rid of beer.

Vendors in tents surrounded the main stage area, with bars at each exit, in the middle, and next to the food court. Motorcyclists would sneak in and ride through, revving their engines to part the sea of people. Bikers with folding lawn chairs were scattered around the grounds, while huge concrete blocks—only movable with the help of a forklift or tractor—demarcated the area for the crowd to watch the bands. Lines of picnic tables filled in the spaces between the vendors and the concrete blocks. There were more people than places to sit.

Kevin found an end seat at a picnic table, sat down, and showed the couple next to him his vast boob album.

ALBERT

Albert was up with the sun, his tent boiling hot. When he awoke, he was in a puddle of liquid and his underwear was wet; he had wet the bed. He was glad he had taken his pants off before he had gone to sleep.

He dressed quickly inside the tent, unzipped the fly, and stepped outside.

The RV and Father's campsite was quiet.

The two Sons of Silence guys were dressed and getting on their Harleys. Albert took his sleeping bag out of his tent and draped it over the top of his motorcycle, so it could dry out. If anyone asked, he would tell them he had spilled beer on it.

As he headed to the shower facility, he heard bikes firing up and someone still in his tent snoring. He saw a guy going for a jog and heard a couple having sex in their tent.

He waited more than forty-five minutes in line, only to take a cold shower in a room that stunk like piss and shit (Albert thought this would be a great place leave Father). He dried off with the paper towels supplied by the Chip then made his way to the main grounds.

Albert walked around the food court area, pricing breakfast burritos, gyros, and breakfast pizzas. He heard a couple of bikers saying they were going to the main entrance, as there was a free breakfast. Albert followed them.

The free breakfast was sponsored by Bikers for Jesus. The bikers had their vests on; they were welcoming people and shaking hands and saying, "God bless you." Albert sat with a group from the Christian Motorcycle Association.

The free breakfast included bacon, eggs, pancakes with lots of butter and syrup, and coffee. Albert went through the line twice and then a third time to take another eight slices of bacon, which he put in the pocket of his leather jacket for later.

A huge man, maybe three hundred pounds, his belly well over his belt, his Harley T-shirt stretched tight but still tucked in, approached him. He handed him a black hardcover Bible with *King James Version* on the cover. He told Albert to just read it and Jesus would talk to him; he should start with the Book of John.

Albert didn't make eye contact. He just said, "Thank you," took the Bible, and walked away.

The enormous man yelled," Thanks for coming!" and told him to please come again. He said they'd be serving free breakfast all week.

Albert decided to stroll through the campground, looking for places to put Father. He checked out the outhouses, shower houses, and dumpsters, all of which were places he had used before. He felt the best place would be close to the RV, maybe behind it, where the two big guys had been pissing. Albert knew the RV had to have a shower, so Father most likely wouldn't go to the shower houses near the RV.

When Albert returned to his campsite and tent space, his sleeping bag was dry. He took his folding chair out from under the tent's fly, unfolded it, and sat facing the road and the orange-and-black RV.

Within the next hour, the annoying little man, Father, came out of the RV. Albert watched as the man cleaned the front of the RV then cleaned the golf cart.

The campsite was empty; the two large linebackers probably were still in the RV, and the two Sons had left. Maybe he should just walk over and pick him right there. He was very close to the road, though, and someone was always driving by: bikers, campers, septic and water staff, security, and the cleaning service. Albert couldn't believe how many service people were at the Chip.

As he mustered the courage to stand and go over to Father, the two linebackers emerged from the RV—Matt first, followed by Jerry. They wore only their undershorts, no shirts. Both were so muscular that their triceps stood out in a horseshoe design, their six-pack abs flexing when they walked.

Albert sat back down.

Father yelled at them about drinking. Jerry wanted aspirin and was pumping something out of a dispenser. Matt went inside the RV to get water.

Albert watched all afternoon. They went in and out of the RV, took showers, then slept in the folding chairs in front of the large fan under the awning of the RV while Albert sat in the sun and sweated.

The two Sons of Silence guys returned around three or four, talking about Devil's Tower and some guy they'd met in Belle Fourche.

The old guy walked over to the RV, and the little guy gave him a couple bottles of water. He came back and handed one to the younger guy, who waved at the guys at the RV. The old guy took some pills and said he was going to lie down.

As evening approached, Father grilled food. The linebackers put out chairs and coolers, turned on bug lights, and set a bunch of bottles of alcohol on the table. Father went around talking to other people in the RVs around them. He didn't come over and talk to Albert.

Albert watched as dozens of people came over to the orange-and-black RV. Father offered them food and beer. The two Sons sat at the picnic table, drinking liquor. There were lots of women. Albert thought about getting up and joining them, eating the free food, and taking a beer, but decided against it. He saw how the men pissed behind the trailer and Father let only the ladies inside the RV.

At one point, Father came out with a bunch of necklaces. When he gave the necklaces to the girls, they'd pull up their T-shirts or zip open their jackets and show Father their breasts.

Albert sat alone but still blushed as he saw his first pair of, as he'd heard Father say, boobies. Father gave the beads to every girl, and most showed him their boobies. Father, grinning wildly the whole time, taking pictures of them with his cell phone.

Albert went into his tent and powered up his phone. He took some pictures from far away and tried to zoom in on as many boobies as he could.

The party went on for several hours, with Albert never summoning the courage to join them. He just sat back and watched.

As the sun set, people started to leave, and the little man began to clean up. Albert thought this might be the time to act—when everyone left and Father was alone, cleaning.

The older Son grabbed a large bottle from the table and headed to his tent. The other Son wandered off with a redheaded lady who wasn't wearing a shirt.

The two linebackers stayed and helped Father clean up. Then they all got on the golf cart. Albert jumped up. He had to follow them, had to find a time when Father was alone.

It was easier to keep up with the golf cart than Albert had thought it would be, but he was still sweating by the time they reached the main gate. The crowds of people walking to the concert made everyone go slow.

Matt did wheelies in the cart, and Father yelled at him. They stopped and picked up a bunch of people. The more people, the slower the cart went.

At the main stage, Albert stayed close but not too close. There were so many people that he could lose sight of the three men very quickly, and with everyone dressed in jeans and black Harley shirts, they all looked alike.

Bald guys stood out well in the crowd, as did tall guys, and there were very few black guys there. But short guys were easily lost in the crowd.

The three men sat down and ate pizza in the food court. Albert sat about four picnic tables to the right of them.

After they were done eating, Matt had Jerry give him something from a small plastic bottle. Matt rubbed his hands together, as did Jerry. Matt then went left and Jerry right. Father went down the middle; Albert followed him.

Father sat at a table to the left of the main stage. He was talking to everyone, showing them pictures on his cell phone. Albert figured they must be photos of all the girls whose pictures he had taken. Some women even saw the pictures then showed him their boobies, and Father took yet more pictures.

Albert heard several loud buzzing noises, as if a swarm of bees was coming after them. He, Father, and several others all looked up. It was a zip line: four people in harnesses, zipping across the campground thirty to forty feet above the crowd. Laughing, Father looked up again and yelled, "I gottadothat!"

Father's laugh—more of a cackle—drove Albert crazy. His voice was demanding; he told people to look at this, to show him their boobs, to get him a drink. Albert wanted to walk right over and thrust his pick into Father's temple and let the world be rid of this heinous little man.

Midway through the 38 Special concert, Father got up, looked to his left and his right, and asked the man next to him something. The man pointed northwest, and Father headed that way.

Albert was a few paces behind him.

Looking ahead, Albert saw signs pointing to the restrooms. He smiled in anticipation. Hurrying his pace, he got within a few feet of Father, with just two people between them.

When Albert and the others turned the corner of the bar to the restrooms, he was disappointed by the long line of men. The restroom was packed. As he entered the men's room, a man with a baseball hat, plastic gloves, and an apron like Mother wore, was directing traffic. "Table for one to the right. You go there," he said, pointing to an open urinal.

Men would pee, and the man with the apron would follow them, wiping down the toilet or urinal. After the men peed, the next line formed in front of the sinks, soap dispensers, hand dryers, and paper towels.

From there the flow of traffic went to the exit, where Albert saw mints in plastic wrappers along with a large bucket that read, "Tips Are Welcome." There were lots of one-dollar bills in the bucket—at Sturgis everyone asked for tips.

Albert followed Father through the maze. As Father exited the men's room, several men got ahead of Albert. He pushed his way to the front, bypassed the sinks and towels, and went to the exit. He expected Father to go back to the picnic tables, but instead of turning left, Father went right, away from the crowd.

Quickening his pace, Albert approached Father from behind with his right hand in the left breast pocket of his leather jacket. Just another twenty yards and Father would be in the alley behind the vendor tents and bathrooms. Albert hadn't scouted this area and was looking around for people, dumpsters, side roads, or a shed, if available.

Father turned back to the right, found a long line of people shuffling along, and fell into a line. Again, he was chattering away, pointing to the zip liners and showing people his cell phone, and again women were lifting up their shirts for him.

Albert got into the line about three people behind Father. He thought Father might even go back in line a few steps, and he might get to see the pictures on his camera. The line moved forward. Looking over Father's shoulder Albert got a glimpse of the line he was in: he was in the line for the zip-line ride.

The tower for the zip was five stories tall—a metal tower with fifteen steps up to a landing, a right turn to another fifteen steps, and so on. They were weighing people; if you weighed more than 250 pounds, you couldn't zip. Right now, Albert wished he were obese. His pulse quickened but not for the excitement of disposing of the little man. Albert hated heights, and the zip line definitely wasn't his idea of fun.

He considered dropping out of line, but he wanted to follow Father, and the zip line would drop him off at the other end of Buffalo Chip Campground.

After weigh-ins, you were forced to sign a disclaimer, dropping all liability against the Chip as well as the people in charge. Everyone was signing; no one was reading. If you passed the weigh-in and were willing to sign the waiver, then they wanted your cash. Cash only, twenty dollars for the first trip and ten for every zip after that for the rest of the rally. A great deal. Albert reluctantly handed over twenty dollars and followed Father up the stairs. They'd been in line for more than thirty minutes.

At the top of the stairs was a platform. The four zip-line employees wore safety harnesses in case they took a wrong step. Four people were allowed on the platform at one time, each assigned to a zip worker. The zip-line guests were harnessed in before they were allowed to walk to the edge of the platform. The harness was a parachute harness; it went between the legs and over the shoulders, with four locks and thick straps that were secured over the belly.

Once the guests were locked and loaded, the zip employees walked them to the edge and pushed them off. Albert turned ghostly white as he watched a group ahead of him leave the platform, all screaming and hollering.

The next four zippers included Father. Albert wasn't in that group. He watched as Father was strapped in and the harness was locked. Father asked the attendant, "How often do you change the harnesses?"

As the zip-line worker pushed him off the ledge, he replied, "Every time they break!"

Father had his cell phone out and was taking pictures or videoing the experience. He had his arms back and his legs spread widely as he leaned back and took photos upside down. Father was screaming as he flew over the Chip crowd and in front of 38 Special, who were still playing on the main stage.

Albert was next, the first one in his group to be harnessed and the first to be pushed off the platform. He tried to lean back and turned to go back to the safety of the platform, but this pushed him into a twist. The twist to the platform was easy; it was the rebound, because for every action there's an equal and opposite reaction. This flung Albert back toward the zip line and made him arch back. He was upside down like Father had wanted to be. Albert, however, did not want that experience.

While zipping, he somehow was able to rearrange himself and sit up straight. He gripped the harness for dear life and made it safely to the two-story platform at the other end of the Chip. It was longest minute of his life.

As he arrived, Father was yelling and high-fiving the zip-line employees and his fellow zippers. Albert couldn't believe he had paid twenty dollars for this, especially since he had to keep such a close watch on his funds.

The zip-line workers greeted Albert with a firm and steady grip, planting him solidly on the platform. Before he could take a step, they unlocked his harness and directed him to the stairs. Albert thanked the guy who had unhooked his harness and started down the two stories of stairs to the ground, holding firmly to the guardrail the entire time. Father was far ahead of him now, blending into the crowd. The last thing he'd heard him say was that he was going to do this again.

Albert was nauseous, dizzy, and light-headed. Once he reached the bottom of the steps, he went straight to the men's room. Afraid he was going to puke, he splashed water on his face. He wanted to lie down. His night was over. Father would have to wait. He kept telling himself the long walk back to the campsite would make him feel better. It didn't.

As he lay down inside his tent, the world was spinning. Albert sat up, unzipped the fly of the tent, lay on his belly, and rested his head outside on the cool ground. Eventually the world slowed down, and he tried to fall asleep.

His dreams were getting worse. He was tired and sick and just wanted to sleep. Motorcycles rumbled as bikers went in and out of the Chip. Campers walked by, talking loudly; hearing is always the first thing to go when you're drinking. A biker a couple of tents over was snoring loudly. How could he sleep through all this? He wanted to go over and crush the guy's head with his tent hammer, like the guy he'd killed in Alliant or Alliance, whatever that shitty little town in Nebraska was called.

Albert dreamt he was back in his closet; Father had put him in there nearly every night. He heard the door slam, the locking sound, then felt the spanking the next day for peeing in the closet. He heard the reprimand from Father: "Don't piss where you sleep, dumbass."

At first the closet was scary. It was dark, and he heard Mother crying, begging Father to let her baby out of the closet. He heard Father slap her, which made him cringe and coil into a little ball. "I'm not having that little bastard ruin a good bed," Father yelled. "When he stops pissing in the closet, he can go back to his bed."

Albert slept in the closet all through second grade and into third. Then one day Father left and never came back. Although Mother put Albert in his bed each night, after she tucked him in, he always went back to his closet. He felt safe in his closet; at least there he could hear Father coming and could prepare to be slapped, prepare to be pulled by his hair, prepare to get a spanking. Albert liked to be prepared.

As he lay in his tent, his head outside, his body inside, he again wet the bed, this time with his pants on.

He wanted so badly to kill Father. He would do it the first chance he got.

Matt was on a mission. He started at the two-story bar by the main entrance. The bar had a winding staircase that was packed with people standing on the steps, all watching the 38 Special concert. Security kept trying to clear the steps, but new people would come and take the space. Matt nudged and pushed his way to the second floor.

Behind the bar, a barback was putting ice into three water tanks, one with Coors Light, another with Bud, the third with Busch Light. Three barmaids also were behind the bar, all very pretty but not the girl Matt had seen last night.

He went past the stripper pole—no stripper—down the west staircase, and back to the grounds of the Chip. He walked past the Buffalo Chip clothing store; the front walls consisted of two garage doors, both open, with a line of people waiting to check out. Next to that was the Chip mercantile store, then food vendors inside a building; each vendor had a line of five or six people.

The tent vendors were next; leathers, boots, massages, coffee, pizza, T-shirts, sunglasses. Matt breezed past these, knowing she wasn't there. He walked up a set of stairs to the next bar—actually four bars on one deck. The railings were lined with people watching 38 Special, and each bar was crowded, mostly with men. There were a few tables, at chest height, no chairs; all of the tables were surrounded with people, most with a drink and engaged in a loud conversation. Matt had to shoulder his way to each bar as if he were ordering; then he'd see the barmaid, turn, and leave.

The upper deck continued with a metal bridge over the crowd to the next bar. The bridge had a railing on each side, with the side facing the concert lined with spectators.

After thirty yards, the metal structure featured a bump-out. A biker, straddling his Harley, sat in the center of the seven-by-five-foot bump-out, his front tire firmly pressed against the metal wall facing 38 Special. Security stopped the walking traffic behind the biker, and the burnout began. The biker went through five gears in seconds, black smoke from the burning tire and the acrid smell of burning rubber filling the air. The crowd at the bar, on the bridge, and below, was all cheering. The biker responded to their cheers as melted rubber sprayed the metal flooring. After thirty or forty seconds and a loud pop, he shut down the motor and raised his arms in triumph. The crowd went nuts. The blown tire was most likely due to a transmission issue, Matt thought. The poor biker would be out more than $500 for his few minutes of Buffalo Chip fame.

Matt delayed his search for a few moments to watch the burnout, shook his head in disbelief, and continued on the metal platform.

He couldn't see the main platform bar; it was surrounded by people, with four barmaids and a barback on each side. He circled the square bar, taking a long glance at each woman, but none of them were the one he was looking for. As he took the ramp down, he passed the biker with the blown tire, who was now all alone, pushing his disabled bike down the ramp.

Matt headed back toward the concert venue. At the center of concert grounds was a three-story wooden structure that housed the lighting, special effects, and sound system technicians. The bottom floor had a bar that faced the stage. Matt went to the bar to see two lovely ladies hustling behind it, opening beers, taking money, making change, throwing dollars into tip buckets as fast as their hands could move. But neither of them was the girl he'd seen last night.

To avoid the shoulder-to-shoulder concert crowd in front of the bar, he decided to go behind the building and work his way to the bar beside the main stage. As he took a shortcut under the steps, he saw her. She was going up the steps, mouse ears in her hair and whiskers painted on her cheeks. Matt went back the way he had come and started up the stairs.

Security met him on the fourth step. "VIP only," said an old man with a gray beard and a bright-yellow shirt with "Staff" embroidered above the right chest pocket.

"How do I become a VIP?" Matt asked.

"Buy the pass at the main gate. A hundred bucks," Staff replied.

"Man, I just want to meet this girl in there," Matt said. "The concert is almost over. How 'bout this?" He handed Staff a twenty-dollar bill. "You keep the change."

"Go," Staff replied, nodding as he stuffed the twenty into his pants pocket.

The bar was packed, with almost everyone facing the stage as 38 Special belted out "Rockin' into the Night."

Matt squeezed between a biker and the wall; his shoulders nudged the biker into a nearby chair. "Hey!" the guy said, turning to Matt. He saw Matt's cauliflower ear and his bulging biceps and followed up with a softer "Hey, bro!"

She was at the bar, opening a beer while mixing a Jack and Coke. She turned her head to the right, saw Matt, and smiled. She took the man's money, offered no change, and said, "Thanks, sweetie." Then she came over to Matt, leaned across the bar, and grabbed him by the back of the neck. She pulled him in and kissed him on the cheek through his red Viking beard.

"Matt! I've been waiting for you!" She smiled and gave him another kiss, this time on the other cheek and the other dimple.

"Nice to see you again," Matt said, giving her his hand.

"Oh, Matt, thank you." She took his hand and placed it on her heart. "You saved me last night."

Matt's knees buckled; the guy beside him was all smiles.

"I'm Jessica," she said, then dashed off to the other end of the bar and made her circular tour, opening beers, mixing drinks, and giving Matt sly smiles as she worked.

Matt settled in at the bar, he wasn't going anywhere. He turned to the guy next to him. "Isn't Sturgis great?"

JERICO

J erico found his lady far easier and faster than Matt did. As Matt went to the main entrance to make a circular search of the premises, Jerico just went to the first bar he could get to.

The metal-platform bar had railings facing the concert stage, along with a burnout platform. The corner of the platform was reserved for "the girls." First, it was the Red Bull girls. Three college-age girls in two-piece outfits, with belly piercings, shoulder tattoos, ankle tattoos, back tattoos, lots of tattoos. They tossed Red Bull koozies, Red Bull T-shirts, and Red Bull hats to the crowd, who were all reaching up to them from the concert grounds. Thirty minutes later, it was the Jägermeister girls, followed by the Fireball girls, the Easy Rider girls, and the Jeremiah Weed girls. All threw out giveaways and posed for pictures.

Jerico enjoyed watching the girls. He even managed to get his picture taken with a few and collected two koozies, which he stuffed into his back pocket. He went to the bar and was ordering a Jack and Diet Coke when he spotted her across the bar.

Four bikers, Budweisers in hand, were standing in front of the bar but not really at the bar. Jerico noticed one guy was wearing a 1980 Sturgis rally T-shirt—that was cool—and two of them had on the same T-shirt, the seventy-fifth Sturgis rally commemorative shirt. Jerico thought they must have bought them today—and why wear a shirt that tells you where you are? He moved forward, stepped between the four guys, said, "Excuse me," and took a place at the bar, right in front of her.

Jerico held out his hand. She took it and tilted her head to the side, as if to ask, "Who are you?"

"I'm Jerico. We met last night at your cabin, before security carried that guy away."

"I'm Ann. And yes, I remember you." She winked at him.

Jerico still held her hand and pulled her in closer. "I had them play this song for you." In the background, 38 Special's lead singer, Don Barnes, was singing, "I'm a fool for you."

"You're good. Nice timing," Ann said as she went back to work.

"Actually, I have been waiting around for ten minutes for it to play!" Jerico smiled.

Keeping his seat at the end of the bar, Matt watched Jessica work the crowd. She had taken off her high heels, so she could move faster; the more she hustled, the more tips she made. Without the heels, she was still at least five foot eight. Her legs were Matt's favorite body part to watch: diamond-cut calves when she tiptoed, a definite muscular cut between her thighs and her hamstrings, and of course the gap and then the little dimples at the base of her lower back. Jessica's belly was a soft six-pack, not defined like a bodybuilder's, but it was there, and her breasts, well…for one, they were real, and two, they were solid. Matt could tell by her triceps and biceps that she was a lifter, by her thighs that she could squat, by her back that she could do pull-ups, and by her chest that she could bench.

Jessica never lost her smile and never forgot an order. No matter how many drinks someone asked for, she got it right the first time. Matt was amazed at how she could make everyone feel special and complimented nearly every guy who came up to her. She never used the same phrases in a row; she spaced them out so each one felt she was talking to just them.

"Hey, blue eyes," "Great smile," "Thanks, sweetie," "Here you go, honey," "Hi ya, darling"—Jessica had several at the ready. She was great at noticing T-shirts too: "Harley-Davidson, Texas. You came all that way just to see me?" "Hey, Chiver, Chive On." "Nebraska Football? That's all you got?"

The weakest tip was a dollar—a four-dollar beer paid for with a five. Two beers for eight dollars, paid with a ten…you get the math. Matt noticed how Jessica made change—a four-dollar beer paid with a ten was six one-dollar bills in change. The tips were rolling in. Twice while Matt sat there, she emptied her tip bucket, stuffed the bills in her purse, and quickly put the bucket back on the bar.

When the band stopped, and the crowd slowed, Jessica created her own crowd. "Hey, big fella! I want your picture!" she yelled at a guy as she took out her cell phone. The biker leaned back against the bar; Jessica leaned forward and took their picture. He took out his camera and did the same, and he gave her five dollars. Once one camera came out, several more followed, with each guy giving her tip. Four guys held her entire body horizontally, like a fresh fish they'd caught off the coast—a guy at her feet, one at her waist, one at her chest, and one supporting her head. That was worth twenty dollars. Two more groups wanted the same shot and tipped the same.

All the while, Jessica and Matt talked between her serving drinks and getting her picture taken. She thanked him repeatedly for being her bodyguard the previous night and asked him to stay at the bar and keep an eye out for creeps and stalkers. She confessed to him that if tonight was anything like last night, she'd be on the next flight back to St. Louis.

By 1:30 a.m., the barbacks had the place locked down, security had taken the cash drawers, and Jake was there to give her a ride back to her cabin. Jessica thought she was carrying more than $2,000 in cash; last night she hit $1,500, and tonight was even bigger and busier.

Jake gave Jessica and Matt a ride to the admin building, where each girl had her own lockbox. The amount of cash these girls made was too much for anyone to leave in a cabin where you could see through the doorjamb.

Matt volunteered to Jessica her back to her cabin, and she happily accepted the offer. She was wearing a jacket, had taken off her mouse ears and cleaned off the whiskers, and had put on tennis shoes. She took Matt by the arm.

Jessica had to be tired after a day on her feet, but Matt enjoyed the long walk to the cabin and was disappointed when they arrived.

At the cabin door, Jessica said "Give me your cell number and I'll text you which bar I am working at tomorrow. Please come back and hang out with me."

They exchanged cell numbers and she kissed him on his beard; Matt didn't make a move—he just accepted the peck on the cheek. Jessica went inside the cabin and shut the door. Matt heard her talking, along with another girl's voice and a deep voice that said, "Hey."

"Everything okay?" Matt called out. "I can stay out here for a bit, just to be sure."

Jessica opened door a crack and said, "Thanks. We're okay."

Within a minute or two, the lights went out, and Matt head back to the RV. It was nearly 2:30 a.m.

Jerico was drunk. He had sat at Ann's bar all night, drank a lot, and tipped even more. He figured she had made at least a hundred dollars in tips just from him. He watched her every move. Jerico loved a small ass, one that could fit in his hands. "If it don't fit, you must acquit," but this one fit, guilty as charged.

Like the other barmaids, Ann could work the crowd and was an expert at flirting. She received several proposals, several come-ons, and several requests for personal services—even more as the night went on as the men (and a couple of women) got drunker and drunker.

The bar was packed all night, primarily with beer drinkers and small tips. A dollar per beer was the average; one guy gave her two quarters. Ann told Jerico that at a dollar a beer, she'd have to open a lot of beers to get $1,000 in tips.

Getting tired of dollar bills, Ann sat on the bar, reached out, and rubbed the bald head of a biker who wore a black vest covered in patches. The patches read, "Loud Pipes Saves lives," "I Rode Mine," "Helmet Laws Suck," "Live Free," and "MIA & POW."

Ann said, "Just for you, big fella, a body shot for twenty-five dollars."

The bald man rubbed his head, looked at Ann, and said, "I don't know what that is sweetie, but I'll take two!"

She reached under the bar and grabbed a can of whipped cream and a bottle of tequila. She lay down on the bar, knocking over another guy's beer with her foot. "Sorry," she said. He smiled and said, "No problem." All eyes were on Ann and what she was going to do next.

She told the biker, "You have to drink it fast—it's a shot!" She was in a sit-up position, her back curved forward, her abs flexing, no belly fat, you could see the striations of her abdominal muscles. She sprayed whipped cream around her belly button. "Ready, cowboy?" she asked. He nodded.

Ann poured a shot of tequila in her belly button; the biker put his mouth on her belly; and she drove his face into the whipped cream, grinding her hips and belly into his face. Tequila ran down the sides of her stomach.

The biker rose, faced the crowd with white froth all over his smiling face, and hollered, "Thank you, miss, and may I have another!"

The second shot was the same as the first, with the bald guy making a show of giving Ann a hundred-dollar bill and proclaiming, "Keep the change!"

She washed off with a wet towel as a line formed for three more body shots. Her tip average was increasing significantly. Jerico laughed and thought about getting in line.

By 1:30 the bar was emptying fast. The barbacks were cleaning up, and security was easily guiding drunk bikers down the ramp. When one of the security guards asked Ann if she was ready, she turned to Jerico and said, "Will you please escort me home?"

"Hell, yeah," Jerico said. The security guy shook his head and high-fived him.

They were back at the cabin within twenty minutes; Jerico nearly carried her. Ann said she wanted to shower first, and Jerico was more than willing. They went to the shower house together—there wasn't much of a line at 1:45 a.m. As they undressed, Jerico said, "My eyes are the only thing I don't want to take off you."

"Oh, Jerico," Ann ribbed him. "Does that line really work?"

He shrugged. "I don't know. You tell me." Jerico had her in a hug. It worked.

KEVIN

After the RV party and pizza, Kevin had discovered the zip line. Twenty dollars for the first trip then ten dollars thereafter. He was on his fifth thereafter trip, zipping above the concert crowd.

Kevin had video footage, pictures of himself sitting up, pictures taken upside down, and pictures from each side of the zip line. This trip he was taking pictures between his legs as he leaned forward, almost in a Superman position. Landing at the platform, he again screamed in delight and fist-bumped the zip-line crew, all of whom recognized him by sight and sound.

After this last zip trip, Kevin headed to the second-floor bar, found a spot next to the stripper pole, and again took out his camera. The dancers didn't start until midnight; his timing was perfect. The girls rotated every fifteen minutes—they weren't totally topless, pasties covering the nipples is the law in South Dakota. That was odd, Kevin thought, as he'd taken more than fifty pictures of boobies, and no one had been arrested yet.

The girls danced, and Kevin tipped generously, one of the few bikers who tipped the dancers—most just watched then walked on. He was getting extra attention; the girls knew who was paying and who was watching.

Girl number three, college aged, blonde, no enhancements necessary, advanced to the pole and immediately focused on Kevin; the girls must have been talking. She got down from the stage and was grinding on Kevin's leg as he sat at the bar, whispering in his ear, and even nibbling his earlobe. Kevin slipped a twenty-dollar bill into her thong. She slid her hand across his cheek as she glided back up to the stage then danced around the pole. When she saw no other takers, she went back to Kevin. He was more than willing, and soon he had her on his lap and was taking a selfie.

The dancer stood, faced him, spread his legs, and put her arms around his neck as she swayed to the music. Just then, a middle-aged, broad-shouldered, big-bellied rather drunk biker—they all looked alike—came up and pushed Kevin off his stool. The dancer grabbed Kevin, and Kevin grabbed the pole to keep himself from hitting the floor.

"Let the rest of us have a shot!" the biker said, grabbing the girl by the arm and spinning her toward him.

When Kevin regained his footing, he stood face-to-face with the guy and said, "Fuck off."

The man pushed the dancer to the side, pushed Kevin in the chest, and said, "I'm gonna rip your head off, you little shit."

As the man approached Kevin, suddenly the man buckled at the knees and fell to the floor. Behind him, smiling at Kevin, was RJ.

RJ had somehow knocked the guy out; no one saw it, as they were all looking at Kevin, wondering whether he was going to fight the larger man or run.

Kevin didn't even see it; he just saw the guy's eyes roll into the back of his head as he hit the floor.

RJ came forward as people were stepping over the fallen man, saying, "He must be really drunk" and "I didn't even see the little guy hit him. Did you?"

"How'd you do that?" Kevin asked, looking at the man lying flat on his belly.

"Little trick I learned in prison, part of my rehabilitation," RJ said as he too stepped over the man on the floor.

Security came and picked the guy up; he reeked of beer. "Must have passed out," one of them said. "Get him to the gate and give him to the county sheriff."

"Thanks, but I had him," Kevin told RJ sharply.

"I know. And I should have stayed out of it. Last thing I need is another trip to prison. I've got two strikes. The next one and they said I will be in for life." RJ said.

"Can I buy you a beer?" Kevin said.

RJ nodded. "Let me buy you one."

Both men gulped down their beer, it was closing time and the Chip staff was guiding people to the exits. The two men walked to the golf cart, driving it to the RV.

"So, what about the redhead?" Kevin smirked as the cart chugged along; he thought the golf cart was running funny.

"Always had a weakness for redheads. My first wife was one. The beauty tonight, well she brought back some old memories." RJ looked at the stars.

Kevin pulled up to the RV and parked the cart.

"That kid is hammered," RJ said, looking at a man half in, half out of the tent that was next to his tent.

Kevin opened the RV and brought out a bottle of Jameson, two glasses, and some ice. He set the radio a local FM station that was cranking Godsmack, getting the crowd ready for Monday night's concert.

Kevin put ice in the glasses and poured the Jameson in, filling each to the top. He slid a glass to RJ, raised his own glass, and said, "Thanks for helping me tonight."

RJ nodded, and said "And to me not going back to jail." They clinked glasses.

A few minutes later, Matt walked up, grabbed a glass, and joined them. The three men sat and drank for another hour. Jerico never showed up.

It was just after 3:00 a.m. Monday morning.

SALAS

The Monday-morning sun creeping into the second floor of the Fort Wayne police station created a dull, gray haze above the detectives' cubicles. Ronnie and Salas were alone in the dusty fog, punching keys on their laptops. With two dead bodies in twenty-four hours, with same cause of death, in different states, the detectives were searching national, state, and local police databases for similar homicides.

Ronnie stood from his chair. He was clad in pinstriped pants—perhaps part of a suit—a white, button-down short-sleeve shirt, and a green tie hanging mid-chest. "I think I have couple of matches, Detective Salas."

Salas didn't look up; he was staring at his own computer. He waited for a few seconds, expecting Ronnie to talk. "Okay…are you going to tell me?"

"Yes, Detective Salas." Another five seconds of silence.

Finally, Salas looked at Ronnie.

Ronnie began, "The first one is from 2011, right here in Fort Wayne. A male, approximately thirty-five years old, five foot four, 140 pounds, was found in a dumpster behind Walmart. You know the one off of Coldwater, close to I-69?"

Salas nodded.

"Well, the case is still unsolved. Don't know why you didn't get that case. It was in this department, Detective Alex Moore." Ronnie looked at Salas for an answer.

"Moore retired in fall 2011," Salas said. "I got his job after that."

"Cause of death was a deep laceration, point of entry under the mandible. The weapon was driven into the brain. It was a serrated knife. So not exactly like these other two cases." Ronnie sat back down and began typing again. "No weapon was found, no fingerprints, no witnesses."

"They ID the body?"

"No. There was no ID, no missing persons report. No one claimed the body." Ronnie continued typing.

Salas stood and walked over to Ronnie's desk. "Time of year…what month and day was the body found?"

"Saturday, July thirtieth, 2011."

"Anything in the report about the belongings of the DB? Watch? Clothes? Hat?" Salas was now standing behind Ronnie, looking at the same screen.

Ronnie typed some more and scrolled down the screen. "Boots, jeans, vest. That's it. No wallet, no watch, no jewelry, no rings. Report said it was a robbery gone bad."

"Okay, this could be crap, but the entry point is the same. Keep it on file. The next one?" Salas was sitting on the edge of Ronnie's desk, his legs crossed at the ankles, his arms crossed at the chest, which made his biceps double in size.

"Moline, Illinois. August first, 2014," Ronnie read from the screen. "White male, age forty-three. Cause of death was a puncture wound under the mandible and through the brain. Most likely weapon was a screwdriver or ice pick. No mention of the DB's clothing. Body identified as Sam Jenkins of Detroit. Left behind a wife and two kids."

"Where did they find him?" asked Salas.

Ronnie typed some more. "A campground! A KOA in Moline. He was found naked in a shower stall."

"How'd they ID the guy?"

"The owner of the campground remembered checking the guy in. They went to his tent and found his wallet and ID there. The tent was about thirty yards from the shower house, per the report."

"Height and weight?" Salas asked

Ronnie's fingers went to work. "Five four, one hundred seventy pounds."

"How did he get to the campground? Was there a car there? A camper?"

More typing. "Toyota Tundra."

"Ronnie, check the DB in 2011 at the Walmart. Any vehicle mentioned there that was abandoned?"

Ronnie went to a different screen and a local database. He shook his head. "No abandoned car."

"Check for motorcycles that week." Salas bent over Ronnie's shoulder and looked at the screen.

"A 2005 Harley-Davidson softtail was impounded on August fifteenth, towed from the Walmart parking lot. Per registration and VIN, the owner was reported as Gregory Lopez of Canton, Ohio. Multiple attempts were made to contact Mr. Lopez. First attempt, though, wasn't until September twenty-third. No response, with Lopez no longer at the address listed on the motorcycle's registration." Ronnie looked at Salas.

Salas looked back. "Check the 2011 DB at Walmart. It's gotta be Greg Lopez from Ohio. And what's the phone number for Sam Jenkins's widow?"

As Ronnie compared the driver's license photo of Greg Lopez from Canton, Ohio, with the pictures of the dead body found at the Walmart in Fort Wayne, Salas called Mrs. Sam Jenkins in Detroit.

After introducing himself and explaining that multiple police units were still investigating the death of her husband, Salas got to the question he was after. "Mrs. Jenkins, where was your husband going? Where was his destination?"

"South Dakota," she said. "He was going to see Mount Rushmore and a rally of some sorts, he had his motorcycle in the back of the truck."

Salas went to his desk. Ronnie was there with the news that the DB at the Moline KOA was indeed Greg Lopez.

"Ronnie, check for any additional cases from here to South Dakota. Check multiple routes. I need to go see a guy. I'll be back in an hour," Salas said, as he grabbed his badge, cell phone, and car keys.

As he left, Ronnie called out, "Why South Dakota?" but got no response.

Fifteen minutes later, Salas was at Lucky Harley-Davison off Illinois Road. He went to the front door and pulled. It was locked; the sign read, CLOSED ON MONDAYS. Salas wasn't happy. He cussed under his breath as he took out his cell, pulled up his GPS, and typed in "motorcycle repair." The GPS told him to go to Biker Bob's Bikes. He was there in fifteen minutes. Everything in Fort Wayne was fifteen minutes away.

Biker Bob's was a white metal building on black asphalt. The door was open, with a concrete block holding it that way. Salas entered, adjusting his eyes to the dark interior of the repair shop. A young kid, maybe sixteen, sat behind the counter looking at his cell phone.

Salas flashed his badge to the kid and asked to speak to Bob. The teenager's eyes welled up as if he might cry. "I didn't do anything. I promise! We were just hanging out." His face was flushed as beads of sweat built on his cheeks.

Salas was confused but kept a poker face. "I need to talk to Bob… now," he said rather loudly.

Tears were streaming down the kid's cheeks. "Well, his name isn't Bob. He bought the place from Bob. It's Charles, and he's my dad. But he isn't here. He went to the rally. He'll be back next week."

"What rally? Where? Tell me now," Salas said as sternly as he could with a straight face.

"The Sturgis motorcycle rally in Sturgis, South Dakota. He and my mom went. I'm just here watching the place." The kid blew his nose into a paper towel.

"Okay, I'll be back next week. You…you clean it up—I mean it. No drugs, no alcohol, no fucking around. Got it?" Salas growled, pointing his finger at the kid.

"Yes, sir. I got it! I promise. Please don't tell Dad," the teenager pleaded.

Salas had no idea what the kid was talking about and didn't want to know. What he did know was this all was leading to the rally in Sturgis.

It was 9:30 a.m. when Salas got back to the station. Ronnie was there, next to Salas's desk, notes in hand, as Salas sat down.

"What you got?" Salas demanded.

"August third, 2013," Ronnie began. "Alliance, Nebraska. Population 8,600. Alliance is the home of Carhenge, built in 1987, thirty-eight vehicles in the same format as Stonehenge of Wiltshire, England. Did you know Stonehenge dates back to 2400 BC and—"

"Ronnie!" Salas interrupted. "I don't give a shit about Stonehenge right now."

"Oh, yes. Perhaps later. Alliance had a dead body found in its city park, August third, 2013. Alliance is approximately 190 miles from

Rapid City, South Dakota. And outside of Rapid City, there were once fifty minuteman missile silos as part of Ellsworth Air Force Base."

"Ronnie!" Salas yelled.

"Yes, perhaps later. Well, the DB was found in his tent, his motorcycle parked beside the tent. They, the city of Alliance PD, figured he'd been dead four or five days. The smell got to the guy mowing the grounds, and he went over to investigate. Cause of death was a blow to the head, perhaps by a hammer or a crowbar. The vic was struck through the tent. The scene, however, was contaminated by the lawn-mower man. No tracks, no weapon, no witnesses. The ID was for James Watson of Manhattan, Kansas. Married with three kids. Per the report, he was on his way to Sturgis, South Dakota, for a motorcycle rally."

"Height and weight?"

Ronnie went back to his computer, typed a few strokes, and replied, "Five foot two, one hundred twenty-five pounds."

Salas went silent, both hands rubbing his bald head.

"I have another one too, Detective Salas," Ronnie said.

"Another? Okay, let me hear it, but no history lessons." Salas sat up straight.

"This one was in Valentine, Nebraska, about three hours from Alliance and four hours from Rapid City. Again, a city park. August fourth, 2012. Local kids walking in the park called in a man next to a body under a small walking bridge over Minnechaduza Creek. Local police arrested a homeless man, Native American. He was kneeling over the dead body. Cause of death was a sharp pointed object driven under the mandible and through the brain, most likely a screwdriver. The weapon was never found, and the case was eventually thrown out. The homeless man wasn't carrying a weapon, and the autopsy showed that the body had been dead three to four days prior to his finding it."

"Give me more, Ronnie. I need height, weight. Was there motorcycle?" Salas demanded.

Looking back at his notes, Ronnie replied, "Five-five, one hundred fifty-five pounds. White male named Jonathan Riley from Dallas. No motorcycle, but per the interview with the DB's ex-wife, she thought he was riding his Harley to South Dakota. At least that's what he told his two children, twin daughters, age eleven."

"Bike was probably stolen after it had sat there for a few days," Salas thought aloud. "Anything else?"

Ronnie nodded. "Yes, one more vic. Also on August 2012. This one is a little different than the rest. DB was found in the back parking lot of a motel in Murdo, South Dakota, right off I-90. DB was in the cab of a Ford F-150 pickup, pulling a camper. No motorcycle."

"So, what was different?" Salas asked

"The murder weapon was still intact. A screwdriver driven under the mandible and lodged into the brain. No fingerprints, and the screwdriver matched the tools in the vic's toolbox," Ronnie stated. "One witness—a clerk—saw the vic helping a guy fix his motorcycle. All the witness could say was that he was short. Both guys were short. The vic was listed at five foot six, and they guy he helped was about same size. The pickup sat in the back of the parking lot for three days before anyone went and checked it out."

"Any investigation?" Salas asked.

"Local and state police went through video of the grounds, but the pickup and trailer were out of the cameras' line of sight. The clerk who saw the short guy couldn't ID anyone from the security videos. Per the DB's wife in Minneapolis, he was headed to Sturgis to meet up with some friends. Nothing but dead ends. Case is still unsolved," Ronnie finished.

Salas looked at the clock; it was 9:33. "Are these cases related, Ronnie?"

"I'd venture to say yes, Detective Salas. All the wounds have the same anatomical point of entry, except for the hammer to the head. Same time of year too. Would be very coincidental." Ronnie crossed his legs and arms, mimicking Salas body gestures.

"The dead bodies have no connections. Five different states, different jobs, not a lot of money, married and divorced, single. Some are bikers, some just campers, some going to South Dakota, some going to Wisconsin. Makes no sense," Salas said to himself with a loud sigh.

"Yes, the campgrounds, the city parks…but also recall, two parking lots. Hmmmm." Ronnie mimicked Salas's vocal inflection and the loud sigh.

"Why didn't anyone pick up on this, discounting the two DBs over the past two days? That's five dead bodies." Salas again rubbed his head.

"Like you said, Detective Salas, five different states. Not to mention small towns, local cops with poor resources, no leads, no witnesses, no follow-up."

"One thing, Ronnie…the body type of the victims. All little people. He's killing little guys." Salas looked at Ronnie.

"He's killing midgets? You never told me that! How could anyone kill a midget?" Ronnie exclaimed.

"Not midgets, Ronnie. Little people. He hasn't killed any midgets." Salas went to his desk.

"I know it's politically correct to call them little people, Detective Salas, but they're still midgets." Ronnie sat down at his desk too.

"Ronnie, the victims are not midgets! They're just short guys." Salas raised both hands in the air.

"Detective, I realize midgets are short. Duh…that's why they're called midgets." Ronnie raised his hands as well.

"Ronnie, shut up," Salas said.

Ronnie did.

"I think we may have a serial killer on our hands," Salas said. "He was killing once a year, all at the same time of year. Now he has two kills in two days. Something has triggered him to be more aggressive. He could kill again. We need—we *have*—to stop him. One thing we know, he's headed to Sturgis for a motorcycle rally.

"Ronnie, get back on your computer. Look for credit card receipts from gas stations and campgrounds. There has to be a common link. This guy isn't a pro—he's just sick. Sick people make mistakes. Check Alliance, Valentine, Murdo, Sioux Falls, Moline, and Fort Wayne. Small towns mean fewer options for fuel, camping, and food." Salas stood. "I'll tell Captain Green we've got a lead."

RJ AND DEUCE

Monday morning came too early. RJ was hungover and had gotten only three hours of sleep. Deuce had gotten more sleep but looked even worse; the bottle of Jack was empty.

"It's so fucking hot in that fucking tent," he announced as he unzipped the fly and crawled out of the tent. He struggled and grimaced as he stood up, placing his left hand on his knee and his right hand on his lower back.

"Let's get your back checked out today. Find a chiropractor in Rapid City. Could do you some good. Why fight it?" RJ was sitting in a folding chair, looking out over the campground.

"Yeah, this isn't getting any better. Nights are the worst. Sweat like a bitch." Deuce opened a bottle of water and drained it. "I need to rehydrate too."

After the trip to the shower house—the mandatory thirty-minute minimum wait time, the five-minute cold shower—fresh clothes, and another bottle of water, the two men were ready to head to Rapid City. They saddled up, hit "start," and let the bikes idle for a few minutes before taking off. A trail of dust followed them to the exit; Deuce always led.

The line of bikes was long for 8:00 a.m. The first stoplight at the Chip turned green, then red, three times, before Deuce and RJ went full throttle and roared through. They caught green lights past the co-op gas station, which was packed with bikers getting gas and groceries.

At Fort Meade, Deuce went south on a clay-and-gravel road. He didn't want to sit in the Sturgis traffic. The winding road was narrow at the curves, with bikes stopping several times to let pickups and cars pass through. The red clay of the road was packed down; a little oil mixed into calm the dust offered some traction.

The road came to an end at I-90 across from Black Hills National Cemetery. Hundreds of bright white crosses on green grass, all in perfect lines, decorated the hillside. A beautiful resting place for hundreds of America's best. Deuce stopped for a few minutes and stared at the landscape.

Deuce and RJ jumped on I-90 for the twenty-mile ride into Rapid City. They rode in a tight formation, with Deuce slightly ahead and RJ's front tire just to the right of Deuce's front foot peg. The two bikers moved in unison—no turn signals, no hand signals. When Deuce passed a car or bike, RJ was in line, never breaking the space between them, as if RJ were a sidecar to Deuce's Harley.

They took the exit to Mount Rushmore Road and downtown Rapid City. Deuce didn't have an appointment; he just figured he could walk in, get his back cracked, and walk out. He didn't even know where a chiropractor was; he just knew they were like a Starbucks, one on every corner.

He pulled his Harley into Rapid City Back Pain Center and backed his bike into a parking slot next to a black Lexus. RJ did the same, only on the other side of the car. A white poodle, a yapper, was barking at them from inside the black car. The window was down about six inches. RJ stuck his fingers in, and the dog licked them. RJ smiled; funny, the things you forget about in prison.

The chiropractor's office had a small waiting room. The right-hand wall had two large posters. One featured a "normal" spine; the other showed an osteoarthritic spine. The two posters lay in total contrast to each other. The "normal" spine vertebrae had smooth lines and were white, with curves in the low back and in the neck. The "abnormal" spine had gray bone spurs and a straight back with no curves. Deuce pointed to the osteoarthritic spine and said, "That's me."

He went to the receptionist and asked if he could see the doctor. She asked him some questions, handed him a clipboard with several pieces of paper and a pen, and took Deuce's insurance ID card.

Deuce filled out the paperwork and gave them back to the young lady. Fifteen minutes later, the door opened, and a man in a white coat, with "Dr. Everett Meyers" embroidered on the left chest, walked through the door. He tilted his head down and peered over the top of his eyeglasses. The doctor looked at Deuce and said, "H.P. Wozniak? Harold P. Wozniak?"

Deuce stood up. RJ quickly got up and grabbed Deuce by the arm. "The great and powerful Woz," he whispered to him.

Deuce turned to RJ. "Ever say that again, and I'll shoot you in your sleep."

RJ smiled. "Got it, Harry."

"Ever say that again, and I'll set you on fire in your sleep." Deuce smiled back.

"Whatever you say, HP." RJ let go of Deuce's arm. The older man followed the doctor, and the door closed.

RJ sat alone in the waiting room. A purple-haired lady came out the door that Deuce had gone through. She thanked the young receptionist and walked out of the office. RJ watched through the big picture window as she got into the black Lexus, the little white poodle jumping into her lap. The lady rolled the window down partway, and the poodle stuck its head out as she drove away.

RJ read a copy of *People* magazine. Some punky-looking kid named Justin with spiked hair and straight pants was on the cover. RJ thought that kid would be popular in prison.

An hour went by. No Deuce. RJ picked up a plastic model of five vertebrae and a butt bone. It had yellow strings sticking out; RJ figured they were nerves. He twisted the spine like the head was turning to look around; one of the yellow nerves fell out and dropped to the floor. RJ tried to put it back together but couldn't. Finally, the door opened, and Deuce came out.

Deuce walked past RJ, out the door to their bikes.

"So how you feel?" RJ asked.

"Okay. No different." Deuce got on his bike.

"And?"

"And what? My back hurts. That's it. Let's go." Deuce started his bike.

Deuce again took the lead. RJ followed about ten feet behind him. He was puzzled but knew better than to ask. They rode to another building, about a mile from the chiropractor's office. They were in the parking lot of the Rapid City Regional Hospital when Deuce stopped, shut off the bike, and put the kickstand down.

Deuce sat motionless. RJ did the same, waiting for him to speak.

"The chiropractor got me an appointment with a doc in there." Deuce pointed to the hospital. "Doc Meyer said I have a tumor—looked like it was into the bone—and I need more tests, like an MRI and blood work. He called some oncologist there. That's who the doc wants me to see. Gotta be bad for him to get me in today. I mean, he made a call and got me in ASAP."

"Let's go then," RJ replied.

"Look, if I got bone cancer in my back, I'm fucked," Deuce said, squinting at the sun through his black Ray-Bans.

"You don't know. Could be a bad X-ray, could be curable, could be you just need some chemo." RJ was walking toward the entrance, not looking back to see if Deuce was following him

They entered the hospital through the main double doors. RJ asked the lady at the information desk where oncology was. She directed them to the third floor.

After exiting the elevator on the third floor, they went right, down a long pasty-white hallway; so much for yellows and blues to help your mood. The door to oncology was plastered with several doctors' names in white block letters. RJ and Deuce were looking for Dr. Samuel Benson.

RJ opened the door for Deuce. He held the door for him while gently nudging him through. Beads of perspiration covered Deuce's forehead. The room was the same color scheme as the hallway, with rows of chairs along two walls and a wheelchair in the corner.

A receptionist, maybe a nurse, dressed in blue hospital scrubs, was standing behind the counter. There was a door to her left—the entrance to the doctors' and nurses' areas, exam rooms, and a laboratory. "Are you Mr. Wozniak?" she asked Deuce.

"Yeah."

"Fill out these forms, please."

Ten minutes later, Deuce followed the nurse through the door. When he came back to the reception area, it was three hours later, and he came back through a different door. He had a white piece of cotton taped to the crease of his left elbow.

Deuce looked at RJ. "Done. Let's roll."

They walked down the hallway, into the elevator, and descended three floors. They left the hospital the way they'd come in.

Neither spoke.

The two men roared away in their Harleys, with Deuce once again in the lead. They took the first exit out of the hospital parking lot and headed west to the Black Hills.

KEVIN

K evin waited until 8:30 a.m. Matt was still asleep, and Jerico hadn't come back yet.

Cranking up the volume on the radio and opening the shades of the RV made Matt roll over but not wake up. "Get your ass out of bed and meet me outside!" Kevin yelled. "I'm making breakfast, and then…by damn we're going to ride today!"

Matt got up, straightened the bedding, stopped in the RV's bathroom, brushed his teeth while he pissed, and then went outside, still in his boxers. He plopped down heavily at the picnic table. "Man, I didn't need that Jameson last night. I maintained pretty good till I came back here. You're a bad influence on me, Uncle Kev."

"I must have done the zip line like five times," Kevin said in a rush.

"Where's Jerico? Where are Deuce and RJ?" Matt's head turned left and right.

"Jerico never came back last night. RJ and Deuce, well they were gone when I came out." Kevin put a plate of bacon, eggs, and grapes, and a cup coffee in front of Matt.

"Thanks, Kev. Where do you want to ride today?" Matt asked, sipping his coffee.

Kevin sat down with his own plate of food. "Let's do Custer State Park. I want to ride by the buffalo."

"It'll be a bitch riding through town. Let's go to Belle Fourche and through Spearfish. That's my favorite ride." Matt was rubbing his temples.

"Well, look who made it home!" Kevin proclaimed as Jerico walked up the dirt road, shirtless. "We were worried about you! Stayed up till three, then went to bed."

"What happened to your arm? Where's your shirt?" Matt asked, looking at the fresh blood and scrapes on Jerico's right forearm.

"Fell into another damn culvert this morning walking back. I couldn't find my shirt this morning," Jerico mumbled as he sanitized his hands.

"Wait a minute. Another culvert? You've fallen into a culvert before?" Kevin asked.

"Yeah. One night I was really drunk walking home from a bar. Today I was on my damn phone and wasn't paying attention. Girlfriend wants me to call more often." A low mumble came out of Jerico's mouth as he started up the steps of the RV. "I need water."

"Wait!" Matt yelled, looking at Jerico's back as he was heading into the RV. "What the hell happened to your back?"

"You get attacked by a mountain lion?" Kevin asked

"Oh, is it bad?" Jerico asked, trying to peer over his shoulder at his back.

"Bad? It looks like it hurts like hell. Gouges, man—she got you with all four fingers like four times." Matt was counting with his fingers and pointing.

"Yeah, she's a scratcher!" Jerico said, smiling at Kevin and Matt as he went into the RV.

Kevin shook his head. "Shit, what's wrong with young people today?"

After breakfast, Kevin cleaned up as Jerico told Matt about his shower experience with Ann and how he'd gone back to her cabin and spent the night.

"I got to meet Jessica at their cabin," Jerico said. "She's pretty. You struck out?"

Matt shrugged. "Didn't really try. She's just amazing. I don't want to rush her. We talk like we've known each other forever."

"Uuugghhh I don't want to hear this Hallmark shit." Jerico said.

By eleven, all three of them were on their Harleys. Out of the Chip, they turned right on Highway 79 and dogged it through the thirty-five-mph-hour zone. Three state patrolmen had pulled some bikes over. Normally the speed limit was sixty mph, but during rally they dropped it to thirty-five.

They rode past Bear Butte, the Drag Pipe Saloon and Campground, and the Broken Spoke Bar and Campground. Both were packed with trailers, tents, and RVs.

Kevin was leading, followed by Matt, with Jerico close behind. Kevin had his speakers cranked to the max; Jerico could hear the music as if it were coming out of his own bike. Kevin was playing Godsmack, prepping for tonight's concert. Neither of the three men noticed the motorcycle far behind them zipping in and out of traffic.

They road past flat lands of alfalfa, cornfields, an irrigation canal, and a field of sunflowers. Turning left just before Newell, South Dakota, on Highway 212, they joined a staggered line of forty to fifty bikes. They didn't notice but in their rear-view mirrors was someone on a motorcycle cutting in and out of traffic even riding on the right shoulder to pass others, trying desperately to catch the others. The progression of bikes moved on like a swarm of bees.

The bikes rolled into Belle Fourche, most took the old road through the residential district, down Main Street, then turned left on Highway 85 to Spearfish. The stop lights in the city of Spearfish are set so you must stop at them all, no way to speed up or ride slow enough to miss them. As Kevin, Matt and Jerico rode through town the biker trailing them did his utmost to catch up. He ran through stop signs and red stop lights, with each block he drew closer and closer to the three men.

Spearfish Canyon is rated as one of the top ten rides in the United States, and today it was tire-to-tire, an endless stream of bikes. Take that back—there was one interruption, some dumbass in a Corvette.

The black, gray, and white granite canyon walls were direct verticals. Pine trees lined the highway, with sneaking views of summer cabins dotted along the left and right sides.

The two-lane road followed a river, with the water level at a seasonal high due to recent rains. Bikers had stopped, off their cyckles taking pictures at Bridal Veil Falls and Spearfish Falls. Kevin sped past; he had no interest in those kinds of scenic photos. Matt and Jerico followed, the speed racing biker who was zipping in and out of traffic was now less than ten bikes behind them.

The three riders stayed in formation, the music now off, enjoying the rumble of the bikes, the serenity of the views, the clear skies, and the bright sun. Kevin slowed momentarily, watching a biker in leather pants, leather vest, and bandana as he was fly-fishing. The serene, back-and-forth rhythmic motion of the fly rod lay in stark contrast to the fisherman's attire.

Approaching Cheyenne Crossing, they were met by two young ladies in swimsuits standing by the entrance of a gas station. They were holding large hand-painted signs above their heads that read, BIKINI BIKE WASH. Kevin made an abrupt left turn and pulled in, the boys following him. Kevin yelled over his shoulder that they should never miss a photo opportunity. The biker playing catch up was riding to fast to make the sudden turn and sped past the exit. He hit the front and rear brakes of his Harley, the bike fished tailed and slid sideways trying to make the stop. The three men that pulled into the parking lot didn't notice.

White canvas tents with five stalls had been constructed, anchored by thick cords wrapped around metal stakes that had been pounded into the black asphalt. Each makeshift stall housed a bikini-laden young lady bent over, washing or drying a motorcycle. Ten dollars for the wash; tips were appreciated.

Kevin was getting his already immaculate bike washed as he was taking more pictures for his album. Matt and Jerico got fuel and watch several men helping a biker off the asphalt. The bike had slid several feet, the rider had blood running down the side of his head. Kevin joined his partners for water as all three watched the state police place the fallen biker in the back of their cruiser. A tow truck was loading the crashed bike. Kevin heard someone say the biker was so drunk they didn't know how he got this far without crashing. Minutes later, the three men were back on the road. They turned left at Highway 85, climbing their way to Lead, South Dakota.

Barren of snow in August, Terry Peak, a popular skiing destination, stood tall at seven thousand feet and was the focus of the steady incline. Down the back side was Homestake Gold Mine and then road construction all through the city of Lead. They took a right on 385, missing Deadwood for a trip to Hills City.

Highway 385 was flatter, with fewer turns; the traffic flow was steady. Both sides of the highway were lined with motorcycles, as well as pines, aspens, cedars, and patches of open hillsides that were pockmarked with charred tree stumps and blackened tree trunks, victims of seasonal forest fires.

Kevin broke formation and pulled into a Pactola Lake lookout area. The boys followed. The deep, clear, blue water of the lake, lined by dark-green trees and clear blue skies was a picture even Kevin had to get. He had Matt and Jerico line up against the concrete rail, lake and view behind them. A few selfies and then the sightseeing was over. Kevin nearly sent the picture to Gloria then recalled her embrace with his best friend. Matt asked why he looked pissy, Kevin ignored him and they were back on 385.

Twenty miles south and they were in Hill City, another small town transformed by the rally. As they rode into town, the smell of freshly cut pine from the sawmill engulfed them; they could practically taste the pine.

Kevin and the boys rode through the three blocks of Main Street, watching the crowd inch along, shoulder-to-shoulder. Pedestrians moved slowly as they peered into storefront windows that offered Black Hills gold jewelry, souvenir plates, cups, maps, books, and of course, rally T-shirts.

After three hours of riding, Kevin finally got to the road he was after: Needles Highway. They rode past Harney Peak, the highest mountain in South Dakota at 7,244 feet—a rocky projection, really. In the depths of winter, it never holds snow at the top, much less a skier. The three bikers started the 360-degree loop up the back side of Mount Rushmore in an endless line of bikes. The man-made tunnels, only twenty or twenty-five yards long, had been driven through solid rock. It was one lane only, with bikers waiting their turn to enter the tunnel. The tunnel walls were scarred from repeated scratches from side mirrors and the bumpers of pickups and cars. Each rider used their left hand to hold the clutch and their right hand to lay on the throttle as they rode through the tunnels, the roar of the bikes echoing off the walls.

After they reached the peak, the descent started, with all the bikes now in first gear; the low gear limited their speed as they rode down Iron Mountain Road, east of Mount Rushmore. Pumping the rear brakes and lightly using the front brakes, the three men eased their way down the mountain to the prairie grass of Custer State Park. With the heavy bike traffic, it would have been a nightmare if it had been a rainy day.

A mile into the prairie, they ran into another traffic stop, which, to Kevin's wonder, it was due to a herd of buffalo crossing the road.

Matt counted forty buffalo, some cows, bulls, and a dozen calves. Most of the bikers shut their engines down to let the majestic creatures cross in peace. The long-bearded bulls, their horns turned down, led the way. Despite the high temperature of this August day, the animals' coats and hides were thickening for winter. The cows, calves in tow, kept a wary eye on the road and the bikes. The buffalo crossed slowly, one or two at a time. Cell-phone cameras were clicking, videos on wide angle.

Kevin left Custer State Park at the Highway 36 exit, with Matt and Jerico on his tail. They took a left at Hermosa on 79 and cranked it up to eighty for the next twenty miles into Rapid City. Connecting to I-90 off US Route 16, they flew by Rushmore Mall and past Blackhawk, Piedmont, and Tilford to exit 34 for Black Hills National Cemetery. Here the road went from white pavement to red clay. The three men maneuvered the twists and turns of the country road and came out at Fort Meade VA Hospital. Another right turn and they sped past the Full Throttle, finally arriving at the Chip and the RV.

"Man, what a ride!" Kevin announced. "That was nearly two hundred miles."

"I need a beer!" Jerico was again sanitizing his hands.

"I'm hungry" was Matt's contribution. He was staring across the road. A short muscular man was returning the stare.

Ronnie rushed to Salas's desk, some papers in hand. "Detective Salas, we did it. We got him." He was flushed and breathing hard.

"Tell me."

Ronnie took a big breath and exclaimed, "Well, I ran credit-card processing for the campground in Fort Wayne and the KOA in Sioux Falls…no hits. But when I ran gas stations near both campgrounds and compared them to the campgrounds' credit cards, I got three matches. But it gets better. I ran the same search for gas stations in Alliance, Nebraska, and one of the names matched the other locations. This puts him in the same town where three of the murders took place." Ronnie stopped for another breath. "So, I figured let's try another. After all, he must be paying for gas with his credit card, right? Sure enough, I got a hit at a Conoco station in Valentine, Nebraska, the same week as the estimated time of death of the guy they found under the bridge."

"You're shitting me," Salas said.

Ronnie tiled his head, confused. "Ah, no, I'm not shitting you, Detective Salas."

"Anything in Murdo or Moline?"

"No, nothing for the Murdo or Moline killings. I can keep digging if you want. But Detective Salas, this has to be him, right?" Ronnie held his hand out for a fist bump.

Salas ignored the fist, walked past Ronnie, stopped, turned, and said, "Well, who is it?"

"Oh, yeah, I got his billing address and ran his name through the Indiana DMV. Our suspect is Albert Christianson of Auburn, Indiana. DOB: June seventeenth, 1987. DMV lists him at five six, one hundred sixty-five pounds, blue eyes, brown hair, organ donor. Albert lives about thirty minutes from here, Detective. Oh, and he has a motorcycle endorsement on his driver's license, but no cars or motorcycles registered in his name."

"Address?" Salas asked.

Ronnie was back in his cubicle, typing. "435 Cedar Street in Auburn. Hold on." He typed some more. "The house is owned by Ted Christianson. Must live with his parents or a brother."

"Nice work, Ronnie. Let's go for a drive and check it out," Salas said, looking at the clock. It was 10:30 a.m.

At the home of Ted Christianson, in Auburn, Salas parked in the driveway behind a sun-faded red Chevy Impala. From the front seat of Salas's Ford, they looked at the two-story home: a broken window at the south dormer, T-lock shingles cracked and curled on the roof. The blue siding was original, hail dented, and cracked in several places, with exposed wood glaring at them.

The detectives exited the Taurus and approached the car in the driveway. The front passenger tire was flat, with rust above both rear wheel wells, and the front windshield was cracked. The two men walked up the five wooden steps to the front porch. Ronnie followed as Salas stepped over the splintered wood and gaping hole in steps two and three.

"House needs a little help," Salas said.

"Yes, and the yard hasn't been mowed for a while or watered. The place looks abandoned," Ronnie added.

Salas knocked on the front screen door and pushed a button for what he assumed was the doorbell. There was no sound inside acknowledging the knock or the sound of a doorbell.

Ronnie cupped his hands around his eyes and peered through the window. "Nothing. Doesn't look like anyone's home. Do you smell something? Like sewage backup?"

"Methane gas to me. Could be dangerous and gives us probable cause, Ronnie." Salas tried the doorknob, but it was locked. He raised his foot and kicked the door in; it didn't take much effort.

Both men pulled their weapons as Salas announced his presence. "Fort Wayne Police. Is everything okay? Please call out if you hear me. Fort Wayne Police."

No response.

They walked through the main floor as a team.

"Ronnie, check out those family pictures, a son and mother. Looks like the picture of the father was cut out." Salas was pointing at some photos on an end table.

"Yeah, you can see the arm of the man, but he was definitely cut out. What do you think that means, Detective Salas?"

"Someone doesn't like Daddy." Salas continued to lead as they entered the kitchen.

"What a mess. Smells horrible," Ronnie said, pulling his shirt up over his nose.

"That's why we entered, Ronnie. Make sure you put that in your notes," Salas said, holstering his weapon.

"Dirty dishes, empty pizza boxes, empty soup cans, dirty clothes. They can't cook or clean," Ronnie said, as he came out of the laundry room.

"Yeah, I tried the faucet. Water's been turned off or shut off. Lights don't work either, and the food in fridge is spoiled, no electricity," Salas said as he left the kitchen, Ronnie at his side. "Let's keep looking."

"For what? A house cleaner?" Ronnie retorted.

The two detectives climbed the steps to the second floor. Ronnie still had his weapon drawn.

"Check that bedroom and the bathroom. I got this one," Salas said as he opened the door to the master bedroom. He heard Ronnie continue to gag.

As soon as Salas entered the room, he saw a dead body on the bed. He checked the closet, under the bed—nothing seemed disturbed or rifled through. "Ronnie, come in here. We got a DB," Salas yelled.

Ronnie ran into the bedroom, went to the window, opened it, and leaned out, sucking in fresh air.

"What's with you?" Salas asked.

"The bathroom. Wait till you see it," Ronnie said, leaning back into the bedroom and pulling the window back to close it.

"Leave it open. Can't bag and tag odor," Salas said. "See what we got here? Has to be the mother, the wife." He pointed to the dead body on the bed.

"She seems at peace," Ronnie said. "Her hair isn't messed up, and her arms are on her chest, fingers crossed as if in prayer. Her dress is in place. Shoes are even on."

"I don't see any bullet wounds, bloodstains on the dress, or stab wounds. Looks like she's been dead a couple of months. Notice the decomposition. The maggots are dead, body fluids gone but the smell isn't," Salas said, as he took out his phone and called the station.

"Maybe she died in her sleep or had a stroke? An aneurysm? Long bout with cancer?" Ronnie was diagnosing.

"What was in the bathroom? Another DB?" Salas asked.

"I wish. Come look," Ronnie said, as he led Salas there.

Even Salas gagged when he entered the bathroom. He took his own shirt and placed it over his nose and mouth. "Shit, it stinks in here. My eyes are watering," he said, the smell of ammonia burning his nose.

"Look at the toilet, then check the bathtub," Ronnie said.

The toilet was overflowing with urine, feces, and toilet paper. The lid was keeping the waste from running to the floor. Salas pulled back the shower curtain. The bathtub also was filled with urine, feces, toilet paper, and paper towels.

"Shit. Seriously. Shit," Salas said as he left the bathroom.

"You think he used the tub as a toilet?" Ronnie asked.

"Good detecting, Detective," Salas responded as they walked down the hall into the second bedroom.

Salas and Ronnie entered the smaller of the two bedrooms. Wooden floor shone with the morning sun reflecting off it. Kids' posters were on the walls: a purple dinosaur named Barney, and Hank the Cowdog. A shelf was lined with Star Wars action figures and green, plastic army men. The bed was made with tight creases, and a teddy bear sat between the pillows.

Ronnie opened the closet. "Look here, Detective Salas." Ronnie pointed to the closet floor.

Inside the closet, against the far wall, were a pillow, a blanket, and a battery-powered alarm clock that read 11:11. The distinctive burning smell of urine clouded the closet.

"Let's check the basement. I gotta get out of this smell before I puke," Salas said as he left the room and headed down the steps.

Ronnie opened the door to the basement, stepped on the first step, and hit the light switch. He flipped the switch four or five times.

"No electricity, Ronnie," Salas said, pulling out his cell phone and activating the flashlight app.

"Oh, yeah, you said that. You go first," Ronnie said, stepping aside.

The basement was dark, dusty, and smelled of mold and mildew but at least no ammonia. Salas scanned the width of the basement with the cell-phone light. Ronnie was breathing on Salas's neck.

"You got a flashlight app?" Salas said, turning around. He placed his hand on Ronnie's chest and pushed him back a few inches.

"No, Detective Salas."

"Make a list of stuff you need, Ronnie: flashlight app, longer pants, breath mints," Salas said, as he scanned the basement's walls and concrete floor. A few metal posts were projecting from the concrete and bolted into the floor joists. In the center of the room was a weightlifting bench and an iron cage for squats and military presses. One wall had racks of dumbbells in pairs, from twenty-five pounds to ninety-five pounds in ten-pound increments.

"Strong little shit. Three fifteen on the bench," Salas said, as he took his index finger and spun a forty-five-pound plate on the bench bar.

"How do you know that, Detective Salas?

"Three forty-five-pound plates on each end of the bar. The bar weighs forty-five pounds too. That's three fifteen."

The two detectives went back up the stairs—Salas counted fifteen of them—then walked through the living room, out the front door, and outside. They needed fresh air.

Two Auburn PD cars pulled up, lights flashing, no sirens. They parked at the curb. An ambulance, AUBURN COUNTY HOSPITAL in gold paint on the side, parked in the middle of the street. Two male paramedics opened the rear doors of the vehicle. They pulled out a metal gurney, white sheets over a thin mattress, and wheeled it to the front porch. One paramedic pushed while the other steered.

Neighbors were gathering across the street: several older men, a couple of ladies and three kids on bicycles. It was a pleasant summer Monday morning—well, at least it was outside the house.

As the city police officers came forward, Salas turned to Ronnie. "The kid sleeps in the closet. My bet is water and electric were shut off for nonpayment. Shut-off date probably was a couple of weeks after the woman died."

Salas continued, "Pictures of the father were cut out or taken down. Dad is dead, gone, or dead and gone. My bet…he's a mama's boy. Now that she's dead, he can't function. He, Albert, was killing once a year, but that doesn't get him off any more. Without Mom, he needs more.'

"And for sure, without Mom, he doesn't know how to clean," Ronnie said, his fingers interlocked behind his head, his elbows extended wide. He was still trying to get more air in his lungs.

"Agreed. That's detecting, Detective. He'll kill again and soon. His world is upside down right now," Salas said, walking down the driveway. "Ronnie, direct the officers and crime-scene techs to the DB. Warn them about the bathroom. I'm going to talk to a few neighbors. And see if you can find the whereabouts of the owner of this fine house, Ted Christianson."

"Will do. And Detective Salas, is this a crime scene?" Ronnie asked. "The woman could have died of natural causes, and shitting in the tub isn't a crime…is it?"

Salas walked across the street. He avoided the onlookers, the kids on the bikes. Three women with their hands cupped to their mouths were talking in a semicircle. He avoided them too and went to the house directly across from what could be—and most likely was—a crime scene.

Salas flipped the latch up on the metal gate and walked into the yard. The grass was lush green—no weeds, no dandelions, no crab grass. The lawn was freshly manicured, with crisp edges where the grass met the sidewalk. Interconnecting red bricks lay in a perfect circle around two pine trees in the center of lawn, with not a single pine needle on the grass.

The blue paint on the cedar siding was new, maybe within the year, and the window trim had fresh white paint. Salas rapped three times on the front door; it opened on the second knock.

An elderly black man, graying at the temples, bald on top, opened the door. "I hear you. What do you want?"

"Sir, I'm Detective Mike Salas, Fort Wayne Police Department. Mind if I ask you a few questions about your neighbor?" Salas asked, his badge facing the man.

"James C. Cooper, officer. Please call me Coop. Thirty-five years with the US Postal Service. Retired now, marine for life." Cooper extended his hand to Salas, who shook it firmly. As Cooper stepped outside, the two men faced the Christianson home.

"He killed her, didn't he?" Cooper asked, his hands on the banister as he leaned forward, scanning the police cars, ambulance, and crowd.

"We don't know for sure yet, but yes, between you and me, Mrs. Christianson is dead. Any idea why Albert would kill her? Salas asked.

"Albert? Hell, he didn't kill her. He loved his mom. But he would have killed his dad if he could have. Ted was the biggest ass in the history of asses. Ted's the killer," Cooper said bluntly.

"Ted lived in the home?"

Cooper shook his head. "No, he left years ago. Went to work one day and never came back. Left the woman, Elaine and boy alone. That was at least eight years ago. I was with at the postal service. This entire block on my route…delivered mail to that house every day, saw it all." Cooper swung his left arm from right to left as if to encircle the entire block then pointed to the Christianson home.

"So why do you think Ted killed her?"

Cooper let out a long sigh. "Hell, he used to beat her, beat her bad. Beat the little boy too. I called the police on the bastard at least ten times. Elaine never filed charges, never admitted he beat her. Never admitted he beat the kid. Always made excuses: she fell down, ran into the door; kid wrecked his bike. We could hear the crying, the screams. Drove my wife, Betty, to an early grave." Cooper crossed his heart, looked up into the clear blue sky, and blew a kiss.

"I'm sorry about your wife's passing. But again, Coop," Salas repeated, "why you think Ted killed her?"

"Ya know, after he left, at first he'd just drive by at night. I'd see him drive by in his minivan. Then a couple of times, when the boy was at school or work he'd go into the house. Must have kept a key. Once Albert got out of high school, he became a muscular little shit. I don't think Ted wanted to mess with him then. But Ted would come over when Albert was at work—again, he'd go into the house. Come out fifteen to twenty minutes later. I know he had to have beaten her, raped her, threaten to kill her. So, ya know, I just figured he came back one day. I must have missed seeing him, and he finally killed her. Haven't seen Elaine for a couple of months. I probably should've gone over and checked for myself." Cooper looked down at his feet

"Why wouldn't Albert have called the police or an ambulance?"

"Albert? I don't know Detective, Albert is a strange kid." Mr. Cooper seemed embarrassed to talk about it.

"Coop, where does Albert work? Do you know?"

"Kid is a janitor at some school. Works nights mostly, I think he just cleans and scrubs the floors. Easy stuff." Cooper added.

"When was the last time you saw him?" Salas asked.

He thought for a moment. "Friday around noon. He cranked up that damn motorcycle. He likes to rev the damn motor. Makes him feel like a big shot. He took off that a way." Cooper pointed west.

Salas thanked the old man and went back to Ronnie, who was waving at Salas, motioning for him to come look at his cell phone.

"I've got a Ted Christianson, Detective Salas, rural route address about twenty-five minutes from here," Ronnie proclaimed loudly as he led Salas to the Taurus.

At 11:54, they were sitting in front of a pea-green single-wide trailer. The bottom skirt had broken off and was lying on the grass. Ronnie and Salas could see the axle and concrete blocks the house sat on. There were no tie-downs or anchors; the fact that the building was still erect defied the laws of nature.

Black, used tires, no tread, had been tossed haphazardly across the dull white roof of the single-wide. All the front windows were cracked, and the siding was held in place with duct tape, wire, nails, and screws. The yard matched the home in Auburn; evidently the Christianson boys weren't green thumbs.

A Ford Aerostar minivan sat in front of the entryway's two wooden steps. The van looked tired.

Salas yelled at the front door; he didn't think he could fit between the van and the steps to knock. "Christianson, Mike Salas, Fort Wayne PD. Come outside please, sir. We need to talk."

The door opened. A pasty fifty-something man in blue jeans stepped out onto the first step and shut the door. His Wranglers were unbuttoned, the zipper partway down. A dull-white wife beater was tucked into his underwear. At first Salas thought Ted's hair, pulled behind his ears, was wet then realized it was just greasy.

"What the fuck?" were Ted's first words.

"Sorry to bother you, sir. Lovely place you have here. Are you the owner of a house at 435 Cedar Street in Auburn?" Salas asked.

"This place is a piece of shit. And yes, I own another piece of shit in Auburn, why? The crazy bitch burn it down?" Ted said. He took out a Pal Mall and lit it up. The first drag off the cigarette was five seconds; Salas counted.

"No, sir. Your wife—or ex-wife—was found dead this morning," Salas said bluntly.

"Bitch is...*was* my wife. Never got a divorce. Lawyers wanted too much fuckin' money," Ted said. He didn't appear shocked or saddened. Another long drag of the cigarette.

"We need you to ID the body as soon as you can get to Ft. Wayne. We need to perform an autopsy, sir. Are you aware of any medical conditions your wife, ex, er, Elaine had?" Salas asked.

"She had headaches all the time, and was on blood pressure crap, really expensive shit." Christianson reached into his back pocket and pulled out a pack of cigarettes.

"Anything you'd like to share with us would save us some time," Salas stepped forward and looked the man in the eye.

"I didn't kill her. Bitch was a good piece of ass. Too bad she had that fuckin' retard of a son or I would've stayed around." Ted's cigarette had burned to nearly halfway up to the filter.

"Not your son, sir?" Ronnie interrupted.

"No, married her when he was two." Ted responded.

"What can you tell us about Albert." Ronnie stated rather than asked. He didn't like this guy.

"Told you not mine. Brick shy of a load." He let out a smoke ring.

"Where did Albert work?" Ronnie continued.

"Hell if I know." Was Ted's response.

"Do you know, did he ride his motorcycle to Sturgis, South Dakota this week?" Ronnie asked

"Hell if I know." Ted repeated. "Paid that house off a few years ago. I'll move back in and kick that fuckin' tard out," Ted said in triumph.

"Good for you, Mr. Christianson," Salas said. "Appreciate your cooperation. I'd recommend that after the investigation you go to your home and take over. Your wife will have funeral expenses, and of course the home is in need of a little upkeep." He turned and got into the car with Ronnie in tow. As they drove off, he heard Ted yell, "I ain't paying for no fuckin' funeral!"

They were back at the office by one. Salas went to talk to Captain Green as Ronnie hit the computer, looking for flights to Sturgis.

Salas knocked on Green's door, peered in. "Tom, I know you'll say no, but hear me out."

Salas sat down and presented his case to Green. Salas was right; Green said no.

"It's a federal case now," Green said. "You know that. Multiple states, multiple murders. You and Ronnie did great work. I agree…it's gotta be this Albert Christianson. Now hand it off. End of story."

Ronnie knocked on the door as Green was opening it for Salas to exit. "Detective Salas, I have a credit card hit on Albert in Sturgis. Buffalo Chip Campground. He charged two hundred fifty dollars on his Visa." Ronnie looked at Salas then at Green.

"See, Tom, we have him. By the time we get the feds involved, do all the paperwork bullshit, he could kill again. We know where he is for, God's sake. Let Ronnie and me fly there, go to the campground, arrest him, and nail the little son of a bitch. We'll be back by Wednesday or Thursday." Salas was pleading.

Ronnie nodded. "There's a flight at three, Detective Salas. Fort Wayne to Chicago on United. Puts us in Rapid City at five. Two-hour time change helps us. I called Sturgis PD. A chief Brannigan said he would welcome the help. They can meet us, surround the camp, and assist in the arrest."

"Okay, okay. Go now before I change my mind. I want a report in my inbox as soon as you get back. You got it, Salas?" Green went back to his desk and sat down. He clearly wasn't expecting a response. "And Salas, I got Davis coming in this week. He IDs you and you are done. So, finish this fast."

Salas shut the captain's door giving the door the finger. He patted Ronnie on the shoulder. "Great work. The timing on the credit card was perfect. Go home, pack your stuff, and get some clothes that blend in. We don't want to look like the police. Meet me at the airport. We're going to Sturgis."

Checking his watch, Salas realized he didn't have time to go home and pack. After parking the car at a nearby Walmart, he emptied his gym duffel in the backseat. Inside the store, he grabbed a basket and went to the men's department. A three-pack of Fruit of the Looms, briefs not boxers—Salas's thighs were so big that boxers bunched up. A three-pack of white V-neck T-shirts, one pair of white socks, and his shopping was complete.

Next stop was the travel section in the toiletry department. Travel toothbrush, toothpaste under than three ounces, solid deodorant, a ninety-nine-cent can of AXE body spray, and Salas was nearly done. He was trying to find a towel when he spotted Angelina and Dan Davis in electronics. Dan Davis had a hard, white, plastic neck brace cupped under his chin, extending to his chest. Salas lowered his boonie hat to the side and tried to walk briskly by. Dan Davis said, "Hey, isn't that the son of a bitch who broke my neck!" then groaned as he tried to turn and look.

Salas heard Angelina: "No, honey, that's not him. Watch it—don't try and turn your head!"

Looking back, Salas made eye contact with Angelina. Dan Davis's back was to Salas. Angelina had her hand in a fist, her thumb extended to her ear, her pinky finger near her lips. She mouthed, "Call me" and smiled.

Membership has its privileges. Salas and Ronnie sped through security—badges, weapons, and all. The local TSA, dressed in customary blue shirts, black pants, and black shoes, all knew Salas and waved him through as the plane was ready to go, wheels up. Less than an hour later, Ronnie and Salas were sprinting through O'Hare to Gate F and on a two-hour flight to Rapid City.

ALBERT

The morning sun was his alarm clock. As the rays of sunshine hit the tent, the rising temperature served as the alarm.

Albert repeated his walk to the free breakfast offered by Bikers for Jesus. Same men, same vests, same menu.

The Bikers for Jesus crew was busy, with a member seated at each picnic table in discussion with other bikers. Albert found an open end at a table, sat quietly, and listened to the men talk. The discussion was about Harleys, makes, models, years, V-twins, and options. Albert kept his mouth full of food, hoping no one would ask him a question—and no one did. Famished, he went through the buffet line twice.

Taking the long way back to his tent space, he walked for nearly an hour. Once or twice he got lost as he headed to the American flag that was on Father's RV, only to find it was an American flag but a different RV.

When he finally saw his campsite, Father and the two linebackers were mounted on their bikes, idling. Albert walked the last thirty yards quickly, trying not to run. He desperately wanted to follow them, perhaps ride with them.

The three men took off in a roar as Albert got to his Harley and jumped on. He hit the start button, but nothing happened. He forgot to turn the barrel key then realized he'd left the key in the tent. After unzipping the front screen, he dove in headfirst on his hands and knees. In a panic, he went through his bag, which only caused more delays. When he finally found the key, he crawled back out and straddled his bike, but Father and the linebackers were out of sight.

He started his Harley, put it in low gear, but popped the clutch too fast, jerking the bike forward, the motor dying. He started it again and put it in gear, not repeating the same mistake.

Once Albert was on the dirt road, he picked up speed and looked for the three men, but a line of a hundred bikes was ahead of him, and he couldn't tell one biker from the next. All the bikes were backed up at the exit, with the delay of the stoplight.

He felt confident he would catch them as they rode into Sturgis. It didn't work out that way, though. As he finally had his turn at the stoplight, two bikers, making the left turn together, smacked handlebars, spilling both men to the asphalt. The two riders jumped up from the highway looking more embarrassed than hurt. This little scene seemed to take forever as other bikers dismounted, parked their bikes, and helped the two fallen riders get their Harleys upright. Men dusted gravel off the shoulders and backs of the fallen riders, then checked the riders and their bikes for injuries.

Once Albert had passed the accident, he sped to town, unaware the three men had taken a right at Highway 79 toward Newell.

An hour later, Albert finally had made it as far as the Easy Rider Saloon in Sturgis and conceded that he wouldn't find the three men he was trying to follow. Too many side streets, too many parking options, too many bars, too many motorcycles, and too many people for him to see them until they were back at the campsite.

Albert rode through town on Lazelle Street, not an easy task. Bikes, RVs, pickups pulling trailers, semis, and flatbeds loaded with combines crowded the road. At every intersection pedestrians would just cross the street, with no concern for oncoming traffic and forcing the caravan of cars and motorcycles to come to a standstill.

Every parking lot, business, and restaurant was packed. As Albert rode past McDonald's, the line to get inside was at least twenty people long, and the drive-thru was backed up to the street. He rode under the I-90 bridge in the right lane and joined a line of motorcycles on the road to Deadwood.

The fourteen-mile ride was congested and slow-going. Turn lanes were full, forcing the traffic on the main road to slow or stop. A car sat on the shoulder with a flat tire. Police had pulled a biker over, and a farmer in an open-cab John Deere tractor was pulling a baler. The tractor had no flashing red lights, no SLOW-MOVING VEHICLE sign, no turn signals.

State police greeted the line of bikers as they rode into Deadwood. Suddenly traffic stopped. Albert heard a police officer tell a biker,

"Deadwood's full. You might want to head north to hit I-90. The truck route on the south side of Deadwood is open, but it's moving at a snail's pace." Albert stayed in line, went south, and confirmed the snail's pace.

The ride through Deadwood usually took three or four minutes; today it took an hour. By the time the line of bikers hit Highway 385 to Hills City, they were ready to lay on the throttle and climb the hill. The state patrol was ready too, with three bikes pulled over a half mile up the incline.

Albert stayed focused on the line of bikes and made sure to stay in his spot in the staggered formation, ten yards behind the biker in front of him. His favorite turn was the swooping right turn into the bright sun and the blue water of Lake Pactola. Every year that Albert made this ride, the view was better and better. He considered stopping and taking some pictures but remembered he'd forgotten his cell phone in the tent. He'd left in too much of a hurry.

After Pactola was Lake Sheridan, then a left turn before Hills City to the gas station where the biker had put Albert's father in the trash can all those years ago. Albert loved this place and had come here every year since he'd passed his motorcycle driver's test. He got fuel at the same pump, next to the same trash can. He backed his bike into a parking spot and headed into the store for a Diet Dr Pepper and a PowerBar. As he sat beside his bike, on the curb, his legs stretched out in front of him, he replayed that day over and over in his mind. The biker giving him the bandana, apologizing to his mother. The biker picking Father up by the neck, right where Albert liked to drive his pick, and stuffing Father into the trash can.

Albert walked to the trash can and looked down inside it as if to see Father. He tossed the empty PowerBar wrapper in the trash then poured the remaining few sips of his soda on top of the silver wrapper. As he smiled and stared, the honk of a motorcycle horn woke him from his trance. "Careful, little buddy!" the biker yelled. "Don't want you to trip over me."

Albert apologized, lowered his head, and headed back to his bike. He took his seat on the curb and watched the bikers pull in and out, getting fuel at three and four gallons at a time; none of the pumps were lonely for long.

The bike traffic from Hills City to Rapid off Highway 16 was light, with most riders opting for Keystone or Needles Highway. Albert rode 16 through a busy residential area, took a left on St. Joe past Murphy's Pub, then hopped on I-90 to head back to Sturgis.

Taking the first Sturgis exit, Albert followed a group of riders past the city hospital and through residential neighborhoods. Tents were set up in yards, with more tents in yards the closer he got to Main Street. This back-roads ride was a first for Albert, and he was surprised when they came out on the highway to the Chip.

Taking the first Chip exit, Albert's pulse quickened as he saw Father's bright-red Harley and the two wide-backed men he rode with. He followed them to their campsite. All three men put their kickstands down together, shut down their rides, and stretched. A long day, a long ride.

Albert heard them talking about food, beer, and tonight's concert. He thought about walking over and introducing himself; maybe they would give him a beer. Instead he crawled inside his tent, took the ice pick out of his leather jacket, and rubbed it, cleaning it with his towel. He could still see the trash can at the gas station and was reliving the moment when the biker had grabbed Father by the neck and had picked him up. Albert was anxious, nervous. He sat in his tent, his legs bent at the knee, his ankles crossed, and watched the three men set up the grill and bring out food, coolers, and whiskey bottles.

Matt and Jerry—or maybe it was Jerico—were talking about the 150,000 people who were expected at the concert tonight. Maybe with that many people around, he could just walk right up to Father and pick him. With that big of a crowd, all pushing and shoving, perhaps they wouldn't even notice. He liked the idea of killing Father where everyone could see, but what he liked most was the look in his victim's eyes the moment the pick hit his skull. He didn't want to share that with anyone. That was his moment, his time and only his.

The flight from Chicago to Rapid City was on schedule, a rarity for United. Ronnie spent the time in flight online at $4.95 for thirty minutes to find a hotel room in Sturgis. Super 8 and Holiday Inn Express had no vacancies in Sturgis or Rapid City. Ronnie tried to use his status at Choice Hotels but was turned down at all their affiliates: Comfort Inn, Marriott, Hilton, Best Western, Econo Lodge. Motel 6 gave him the same answer: no availability. Ronnie couldn't think of any additional hotel chains, so he tried some mom-and-pop motels and was turned away from the Foothills, Dakota Pines, Big Sky, and Alex Johnson.

"Detective Salas, I got us a rental car, but no luck with a hotel, and I've tried more than a dozen."

"What the heck? That's can't be right. It's little town in the middle of nowhere. Keep trying." Salas went back to his book, where Jack Reacher was in a gun battle.

After picking up the rental car at the Rapid City Regional Airport, Salas drove the Toyota Camry off Highway 44 to North Elk Vale Road. The first hotel he saw was a La Quinta. "You try those guys?" Salas asked, pointing at the hotel.

"No, Detective. I didn't try La Quinta. Frankly I've never heard of them." Ronnie had his cell phone out and was punching keys.

"I got it," Salas said. He pulled under the canopy, put the Toyota in park, and walked into the foyer.

Salas flashed his badge to the young woman behind the counter. "I need two rooms this evening, miss. Most likely two nights."

"Sorry, sir…er, Officer. We don't have any vacancies for the rest of the week, but usually with the rally, we get a few who leave early, so we might have a room for you by Thursday. Would that work?" Her name tag said, "Judy from Minnesota."

"No, I need them tonight. Can you check the surrounding hotels for an opening, please? I'd appreciate it." It was more of an order than a request.

"Oh, Officer, you're not going to find a hotel room in the area tonight. It's rally week. We've been booked full for a year. It's the seventy-fifth year of Sturgis—this is the largest rally ever. There are a million people here," Judy said with a smile.

"Are you shitting…sorry, are you kidding me? A million? I thought this was just a motorcycle rally."

"It is, sir. The largest in the world. You might want to buy a tent! Good luck!" Judy left Salas standing at the counter.

Back in the Camry, Salas turned to Ronnie. "This is a really big rally. No rooms in the area. She told us to get a tent."

"Yes, Detective Salas. I was just reading about it." Ronnie showed Salas his cell phone. "The Sturgis event started in 1938. Thus, this is the seventy-fifth year. A motorcycle club called the Jackpine Gypsies held motorcycle races and stunts. Today it's one of the largest rallies in the world, attracting hundreds of thousands of motorcycle enthusiasts from across the globe."

"Ronnie, maybe that would have been good information to know a little earlier today. Thank God Albert Christianson is at a little campground. That'll make it way easier to grab him. Let's go buy a tent. We'll stay at the same campground where he checked in." He pointed to Ronnie's cell phone. "Find a place to buy tents on that thing." Salas started the car and pulled out of the parking lot.

The two detectives arrived at Cabela's five minutes later. Motorcycles were backed into the front parking spaces, front tires facing the store. Salas found a parking spot on the west side in a lot filled with pickups pulling trailers and RVs.

Entering the store, Salas suddenly stopped walking and looked up; Ronnie bumped into him from behind. "Look at all this taxidermy work. There are a lot of dead animals in here," Ronnie stated, not even realizing he had walked into Salas.

"Look at the fish tanks. Those are some huge fish," Salas said as he headed to a store clerk to ask where the tents were.

"Look at that one, Detective Salas. A mountain Lion attacking a deer." Ronnie took a picture with his cell phone.

Salas pointed upward. "I like that flock of geese hanging from the ceiling. Looks like they're going to land on us."

Salas picked out a basic Cabela's two-man tent, two light-weight sleeping bags, and a mattress pad for himself. They checked out and were back on I-90 within thirty minutes.

Ronnie's phone was talking to them, telling Salas to stay in the right lane and take the first Sturgis exit. Salas followed orders, took the exit, and came to a stop. Looking ahead, he saw a continuous line of cars, trailers, and motorcycles for as far as he could see.

"What the fuck are all these people doing here?" Salas asked Ronnie, not expecting an answer.

"Oh, God, the noise, Detective. It's a constant roaring groan!" Ronnie had to talk loudly as his window was down and bikes lined both sides of the car.

The phone told them to turn right. They did, still following a line of bikes.

Salas shook his head in amazement. "I had no idea this existed. I've never seen so many motorcycles in one place."

"Looks like we have about three more miles, as per the GPS. Up here to the right." Ronnie pointed straight ahead.

"Only an hour away!" Salas laughed as they sat stalled in traffic.

They finally pulled into the Buffalo Chip Campground at seven-thirty. Salas parked the car near the west entrance and headed to the white admin building. The building was on skids, evidently a mobile structure. Salas looked east and at the southern horizon—nothing but campers, tents, motorcycles, and RVs.

Salas approached a young man wearing a bright yellow T-shirt with "Security" on the back and "Buffalo Chip" on the front.

Salas showed him his badge. "I need to talk to the head of security."

The young security guy said, "That'd be Marvin. He's at the campground. You'll have to go in there to find him." He was pointing east.

"Marvin? Marvin what? Take me to him," Salas demanded.

"Marv Kezler. Can't. Supposed to stay here," the guy responded, pointing to the floor. "Go talk to Donna in the white building over there." Now he was pointing to another building.

Salas went as directed. There was a line. He stood in it. Ten minutes later, he was talking to Donna.

"Donna, I need to get into the campground. We're looking for a possible felon." Salas placed his badge on the counter. Donna stood behind a clear plastic window, her hair was cut short, manly short, Salas expected sideburns. There was a small hole in the window where she spoke and another on the counter so she could take your money.

"Indiana PD…long ways from home. It's two hundred fifty dollars to tent, seven hundred fifty for a camper, higher for an RV. What you got?" Donna looked Salas in the eye.

"A tent, but I really need to meet Marvin, the head of security," Salas said.

"Two hundred fifty gets you in—that and this wristband. No wristband, no entry." Donna was looking over Salas's shoulder at the line of people behind him.

"Okay, I need two wristbands," Salas said.

"That'll be five hundred. Cash or credit card?" Donna asked.

"Five hundred! We just want to camp one night! We'll be gone this time tomorrow," Salas fumed, staring Donna in the eye.

"Five hundred dollars, or please leave the line, sir. I have folks behind you wanting to get in." Donna smirked as Salas gave her his credit card. "I need your left wrist. Place it under the glass." Salas struggled to get his hand through the space. Donna connected the wristband; it was tight.

Salas motioned Ronnie to the window. "She needs to put a wristband on you. Slide your hand through there." Salas nodded to the open slot. Ronnie's placed his hand, wrist, forearm, and elbow through the opening. Donna put the wristband on; it rolled around Ronnie's wrist. "Don't lose that!" she said.

"Where do we set up our tent?" Salas asked.

"Anywhere you want, but be careful if you tent behind a vehicle. I'd hate to see you get run over. Next!" Donna said, dismissing them.

Salas and Ronnie drove through the Chip, an ever-winding entanglement of roads, lanes, paths, and walkways to tent sites, RV lanes with concrete pads, and rows of log cabins on concrete slabs. Motorcycles stood leaning to the left at every tent, trailer, RV, and cabin.

"You've got to be shitting me," Salas steamed. "I thought we could walk in and pick up this guy. This place is a cluster fuck. Gotta be a hundred thousand people here!"

"The rigs these people drive," Ronnie went on. "How can they afford these things? What do they do for a living? That's a Ford F-350 Dually king cab pulling a fifth-wheel trailer that's bigger than my mom's house." Ronnie was taking pictures with his cell. "Look, that one has a walk-out deck with a hot tub on it."

They found a hole in the mass of people, a small space to park the car off the dirt road to pitch the tent.

"Ronnie, set up the tent…like that guy's," Salas said, pointing to a tent. "Evening!" he called out, approaching the tent next to their Toyota.

"Hotter than hell today, boys. Hotter than hell. Welcome to the Chip!" said the old man, his gray hair pulled back in a ponytail. His scraggly gray beard came to a point at his chest. The old man had his left hand on his beard, squeezing and twisting it. His right-hand index and thumb were yellow, Salas figured from years of nicotine. He was smoking now, but it wasn't a cigarette.

"Great view you got." Salas was looking west with the old guy, at the setting sun.

The old man sat in front of his tent in a large fold-out lawn chair. He had on faded blue jeans and black boots with silver tips. His frail body was crumpled in the chair. A black unbuttoned vest, no shirt, revealed folds of skin as a belly. A faded black tattoo on his right shoulder said, "Live Free or Die Trying." Black sunglasses hid his eyes.

"What ya smokin' there, bro?" Salas asked.

"It's medicinal. Helps my…glue coma?" The old man smiled. "Want a hit?" The old stoner held out his hand to Salas.

"No, thanks. I don't have glaucoma." Salas smiled back.

"Nice to see you boys here at the Chip. Mind you, though…your lifestyle ain't real popular here, not that there's anything wrong with that, anything wrong at all." The stoner continued to look at the setting sun.

"Oh, no, sir. We're not together. He's my partner. We're here to find someone." Salas was defensive.

"Sure, boy. Your partner. It's fine with me, fine with me." Stoner's right cheek was raised in a grin. "Nice boat shoes, boy," he yelled at Ronnie.

"No, really. We just work together." Salas said.

"Reality is for people who can't handle drugs. Somebody famous said that once."

Salas peered inside the stoner's tent. Lying on her side was elderly woman asleep on an air mattress. She was in jeans, with no top or bra, and was snoring lightly. Both her breasts touched the air mattress. A battery-powered fan was pointed at her belly.

"She okay?" Salas asked.

"Oh, yeah. She hit it hard early. But she will rally. She will rally." Stoner never took his eyes off the setting sun.

Ronnie was struggling with the tent poles; Salas ignored him.

"You been here before, I take it, sir?" Salas asked.

"That I have, bro. That I have," Stoner replied.

"Where's a good place to eat?" Salas asked, still looking at the snoring woman.

Stoner took another dose of his medication. "Big concert tonight, Godsmack. Never heard of 'em. Feels like rain's comin'."

"Too damn hot to rain," Salas said. "Godsmack, huh? I'll have to check it out."

Salas turned his attention to the tent. "Ronnie, you got that damn thing ready?"

"Well, I hope so. It's the first time I've ever set up a tent. Like I said, I prefer a midlevel hotel chain." Ronnie was sweating from the tent exercise.

Salas headed back over to their tent. "Let's head to the main camp area. I want to find security, that Marvin guy. And you need to change clothes." Salas and Ronnie walked away.

Stoner never moved, never changed his line of sight.

After a thirty-minute walk, Salas and Ronnie found the admin building near the main east entrance. Salas knocked on the back door; it took three more hard raps before anyone answered. A brunette with a headset on, a microphone near her mouth, opened the door. Salas flashed his badge and asked for Marvin. She shut the door in Salas's face. Salas was ready to knock again when the door opened. A figure emerged, filling the entire doorway. Salas couldn't see the room behind him, much less the brunette. "Marvin" was the name on his button-up shirt. A security bowling shirt, the buttons were stressed. Marv turned sideways to get through the doorway. He had no neck, just two large chins.

"What?"

At least he can speak, thought Salas. "Detective Mike Salas, Fort Wayne, Indiana, PD," Salas said, sticking out his right hand in an offer to shake. "I'm here looking for a guy who registered Sunday with a credit card. He's in a tent."

Marvin didn't shake his hand; he was punching keys on his cell phone. "And what do you want me to do?"

"I need the assistance of your security team to help me track him down, so I can arrest him. *Today*," Salas stated.

"Dude, Salas, there are over 150,000 people here, man. That's like looking for a needle in a haystack." Marvin was chuckling and sweating. "I'm knee-deep in shit already, and the concert hasn't even started. I got drunk adults, drunk kids, drunk people driving cycles, and drunks driving four-wheelers. I have four state patrol officers here arresting two guys for dealing and another for stealing a Harley. I just busted a camper of three hookers. They're sitting over there, waiting for more state P's to take them to town. Sorry, bro. You're on your own." Marvin turned to go back inside.

"Marv, here's a picture of him, and here's my card. The man is armed and dangerous." Salas handed him a black-and-white photograph and a glossy business card.

"What'd he do?" Marvin asked, looking at the picture and putting the card in his shirt pocket.

"Killed someone. He's armed with a knife," Salas said.

"Detective, nearly everyone here is armed with a knife. A knife is the least of my worries. If we see him or he walks in and confesses, we'll call you. No promises." Marvin opened the door, turned to the side, and went back inside the small building, his belly and back smacking the doorframe.

"Great. This is going to be harder than I thought, Ronnie. I don't know what I'm going to tell Green," Salas said as he turned and walked back to the crowd. "Let's get you some jeans and boots. You look like a douche bag."

"Where are Deuce and RJ?" Matt asked as they sat down for steaks.

Kevin had T-bones ready for the two Sons of Silence, but they were a no-show.

"Don't know. They rode off early. Figured they be back by now," Kevin said as he joined Jerico and Matt at the picnic table.

The three men tore into the T-bones, medium rare, along with Texas toast, beer, and some welcomed shots of Fireball.

Tonight's game plan was the same as last night's. Matt was going to Jessica's bar, the one where they did burnouts, and Jerico would head over to Ann's bar at the main entrance. Kevin relayed that he had big plans to double his booby album.

The sun was setting when they finished eating and cleaning up. Then they piled into the golf cart.

Matt eventually found Jessica behind the bar—no shoes, sprinting from biker to biker. He nudged his way in so he could lean against the end of the bar; when Matt nudged, people moved. Jessica was in her schoolgirl outfit: a plaid skirt that was so short it revealed her butt cheeks, a white long-sleeve shirt tied in a knot below her breasts, a plaid bow in her hair, and dark-red plastic-rimmed glasses. Matt liked the glasses.

Jessica came up to Matt, grabbed his beard with both hands, pulled him forward, and kissed him on the mouth. Matt blushed; Jessica laughed. Several bikers asked for their kiss. Matt ordered a double Jack and Diet Coke and gave her a ten-dollar tip.

Jessica leaned forward and spoke in Matt's left ear. "Last night was horrible! Summer came in at three with some smelly guy. Her bed is right against my bed, at my feet. Get this…they start doing it, and her head was against my foot! My foot was like a headboard! Thank God he was quick!"

Jessica went back to the other end of the bar. Matt counted as she opened three Buds, two Busch Lights, and four Coors Lights. She mixed two Jack and Cokes and poured three shots of Jäger. He thought she'd collected at least at twenty dollars in tips; she was gone less than a minute.

"And then Ann brought in your friend, Jerico!" Jessica said when she returned. "They fooled around a while then fell asleep. She did him this morning, though."

Another round right to left, another twenty dollars in ones, and she was back to Matt. "I don't think I got three hours of sleep! I'm all Red Bulled up!" Another round, another bunch of ones.

"Don't take this the wrong way, Jess, but…come stay with me tonight. We have a huge RV with indoor plumbing. You could take a long bath. By yourself. We have air conditioning and food—real food. Let me make you breakfast. Just think about it." Matt smiled and followed up with, "You can trust me."

"Let me think about it. Let's see if you behave!" Jessica said, then continued her rounds.

JERICO

J erico didn't go straight to Ann's bar. Instead, he spent some time at a bar next to the main stage. Twisted Sister was opening for Godsmack, and Dee Snider was belting out, "I wanna rock, rock!"

Jerico spied a shapely barmaid, with nice breasts in a push-up Walmart bra; her black fishnet tights had a hole in the left thigh. He ordered a Coors Light and introduced himself. "Hey, I'm Jerico," he said, sticking out his right hand.

"Sarah" was the reply, his hand in now in hers.

Jerico pulled her forward, his mouth in her ear. "Sarah with an 'a' or ending in an 'h'?"

"I've never been asked that before!" Sarah smiled, handed Jerico his beer, and said, "An 'h'!"

Sarah, with an 'h,' went left to right then right to left, opening beer, mixing drinks, and a pouring a vodka shot.

Jerico reached out again. She took his hand.

"Where are you from?" Jerico asked, his mouth back to her ear.

"Right here in Sturgis!" She smiled as she pulled away then opened more beers, poured a shot of Crown, and threw dollar bills into her tip bucket. Sarah made her trip around the bar—more beer orders than anything else. Several patrons already were too drunk to walk. "Man, that guy's hammered, and it's only nine p.m.!" she said, pointing a heavy-lidded biker leaning against the bar.

"You know what they say, you're not drunk as long as you can lie on the ground and hang on!" Jerico said, and they both laughed.

"You ever heard of the wrestler Les Sigman?" Jerico asked.

"Of course! He's a legend around here. Just about made the Olympics! You know him?" Sarah said.

"Yeah, me and my good friend hang with him. Great guy." Jerry acted as if he knew Les personally.

Jerico stayed with Sarah another hour. He wrote his number on a bar napkin. "Text me if you want to hang out later," he said.

"I'd love to. But how will you know it's me?" Sarah asked, wide-eyed.

"You're the only one I've given my number to!" Jerico yelled over the background vocals of Snider.

Ann's bar was just a few yards away. Jerico made his way to the center of the bar, claimed a spot for himself, and waved a twenty-dollar bill in the air. Ann saw him, laughed, and poured him a Jack and Diet Coke. "This one's on me for last night," she said. "You and I need to take another shower."

Jerico stayed at Ann's bar the rest of the night. When the rain came and the wind blew, she was the first to shut down the bar. She ordered the barback to clean the place up and had security take the cash drawers as she and Jerico sprinted through the downpour.

Jerico was running with a slight limp and in obvious pain but kept up with Ann. She was in great shape, and Jerico thought he needed to talk to her more to see what she did for fun, where she worked, if she worked out, and what her last name was.

It was nearly a mile run to the shower house near the RV. By the time they entered the stall and closed and locked the door, they were wet from head to toe. Ann tore Jerico's T-shirt off, leaving a red mark on his neck. Two hookups with Ann, and he was out two shirts.

He couldn't get his boots off; they were the slip-on type, with a small side zipper. The rain had drenched him, and the water inside his boots had worked like glue to stick the boots to his socks. Ann was already naked. She had Jerico sit on the wooden bench in the shower stall as she straddled his right leg. With her bare butt in his face, she gripped his right boot with both hands, trying to pull it off. She tugged; they laughed; the boot came off. After she got the left boot off, they turned on the shower. Warmish water streamed down on them, much nicer than the cold rain but just as wet. They drained the hot-water heater then toweled off with paper towels from the dispenser. Ann dried Jerico as Jerico dried Ann. That led to round two.

Round three was in the cabin. Three of the four beds were occupied; all were busy, and all finished about the same time.

Jerico had the best night's sleep since he'd left O'Neill.

KEVIN

Kevin walked around the entire open field in front of the main stage, looking for the perfect spot to watch the concert, and decided the VIP bar where they housed the lighting crew was worth the hundred-dollar fee. He paid in cash and walked up the wooden steps to the second-story bar.

The lighting and special-effects crews were on the third floor, blocked off from the VIP crowd. Kevin found an open stool on the rail with a center-stage view. The three-story wooden frame building was fifty yards from the Wolfman Jack main stage, which had enough room for several thousand people.

The crowd for Twisted Sister was shoulder to shoulder, with more and more bodies cramming in every minute. The waitress told Kevin they'd sold 150,000 tickets for Godsmack; the barback told him 200,000. Either way, there were way too many people packed in there. Kevin was glad he had a chair and wasn't in the midst of the mass of humanity before him. This VIP ticket was well worth the entry fee, as were the higher priced drinks.

Kevin scanned the crowd for Matt, Jerico, RJ, and Deuce. There were so many people, though, and so many were dressed alike that all the bodies and faces melted together. The more tattoos the person had, it seemed, the less clothing he or she wore. Many of the ladies wore half shirts, showing off their tramp stamps. The guys with shoulder tats wore tank tops or wife beaters. If they had calf tattoos, they were in shorts; thigh tats, the girls wore shorter shorts, and the guys wore jeans with strategically placed rips. Ankle or feet tattoos, they wore sandals. Back and chest tattoos, well, they went shirtless, even though the tats probably looked good when they were skinny, but now the expanded/extended tats needed be covered.

The VIP crowd grew as Twisted Sister left stage and preparations for Godsmack were underway. Kevin was glad he'd gotten there early for the barstool and rail seat; he was too short to see anything from three or four bodies back in line. A couple from Dallas took the spots next to him, the lady on the stool and her husband behind her, his hands on her shoulders. They made small talk with Kevin about the crowd, Texas football, and the dark clouds in the sky.

Boston's best—aside from the Patriots, Bruins, Celtics, and Sox—Godsmack came onstage about forty-five minutes later. The crowd went into vocal overdrive, out yelling even the lead singer, Sully Erna, who was mic'd up. The music started, and the wind joined in. Three songs into the first set, and the first raindrops fell from the sky but never hit ground, as it was covered with people, their arms in the air as they cheered the band.

Eight songs in, and it was a downpour. Most people over forty ran for cover while the younger crowd inched their way closer to the stage. Two more songs, and they stopped the music. The wind, rain, lightning, and thunder were the entertainment. Fifteen minutes later, Sully brought his boys back onstage and started another song, but security, safety, and common sense prevailed. The band exited to the comfort, warmth, and dryness of their motor home.

The VIP section was protected only in the back half of the wooden building. Kevin's front-row stool was covered in water, as was Kevin. Several people left the bar, descending the wet staircase slowly, then made a mad dash for their campers, vehicles, and tents. As more people left the bar, a waitress yelled, "Half-price beer!" Thirty or so men and women stayed on the second floor, cash in hand, as two waitresses opened beer cans as fast as they could.

For Kevin, one beer quickly became ten. He was swaying, staggering in his steps and speech. That's when the booby camera came out. He wasn't alone in his massive beer consumption; the entire second-story crowd was drunk.

Two ladies began to dance together, although no music was playing. A short-haired blonde, her wet hair swept back over her head, was dressed in short jean cut-offs with frayed white fabric dangling around the pockets. Her partner wore jeans; biker boots; a bandana as a top, tied in a knot midback; and another bandana covering her hair. It was a slow-motion, steady bump-and-grind, with an occasional kiss as they moved in sync.

A group of men formed a small circle around them, dutifully cheering them on. Kevin was at the forefront, cell phone in hand, video mode.

The cheering hushed as the two women embraced and kissed passionately, their eyes closed, their mouths connected by two tongues. The bump-and-grind slowed to groping, fondling, and caressing. They were definitely making out, on their feet.

Both their hands went down to the opposite's zippers as if they'd discussed it. Pants were unbuttoned, zippers were down, and fingers were sliding. The bandana top was off; the cut-off jeans were down to the floor. Both women were exposing a little too much.

The husband/boyfriend of the woman in the cut-offs stepped into the circle first, prying his arm between them.

The husband/boyfriend of bandana girl put his jacket over his woman's shoulders. The crowd groaned in exasperation as the two men walked the women down the stairs, the girls laughing and holding hands. The rain continued; they were discussing which camper to go to.

Loosened up by the two girls, Kevin encouraged other women to at least show him their boobies; six ladies were still on the second floor. One by one, Kevin was getting his way and taking individual and group pictures.

Kevin's fifth target was standing next to her man, leaning against the bar, just out of reach of the rain. "What did you think of those two ladies' extreme dance moves?" she asked him.

"I'm getting pictures of all the ladies on the floor, just their boobies! Can I get yours?"

The bosomy brunette, wearing a 2012 Sturgis rally T-shirt, smiled back and said, "Well, sure!" and pulled her T-shirt out of her pants. A right arm across her body stopped her from going any further.

Her man, who was leaning against the bar, stood erect, as if he'd been hit by a lightning bolt. His right arm still across his wife, he grabbed Kevin by the collar with his left hand and pulled him toward his beer breath. He raised a closed fist. "You rotten little shit," he said. "Who the fuck you think you are, asking to see my wife's tits?"

Kevin closed his eyes, preparing for a punch to the face and knowing he deserved it. But the punch never came. He opened his left eye first then his right to see the man leaning to his left, his right ear touching his right shoulder. The man was grimacing in pain. Behind him was RJ.

RJ had his right finger and thumb deeply embedded in the man's right trap muscle. The grip was a vice, as it forced the man down to his right knee. His face was flushed; he was clearly in pain. In fact, the man was begging for the pain to go away. His wife had both her hands up to her mouth.

"Now, the little feller meant no harm," RJ said. "He was just being nice to your lady. And your lady is a fine-looking thing. You should be proud of her." RJ released his grip; the man stayed on his right knee. "Let's go, Kevin. The rain's died down. Let's head back before it gets worse." RJ turned and walked down the stairs.

Kevin stopped at the top of the stairs then turned to the man and woman. The man was still on one knee, rubbing his right shoulder and neck.

With a shrug, Kevin said, "Sorry!" then followed RJ out of the bar.

"For a guy that don't want to go back to jail you sure do press the issue. They call security and you go to jail. I had that covered." Kevin told RJ.

"Yeah, I know. I should have stayed out of it. That's how I went to prison the first to times." RJ said as they made their walk back to the RV.

Matt was still in his place, both arms resting on the wooden slab that served as a bar. A muscular, bald, middle-aged guy with enormous arms walked up and leaned against the bar, mimicking Matt's stance. The new arrival looked at Matt's shoulder tattoo and said, "Nice ink. Must have a story. Tell me."

"My mom's a breast cancer survivor. See the cancer loop?" Matt said, pointing at his shoulder. "The two roses are for my sisters."

"That's cool, my friend. Wish I had a story for mine, but it's just barbed wire." the bald guy said, rubbing his biceps.

"Yeah, well, you got the biceps to pull it off. What about the rosary tat on your wrist? You Catholic?"

He shook his head. "Nah, my mom was. I got this for her. She likes it but doesn't like tattoos. I take it you wrestled or did MMA?" Biceps Man asked, looking at Matt's deformed ear.

"Yeah, wrestled. Forty pounds ago. Minnesota. How 'bout you?"

"Yeah. Nebraska back in the day. When they were Big Eight not the Big Ten."

"Tough conference, lots of history. OU, OSU, the Tigers, Cyclones," Matt said as he raised his cup.

"Salas, Mike Salas," said Biceps Man, extending his hand.

"Matt Buckles." The two shook hands.

Jessica came up, again grabbed Matt by the beard, and planted a kiss on his lips. "I'm with you tonight, sweetie," she said into his ear.

Salas ordered a Coors Light and looked at Matt. "She with you?"

Matt smiled. "Yeah, I guess."

"Lucky fucker." Salas raised his beer, touching Matt's plastic cup. Salas pulled out his cell phone, turned to Matt, and said, "Gotta take this. Save my place, Ronnie! Order a drink. I'm buying." Salas walked off, his cell phone to one ear, his finger in the other.

Salas walked with a phone to his ear, his other hand and finger plugging the opposite ear. "Yeah, Salas here." He yelled into the phone.

"Salas. Davis positively ID'd your photograph. You are to get your ass home tonight if possible." It was Captain Green. "You are done Salas, off the force."

"What?" Salas yelled. "I can't here you. Let me call you in the morning." Salas shut off his phone. "You got to be shitting me." He said as he walked the length of the concert stage thinking of what to do next.

Ronnie, the skinny guy Salas had yelled at, stepped into Salas's gap at the bar. Ronnie rubbed his hands together as he looked at Jessica. He pulled his shaggy hair back over his forehead and puffed out his chest. His new 75th anniversary Sturgis T shirt sagging on his shoulders. His new blue jeans were buttoned over his belly button.

"What can I get you, sweetie?" Jessica asked. "Nice boots."

"Why thank you I just got them at a vendor here at the Chip. I was torn between lace ups and zippers." Ronnie replied.

"Drink sweetie, what would you like?" Jessica cut him short.

"Hmmm." Ronnie was still rubbing his hands together. "I've always wanted to try a mojito."

"Sorry, sweetie. This is Sturgis, not Cancun. No mojitos here." Jessica looked him over.

"I see. A mojito is a tropical drink. How about a mimosa?" Ronnie looked at Jessica then Matt.

"Oh, sweetie, you're so cute. We don't have any champagne. How 'bout I introduce you to our three most popular gentlemen here? Jim, Jack, and Johnny." Jessica placed three bottles on the bar. "Meet Jim Beam," she said, as she held the bottle in front of Ronnie then picked up the bottle of Jack and rolled it in her grip. "Meet Jack Daniels." She placed the bottle in front of him then grabbed the third bottle and said, "And meet my personal favorite, Johnny Walker."

"Interesting. These are the most popular drinks here at Sturgis?" Ronnie asked.

"Yep, sweetie. These are what the guys are drinking," Jessica said, smiling at Ronnie and Matt.

Ronnie turned to Matt. "Which do you recommend?"

"Try all three. Your buddy, Mike, said he was buying," Matt replied.

"That he did, so let's do it. I'll have a glass of all three, please." Ronnie was so polite.

"How about a shot, sweetie, not a full glass. You try all three and see which one you like, and then you can have a bigger glass if you want." Jessica was pouring three shots. "Now listen, sweetie. This is a shot. Drink it all at once. This ain't sipping whiskey."

Ronnie took the first shot glass, which was filled with Jim Beam, and held it firmly between his thumb and index finger, his pinkie pointed up. After taking a whiff of the liquid, he pulled the shot away from his nose, spilling some of it on his thumb and finger. "My Lord, this smells horrible! Are you sure people drink this?"

"Don't smell it, man! Drink it!" a burly biker standing next to Ronnie yelled.

Ronnie put the glass to his lips and drank it fast. As soon as he put the glass on the wooden bar, he put his hand to his mouth and gagged, bending at the waist; he was wheezing for air.

Jessica stepped back. "Keep it down, sweetie. No puking at the bar!"

"That burns. It came up my nose!" Ronnie's eyes were watering, a tear rolling down his cheek.

Jessica handed him another shot glass. "This one's Jack. You'll like it better."

"I love Jack. That's what I got," the burly biker yelled as he downed a shot of Jack himself.

Ronnie looked at the biker, grabbed the shot of Jack, and downed it. Onstage, Dee Snider walked off as the announcer was saying something about Godsmack.

"Uuuuugggghhhhh, oh, my…oh, my." Ronnie was gagging again, his hand at his mouth.

"It's an acquired taste!" The biker slapped him on the back. "Give him his third shot. Everyone loves Johnny. Drink 'er down, junior."

Ronnie held the full shot glass in his hand and stared at it.

"Don't think about it. Just do it," Matt said.

Ronnie shot it. He wheezed again then grabbed Salas's beer and drank it down. He placed the beer can on the bar and was gasping for air as if he were running a marathon. "I can say I don't care for any of those gentlemen!"

Matt turned to Ronnie. "Well, my favorite shot is Fireball. Try one of those."

Ronnie's face was flushed as clear snot ran down his lip under his nose.

"Young lady, a Fireball shot for me and my two friends," Ronnie said, pointing at the biker and Matt.

"You got it, sweetie. Three shots of fireball!" Jessica said as she poured the shots.

The three men raised their shot glasses in the air above their heads and clinked them together.

"*Salud*," said Matt.

"Here's to Sturgis," said the biker.

"Toast," said Ronnie.

The three drained their glasses.

"I like that one!" yelled Ronnie. "I'd like another."

"How about we have a glass of water?" Matt offered, as Jessica gave him a plastic cup of clear H2O.

"Sure! Let's make it a shot of water!" As Ronnie drained the glass, water dribbled down both sides of his mouth to his shirt. The biker wandered off after the water shot, not wanting to participate.

"Okay, another Fireball. It's ciminommy," Ronnie slurred.

Jessica poured him a shot. Ronnie didn't hesitate; he downed it and slammed the shot glass back on the bar, eliciting laughter from Matt and others.

Salas returned, his phone in his front pocket.

"Trouble back home Ronnie." Salas said, looking at the shot glass. "A shot? We having shots? Great idea. I need one. Ronnie, you ever try a shot?" Salas looked at Ronnie, who didn't have a glass in his hand. Salas forgot about the missing beer.

"Two shots of Jäger, please," Salas said, giving a peace sign to Jessica.

Ronnie and Salas did the Jäger shots.

"Tastes like licorice!" Ronnie yelled. "I like it."

"One more for me too," Salas said, again the peace sign to Jessica.

Ronnie had his shot down before Salas got the glass to his lips. Salas gave Ronnie a sideways glance, his eyebrow raised.

"Hey, you wouldn't happen to have any Jameson back there, would you?" Salas asked Jessica, as he leaned over the bar, looking at the bottles under the wooden slab.

Jessica looked at Salas and then at Matt. "You know, you two could be related. And yes, we have Jameson."

"All bald guys look alike," Salas said, his arm on Matt's shoulder. "Give us each a shot of Jameson, and then I'm done." Thunder was echoing in the background; Godsmack was echoing in front.

The three men took their shots and again clinked glasses. Ronnie stumbled sideways, hitting shoulders with Salas but not spilling any Jameson. They drained their glasses.

"Gotta run!" Salas announced. "What do I owe you?"

"Defective Dallas?" Ronnie's eyes were bloodshot.

"Ronnie? Are you drunk?" Salas asked.

"I think I'm gonna regurgitate." Ronnie was pale.

"Twelve shots is eighty-four dollars, and the beer makes it eighty-nine," Jessica said, holding her hand out.

"Twelve shots? What the hell? Ronnie, we haven't even been here an hour," Salas said, as Ronnie leaned his head on Salas's shoulder, his eyes closed. It started to rain; the wind was howling north to south.

Salas handed Jessica a hundred-dollar bill and a ten-dollar bill and said, "Keep it." He turned to Matt, smiling. "I'd better put him to bed. Nice talking to you." He hoisted Ronnie over his shoulder like a bag of potatoes and walked away in the rain.

The rain and wind picked up, with sheets of water falling left to right. Narrow rivers of water ran down any and all inclines at the campground. People were scattering, hurrying to their tents and RVs with their hands over their heads. Godsmack exited the stage as the downpour continued.

Security cleared off the top floor of the metal platform, grabbing the cash drawers as barbacks locked down the alcohol. Stragglers in the bar were warned of the dangers of lightning on metal, which prompted many of them to rush down the steps. Some were running back to their campers and tents, while others sought immediate shelter from the rain and blistering wind.

Matt took Jessica, arm-in -arm, off the bar platform and ran to a vendor's tent. The business advertising leather boots and leather gloves was closed, with the front flap rolled down and locked with three metal clasps.

The white tent glowed yellow from an interior light. Matt yelled as he unclasped two of the front rings, ducked, and stepped into the tent. "Can we stand here with you?" he asked the vendor.

"No, we're closed!" the man yelled, putting his hands on Matt's chest and pushing him back.

Jessica stepped in beside Matt, away from the driving rain. The fierce wind was banging the tent's canvas against the steel poles like a jackhammer on concrete. The vendor saw Jessica, clad in her short skirt and white wet shirt that hugged her chest, and said, "Please, please come in! Let me get you a towel!"

ALBERT

He had followed Father since he and the linebackers had left the camp area. Albert took the stairs soon after Father ascended them to reach the second floor of the VIP bar. A large hand was placed on Albert's chest; the hand and fingers more than covered the decal from the seventy-fourth annual Sturgis rally T-shirt Albert had on. The security guard was palming Albert's chest like Jordan could a basketball.

"Need to see your wristband, please."

Albert showed the guard his right wrist, the one with the wristband allowing him access to the Buffalo Chip.

"Not that one, the VIP one. No wristband, no entrance."

"How much is it?" Albert asked.

"A hundred bucks."

Albert walked away; he didn't have that kind of money. He went to the first picnic table that had a direct line of vision to the steps. The table stood behind the three-story bar. No one was sitting there. He sat down—no view of the stage, thus the free seat.

Albert was growing increasingly impatient; he wanted to make his kill. He was tired of hearing Father's laugh, his bossy voice; seeing him pull out the booby camera. He stared at the steps to the VIP bar as Godsmack walked onstage, the roar of the crowd drowning out his inner voice.

When the rain started, Albert sat motionless as the first wave of concertgoers gave up early and ran for cover. As the storm increased in intensity, people were yelling and running from the main stage. Albert liked the chaos and thought this was perfect; he could run behind Father as the little guy ran for cover, perhaps picking him as he got on his golf cart, or maybe he'd follow him to the RV and pick him when he parked the cart.

The storm was a blessing. Albert sat and watched the steps. A few minutes later, he was drenched, sitting in a puddle of water. Rainwater was pooling in his shoes and dripping down the back of his neck.

Several people scurried out of the VIP bar, but none of them were Father. A couple of men went upstairs; Albert considered joining them, but he could still see the large-handed security guard on the steps, under a single light bulb. The guard was dry and out of the rain.

Albert was the last remaining person on the concert grounds. A solitary figure, motionless, staring at the steps. He didn't know what time it was; his cell phone was in his tent, probably with a dead battery. He was content to sit there and wait. The rain and wind were worth the opportunity.

Eventually the rain eased up, the nearby US flag no longer pointing south but lying flat against the pole. The rain was a sprinkle, small dots created on little ponds.

Two men came down the steps. The larger man shook hands with security; the smaller man was Father. Albert's pulse quickened; his plan was becoming real. He watched as the two men walked west to the opposite entrance of the Chip.

Albert waited for what seemed a minute but was less than ten seconds, giving the two men a fifty-foot head start to Albert's stalking.

Father and the other man walked quickly to the exit. As Albert got closer, he heard them talking but not what they were saying. His heart sank as the large man got on the golf cart with Father. Father started the cart, turning on the small gas engine, and made a U-turn to head toward camp. Albert now realized who the passenger was. It was one of the Sons of Silence.

He walked back to camp, the muddy road burdened with ruts, washed out by the rain. He walked slowly, occasionally kicking a rock with his right foot, watching the pebble roll into the darkness. He stopped inside the shower house, where he heard a man and a woman giggling in a stall. Albert relieved himself and, as he washed his hands, caught a glimpse of himself in the mirror. He stopped, looking the man in the mirror directly in the eyes. The man in the mirror was weak, he thought; he couldn't get the job done. He was a loser. The man in the mirror wet his bed, peed in the closet, lived with his mother. Albert hated that man in the mirror and wanted to kill the man who had made him that way. He had to kill Father and kill him soon. "Tomorrow you will die," he said under his breath.

By the time he reached his tent space, the RV was quiet, a lone outdoor light shining down on its steps. Were the two linebackers there or did Father keep the light on for them? Was the Son of Silence in the RV? Albert thought he could knock on the door. If Father was alone, he could pick him on the steps and push him into the RV. But what if the Son was there or one of the linebackers?

Albert went to his tent; again, his spirits sank. He had left the screen door open, uncovered by the rain shield. He crawled inside the tent, his clothes still wet from the storm. He felt his sleeping bag; it too was drenched. He felt his extra clothes; they were soaked. As he lifted his bag, water drained out of it. His third night in Sturgis, his third night sleeping in wet clothes—at least this time he hadn't wet the bed.

Carrying Ronnie on his shoulder was light work. The comments from the crowd—now those were brutal: "Carrying your boy home?" "Cute couple." "Junior can't handle the big boy." "Had to get him hammered to get him home." "Take it easy on him." Salas ignored all these remarks. But when he heard "Gross. He's puking," he stopped and put Ronnie on the ground, next to the port-a-potties.

The rain and wind were picking up. Salas was looking for cover and decided, *What the heck?* He put Ronnie in a green outhouse, sat him upright, leaned his head against the wall, and shut the door.

Salas entered the port-a-potty next to Ronnie's and did his own business. He stood in the john, listening as others had the same idea. "Let's hit the toilets and get out of the rain! Dude! Lock the door!" Salas laughed as they slammed the door to Ronnie's toilet. Within seconds, the door opened again." Sorry, man. You should lock the door." Again. "Oops, sorry." Again. "Lock the fucking door, mister."

The rain was pelting the port-a-potty, echoing within its small confines—a constant tapping, with water coming through the side vents from the wind gusts and running down the interior walls. The water didn't affect the smell, Salas opened the door letting as much air in and as much water out as he could.

They weathered the storm; as the noise died down, so did the rain. Salas heard others leave their makeshift shelters, proclaiming the storm was over.

He exited the toilet; the rain had stopped. When he opened the door to Ronnie's stall, he was in the same position that Salas had left him in. Salas hoisted Ronnie over his shoulder, in a fireman's carry. The walk back to camp was minus the comments and insults, just Salas and Ronnie in the cold wind, a muddy road, and wet grass.

As Salas approached the rental car, he spotted their neighbor, the stoner in his chair, smoking, his sunglasses still on.

"Hey, old-timer. How was your evening?" Salas asked, as he walked around the car, Ronnie's butt pointing at the old man.

"Rained like hell, rained like hell," Stoner said. "Your partner okay?"

"Yeah, he's a lightweight."

"Ha! Broke his cherry at Sturgis."

Salas looked left, then right, doing a pirouette. "What happened to our tent? Somebody steal it?"

"Nope," Stoner said. "Last I saw, it was flying that a way." He was pointing south.

"It blew away?" Salas asked.

"Yep, soared like an eagle. In the storms of life, may your heart soar like an eagle. Somebody famous said that once."

"You got to be shitting me."

"Gotta stake a tent down, bro. Gotta stake 'er down."

"Great."

Salas was still looking south as he reached into his pants pocket and brought out the car keys. He held Ronnie with his right arm while he unlocked the rental with his left. He pushed the "unlock" button twice with his index finger to open the back doors. He laid Ronnie in the backseat, on his belly, his face and mouth toward the floorboard. He had to fold Ronnie's legs to the side in order to shut the door.

Salas opened the trunk and brought out the two sleeping bags. He laid one on the hood of the car and pulled the other out of its stuff sack and placed it on top of Ronnie. Salas then put the key in the ignition, turned the key to "on" without starting the car, and brought each window down about four inches. Salas even opened the sunroof to let in more air.

Stoner lit up another doobie. "Need some of this, bro?" Stoner asked, handing the joint to Salas.

Salas shook his head. "No, thanks. I heard that stuff can hurt your brain, damage your memory."

"I'm sleeping in my tent. Staked 'er down," Stoner said.

"You got me there."

Salas walked over to Stoner's tent and, with his cell-phone flashlight, peered into Stoner's tent. "She okay?" Stoner's wife was lying naked inside the tent, on top of the air mattress, no covers, no clothes.

"Yep, she hit it hard tonight, bro. Hit it hard. She'll be okay in the morning." Stoner took a long drag off his joint, half of it burning into a glowing ember, ashes falling onto his lap.

"Okay, hope to meet her tomorrow."

"Iron sharpens iron, scholar the scholar. Somebody famous said that once."

"Okay...thanks. Well, looks like I'm sleeping in the front seat," Salas remarked, taking his sleeping bag off the hood of the car.

He opened the passenger side door and hit the electronic seat buttons, taking the seat as far back as possible. The next button laid the backrest down, at a 150-degree angle. After he took the key out of the ignition, he leaned back. Ronnie's head was right behind his; Salas could hear him snoring lightly. "He'll be hurting in the morning," he said softly.

"You got that right, bro. You got that right," said Stoner.

Jessica and Matt left the vendor's tent when the rain slowed. The vendor thanked them—well, Jessica really—for stopping.

They jogged to Jessica's cabin to get her some dry clothes before they went to the RV. They skipped the admin building, as Matt told Jessica they had a safe in the RV to lock up her cash.

When they arrived at the cabin, Jessica used her key to get in. She went in first, with Matt following her. She turned on the light. Summer and an acquaintance were wrestling under the covers. The light signaled the end of the match as both heads peeked over the edge of the blanket.

"What a storm, huh, Jessica?" Summer said with a smile.

Her man sat up: no shirt, hairless chest—looked like he had shaved it—a tattoo of what looked like Elvis on the right pec. A skinny Elvis. The guy nodded at Matt, who returned the nod.

"Wicked storm!" Jessica replied, looking at the other bed. Shelly was sitting up—bare chested, no tattoos.

"Hey, Jess." Shelly's face was bright red, as was Matt's.

"Hey, Shell. What ya got under the covers?" Jessica was smiling too.

A demure brunette wiggled her way to Shelly's belly, laying her head on Shelly's lap. When she looked up, Jessica said, "Hi, Karen." Karen's hair was cut in a bob, and she had a single dimple on one cheek. No smile. Her body was covered by the blanket, except for her bare back, which was covered with several tattoos in red, blue, and yellow. She licked Shelly's belly while she looked Jessica in the eye.

Jessica threw her clothes into her bag, not bothering to fold them. "Tell Ann I'm staying with Matt for a few days, and don't leave without me!" She and Matt went outside and shut the door.

"Well, that was awkward," Matt said, taking Jessica's bag.

She kissed him on the cheek then jumped onto his back for a piggyback ride.

Once they were in the RV, Jessica took a welcomed warm bath, washed her hair, and slipped into one of Matt's Minnesota Golden Gopher Wrestling T-shirts, an XL. While toweling off, she heard Matt talking to another man, and then she heard the guy walk past the bathroom; he said good night and closed the door to the back bedroom.

When she came out into the living room, Matt had several candles burning and soft music playing on the radio; she didn't know the artist. A glass of red wine was greeting her.

They sat toward the front of the RV in black leather swivel chairs. Matt handed Jessica her wineglass as well as a plate of chips, crackers, and cheese. Jessica smiled and crossed her legs, the definition between her thighs and hamstrings even more pronounced. Her brunette hair was pulled back, still wet from the bath. They talked for several minutes, with Jessica speaking about her ex and her future, fatigue settling in on both of them. Matt knew she was probably using him. After that first night, when she was attacked, she was scared, and Matt was a full-size portable security system. But he didn't care—he wanted to be with her. He committed to taking care of her for the next few days and then would let the future play itself out.

He stripped down to his boxers, and they crawled into the queen-size bed. He wished it were a single. They settled under the covers. Matt didn't make any moves, didn't grope her, didn't try to kiss her. Jessica snuggled into him, his arm around her, her head on his chest. She let out a long sigh as she rubbed his belly.

Matt sang softly, "I could stay awake to hear you breathing. Watch your smile while you're sleeping, while you're far away and dreaming. I could spend my life in this sweet something. Don't want to close my eyes. I don't want to fall asleep, because I miss you, baby, and I don't want to miss a thing."

Jessica sat up and grabbed Matt's beard with both hands; she liked to do that. She pulled his lips to hers and kissed him. It was a long kiss, a simple kiss, a passionate kiss. Then she pulled away, again folded into his arms, and fell asleep.

O n Tuesday morning, Kevin was awake by nine—another short night. "These late nights are killing me!" he proclaimed, rolling out of bed.

After checking his e-mail, he checked the surveillance cameras and stayed on the rear entrance of Skip's bar for nearly thirty minutes. No one entered, and no one left. He pushed the re-wind button then fast forwarded the video from midnight to 9 AM. He saw what he didn't want to see. Gloria and Skip leaving the bar at one in the morning, both getting in Gloria's car and driving away. Skip hadn't returned to the bar / apartment. He decided Skip and Gloria were going to be evicted.

Walking through the RV, Kevin first noticed that Jerico's bed was empty and didn't look slept in. He stopped and stared a little too long at the young lady asleep next to Matt. She was on her side, her right leg over Matt's legs. Her T-shirt was riding above her hips, and she had no shorts or underwear on. The curve of her lower back, her right leg at a ninety-degree angle over Matt, her bare right buttock, her hips and thighs—all of them looked soft but muscular. He wanted to take a picture of her but decided against it.

From the fridge, Kevin grabbed some eggs, bacon, bread, and fruit. Outside, he started the grill and prepared breakfast. He waved at Deuce and RJ to come over and went back inside to turn on the music—the inside and outside speakers. As he opened the door to the RV, he yelled at Matt to get out of bed and said breakfast was ready.

Deuce and RJ were sitting at the picnic table, facing the RV. RJ had brought over a case of water and two jugs of orange juice.

Kevin filled two plates and placed them in front of the men as Matt came out of the RV. Matt sat across from RJ, grabbed the OJ, and drank directly from the jug, which elicited objections from all. Matt kept the jug for himself.

The RV door opened, and Jessica stepped out onto the first step. She raised her arms above her head and stretched like a cat, her fingers wiggling, her head arched back. She let out a loud yawn.

Deuce and RJ stopped eating and stared at the girl. As she stretched, the T-shirt went above her hips; she unknowingly exposed herself and her Brazilian cut to the Sons. Deuce elbowed RJ, who elbowed back.

Kevin missed it, as did Matt. Deuce and RJ were speechless as Jessica sat down beside Matt, across from the two men.

"Hi! I'm Jess," she said, reaching her hand out to shake Deuce's.

"Deuce," he said, shaking her hand. "Nice to meet you."

"RJ." As RJ held out his hand, Deuce was still holding hers.

Kevin put plates of food down in front of Matt and Jessica, got himself a plate, and sat down beside RJ.

No one was talking.

Kevin finally broke the silence. "I say we ride to the Spoke today and sit by the pool, watch the people."

"Sounds good to me. What time do you have to be at work, Jess?" Matt asked.

"Two. I'm sure it'll be a huge crowd tonight for Lynyrd Skynyrd," she said, devouring her plate of food.

"We got work in town," Deuce said, still looking at Jessica...as was RJ, as was Kevin, as was Matt.

Just then, Jerico arrived, walking up the dirt road, shirtless again. No one noticed him until he sat down next to Matt.

"Hello!" he said.

"Hey, help yourself to some food." Kevin said.

They told Jerico about their plans for the day, and then to hit the concert later tonight. After further discussion, they decided to go into Sturgis on Wednesday night to catch the city scene. RJ told them about Da Bus, a private bus service that rode through the campgrounds on a regular basis and picked people up and dropped them off downtown. Every hour on the hour, all day. The last bus out of Sturgis was at one in the morning.

It was just past one o'clock when Jessica announced she was heading into the RV to get dressed. When she stood up and went up the steps, all eyes were on deck. She opened the door and said, "Hey, a quarter!" then bent over to pick it up from the RV's floor.

Matt turned to see what she was talking about, as did Kevin. Deuce and RJ were already staring. Jerico was still eating. As she bent over, she again gave the boys a bird's-eye view. She accidentally dropped the quarter and stayed bent over to pick it up. Matt blushed; Kevin, Deuce and RJ remained quiet but didn't turn away. Jerico was still eating.

Matt left the table and followed Jessica into the RV. He had his hand on her hip as he shut the door of the RV. "Oh, no!" the men heard her yell. Evidently Matt told her what had happened.

Jerico said, "What was that all about?"

Jessica stayed inside the RV while the boys prepped their bikes. She didn't come out until she heard Matt, Kevin, and Jerico ride off.

The ride to the Spoke took twenty minutes. The speed trap on Highway 79 was in full force; two state patrolmen had pulled five bikes over on the side of the highway, lights flashing, speeding tickets being issued—you couldn't talk your way out of it.

At the entrance to the campground, security directed them to the Broken Spoke Convenience Store, a quick right turn from the entrance. Matt and Jerico sat on their bikes while Kevin went inside and bought day passes at ten dollars apiece. They rode their bikes less than a hundred yards and parked in front of the Broken Spoke Saloon.

In front of the saloon was an outdoor bar, located under a second-story wooden deck. Picnic tables had been haphazardly arranged in front of the bar and at various angles in front of the vendors. On the west side of the bike parking lot were white canvas tents with vendors offering pizza, hamburgers, barbecue, jewelry, lingerie, and oil changes. There was a custom bike builder there from Lincoln, Nebraska.

As Kevin, Matt, and Jerico entered the bar—more like a three-story barn—they were greeted by the Broken Spoke T-shirt shop to the left and restrooms to the right. Three ladies in short shorts and low-cut tank tops were offering shoeshines and selling boot wax. The girls were busy; Kevin stopped there first to get his boots shined while Matt and Jerico went to the center bar for drinks.

The stage was at the east end of the bar, while the west end featured an open double-wide garage door, blue skies on the horizon. Bikers entered the west end of the bar on their bikes, went through the open garage door, dropped the throttle, and cruised through the bar, exiting via the front entrance—a steady stream of bikes and the roar of Harleys echoing throughout the place.

The bar where Matt and Jerico were ordering, was a large rectangular structure with stools lined along the wooden counter tops. Four barmaids manned each section, with two male barbacks dumping ice and beer into the water tanks. A stripper pole on a wooden stage was strategically placed in the middle of the room, with a swing hanging from the ceiling, that was accessible from the stripper pole.

The barmaids, all dressed in plaid skirts and white shirts tied at the belly, took turns at the pole and on the swing. Kevin, his boots now glistening, had his camera out.

After they all downed a beer, they walked up the east steps to the second story of the bar. The west-end steps led to the second floor as well; on that end was a tattoo parlor and of course another bar.

At the top of the east second-floor steps, the bar appeared, along with a massage parlor, and at the west end—and to their surprise—an art gallery. The three men went inside the gallery. Along with paintings of motorcycles, bikes on landscapes, and bikers riding through the Black Hills was a poster advertising a meet-and-greet with the *Sons of Anarchy* cast.

The north side of the second floor supported a handrail that looked over the stage and the floor of the bar. A great place to watch the barmaids, the stripper pole, and the swing. Steps led up to a third-floor, where the bar was closed, but several bikers were lined along the north railing there, watching the scene below.

The second floor featured an outside exit with yet another bar, strategically placed against the rear wall. Steps going down to the parking lot below were located at each end of the deck, and a handrail went across the entire length of the bar. The rail was packed, with no open spaces left, as bikers, drinks in hand, leaned against it, watching the crowd.

Another Coors Light each, and they went to the pool, the reason for their day passes. Security let them through to an Olympic-size pool. The water, a crisp blue, was filled with men and women, most of whom were shirtless. Pasties were the proper attire, but few females obeyed the rule.

An inflatable female doll, its mouth in an O, was clearly a favorite for a man with a goatee, nose ring, and a snake tattoo climbing up his neck. Four men, two at each end of the pool, were throwing a football while Jasmine Cain wailed away onstage.

The pool was located at the top of a small plateau overlooking the campground and offering a beautiful view of Bear Butte. Local Native American tribes were rumored to have been against the bar and campground being so close to their sacred mountain, but capitalism had won out.

Jerico got a massage, a phone number from the masseuse, and her promise to go on a ride with him on Wednesday, while Matt and Kevin sat down at a picnic table with an umbrella and downed more Coors Lights and pulled pork sandwiches.

As more beer was consumed, more ladies dropped their tops, and the busier Kevin was with his cell-phone camera.

An intense belly-buster contest was won by a four-hundred-pounder in a Speedo. The loser had "Sturgis 2015" shaved into the hair on his back. The cheering from the crowd decided the winner, who won nothing but the adoration of the crowd.

A drunken blonde in a thong, with sleeve tattoos and dreadlocks, slowly danced her way around the pool, bumping and grinding a few females on the way. Seven men and four women were in the two hot tubs, beers in hand; no one seemed to ever leave to go to the bathroom.

Three tiki bars were at the pool level. All three bars were packed with people standing in line for a drink while three waitresses worked the crowd. Aluminum beer bottles and plastic cups were being picked up by security as they made their rounds. A lifeguard in a tall white wooden tower stood watch

Kevin insisted they switch to water. "No drunk riding" was the rule, though four Coors Lights apiece to Matt and Jerico was like drinking water. Kevin went back to the vendors in the parking lot and brought back a pizza; in that time, Matt and Jerico finished another beer each.

After they finished eating, they saw a semi with a trailer pull through the campground parking lot. The trailer was open on the sides, with a metal rail and counter tops running the entire length and a metal roof providing cover from the sun. Several people were riding in the trailer, standing against the counter tops. At the front end was a bar, with steps to climb into the vehicle.

Kevin proclaimed they were riding it, and the three men jogged to the trailer and hopped on while it was moving. The driver of the rig never went over five miles an hour; music was blasting from the speakers.

The truck went around the campground. Although the Spoke wasn't nearly as big as the Chip, Kevin liked it better. It was cleaner, not as congested; had more shower houses, water and electrical hookups, and level RV parking spaces; and the tenters were sectioned off from the RVs. As the semi went up and down the lanes, the three men got a tour of the cabins, campers, pickups, trailers, RVs, and bikes. One more Coors light was allowed, Kevin told the boys.

At the end of their tour, they jumped off near the main campground exit, hit the restrooms, then found their bikes and rode back to the Chip. Kevin led, taking extra precaution to obey the speed limit, especially in the speed-trap zone, although all three patrolmen were busy as they rode by.

Back at the RV, Matt and Jerico set up the grill and brought out the beer and whiskey as Kevin made his rounds inviting their neighbors over for a party. Within thirty minutes, there were thirty people. The beaded necklaces came back out; Kevin was happy.

Matt walked away after letting Jerico know he was heading to Jessica's bar. Jerico was texting the masseuse, his girl in O'Neill, Ann, and Sarah.

By ten o'clock on Tuesday morning, Salas had missed two calls, both from Captain Green, demanding his immediate return to Indiana. Salas chose to ignore them; he'd think of something when he got back.

He'd been awake since six, and waiting in line to shit, shower, and shave had him in a bad mood. He'd been walking the tent areas since seven, looking for short people, memorizing the photo of Albert Christianson.

Ronnie was awake, drenched in sweat, the interior of the car as bad as a tent in terms of capturing the morning sun. The car sauna did him good, however, ridding his body of the evil toxins he'd consumed the previous night.

When Salas got back to the car, Ronnie had showered and was ready to go.

"Detective Salas," he said, "I have an amazing headache."

"You must have slept wrong. Maybe your head was at a bad angle."

Salas stopped by Stoner's tent. He was sitting in his folding chair, sunglasses on, smoking a joint. Salas peered inside the tent again. Stoner's wife lay naked on the air mattress. She was on her back, her breasts off to each side, her legs spread. She was snoring loudly, her mouth wide open.

"How's she doing? Sure she's okay?" Salas asked the old-timer.

"Can't snore like that, bro, unless you're healthy. Can't snore like that. It is health that is real wealth, bro, not pieces of gold and silver. Somebody famous said that once."

"We're headed into town. You need anything? Could bring you back a sandwich, case of water. What do you need?"

"Got all I need here, bro, right here," Stoner said, holding his joint in the air.

"Save our space, okay? Don't let anyone park here."

"Lay your sleeping bags on the ground. Put some rocks on them. They will stay. Never know where I'll be. Never know."

Salas did as told. With Ronnie in the passenger seat and Salas driving, they left the Chip for the Sturgis Police Department. It took more than an hour to travel the ten miles into town. Stop-and-go traffic, mostly stop.

Once they were in Sturgis, the game was where to park. Salas took the first option he could see and pulled into Sturgis Liquor and parked the car. As he and Ronnie got out, a teenager, peach fuzz on his face, approached them. The kid wore a red T-shirt with Che Guevara on the front, baggy shorts with big side pockets, his red-and-black plaid underwear sticking out the back.

"You can only park here if you're buying something at Sturgis Liquor, sir," the kid announced. Both of his hands were on his hips.

"I'll only be here an hour or so. We're good," Salas said, walking off.

"Sir, if you don't go into the liquor store, I'll have your vehicle towed," Peach Fuzz barked out in a squeaky voice; he was maybe fifteen or sixteen.

Salas pulled out his badge and held it right in front of the kid's face. "I'm a cop. If this car isn't here when I get back, I'll have this store shut down, audited by the IRS, and have you arrested, and your house searched for contraband. You understand what I just said?"

Tears were in the boy's eyes; Salas had that effect on kids.

The teenager nodded vigorously. "Yes, sir."

"And take that fucking shirt off. Che Guevara was communist, a murderer—he killed people. Read a book before you wear shit like that." Salas and Ronnie walked away as the kid was taking his shirt off.

They headed to the west end of Main Street. Salas quickly tired of the slow-moving sidewalk traffic and went into the street, walking beside the motorcycles that were inching down Main. A Sturgis police officer stopped him at the first intersection and put a hand on Salas's chest. "You can't walk down the middle of the street, sir. It isn't safe."

"Thank you, Officer." Salas had his badge out. "Please direct me to your chief of police. And what's his name?"

The officer pointed to a brown brick building with sloping green grass on the southwest corner. "Chief is Ben Brannigan."

Salas shook the officer's hand, said "Thank you," and walked into the police station, Ronnie on his heels. A middle-aged woman sat behind a glass partition. She was locked and loaded in her office chair; if she stood the chair would rise with her. Her name tag said, "Peggy." After Salas asked to see the chief, she pointed him to the double steel doors, where an officer let him and Ronnie in.

Chief Brannigan's office was in the far-right corner, with a view of Main Street. He was sitting at his desk, looking at a report, his belly touching the desk. His forearms were the size of Salas's calves, and he had two chins.

"Chief, Detectives Mike Salas and Ronnie Higginbotham. Here from Fort Wayne, Indiana, sir," Salas stuck out his hand; Brannigan shook it, remaining seated.

"Long ways from home," Brannigan said. He gestured for Salas and Ronnie to sit down. "I take it this isn't for fun."

"No, sir," Salas said. "We have a murder suspect we've tracked to Sturgis. Honestly, I didn't know the rally was of this magnitude. I thought we would have arrested him by now. We know he's staying at the Buffalo Chip, but so far, we haven't had any luck finding him."

Brannigan nodded, his chins jiggling. "I understand. Unless you're in the biker world, you probably wouldn't know about this rally. We get complaints from tourists every year, as if we're at fault for their vacation being ruined. So, what can I do for you, Detective?"

"I'd like your team to have a look at this photo. Name is Albert Christianson. If you see him or arrest him on any charge, please call me. He carries a knife or some type of pick." Salas handed him a copy of the picture and his business card with his cell-phone number.

"Detective, Salas"—Brannigan was looking at the business card— "during this rally, we'll have over two hundred bikes stolen, three hundred DUIs, a dozen deaths, hundreds of accidents, fights, domestic disputes, and drunk and disorderlies. Unless this Christianson comes up and introduces himself, we won't be of much help."

"I understand, sir. We know we can get him back in Indiana, but my gut tells me he'll kill again and kill this week. We have to try."

"I'll send his photo and name out to all our officers and to report any knife fights. Good luck." Brannigan lowered his head back to his file; Salas and Ronnie were dismissed.

They stopped at a gyro truck for lunch, the greasy meat and yogurt sauce dripping down their chins. They took their waters to go.

The rental car was still sitting in the parking lot of Sturgis Liquor. The teenager had his red shirt on inside out, the white tag flapping at the base of his neck. He saw Salas and immediately went inside the store.

Salas followed the kid, who hurried to the back of the store, opened the door that read PRIVATE, went in, and shut the door hard. Salas grabbed a case of water off the bottom shelf, a couple of Snickers bars, a bag of chips, and some beef jerky, then paid and left.

At the parking-lot exit, he waited more than ten minutes before ordering Ronnie to create an opening to turn left so they could get on the street and head back to the Chip. Ronnie got out of the car and stopped traffic with his right arm extended, waving Salas in. This clearly wasn't his strong suit; he was too skinny to be a traffic cop. Bikers yelled, honked their horns, and revved their engines. The crowd on the street hollered their disapproval as well.

Traffic was worse than when they'd driven here, the crowd having doubled from earlier. Salas was able to screen the crowd as they sat in line, with every short male being scrutinized. He was hoping for a lucky break but didn't get one.

A crowd had gathered in front of the Easy Rider Saloon. A guy on the third floor holding a sign that said, SHOW YOUR TITS was getting favorable responses. Sturgis PD was on the case.

Rock music was blaring from the Knuckle. Salas glanced at a waitress outside the bar. Her rear, facing the street, was in a thong and black leather butt-less chaps. Salas thought maybe he should buy a bike and retire.

Salas wanted to pull into the Full Throttle to look for Albert, but security stopped him, as no cars were allowed. The man in the bright-yellow polo pointed Salas to the back exit on the other side of the maze of cabins and told him to turn right after the gas station. Salas did as directed, parking the car and walking to the Throttle. Ronnie was hoping they'd see the guy from the *Full Throttle Saloon* reality show.

Salas was more interested in the crowd; looking for short guys was the theme.

Ronnie bought a long-sleeve *FTS* shirt while Salas continued his search. Two hours and zero leads later, they drove out the back exit and took a right turn toward the Chip.

Back at the Chip, Salas parked at the CrossRoads, The CrossRoads was a mini-event center outside of the campground. The lot was corner to corner vendors, bikes and bikers. Salas and Ronnie headed into a little bar called Jumpers that offered free Wi-Fi. Ronnie got his phone online, checking databases for Albert's credit card usage, DMV hits, anything new he could find on Albert Christianson.

Outside, Salas walked through a field of flags—more than a thousand US flags in honor of fallen veterans—and stopped at a fifty-foot-tall sculpture of a V-twin engine. After petting the nose of one of the Budweiser Clydesdales, he strolled through the Rat's Hole Custom Bike Show. He had another urge to buy a bike but saw the prices and walked away.

Ronnie and Salas ate dinner at Jumpers—burgers, fries, and water—then drove back to the campground. Their sleeping bags were still there, as was Stoner, who was in the same spot he'd been in when Salas had left, sunglasses still on, joint in hand. Salas wondered why he and Ronnie had even gone back to this spot; they didn't have a tent and were sleeping in a car.

Salas grabbed the case of water, the Snickers bars, chips, and beef jerky and took them to the old man in the chair.

"Here. Got you some goods. Thanks for watching our spot."

"No problem, bro. No problem."

"You go for a ride today?"

"No bike, bro. Just here to party, just here to party."

Salas laid the groceries by the tent and looked inside. Stoner's "old lady" was on her side, her back to Salas, her bare back and butt pointing toward the front of the tent.

"How's your wife doing?"

"She hit it hard this afternoon, bro, but she will rally."

"She hit it hard yesterday too. She okay?"

"Each day is a scholar of yesterday, bro. Somebody famous said that once."

Salas and Ronnie left for the main stage, Salas feeling this was a waste of time; they should just pack up, go back to Fort Wayne, probably get fired and wait for Albert to come home. But Salas also had a bad feeling that Albert was going to kill again—if he hadn't already—and would add a fourth dead body on the ride back to Indiana.

They stayed together at the Lynyrd Skynyrd concert. There were too many people for Salas and Ronnie to split up and ever find each other again. Their cell phones were useless—too many people on too few satellites.

No beer, no shots tonight—they were hunting, Salas grabbed every short guy and looked him in the face. "Sorry. Thought you were my little brother" was his standard response.

Salas and Ronnie walked the entire perimeter of the concert four or five times. At one point, they tried to cut through the middle of the crowd but gave up quickly. Everyone was shoulder to shoulder, arms raised, dancing to the music. Salas knew the songs: "Simple Man," "Sweet Home Alabama," "Tuesday's Gone," "Gimme Three Steps," "That Smell."

They headed to the food court but had no luck there either. They went past the port-a-potties, the dumpsters, the back alleys of the Chip. They checked out the loading/unloading zones for beer trucks and vendors. He and Ronnie flashed their badges to enter the VIP section behind the Wolfman Jack main stage and again to access the band's loading area. Any place with few people, poor lighting, and poor security. Nothing.

Johnny Van Zant left the stage with one song left to go; the crowd was chanting "Free Bird." Salas and Ronnie headed to the west exit of the concert grounds to take position, eyeing everyone leaving the grounds from that exit. Van Zant returned, Confederate flag in hand and the familiar chords of "Free Bird" began.

Ronnie and Salas were at opposite ends of the exit: Salas south, Ronnie North.

The exodus began, thousands of people, a swarm of locusts. Singing; arm in arm; drunk; puking, stumbling, yelling; carrying folding chairs, coolers, each other.

Nothing. No Albert.

When the crowd had dwindled down to less than five or ten people a minute, Salas waved at Ronnie, and they gave up for the night. Tomorrow would most likely be their last day, and then they'd fly back on Thursday. Salas had to get back to Captain Green, he'd turn this over to the feds.

When they walked to their car, it was after two. Salas wasn't looking forward to sleeping in the car again, but that was their only option. Glancing at his watch, he knew if they were lucky they would get three or four hours of sleep before the sun came up. Salas was tired; he felt hungover, but he hadn't drunk anything except for a few shots last night. A slow, dull headache.

Ronnie checked his e-mail on his phone. He told Salas they'd gotten the autopsy results for Elaine Christianson. Cerebral aneurysm. "Probably laid down with a headache, died soon after."

"Well, at least he didn't kill his mom."

They found their car. Stoner was still in his chair, smoking. The case of water hadn't been opened, but the Snickers bars were gone.

"What'd you do tonight, sir? Hit the concert?" Salas asked Stoner.

"Nope. I'm not a concert man. Stayed here, relaxed a little. Stayed here."

"How's the wife. She up and at it?"

"Nope, she went down early tonight, bro. Down early. She liked the candy bar, bro."

Salas lay down in the front seat, Ronnie in the back, windows down, sunroof open. Salas looked up at the stars and wondered where the hell Albert Christianson was camping.

Tuesday was Albert's day to ride. He had watched Father long enough to know he spent his days with the two linebackers, thus no opportunity to pick him.

He was up with the sun. He put on his damp clothes and laid his sleeping bag on top of the tent, hoping the sun would dry it out. He tied the ends of his sleeping bag to the tent stakes in case the wind picked up.

Albert fired up his Harley, letting it warm up, then gassed the throttle several times, to the dismay of his fellow campers: "Are you serious?" "Can't you just ride away?" "Shut the fuck up!" "Is that necessary?"

He rode through the city of Sturgis then Albert rode his Harley on to I-90 west, the Spearfish exit, to take Spearfish Canyon Road through the Black Hills. A line of thirty bikes, mostly Harleys, were starting the ride through the early-morning sun of the canyon.

A lot of couples—men in the front, their ladies on the back—were riding together this morning. Albert envied those bikers. He thought one day he would have his lady ride with him, but first he had to find a lady. Albert had talked to a girl at work once, and he liked the girl at the convenience store where he got fuel, but he hadn't talked to her yet. His mother had wanted to ride with him the first year he had ridden to Sturgis. They argued, his mother not wanting him to go by himself. He doubted any of these bikers were riding with their moms.

Albert focused on the ride, the steep canyon walls, the slow turns, as he stayed in formation with the line of bikes. He rode Highway 14 to Cheyenne Crossing then took 85 to Lead. He turned right at Lead on 355 to Hills City.

After the incline off 355, Albert stopped at Lake Pactola, along with most of the bikers in line. Bikers were taking pictures of the crystal-blue lake, the water as smooth as glass; it was too early in the day for boaters and tubers. If Albert's phone wasn't dead, he might have taken a few selfies.

The ride past Lake Sheridan slowed as three mountain goats were grazing on the vertical cliffs across from the lake, unfazed by the noise and bikers below. The steep canyon walls somehow provided footing for the goats, a definite photo opportunity for the bikers. In awe of the goats' grip on the rocks, Albert stopped and watched them for several minutes.

After turning at Rockerville, off of Highway 16, he rode past the Bear Country, U.S.A. exit but didn't see any bears. He considered stopping at Reptile Gardens, but the parking lot was already packed by 10:00 a.m.

He stayed on the highway, taking I-90 west. Then he took the Deadwood Avenue exit to the Rapid City Harley-Davidson.

A continuous line of bikes was forming—no cars—as he rode on the south side of the parking lot behind the line of semis and trailers that served as vendor spaces on the other side. A guy clicking pictures of each passing biker, his camera on a tripod, had an assistant handing out business cards. Albert grabbed the card as he rode by then tossed it onto the pavement.

As he turned left at the end of the line of trucks and trailers, he saw that the biker parking lot was three-quarters full. Albert had never seen so many bikes in one place. Endless rows of motorcycles. Security guided him to a parking spot. He pulled in, front tire first like everyone else. Albert locked the bike with his barrel key, the handlebars turned to the left. As he headed to the entrance of Rapid City Harley, he wondered if he'd be able to find his bike when he was ready to leave. Albert counted the number of rows of bikes. He was in row fifteen near a center light pole.

Walking from north to south, he covered every vendor space. There were more bike vendors than T-shirt and food vendors. Albert stopped by the exhaust pipes and stereos but ignored the LED lights, seats, paint, and jetting carburetors. The Ape Hangers sunglasses and GPS systems were cool; the motorcycle trailers, trike conversion kits, and Boss Hog bikes not so much. He stared at the custom choppers and bike builders for a long time, envious of the bikes and the ability of their builders. The last few rows of vendor stalls before the food trucks contained leathers, saddlebags, sunglasses, boot polish, Black Hills Jewelry, and copper bracelets.

He stopped at the center tent, the Harley-Davidson tent, where he purchased an official seventy-fifth anniversary T-shirt. It cost twenty-five dollars, but it was official. He put the shirt on his credit card; he'd figure how to pay for it later. The lady at the cash register told him it was prewashed and wouldn't shrink.

Albert left the tent, removed his leather jacket, took off his T-shirt, and put the official T-shirt on. The sleeves hugged his biceps; he liked that. He threw his old T-shirt into a trash can and put his leather jacket back on.

When he went inside the actual store, he was greeted by a cute young lady in black jeans and a Rapid City Harley-Davidson tank top that was very tight across her chest. "Welcome to Rapid City Harley!" she proclaimed. "Let me know if you need anything." Albert stared at her chest; he didn't speak. The young lady quickly turned, thankful to greet the next person entering.

Albert lowered his head, eyes on the floor. The store was air conditioned, with bikers in every aisle, at every shelf, and every rack of clothes. He took advantage of the clean, air-conditioned restroom and soft toilet paper.

At a food stall, Albert ordered an eight-dollar hamburger with everything, a two-dollar bag of chips, and a three-dollar bottle of water. He nearly emptied the relish, onion, pickle, ketchup, and mustard containers. This would be his only meal today, so he decided to take advantage of the free condiments. Albert remembered he'd forgotten to go the Bikers for Jesus free breakfast today. He would go again tomorrow morning.

The ride out of Rapid City Harley-Davidson went past the Harley repair shop at the back side of the store. The line of riders wanting their bikes serviced extended into the parking lot. Albert rode past, then took the first left then a right onto I-90 for the twenty-mile ride to Sturgis.

He took the back road past the Sturgis hospital, like he'd learned on Saturday, followed by a right turn at Jack's Campers and to the Chip.

When Albert got back to his tent, Father was hosting another party at the RV; the smell of the grill made his stomach rumble. He debated again about going to the party. He could take off his jacket and compare biceps with the two linebackers.

Girls were showing their boobies to Father, and he was laughing loudly, the cackle infuriating Albert.

The Sons' bikes were gone, one less thing to worry about.

Albert sat in his lawn chair, his leather jacket off, flexing his biceps. He watched the party, watched the linebackers, watched Father. "Tonight, you'll die, Father," he murmured.

The RV party went on for a couple of hours; the Sons never showed. People started to leave as the sun went down. Eventually Father shut down the festivities, proclaiming everyone needed to go hear "Free Bird." The linebackers were first to go. They took the golf cart and sped away as Father cleaned up the empty beer cans, bottles, and paper plates.

Following Father down the lane to concert venue, Albert looked for opportunities. Father stayed on the road, surrounded by others walking to the concert. It seemed there were more people here tonight than last night for Godsmack.

A guy on his Harley rode by very slowly. His lady was topless; she was lying on the bike, her back on the gas tank, her legs spread around the man, her ankles crossed behind his lower back. Father was taking pictures.

Father stopped at the food court, bought a plastic bottle of Diet Pepsi, and sat at the end of a picnic table, across from an older couple. The lady was wearing a brown leather jacket with brown leather pants and brown leather boots. Her husband was in matching attire. Father drank half the Pepsi then took out a flask, poured some liquor into the plastic bottle, and swirled it around.

Albert took a seat at a nearby table, with Father's back to him. He heard them talking: politics, the next president, Hillary, Bush, Obamacare. Albert didn't know much about that stuff and couldn't follow the conversation very well. He heard the older man say something about Jesse Ventura; Albert did know about him and liked his character in *Predator.*

Listening to the music, he didn't know any of the songs from the opening acts, Shinedown and Lukas Nelson. The old man said Lukas sounded just like his dad.

Albert sat patiently, listening to Father, not to Lynyrd Skynyrd. Father cheered and hollered when the band finally played "Free Bird" as their last song. He didn't know why people were holding their lighters in the air, flames burning.

He sat quietly, ready to follow Father as the band thanked the crowd and walked offstage. Thousands of bikers flooded out of the concert grounds.

Father was much louder than usual. Albert noticed that he had drained the Pepsi and was drinking the last drops of liquid directly from the flask. He hoped Father was drunk; this would be the opportunity he needed.

The older couple shook hands with Father and walked away hand in hand. Father sat at the table alone, looking at his cell phone. Albert was alone as well, looking at Father.

The last of the partiers were leaving the concert grounds when Father decided to leave. He stood up and headed west toward the exit, with Albert several feet behind him.

The lighting was good near the exits, the left turn on the road to the RV not so much. Albert followed, careful not to make a sound. Father was using his cell phone as a flashlight on the washed-out road.

Past the shower house was a dark stretch of forty or fifty yards of open road. This was it; the crowd was gone. With no one on the road, darkness was his friend.

Albert quickened his pace as he pulled the pick from his left breast pocket. The plan was to approach Father, ask him for a light, then pick him on the road, leaving the body there. Then he would walk to his tent and go to sleep. It would all happen so fast.

Albert closed the distance from twenty yards to fifteen to ten to five, the pick tight in his fist. Suddenly someone behind him yelled, "Kevin, wait up!" Father stopped and turned, looking directly at Albert.

Albert put the pick back in his leather jacket and said, "Excuse me" to Father as they grazed shoulders.

He heard RJ say, "Thought that was you." Albert walked off into the darkness.

He crawled into his tent, cussing under his breath. How could Father be so lucky to have that damn biker walking down the road? He heard Father laughing at him, ridiculing him, mocking him. "Don't piss your bed, you little tard. I'll let Mommy wipe your ass, you little pussy."

Albert lay on his belly inside the tent, the sleeping bag still tied to the stakes. The tent canvas was cool, his left cheek sticking to the floor. He closed his eyes to get Father out of his mind, out of his sight. As he lay there, eyes closed, he saw himself walking out of school, backpack around his shoulders. He saw his father at the curb, sitting in the minivan, smoking. Albert waved at his dad, smiling. He walked up to the van to ask him if he could play with his friends. They were little boys like him, first graders full of energy and life, unprepared for the cruel world that would grow with them.

Father yelled, "Hey, Al-bert. Did you tell your little buddies how you pissed the bed last night, Al-bert? How you wear diapers? Huh, you tell them that? Tell 'em, Al-bert."

The boys all laughed. Albert lowered his head, ashamed. He got into the van, and Father drove away, windows up. A gray, smoky haze engulfed them.

Albert thrashed about. He sat up, startled, the roar of a Harley passing by.

He went to the shower house, towel in hand. He took a long shower, crying as the water hit his face, mixing his tears with water.

He didn't sleep the rest of the night.

MATT

Matt and Jerico spent the night at the Top Shelf Bar, where Jessica and Ann were working together.

The Lynyrd Skynyrd concert was a hit—thousands of people and no rain. The girls were bringing in one and five-dollar bills by the second.

After the concert, the boys knew the routine. Jerico took Ann to the admin building, where she locked away her cash. They would then they hit the showers before heading to Ann's cabin.

Matt and Jessica took a slow walk, hand in hand, to the RV.

Jessica was in the shower. Matt was making her a sandwich when Kevin entered the RV and plopped down in one of the leather chairs. Jessica came out of the shower in Matt's wrestling shirt and was putting a towel on her head. Kevin stared. Matt blushed as Jessica raised her hands over her head, wrapping the towel in place, the T-shirt once again above her hips, her bare crotch staring at Kevin.

"Uh…Jess, my uncle's here," Matt said, pointing to Kevin.

"Oh, hi, Kevin. Thanks again for letting me use your shower; it's so nice. I love your RV." Jessica didn't know what they had seen.

They sat together while Jessica ate. They listened to music and talked about the concert, the bikers, the storm, and today's ride through the Black Hills.

Jessica told Matt she wanted to ride with him before she had to leave for St. Louis. Matt didn't want that day to come. He wanted Sturgis to last forever.

Kevin's buzz turned into that feeling thirty minutes after you take NyQuil. He excused himself and went to the back bedroom to get some sleep.

Matt closed the curtains, turned off the lights, and followed Jessica to bed—Jessica in a T-shirt, Matt in his boxers. He lay on his back just like the night before. Jessica crawled in, put one leg over Matt, then stopped. She lay on top of him, one knee on both sides of his hips. She kissed him while they interlaced their fingers, palm to palm, their hands above Matt's head.

Matt rolled to his side with Jessica's leg still over him. Jessica released his fingers and took off Matt's boxers.

Kevin smiled as he heard them making love. "Lucky little shit," he muttered. He was asleep in two minutes.

RJ AND DEUCE

On Wednesday morning, RJ and Deuce were sitting at the picnic table outside the RV, waiting for Kevin to wake up. Actually, they were waiting for Jessica to wake up and come outside.

RJ had waited patiently since Monday afternoon for Deuce to tell him what the oncologist had said. As he was mustering the courage to ask, Deuce's cell phone rang. Deuce took the call, stood up, and walked away from the RV, closer to their tent. He wasn't talking, just listening, with the cell phone to his right ear.

Deuce was back within ten minutes and sat down across from RJ. "Well, that was the doc. The cancer doc."

"Yeah?"

"Doc says high-grade osteosarcoma, advanced. He says it's pretty rare for a guy my age, more common in kids. It's in my lungs too. He thinks it started in my leg bone and moved to my pelvis and lower vertebrae."

RJ said nothing. He just looked at Deuce.

"He wrote me a script for pain pills. I'll go get them today."

"That's it?"

"Could do chemo, maybe take off the leg. Radiate my spine. But screw that. I'm not going through chemo, and they are not removing my leg." Deuce was solid.

"What'll happen if you don't go through chemo?"

"Six months, tops."

"We gotta try." RJ had tears in his eyes.

"RJ, I just wanna ride. Let's go on a two- or three-month ride, head to the coast." Deuce was looking at the sun. "I got a life insurance policy, for my girls. Get my house in Boulder signed over to you. Get you up to speed on the club business."

RJ had his head in his hands. "Give the house to your girls, Deuce. I can get by."

"No, I decided this long ago, before I knew this."

"I can't run no business. And what if I go back to jail. Third timers are lifers."

"You ain't going back to jail. Now give up that talk. You know those warehouses in Boulder we got men at?"

"Yeah," RJ said, looking back up at Deuce.

"It's called Clover Security. No one seems to bother us. Easy money. Make sure we have two or three guys at each location every night. We just walk around and keep people out," Deuce said with a smile.

"What's in the warehouses?" RJ asked.

"That's the funny part. You guys always talk like it's guns or drugs. One's electronics—TVs and shit. The one on Fort Street is fireworks. The big one downtown is school supplies."

"School supplies?" RJ shook his head and laughed. "Hell, I thought we were guarding something badass."

They sat in silence for several seconds.

"I gotta know one thing, RJ," Deuce said.

"You got it."

"Just what does 'RJ' stand for?" Deuce was smiling now.

"Like I told Kevin the other day, just R and just J. At least that's what I was told." RJ shrugged. "And where the hell did you come up with 'Deuce'?"

"I flew the Deuce in Nam. The Delta Dagger, an F-102. I was one of the last to fly the Deuce in the late sixties out of Da Nang Air Base. They put her to bed in the seventies. Guys called me 'Deuce' 'cuz I flew the Deuce. It stuck."

"Sounds better than 'Harold.'" RJ laughed again, leaned over the table, and gave Deuce a hug.

Kevin came out of the RV. "What the hell, boys!" He walked down the steps and put his arms around the two of them, his face against RJ's back.

The grill was fired up. Deuce brought out a cooler filled with bacon, breakfast steaks, eggs, and more orange juice.

"You didn't have to do that. I got plenty in the RV," Kevin said.

"I know," Deuce replied, opening the packages of meat and bacon.

Kevin went back into the RV to put on some music. When he opened the door, Jessica was straddling Matt, her back arched, her eyes closed. Kevin blushed and yelled, "Get a room!"

Ten minutes later, Matt joined them outside, Jessica five minutes after that. Deuce and RJ were standing at attention when she opened the door and came down the steps. No yawn, no bending over. Jessica was dressed in the same wrestling T-shirt, tied at the waist, and a pair of gym shorts. Both men let out a groan.

"Plans for the day, boys?" Kevin asked the Sons.

"Riding into Rapid," RJ stated while cutting a steak. "You?"

"Stone House. On the other side of Belle Fourche. Is the destination. Then tonight we're on Da Bus to Sturgis! Join us if you wish!" Kevin announced.

Jerico walked up the lane to the RV; he actually had a shirt on this time.

"How was your night?" Matt asked him.

"Short. Didn't sleep much," Jerico mumbled but with a smile. He pumped two squirts of gel out of the bottle of Purell Kevin had on the center of the table.

Kevin placed a plate of food on the table and told Jerico to sit. He did.

"So, how's Ann?" Jessica asked. She was holding Matt's hand against her inner thigh under the table.

"She's good," Jerico said between bites.

Deuce announced they were headed out and thanked Kevin for breakfast. He was still in obvious pain when he stood.

The Sons walked to their Harleys, started them, idled briefly, then rode down the lane. All four watched them leave as the dust settled.

Jessica was up next. She went into the RV; Matt followed her inside.

"You're going downtown tonight?" Jessica asked him.

"Yeah, the guys want to check out downtown Sturgis."

"Well, I'm in the VIP section again tonight, second floor."

"I plan on being there later on. I'll take care of you," Matt promised.

Jessica stood on her toes, put her arms around his neck, and pulled him to her. "Oh, Matt," she said, "I needed to hear that."

Matt looked her deeply in the eyes. "Jess."

They kissed.

Jessica said she needed a nap and lay down on the bed. She curled up in the blanket facing the window. She was asleep, ear buds in, when Kevin and Jerico came in to get dressed.

Matt sat at the edge of the bed and just stared. Jessica's body wrapped in a white sheet, her hands under her chin. His mind didn't want to get past today, this very moment but he knew this would end.

KEVIN

About twenty minutes later, Kevin, Matt, and Jerico were riding down the dirt lane, the same one Deuce and RJ were riding.

They headed north on 79, went thirty in the thirty-five-mph zone, and spotted just one biker pulled over this time. Two state patrolmen in their cars—windows up, AC on, radar guns pointing both directions—were sitting at the exit to the racetrack.

The highway past the Spoke went on for fifteen miles then veered left just before Newell on 212 to Belle Fourche.

Forty minutes later, they were in the geographic center of the United Sates.

They took the old downtown exit, not the truck bypass. Cruised through Old Town Belle, passed some beautiful old pink stone houses, and popped out on Highway 85, turning south to Spearfish. They stopped at Stadium Grill and parked their Harleys, as Kevin announced he had to shit. They went inside. Their first Coors Light.

Back on the road, they headed south and took the right turn on Highway 34. Ten minutes later, they were at the Stone House Bar and Grill.

At the entrance of the Stone House, they were greeted by a cowboy on horseback. The gentle quarter horse, a bay mare, held her ears back as the bikes roared by and the cowboy, baseball hat on, a plug of chew in his cheek, pointed to the east, working the bikers instead of cattle.

A second cowboy guarded the exit—red scarf covering his mouth, the dust rolling from the bikes, and a white straw hat pulled low. He sat on a red roan, another quarter horse, and was guiding bikers out the exit.

The three men parked their Harleys on a slight incline facing the highway. Matt and Jerico used their keys to lock their bikes. Kevin pushed a button, and his bike honked that it was locked.

They walked north under the camouflage netting of the outdoor bar. At the far north side, the end of the camo was attached to the roof of a wooden-framed building. It housed T-shirts, baseball hats, key chains, koozies, and other souvenirs adorned with the Stone House logo. A virtual mall in a pasture.

At the south end was a wooden stage where a five-man country band was doing a pretty good rendition of Garth Brooks' hit song, "Friends in Low Places."

To the west was the Stone House, an actual stone house, long since abandoned. The deck was now a bar and grill. Young ladies in jean cut-offs and half shirts with "Stone House" on the left chest were grilling hot dogs, burgers, brats, and veggies. Walking tacos were available in Doritos bags, and beer stands had been set up on each corner. Dozens of horse tanks were filled with beer and ice, with top-shelf whiskey under the counter.

Matt bought the Coors Lights and Kevin the burgers, while Jerico got a table. The tables were abandoned wooden spools for electrical cables; the chairs were tree stumps—cheap, readily available, and able to survive the weather.

Each table had a black permanent marker on it. Kevin wrote their names and the date in block letters in the center of the spool.

The music only got better, and the crowd grew in numbers.

The tree stumps were big enough for two medium-size butts. Jerico found two women to share his and Matt's seats. Jerico collected phone numbers like Kevin collected booby pictures.

Having the girls sit with them extended their stay. The ladies were locals, students at Black Hills State University in Spearfish. They were too young for the boys, but they liked the free beer Jerico was buying. Kevin hoped they were of age; nobody was carding.

One Coors light turned into several. Kevin putting the stop at four, and then mass consumption of water followed.

Back on their Harleys, they waved to the cowboy who was pointing south. They rode under Highway 34 through a culvert. Concrete blocks in a V lined the entrance and exit, with clay covering the metal floor. Kevin stopped in the makeshift tunnel and laid on the throttle, filling the entrance with smoke and dust.

Retracing their ride through Belle Fourche, they headed back to the Chip on Highway 212. Lines of bikes were coming into Belle, lines of bikes leaving. The three men rode in a pack of ten to fifteen bikers, cruising at sixty miles an hour.

The right at Newell was seamless; they barely had to slow down as the wide curve merged with traffic. Heading due south, they passed the Broken Spoke. The campground was full, with the parking lot to the bar and vendor stalls crowded with bikes. The parking lot concrete wasn't even visible.

They passed Bear Butte on the left, Bear Butte Lake on the right, and rolled past more campgrounds, with rows and rows of campers and tents on every level piece of ground.

Bikes were backed up at the Highway 34 exit off 79. Two EMTs were loading a man into an ambulance with STURGIS REGIONAL HOSPITAL on the side panel, while a motorcycle was being loaded onto a flatbed tow truck.

After the left at the light, and the right to the Chip, they raised their arms, showing off their Chip passes, and rolled through security. A 150-mile ride.

Once they were back at the RV, the coolers came back out, with Kevin announcing the day's riding was finished and they were free to drink.

Jerico passed the bottle of Purell to Kevin and Matt; who all participated. The Heineken and Stella were gone, so tonight, Guinness was the beer of choice. They raised their cans of Irish stout in a toast.

"May you be in heaven a full half hour before the Devil knows you're dead!" Kevin exclaimed.

"Here's to being single, drinking double, and seeing triple!" Jerico chimed in.

"May you die in bed at ninety-five, shot by a jealous spouse," Matt said with a grin.

They all laughed, touched glasses, and drank.

"You gotta believe in something, and I believe I'll have another beer. Can I get you one, my friends?" Kevin asked.

They drank for another hour. The sun was setting.

Kevin got into the RV shower while the boys went to the shower house. After washing up, they all put on clean jeans, clean underwear, and their best T-shirts.

Tonight, they were hitting downtown Sturgis.

On Wednesday morning, Salas woke up in the front seat of the rental; he was sweating, the sun peering through the front windshield. He woke up because someone was yelling, not because of the heat.

He got out of the car, stretched, yawned, and walked over to Stoner, who was sitting in his chair, sunglasses on, smoking.

"What's all the yelling about?" Salas asked Stoner.

"Appears to me, the missus of that young fella isn't where she's supposed to be this fine morning. Appears to me."

Salas observed the situation. A bare-chested, white male, with a beer belly you could sit a cup on, was barefoot in blue Levi's. His jeans hung on his body, as he didn't have an ass, just a crack. The missus, obviously named Barb, as per his yelling, wasn't where she was supposed to be.

His Chip home was a faded white Scotsman single-axle travel trailer. A window AC unit was hanging out the side, with a power cord running to a generator sitting in an '80 or '81 Dodge Power Wagon.

"Barb, Barb!" This was Beer Belly's third attempt. Barb wasn't replying.

The concerned husband walked to the front of the Power Wagon, stopped, made a fist, and knocked on the closed window of the Dodge. "Barb! You whore!" He tried the door, but it was locked.

Salas watched as the window came down a few inches. Something was said from inside the pickup.

"Nothing happened? Nothing happened?" Beer Belly yelled. "You're naked in my truck with some asshole!" People were gathering around the Scotsman.

A head appeared above the steering wheel—black hair and either a lot of eyeliner or two black eyes. She was saying something.

"You didn't do anything? Yeah, right!" Beer Belly hollered. "You just like to sit naked in trucks with other men. I believe you, honey."

"Mom! Mom! What the hell, Mom?" A boy, maybe thirteen, came out of the Scotsman. He was bare chested too, built like Ronnie but even skinnier.

A family vacation gone awry.

The door of the Dodge creaked open, and a naked mom stepped out. This family did not believe in shirts. She bent over to pull on her pants, her bare white ass shining in the morning sun. She twisted her hips right and left as she pulled her pants up. Salas got an eyeful.

Mom stood there, pants on, no top. She held out her arms to her husband.

"I was really drunk, and he was too drunk to get it up. Look at him…he's still passed out!" Mom made a good point.

"I'd never, ever do something like this sober, honey. You know I only love you." Mom had her arms open for Beer Belly. He went to her; then they hugged Junior and went inside the trailer. The crowd dispersed. The drunk guy was still in the pickup.

Salas shook his head and walked to the main concert area to grab some coffee. It was seven in Sturgis, nine in Fort Wayne. He had a text from his boss, Captain Green. It read "Get your ass back here." Salas decided he'd better give the Captain a call. He punched a few keys on his cell phone. The call went straight to voice mail. Salas smiled.

"Hey, Captain, Salas here. We 'bout got him. Narrowed it down. Lots of people here, and he's laying low. We'll get him tonight, be home Friday." He hung up the phone.

Salas grabbed three coffees to go and three pastries that looked stale, but had lemon filling, and walked back to the car.

Ronnie was sitting cross-legged, on his rear, in front of Stoner, and they were talking. Salas handed them each a cup of coffee and a lemon pastry.

"Thanks, Detective." Ronnie eyes were glued on Stoner.

"No, thank you, bro. Not a coffee drinker. I'll save the doughnut for the missus. She likes that stuff, she does."

"Detective, Mr. Pierce here is quite the observer. It seems he doesn't sleep well and thus spends a great deal of time in this chair, observing. He feels he may have seen our suspect."

"Please, Ronnie, tell me more," Salas said sarcastically.

"I described our suspect and told him about the dead body in Fort Wayne. I mentioned that he has perhaps killed several people. Listen to what Mr. Pierce has to say."

"Son, I evaluate things and people, which helps me avoid mistakes. Somebody famous said that once," Stoner said, lighting up again. "Yeah, I've seen him. 'Bout five foot four or five-five. Stocky little feller, like a weightlifter. Wears a leather jacket. Young man, baby-faced. Maybe a little slow around the edges. You know what I mean?"

He had Salas's attention.

"He's walked by here a couple of times—early, about now or earlier, I'd say." Stoner was pointing behind him, not looking, just pointing toward a big tent. "Missed him yesterday."

"Why do you think he's a little slow?" Salas asked. He'd been thinking this as well, especially because of what James Cooper and Ted Christianson had told him.

"Talks to himself. Eyes are a little crossed when he looks at ya. Won't look you in the eyes. Blushed like a baby when he saw my old lady without her top. I always take blushing as a sign of guilt or ill-breeding. Somebody famous said that once."

"Does he walk back this way or just go toward the tent?" Salas asked.

"One way, bro. One way."

"What's at the tent?"

"Damned if I know, bro."

"Ronnie, I'm headed to the tent. Stay here and see if he walks by. Stoner—er, Mr. Pierce—would you recognize him if I showed you his picture?"

"Sure would. We don't remember days—we remember moments. Somebody famous said that once."

Salas took a picture of his nephew out of his wallet and showed it to Stoner. "This him? Maybe a little younger version?"

"No, sir. That's not him."

"How about this guy?" Salas showed him a picture of Albert.

"That's your boy." Stoner gave him a thumbs-up.

Salas thanked the old man for his help and headed northeast.

A white banner was hung over the entrance to the tent, with blue letters that read, BIKERS FOR JESUS. The smell of bacon permeated the air. Salas's stomach grumbled in anticipation.

He lowered his head to enter, stopped, and looked right to left. The prairie grass was matted down; twelve rectangular folding tables were set up in four rows of three, eight chairs per table, all of which were covered in white plastic tablecloths.

Most of the chairs were occupied by bikers of various sizes and shapes, with only a couple of women there. A buffet had been set up on the east side of the tent, with bacon, eggs, sausage, pancakes, syrup, orange juice, and coffee. Behind the buffet, three guys and two women were cooking, flipping pancakes, and pouring coffee.

Salas went to the first row of tables and stood at the front. He placed his arm on the shoulder of the biker sitting to his right and looked up and down the row of men. "Thank you, guys, for being here today, and thanks to Bikers for Jesus for setting up this breakfast." Salas made eye contact with each person. The group responded with a few nods and some verbal thanks. No Albert.

Salas repeated the same greeting at the second row of tables: more nods, more thanks. No Albert.

A short man stood up. He had a large belly, a goatee, hair pulled back in a ponytail, and a leather vest with "Bikers for Jesus" embroidered on the left and "Billy" on the right. He approached, stuck out his right hand, and firmly shook hands with Salas.

"Thank you as well, brother. We appreciate you coming in this morning." He followed Salas to the third row of tables.

"Are you with a state chapter of Bikers for Jesus or a member of the Christian Motorcycle Association?" Billy asked Salas.

"No, just appreciate what you guys are doing—your service and your faith." Salas was looking over the third row; he made no announcement at table three. Albert wasn't there.

Table four was closest to the buffet. Salas scanned each face, making eye contact with each man. Still no Albert. "You been here all week?" Salas asked Billy.

"No, got here yesterday, from North Dakota. A quick ride. Yourself?"

"Indiana. Got here Monday in time for the storm. Anyone on your team been here all week? I'm looking for a guy."

"Yeah, Jimmy's been here since last week. He helped set up the tent, bring in the supplies. It's his tables, his grill."

Billy took Salas over to Jimmy, who was working the buffet line. Jimmy was a rotund dude wearing a white apron, a blue bandana tied around his forehead. Pancake powder covered his beard, eyebrows, and the top of his head. He looked like the Stay Puft Marshmallow Man from *Ghostbusters*.

"Jimmy, Mike Salas. Nice to meet you."

They shook hands.

"Nice to meet you too, Mike. Thanks for coming."

"Listen, I'm looking for a guy, figured he might have stopped in. You recognize him?" Salas showed Jimmy a picture of Albert.

Jimmy nodded. "Yeah, he's been in a couple of times. He was in earlier this morning. Real quiet little guy, shy. Standoffish. He took a handful of bacon and put it in his pocket. Ya know, we don't care. Tomorrow I'll wrap up a meal for him to take back. He probably doesn't have a lot of money, and you know how expensive everything here is."

"Yeah, I know. He's a friend of mine, and I really need to find him. A family thing. Did you happen to see which way he went? This place is so big."

"Sorry, no. I saw him take the bacon and walk out, didn't see the direction. Had to have burned his hand, though. That bacon was fresh off the grill."

"Thanks, Jimmy. And again, this is a great service you're doing here."

"Each one must give as he has decided in his heart, not reluctantly or under compulsion, for God loves a cheerful giver. Second Corinthians."

Salas left the tent and went left, the opposite way he had come. "If I had a dog that could smell out the bacon," he muttered, "I could bust this guy."

He walked around the camp, through an endless number of tents—rows and rows of freaking tents.

Salas knew it was worthless. Like Chief Brannigan had told him, Albert would have to walk up to Salas and give himself up in order to be found.

He eventually located his car, Ronnie, and Mr. Pierce. They hadn't seen Albert either. It was nearly noon. Mrs. Pierce was still sleeping, although she had moved. She was lying with her head outside the tent, her face up and shoulders on the ground. Her pelvis was still on the air mattress, putting her head at a downward angle, below the level of her hips. She was topless, her breasts hanging past each side of her chin.

"She okay?" Salas asked.

"Had one of them flashes." Stoner was rolling a cigarette, licking the paper, twisting each end. He took a blue Bic out of the cup holder of the folding chair and lit up. "She'll be good soon. She's excited for tonight. Hump day, bro. Hump day." The old man took a long first drag, held the smoke in, and breathed out. No smoke exited. "Didn't find your boy, huh?"

"Nope. I was close, though. I'll get him in the morning. They're giving out free breakfast at that tent. He goes there for food."

"Lion is most handsome when looking for food. Somebody famous said that once."

"And don't expect a lion not to eat you just because you didn't eat him. Somebody famous said that too," Salas said.

Stoner grinned. "I like it."

"Where's Ronnie?"

"Don't know, bro. Don't know. He turned bright red when the old lady rolled out. Must be guilty, though it could be the breeding, I guess."

Salas found Ronnie on the way to the shower house. Ronnie still in his rally shirt, hair pulled back. Boots with some grit on them. He was starting to blend in.

A biker rushed passed them on his Harley. Ronnie nearly jump into Salas's arms.

"Guy's in a hurry!" Ronnie said, as Salas gave the guy the middle finger and yelled at the biker to slow down.

After a shower and shave, Salas felt somewhat refreshed, though he'd give anything for a Hampton Inn bed. He met Ronnie at the car. Stoner hadn't moved, and neither had his wife.

Salas and Ronnie walked back to the CrossRoads and Jumpers Bar. Ronnie was back online, checking databases. Salas was on his cell; he called Green again and was relieved when it went to voice mail again. He left a message that the suspect had been located, and an arrest would be made tonight or first thing in the morning. Short and sweet.

Salas called Chief Brannigan of the Sturgis PD, who confirmed there had been no dead bodies at the campground this week—a stat he didn't have to look up.

His third call was to the Buffalo Chip Campground 1-800 number.

"Hello, the Chip. How may I help you?"

"Yeah, I'm trying to find a friend of mine. When people leave the Chip, vacation over, do they check out?"

"If they've rented a cabin, they're supposed to check out and leave us the key or we charge them a fifty-dollar lock-change fee. Is your friend staying in a cabin, sir?"

"No, he's in a tent."

"Then no, sir, there would be no need for your friend to check out. Tenters get a receipt when they check in."

Ronnie cut in as Salas hung up the phone. "Confirmed. Albert used his credit card yesterday afternoon at Rapid City Harley-Davidson. Purchased a T-shirt."

"Well, I hope that means he hasn't killed anyone. My feeling is that when he kills, he rides away."

"Maybe he's had enough. Maybe it's out of his system until next year."

Salas shook his head. "With Mom gone, I doubt it. He won't make it home without another one. Once he's at the free breakfast tomorrow morning, we'll have him, but for someone it might be a day too late."

"Tonight, the band Social Distortion is on the main stage," Ronnie said. "Personally, they band's one of my favorites. They're similar to the Sex Pistols, with a little Johnny Cash mixed in."

"Great. Can't wait."

"If Albert doesn't kill tonight, Detective Salas, he might not. He has a two-day ride back to Indiana. So, he'll have to be leaving tomorrow or early Friday morning if he has to go to work on Monday."

"Yeah. Let's work the entrance to the concert from the same sides again tonight and hope for the best. If not, we get him at breakfast. And put your Full Throttle T-shirt on."

That night, Salas and Ronnie took their positions. Salas could see Ronnie across the entrance. He looked better in the FTS long-sleeve shirt, the jeans were wrinkled and with the dirt on the new boots Ronnie looked like a biker.

They scanned the crowd—left to right, then right to left—people coming, people going. The crowd wasn't as large as it had been the previous two nights. Salas thought it should be easier to spot Albert if he was still at the Chip—the key word being *if.*

One thing Salas knew for sure: it was going to be a long night.

ALBERT

Well, he didn't wet the bed, but he didn't sleep. On Wednesday, Albert got out of the tent before the sun was up. He sat in his folding chair and stared at the RV, rubbing his chin with his right hand. Calluses from weightlifting, prominent on his index and middle fingers, scraped against his skin.

He stood and stretched his arms above his head, arching his back. He looked at the RV, then at the Sons' tent. The RV was quiet; the tent flap was zipped shut.

Taking short steps, Albert slowly walked over to the RV. He stood by the picnic table, staring at the front door. A bike fired up a few campers down, startling him and breaking his stare. He walked to the front of the RV and looked at the front windshield. A curtain blocked the view inside.

As he walked around the back side of the RV, he peered into every window; each one was covered with a curtain. The hum of the air conditioner concealed any noise from his shoes hitting the grass. He stopped at the trailer hitch, which was unattached to the RV. It had an electrical motor lift kit to raise and lower the hitch, not a hand crank.

At the end of the bike trailer, Albert stopped again, unbuttoned his pants, undid his zipper, and peed on the trailer tire. When he finished, he zipped and buttoned up then continued his walk. He stood and stared at the back of the trailer. A Master Lock was in place, securing the ramp to the trailer. He noticed a small, brown, circular piece of glass in the center of the trailer, above the ramp door. *A trailer light*, he thought, not knowing it was the camera that helped Kevin back up the RV and trailer.

Albert walked back to his tent, turned, and looked at the trailer again. Then he looked at the Sons' tent. The tent fly was open.

With the free Bikers for Jesus breakfast on his mind, he made an early-morning walk to the big white tent. As he walked along, it was the quietest of any of his days at the rally. The sun wasn't up yet, just a faint glow of sun trying to peak out, a gray morning.

Albert walked into the tent, not having to lower his head to enter. Two or three bikers were at each table, some with their heads bowed in prayer, their lips moving. The big guy who had first talked to him was behind the buffet table. Wearing a white apron, he was making pancakes, smiling, and singing. His deep voice echoed inside the tent. *"El-Shaddai, El-Shaddai, El-Elyon na Adonai.* Age to age, you're still the same by the power of your name." He stopped singing when Albert came forward.

Grabbing a plate and white fork, Albert kept his head down, stacking bacon and fresh pancakes onto the plastic plate.

"'Morning. Glad to see you're back." The man in the apron smiled at Albert.

Albert said nothing, didn't make eye contact. He picked up a cup of orange juice, drank it all while he stood there, and took another cup with him. He chose the back table and sat at the opposite end, where two men were in prayer. He ate quickly. He hurried for another trip through the buffet line, while the cook in the white apron was busy talking to two bikers next to the coffee station.

Albert ate his second helping faster than the first. He gobbled it down, stood, and tossed the plastic fork and plate into the black trash barrel. He stopped by the exit, looked back, and saw the cook still in conversation with the bikers. Albert walked quickly back to the buffet table, grabbed a handful of bacon, stuffed it into his pocket, and walked out, this time not looking back.

Walking to his tent, he ate the bacon, licking his fingers after each strip.

Albert stopped at the shower house, which was just now coming to life with the early-morning sun. He washed up and returned to his one-man tent. The RV was quiet, with no activity outside or in. The Sons' bikes were still there; the tent flap was still open.

Albert lay down in front of his tent and did a hundred push-ups. He lay flat until his breathing was normal then did a hundred more, again lying flat, until his breathing slowed. After rolling over, he laid on his back, hands locked behind his head, his feet pointed east. He watched the sun climb higher in the sky. *Tonight is the night*, he thought. *Today is Father's last day.* Albert committed to the kill, even if it meant picking Father right in front of the RV, right in front of the linebackers. Thursday, he wanted to leave for the two day ride back to Indiana; tonight would be the night.

He dozed off, lying in front of the tent. A full belly took the blood from his brain to his stomach. He slept for a couple of hours before waking to the sound of Father's voice. "What the hell, boys!" He turned his head to the left to see Father hugging the Sons. Incensed, Albert sat upright. He'd never had a hug from Father. How could Father hug two men from a biker gang and not hug his own son?

Albert dug his fingers into the ground, through grass, rocks, and soil. A fingernail was ripped off his index finger as he balled a fistful of dirt in his hands. Small splatters of blood dripped onto the grass below his hands. He was holding his breath. He stood and opened his fists, the dirt falling to the ground. After Albert straddled his Harley, he hit the ignition, and the V-twin roared to life. He pulled forward, saw no foot traffic or bikes coming, and rode out onto the dirt road.

Albert laid on the throttle, popped it into first, and slowly released the clutch, gravel and dirt flying behind his bike. He shot forward and sped out of the camp area. He stayed heavy on the throttle through the campground, with bikers, people on foot, and campers yelling their disapproval about how fast he was going. A security guard stepped out on the road at the west exit, his hand up for Albert to slow down. Albert lowered his head, swerved left, missed the guard, and peeled out onto the asphalt.

He laid scratch when he hit second gear, ran the red light at the corner as he turned left, and sped to Highway 79. Albert laid into the hard-right turn at more than fifty miles an hour, his tailpipes sparking from contact with the highway. As the road straightened, he came out of the curve and hit the brakes hard, both the foot brake and hand brake. The Harley screeched to a halt. A state patrolwoman, a ponytail sticking out the back of her blue hat, had pulled a bike over. Albert slipped into first gear and rode slowly past the patrolwoman as she was handing the biker a slip of paper. The state trooper made eye contact with Albert as he went past; he knew she knew, and he regained his composure.

Albert rode to Bear Butte State Park, just another five miles down the highway. He paid the four-dollar entry fee, parked his bike, then walked through the education center. His pulse was still racing, and he was thankful he hadn't gotten a speeding or reckless driving ticket. He looked at artifacts, pictures of Indians and the governor of South Dakota, and read about the religious history of the mountain, how it was a sacred place for the Cheyenne, Lakota, and other Native American tribes.

Great fighters like Red Cloud, Crazy Horse, Sitting Bull, and George Custer had been right here, right where he was standing. These men were all fighters. Albert would be a fighter too. Albert would rid the world of Father. He was calm now, his face no longer red, his hands relaxed. He licked the blood off his index finger; it tasted of dirt.

Albert walked back to his bike. He liked the small scars on the bottom of the tailpipe; dragging pipe was kind of cool. Dirt was caked under his rear fender, and blood was on the right handlebar and grip. He swung his right leg over the leather seat then started the bike and made a wide U-turn with the Harley. He rode slowly as the park ranger in the little brown wooden building tipped his hat and said, "Thanks for coming" as Albert passed.

Riding back to the Chip, he pulled into the Full Throttle. Security directed him left, then right, and guided him to a place to park. He waited before pulling in, giving the biker next to him time to get off his bike, lock the handlebars, take off his jacket, and stuff his Harley-Davidson windbreaker into his saddlebags. When Albert parked his bike, the next guy in line gave him the same courtesy.

Inside the Throttle, he made his way to the second story. The deck overlooked the highway, endless rows of parked bikes, and a parade of bikers coming and going. He leaned against the chest-high rail and watched the scene below. After a time, a barstool opened up at the bar. Albert made his way through the crowd of men, climbed onto the stool, and placed his elbows on the wooden countertop. A blonde, with pigtails sticking out of the sides of her head, was working the bar. She wore a pink halter top—nipples erect—and had flat belly with a silver ring in her navel. She asked Albert what he wanted to drink. Speechless, he stared at her, his mouth open wide.

"Honey! Look up here, honey." She grabbed his chin with her right hand and squeezed it as she pushed upward. "Look, honey, I have eyes too!"

The men at the bar laughed. Someone yelled, "This the first set of titties you ever laid eyes on, little buddy?"

Albert's cheeks turned bright red. He slapped the girl's hand off his chin—it took two swats.

He didn't look at the other men. Instead he lowered his head and stepped off the stool. As he walked away, he heard, "That boy is scared of titties!" and "I don't think he's old enough to be here. What's the drinking age in South Dakota?"

He hurried down the steps, two at a time.

Just before the exit, Albert went into the men's room and peed at the first urinal. Then he went to the sink. As he turned the faucet on, the water splashed onto his jeans. He stood in front of the mirror inspecting himself; it looked like he had wet his pants. He hurried into an open stall, closed the door, and rubbed his crotch fiercely, trying to get the dark denim to a light blue to match the rest of his jeans.

A voice came from the next stall. "You piss your pants again, boy?" Father said, cackling.

Albert yelled, "Shut up!"

There was no one in the next stall, of course. The bathroom was empty except for Albert.

Crying, Albert ran out of the bathroom, out the bar, and to his bike. He stood next to his bike for a long time. He hated Father. Finally, he rode out the back entrance of the Throttle, past rows of cars, campers, pickups, and trailers. He rode slowly, took the right at the light, and headed to the Chip.

The sun was nearing the horizon as he parked his bike next to his tent. He saw Father and the two linebackers sitting at the picnic table, each with a beer in front of them. Shutting off the Harley's engine, he heard them talking loudly, laughing. Albert knew they were laughing at him. He looked at his crotch; it was still slightly darker in color than the rest of his jeans. He sat in his chair and watched them, still waiting for his pants to dry.

Albert ate the last of his breakfast bars and found a piece of bacon in his leather jacket. He didn't have any water and had drunk what little whiskey he had brought. He thought about joining Father, just to get close to them; maybe they would give him a beer. Father gave everyone a beer, but Father never had invited Albert to the RV parties. He always left Albert alone at his tent; he never gave Albert a beer.

He sat and watched as they drank, then watched Father go into the RV and shut the door. Albert stood as the two linebackers took off in the golf cart, towels in hand.

He walked to the RV and stood by the picnic table, his heart racing. Then he went to the door of the RV, where he turned and look left then right. No linebackers, no Sons, no traffic. He grabbed the grip to the left of the door and pulled himself up the first step. He put his hand on the door handle and pushed down. The handle didn't move. It was locked. Father had locked the door.

A golf cart pulled up. Albert froze.

"Hey! You guys gonna have a party here again tonight?" It was two girls, a redhead and a brunette. Albert recognized them; he thought he had a picture of the redhead's boobs. He blushed the color of her hair. He came down off the steps and headed back to his tent.

"You gonna party or not?" the redhead asked again.

"No" was all Albert could say. He didn't look at them.

"Well, hello to you too, little man." When she put the cart in reverse, a *beep beep beep* came from the cart. When she put it in drive, the noise went away, and the two girls did too.

Albert sat in his folding chair, his heart pounding, his palms sweating.

A few minutes later, the linebackers pulled up in their golf cart. Matt tried the door to the RV, but it was locked. He knocked on the door then pushed a button on the side of it. "What the hell, Kevin!" he yelled. "You locked us out!"

Father opened the door. "Damn right I did!" he yelled. "I don't trust you two little peckerwoods! Figured you'd dump cold water on me!"

Albert took out his pick. He rubbed it and shined it with his towel. Fifteen minutes later, as Father and the two linebackers walked past his tent, he put the pick back into his left breast pocket.

The pick was ready, and so was Albert.

He followed them as they walked to the west exit, staying far back.

Albert saw Da Bus before they got to the exit and now realized they were going downtown. Da Bus was an old-school bus with a shitty paint job, a smiling driver, loud music, and lots of beer. He watched as Jerico paid the entry fee and the three men climbed the one step and boarded the bus. They took seats in the back.

Albert waited a few minutes, and then he too paid the fifteen-dollar fee and climbed aboard; it was expensive, but it would be worth it. He took a seat in the first row from the front, behind the driver. As he sat, at an angle, so he would be able to see Father with a short right turn of his head, Father lifted a jug of Fireball, took the first swig, and passed it to Matt. After a short pull and a loud "Hell, yeah!" the bottle went to Jerico, who followed suit and passed the bottle to the guy in the next seat over.

A man in a plain leather jacket—no decals, no patches—grabbed the bottle. His wife—or girlfriend—wore a matching black leather jacket, tight leather pants, and a red bandana tied in a knot on her forehead. Under her leather jacket, she was topless; her cleavage attracted Albert's eyes. The biker wiped the mouth of the bottle off with the tail of his shirt and took a long pull. He handed it to the woman, who took a long swig as well.

Father yelled out another "Hell, yeah!" with a laugh that set Albert on edge. The bottle made its round to the front of the bus. The driver passed on the offer. When the bottle came to Albert, he took a long swig, one like Matt took. He gagged and nearly barfed as the red-hot cinnamon coursed through his body. He gasped for air as the others laughed.

Albert passed the bottle along. Four or five other willing partners took a pull of the Fireball. Evidently, they felt the alcohol would kill any of the germs that were being passed around. The bottle made it back to Father, who held it up—more than half was gone, and they hadn't even left the parking lot.

After making stops at the Broken Spoke and Glencoe campgrounds, Da Bus was now full. Kevin greeted the new recruits with the last of the Fireball. Announcing its demise, he pulled a travel bottle of Johnny Walker Blue from the back of his pants. He took a halfhearted sip then passed Johnny to Matt, Jerico, and the rest of the bus. Kevin noticed the last shot went to the short guy behind the driver, who struggled to keep the shot down, turning red and coughing in fits. This made Kevin laugh as he pointed and told Matt the guy was probably going to puke.

The final stop was the parking lot of Sturgis Liquor. Da Bus came to a halt, and bikers stumbled out. Groups of two and three went right to the Easy Rider Saloon, left to the tent vendors, across the street to the Knuckle, or south one block to Main Street.

Kevin led the way as Jerico and Matt were shoulder to shoulder, talking about Ann and Jessica. The mob was intense, with the boys struggling to keep up with Kevin, especially since he was so short, and the crowd was so big. Their conversation quickly ended.

The plan, as Kevin called it, was three stops: first the Dungeon, then One-Eyed Jacks, and finally Loud American Roadhouse. All on Main Street. The final phase of the plan was to board Da Bus at 1:00 a.m.—if you missed it, you were on your own to get back to the campground. Matt, of course, would be leaving early to head over to Jessica's bar.

The doorman at the Dungeon sat on a barstool—no back support, just a round seat on a three-legged stool. The man wore no shirt, had no body hair, and wore jeans and black lace-up boots. The jeans looked as if they hadn't been off his body for several days. Tattoos covered every inch of his torso, and full sleeve tats went past his wrists. The knuckles on his right hand read, "Life," and the left knuckles read, "Love." Ink rockets with black flames went up his neck and into his scalp. His head was shaved to show off his cranial tattoos. A huge bullring went through the septum of his nose, and each earlobe and eyebrow sported multiple piercings, all small round silver loops. His nipples were pierced, and again, one wasn't enough; evidently nipples could support five silver loops.

Kevin was taking pictures of the guy's tattoos: black-ink lightning bolts, hearts, a German shepherd, a black lab, a kitten, crosses, the Devil, Buddha, Jesus with a crown of thorns, Jesus on a cross, a temple, pyramids. No reason, no rhyme—just lots and lots of tats.

"Dude, you're crazy," Kevin said. "Which one's your favorite?"

"The one of my ex."

"Show me. Where is it?" Kevin wanted a picture.

"It's on my ass. I sit on the bitch's face every day."

Kevin laughed hysterically, the belly-buster laugh of Woody Woodpecker.

He and the boys headed downstairs to the Dungeon's basement. The red light bulbs cast a devilish glow on the walls, the floor, the people. One-dollar bills were stapled to the wall—expensive wallpaper. In black ink, each one was marked with the name and date of the posting party.

Kevin's lips were nearly touching Matt's ear as yelled for a beer. "What?" Matt said. The vibration from the speakers made the dollar bills on the walls shake. There was no room to sit, no room to stand, and they couldn't get to the bar. Kevin grabbed Matt by the arm, and tapped Jerico, who was looking at his cell phone, on the shoulder. He gave the head signal for them to go up the steps. Kevin led up the boys upstairs as more people were coming down.

Outside, Kevin went up to the doorman. "Dude, there's way too many people in there. Has to be a fire code violation. You can't let any more people in there, bro."

"I don't work here, man," Tattoo Man said, then turned to get his picture taken with two girls, his arms around their waists.

Next, they battled the flood of people in the street on their way to One-Eyed Jacks. The three men walked in single file. One-Eyed Jacks was surrounded by food vendors, with gyros being the most popular. Once they were inside Jacks, they were hit with the T-shirt shop, beer stations, numerous bars with scantily clad waitresses, a dance floor, and a live band.

Kevin took pictures of a waitress taking a shot off a guy's hairy belly. Girls were dancing on the bar countertops, with dollar bills in their chaps and halter tops, with bikers—men and women—waiting to give them more cash.

They found counter space for three at the back of the bar. Their waitress wore black nylons with holes in the knees, a black thong, and a black bra. Her shoulder was tattooed with small blue footprints; Kevin found out they were her little boy's prints.

Beers—no shots—went around three times. Kevin tipped well.

They checked out the dance floor, the band playing AC/DC's "Thunderstruck," the swarm of people too dense to enter. The floor was landlocked, blocked off by the stage, with wooden steps to the second floor and a bar. Only one way in or out, which was blocked by bikers standing and watching.

Around eleven, they wedged their way out of Jacks and walked east on Main, across the street to Loud American Roadhouse. The west bar was playing country, the east bar rock—live bands at both ends.

Jerico ordered three double Jacks and Diet Coke in black Jack Daniels souvenir cups. Matt slammed his down, said his good-byes to Jerico and Kevin, and left for Da Bus. He had Jessica to take care of.

Kevin stayed at the bar while Jerico literally pounded his way through the back of the dance floor. He had seen something or someone and was on a mission. Kevin was standing on the footrail, which made him about six feet tall; he could use this view. Jerico made eye contact with two dancing women, smoothed down his jet-black crew cut, and stepped between them. He hugged them both at once, a hand on each of their asses, as he kissed the brunette. It was the two ladies they met on the ride to Sturgis at Wall Drug. Kevin knew he wouldn't see Jerico until the morning. Kevin thought of Gloria, then of Skip, then of Gloria with Skip. He needed air.

After dropping off the footrail, he went to the exit, thanked the doorman, and headed outside, souvenir cup in hand. He didn't walk ten feet before a couple stopped him—a man and a woman, dressed in black pants, black military-style lace-ups, and gray polos that said, "Sturgis Police" across the back. Their Glocks were holstered on their waists; the male officer's polo was stretched tightly across his belly, which hung over his belt.

The female officer, Kevin thought she looked a little like Gloria had her hair bobby pinned at each graying temple, was first to speak. "Sir, we have a law in this town, no open containers." She took the souvenir cup from Kevin's hand, walked over to a trash can, and dumped out the booze.

"Oh, sorry, Officer. The doorman didn't say anything," Kevin said.

"Sir, you're in violation of Sturgis city ordinance. I have to cite you for having an open container. Please follow me." It was the tight-polo officer, he was Kevin's height, as tall as he was wide.

"Cite me? Like give me a ticket?"

"Yes, sir. You broke the law." The two officers had him by the back of the arms and were walking him to a white trailer parked along a side street.

"But the doorman didn't tell me. He didn't even try to stop me, and I stopped and talked to him."

"This way, sir. Please walk up those steps, and the officer inside will issue you a citation. Thank you for your cooperation." The two officers were now pushing Kevin up the three steps that led to the trailer.

Inside were two desks. The back desk was occupied by an officer, in a standard-issue, rather snug black-and-gray uniform. The officer was behind the desk with a biker in front. The biker was taking cash out of his wallet. The front desk had another officer, with the same attire as the others, but no biker. Kevin was told to sit at that desk.

"Your ID, please." The officer had parted gray hair, a black goatee, and a shirt that was a size or two too small for him. Kevin thought there must be a sit-up problem at the Sturgis PD.

He took out his wallet and handed his ID to the cop. The officer filled in each blank on the white paper, then turned the paper over and said, "Sign here." A small red X next to a long blue line indicated the spot.

Kevin signed as instructed.

"That'll be eighty-five dollars. No checks…cash only."

"Eighty-five dollars cash? Do I get a receipt?"

"Yes, sir. Cash, please."

"What kind of racket is this? I walked out of the bar, and the doorman didn't stop me. You took my cup and emptied it. It was a Diet coke. Can't we walk around Sturgis with a Diet freaking Coke?"

"Sir, we have reason to believe it was an alcoholic beverage."

"Did you test it? Did you taste it? Did you ask the bartender who filled it with Diet Coke?"

"Sir, you can pay the fine, or you can spend the night in jail. The night in jail will offset the eighty-five dollars. If you pay the fine and wish to argue it, you may. You'll be scheduled to be in front of the judge tomorrow morning at eight to state your case."

"This is total bullshit. It was a Diet Coke. This is extortion. Here—here's your eighty-five bucks." Kevin tossed four twenties and a five on the table. Now give me my receipt so I can get the hell out of here."

"Sir, if you'd like to spend the night in a cell, we can still arrange that. I recommend you lower your voice or don't talk at all."

"Receipt, please. Thank you for serving and protecting," Kevin said, this time more quietly. He stood, grabbed his receipt, and left the trailer.

After walking across the street in a huff, he went into the Oasis Bar. A Kenny Rogers song, "The Gambler", was playing. The singer wasn't Kenny, though. It was karaoke night at the Oasis. Kevin found a wall that needed support and leaned against it, still fuming a little over the eighty-five dollars. He smiled as the biker ended the song and joined the others, who were all clapping for his courage.

Next up was a bald, fifty-something guy with a dusty beard—a Santa Claus type minus the red pants and coat. He stood calmly in front of the crowd as the music loaded, his chin down. As soon as the music started, he started to jump. Little hops at first, and then, as the music got louder—the DJ was cranking it—the old boy was belting out House of Pain's "Jump Around." He was singing something about jumping on the ceiling, throw your hands up then pack it up or buck it up. Kevin couldn't hear the words above the yelling and cheering.

The Oasis crowd went bananas. A senior citizen biker rapping House of Pain and jumping with the energy of a toddler. "Jump around, jump around." The entire bar stood, hands in the air. "Jump, jump, jump, jump." The song went on— "Jump, jump, jump"—and the crowd jumped along. The DJ was jumping; the waitresses, Kevin, the owner—they were all jumping. Kevin forgot about the eighty-five dollars. The music stopped, but the crowd still stood and continued to cheer for the rapper as he went back to his table, receiving high-fives and fist bumps along the way.

Kevin downed a couple more Coors Lights. No one wanted to follow the rapper's performance, so the DJ sang a few songs, trying to keep the crowd engaged. Songs with a little more speed than Kenny Rogers.

Kevin checked his cell phone: it was 12:34. Time to pee and get back to the parking lot of Sturgis Liquor. He didn't want to miss Da Bus back to the Chip. He worked his way through the party crowd, spotted the back exit past the Asian Fusion food vendor, and decided that was the fastest route to the parking lot.

Asian Fusion was well lit, with the vendor's lights focused on the tables, cash register, and entrance into the Oasis. Kevin took off down the alley. Glancing back, he could clearly see everyone in the tent. As he looked forward, however, all he saw was the darkness of the alley. To the right were the backs of the Main Street buildings—back entrances with no lights—and parking spots for the owners and workers. To the left were trash bins, storage sheds, a row of trees, more parking spots, and three port-a-potties. Just what Kevin was looking for and there wasn't a line.

He went to the first urinal, took one step up, went in, and locked the door.

The Fireball shot ran up through his sinuses. He couldn't hold back the tears that welled up, and he thought he would puke. Father continued to ridicule him as others on the bus laughed along.

The bus made two stops, and more people climbed aboard. Through the rumbling of the diesel motor, the music, and people talking, Father's high-pitched laugh still rang out, like a car alarm in a Walmart parking lot.

Father raised yet another bottle and showed it to the crowd. He twisted off the cap, threw it onto the floor of the bus, took a swig, and passed the bottle to Matt and Jerico. The two linebackers took long drinks—they made it look easy. Maybe this one tasted better than the last. The bottle made its way forward to Albert. The label read "Johnny Walker." Albert smelled it first—no cinnamon. He took a long pull, gulped it down. He couldn't hold back his reaction. Putting his hand to his mouth, he struggled to keep the liquid in his body. A coughing fit started next, a hacking smoker's bark. Father was laughing and pointing at Albert, while others looked and laughed too. Albert sat low in his seat, head down. He promised himself he wasn't going to puke. Father was always laughing at him.

The bus stopped in the city of Sturgis. Albert was the second one to step into the parking lot of Sturgis Liquor. Waiting for Father, he leaned against the side of the bus as others exited.

It was difficult to follow them. People cutting in between, people zigging and zagging, an endless hedge maze of black and leather. They crossed Lazelle, dodging bikes, cars, and people. At Main Street, a police officer was directing traffic—his arm extended, palm up in a circular wave to go forward. Albert jogged to cross with Father and the two linebackers.

At a bar, Father stopped and took some pictures of a shirtless man covered in tattoos and body piercings. A skull-and-crossbones on his chest, flaming rockets on his neck, a sunburst on his forehead. Nipple rings, earrings, a hook in his nose, a metal bar through the bridge of his nose. It looked painful.

Albert looked up. The sign read, THE DUNGEON. Father and the boys entered. Albert elected to stay outside and wait for them to come back out, he rested his shoulder against a light pole. A large green dumpster stood next to him, with people stopping, lifting the lid, tossing cans and plastic bottles inside. Albert thought it smelled like his bathroom in Auburn: shitty.

Surprised that they didn't stay in the Dungeon very long, Albert turned his face away from Father as he stepped onto the sidewalk. Father cackled as he talked to the tattooed man. The high-pitch laugh made Albert twinge.

The three men turned left—again a chaotic procession of bodies with no rules for walking, stopping, or yielding to others.

Albert followed them into One-Eyed Jacks. Father and his bodyguards headed to the back of the bar, where they ordered beers and talked to the waitress. Albert took a stool at a bar in the corner between two men, their backs to each other. Neither looked at him when he sat down. He stared at Father. The waitress asked, "What can I get you, honey?" Albert waved her off as if she were a mosquito.

Father kept teasing Albert about pissing his pants, calling him "Al-bert." He squinted his eyes tightly, rubbed his temples, willing the voice out of his head.

When Father and the boys left and went into Loud American Roadhouse, Albert again waited outside. It was just too crowded, and as short as Albert was, he wouldn't be able to see anything anyway. The bar's front wall was open to Main street, a large garage door rolled up so he could see Father's back, his belly to the bar. Father was standing on a footrail, overlooking the crowd. Albert watched as Matt shook Father's hand, patted him on the back, then went out the side door. Matt took a left and vanished into the throng of people. Albert couldn't see the guy they called Jerico. He wasn't standing next to Father, and Albert hadn't seen him leave the building.

Father exited the Roadhouse. He stopped and talked to security then headed directly toward Albert. Two uniformed police officers, a female and a short chubby cop blocked his path. Albert watched as they dumped the liquid that was in Father's cup into the trash; he was confused when the officers grabbed him by his arms and directed him to a white trailer. He could tell Father wasn't happy, which made him smile.

About fifteen minutes later, Father came out of the trailer looking disgusted. Albert stayed in the shadows as Father crossed the street and proceeded down the sidewalk.

In step with Father's footsteps, he was two people behind when Father entered the Oasis Bar. The bar smelled of beer, sweat, and a hint of new carpet. As with all of Sturgis, the bar was crowded. Wooden picnic tables lined the entryway, with bars to the right and to the left of the stage, where a man was singing. Every available chair was taken, every spot against the wall occupied. Waitresses struggled to carry their trays through the mass of people.

Albert didn't recognize the singer but thought he'd heard the song before. Father found a spot to lean his shoulder against a wall; he wasn't talking to anyone. Albert stayed directly across from him, near the stage and the front door. He was glad when the song was over.

A new person came onstage. He briefly spoke to the DJ then stood in the middle of the floor, all eyes were on him. Albert thought the guy who took the microphone looked too old to get up there and sing; he walked with a limp and had to put his hand on his knee to overcome the one step to the stage. The music grew louder and louder as the singer, the decrepit guy, was jumping in place, up and down. He wasn't jumping very high, but he was getting both feet off the ground. He was singing about jumping, telling everyone to jump, and they did. Old people, young people, bikers, the entire crowd, even Father—everyone was jumping, their hands in the air. Albert stood still, both feet planted, his arms crossed. When the song ended, people cheered; they were congratulating the old man for jumping and singing the jump song.

From his spot by the stage, Albert had a good view of the bar and was able to work his way through the crowd. He bumped shoulders with people and said, "Excuse me, excuse me" as he followed Father to the back exit. Outside, the smell of ramen noodles filled the air.

Albert watched as Father sidestepped through the buffet line, past the cash register, and into the darkness of the alley. He was under the tent lights, both hands on a tent pole, when Father stopped, turned, and faced Albert. They looked each other in the eyes; Albert knew this was the time. Father pivoted and headed into the darkness. Albert wasn't as polite as Father when he moved through the buffet crowd; he was in a hurry and didn't say "Excuse me" as he pushed his way through the alley.

He was speed walking, trying not to run but in a definite hurry. Once engulfed in the same darkness as Father, Albert slowed his pace.

Clouds concealed any moonlight, and no light came from any of the rear exits of the Main Street buildings. A row of trees lining the north end of the alley effectively blocked the glow from Lazelle Street. Albert was gaining on Father, who turned left and stepped into a port-a-potty. Albert smiled; his plan was working.

He heard liquid running down a pipe, more water splattering, then Father uttering, "Awwwww." Albert, holding his breath, was standing in front of the door of the urinal. He pulled the ice pick out of the inside breast pocket of his leather jacket, the wooden handgrip of the pick tight in his right fist.

He heard a zipper being zipped.

Feet shuffling.

The door opened. Albert stepped forward.

"Oh, excuse me," Father said.

Opening the door of the urinal, he faced the dark shadow of another guy who was in line to use the toilet. Their eyes met. Kevin said, "Oh, excuse me" then jumped back into the toilet as the man crumpled to the ground.

"What the hell?" Kevin said, now staring eye to eye at RJ.

RJ was calm, his voice subdued. "This guy's been following you for a few days. He was gonna kill you." RJ held his pistol by the barrel. He bent at the knees and felt the man's carotid artery. The man he'd hit with the butt of his pistol was unconscious but breathing, his pulse steady. "See his ice pick there?"

"Kill me? Why?"

Kevin stepped out of the port-a-potty and knelt by RJ, his hands on his knees. He reached for the ice pick.

"Don't touch it. Leave it for the cops."

A door opened behind RJ. A light came on as a man in an apron and hairnet came out, a pack of cigarettes and a lighter in his hands. He saw RJ and Kevin kneeling over the man on the ground. "Hey! What did you do to that guy?" he yelled.

"Shit, I don't need this. I'll be back in prison." RJ said.

"Get out of here now. I got this," Kevin ordered RJ.

RJ didn't need to be told twice. He slipped behind the port-a-potties, ducked through the row of trees, and into the darkness, blending into the mob on Lazelle.

The man in the hairnet kept yelling. Yelling attracted attention in Sturgis, which had a cop on every corner with Vulcan hearing. Lights suddenly came on; the back alley offered better lighting than the field at Fenway Park.

Kevin saw and heard people running toward him, white light from flashlights bouncing on the ground, boots hitting pavement. He was told to freeze. Kevin stood with both hands in the air.

An officer told him to lie on the ground, hands behind his back. Kevin did as told. He heard the officer breathing heavily, Kevin looked up, it was the short chubby one. He was handcuffed with plastic ties, zipped tightly. The officer helped him to his feet as the female officer shone her flashlight on the unconscious guy.

"He has an ice pick in his hand," the female officer announced.

"Yeah, he was going to kill me with that thing," Kevin said.

"He's unconscious, blood on the back of his head. We need an ambulance." The female officer got on her radio. More officers arrived on foot.

"I was in there peeing, came out, and he attacked me. I knocked him out. I'm lucky to be alive," Kevin said. "Hey, you two are the ones who got me for open container!"

"Shut up," said the heavy breather.

The man in the hairnet came forward and stood next to Kevin. "There was another guy here, a big guy."

Kevin stayed quiet.

The unconscious man was groaning and tried to roll over. The officer stopped him by placing her foot between his shoulder blades. A third officer came forward, bent down, pulled the man's hands behind his back, and cuffed him with more plastic ties.

The guy on his belly—Kevin heard them call him "the suspect"—tried to stand. He planted his forehead on the ground while he went to both knees. The female officer ordered him to stay down. Again, she pressed her foot squarely between his shoulders. "Stay down, sir. You're under arrest."

A small crowd gathered as two police cars arrived, their sirens screaming. The ambulance was next just as the sirens were shut off. The paramedics went to work on the guy with the bleeding skull while pictures and notes were taken.

Two officers helped the suspect, his head now wrapped in a bandage, into the ambulance. Kevin finally saw the face of his attacker and said, "Hey, hey! That guy's camping across from me at the Buffalo Chip. I've seen him!"

A paramedic took the driver's seat, and the ambulance went down the alley. It passed a large crowd that had gathered at the Asian food tent behind the Oasis; assaults were good for business. Kevin was placed in one patrol car, the eyewitness in the other. Both cars went straight to the Sturgis police station.

Kevin, still cuffed, was taken to an office and told to sit. He did sit for a while. Restlessness, uncertainty, and nervousness got him fidgeting, then walking in circles and talking to himself. At least he wasn't thinking of Gloria and Skip doing it. What he was going to say, and what the hell actually happened?

Twenty minutes later, a rotund officer with a barrel chest in a khaki-colored uniform, more off-brown, opened the door and told Kevin to sit. He sat behind the desk. His name tag read, "Chief Brannigan." The arresting officer, the short heavy breather, also came into the office. He stood by the door with his arms crossed like a bouncer.

"You've had a busy night. Uncuff him, please," Chief Brannigan ordered the cop. The officer came forward behind Kevin and cut the plastic with a pair of scissors.

Kevin rubbed his wrists and hands. "Well, the open container, now that was total bullshit. But this…some guy tried to kill me. I just defended myself. I'm lucky to be alive."

"Yeah, we have his weapon. And you're lucky. The guy who attacked you is wanted for questioning regarding several murders."

Kevin's eyes grew wide. "No way."

Heavy breather interrupted. "Yeah, you're lucky. Tell us about the big guy who was with you. We have a witness who claims another guy was there. Who was he?"

"I don't know anything about a big guy." Kevin and the chief were looking eye to eye. "It was dark in that alley. Hell, I didn't even know the police were there until I heard Chubby Boy here breathing."

"Fuck you, you mouthy ass."

"Quiet! Mr. Buckles, we have a witness," the chief said.

Kevin shrugged. "Can't help you there, Chief. I knocked the guy out myself."

"Now that's total bullshit. There's no way you knocked that guy out by yourself," the short heavyset officer said.

"Sir?" Kevin was addressing the chief. "May I demonstrate?"

"Sure, I'd like to know." Chief Brannigan sat back in his chair and interlocked his fingers, his hands behind his head.

Kevin stood up and turned to the heavyset cop. "Come at me, Officer."

"Officer Dinkel," the cop said.

"Of course, Officer Dinkel. Come at me with your right arm extended, like you're going to stab me."

"Gladly." Officer Dinkel extended his right arm and rushed toward Kevin.

Kevin reached out with his right hand, crossing his own body, and grabbed the Dinkel's palm. He turned it clockwise hard, with a thrust down then up, as he stepped to the left. The movement locked Dinkel's wrist down and in. Dinkel's elbow bent as Kevin lifted the arm up behind Dinkel's back. This made Dinkel grab his right shoulder with his left hand, in obvious pain, and bend at the waist to avoid the pressure from the wrist and elbow lock. As Dinkel bent over—a natural reaction to avoid pain—Kevin slapped him hard on the back of the head with his left hand. Dinkel's forehead bounced off the chief's desk. Finding that bending didn't alleviate the pain, Dinkel then stood straight up to try to avoid the wristlock. He was howling in high-pitched agony. Kevin slapped him on the back of the head again and let him go.

"There you go," Kevin said.

Dinkel stood in front of the chief, a red mark on his forehead from having hit the desk. He was rubbing his wrist as sweat rolled down his face, his gray shirt black at the armpits.

"I see." Chief Brannigan was smiling.

Dinkel said, "Yeah, well, I wasn't ready."

"I didn't say, 'Ready, set, go to the guy who tried to kill me either," Kevin said.

"Explain the gouge in the back of his head then." Dinkel was breathing hard. "You didn't do that to the guy with your fist," he, still rubbing his wrist.

"I slapped you." Long pause. "I didn't use my fist." Kevin smiled. "But since you asked, when I was in the john, I stepped on something, picked it up, and saw that it was a rock. So, I took it with me and was going to throw it out. Probably not the most hygienic idea to pick up something from the floor of a urinal."

"Well, where's the rock?" Dinkel asked.

"Still in the alley, I guess. I was handcuffed. By you. And told to shut up. By you."

"Enough," the chief interjected.

No one spoke. The chief was thinking, the officer recovering, and Kevin in deep thought.

Kevin sat back down, across from the chief. "Why me?" he asked.

"Good question," Chief Brannigan said. "We'll find out later tonight. A detective from Indiana is on his way. He should have the answers. I imagine you just fit his profile."

Kevin was quiet.

"You're free to go," the chief said. "Officer Dinkel here will get your official statement. I imagine the detective from Indiana will want to talk with you as well."

"Okay, I'm not going anywhere until I head home on Friday."

"Dinkel will bring him to you. I think the Indiana cop is staying at the Chip too. Officer Dinkel, please have another officer take Kevin back to the campground when you're done."

The ride to the chip was quiet. Kevin leaned against the passenger side window and closed his eyes. Where have I seen that guy before? Why did he want to kill me? Why doesn't he like me? What did I do? All of these questions ran through his head.

The roar of motorcycles passing the cruiser opened his eyes. Kevin thought this city never shuts down. This rally was crazy and there are crazy people here. For the first time, Kevin wanted to go home.

T he call came at 1:00 a.m. Salas was standing by the east exit, watching people leave the concert grounds. He had maintained this position for four hours, with Ronnie straight across from him. Salas felt the vibration in his front pants pocket, pulled out his phone, and swiped it to answer. "Salas."

"Detective, Chief Brannigan here, Sturgis PD. We have a young man here in holding. Driver's license says an Albert Christianson. You told us to call you. You got lucky, Salas—he tried to kill someone tonight. It didn't go as planned."

"Keep him there! Don't try and talk to him," Salas yelled into the phone.

"He ain't talking" Brannigan replied.

"I'll be right there."

Salas put the phone back in his pocket and waved frantically at Ronnie. They met in the middle of the dirt road, an endless swarm of bodies passing them.

"They got him, Ronnie. He tried to kill someone tonight. He's at Sturgis PD."

"Did he kill someone?" Ronnie shot back.

"Nope, tried and missed. The vic got lucky and so did we."

The two men left the east exit to get to their car. Salas, in the lead, was looking ahead at the line of traffic.

"Shit, look at that line, Ronnie. We won't get the car out of here for an hour."

"If we had a motorcycle, Detective Salas, you could ride on the side of the road, bypass all the bikes, and get out of here ASAP. A car is just too wide to try."

Salas stopped the first motorcycle he could and put his badge in the face of the biker. "Need your bike. Police emergency."

"Right. You'll have to shoot me to get my bike, man," the burly biker said.

He tried another biker and another. Same result. "These guys would rather die than let you borrow their bike!" he exclaimed.

Salas continued to walk down the row of idling bikes that were in line to leave the Chip. Suddenly a bike cut in front of him, nearly hitting Ronnie. The rider made a sharp right to go down a dirt lane to a section of tents. The bike and biker leaned too far into the turn and laid the bike on its side. Salas jogged ahead to help. He immediately noticed the biker was a woman, a rather attractive one, sporting a pink bandana and butt-less leather chaps. As she stood, Salas read the print on her panties: "Crazy Bitch." She turned and faced Salas; her tank top bore the same slogan. Evidently, she was a crazy bitch.

Salas dusted off her shoulders and back as she stood next to her bike. She had dirty blonde hair, nice cheek bones and the perfect butt for those butt-less chaps. "You okay?"

"Yeah, I'm good! Pry too good!" Crazy Bitch was drunk.

"Miss…" Salas pulled out his badge and showed it to her. "Sorry, miss. I'm going to have to impound your motorcycle. You're obviously driving while intoxicated."

"I'm good to ride, Officer, and you can ride my Harley too!" Her right hand was rubbing Salas's chest.

Salas pushed her hand down? "Now, miss, I'll be taking your bike. This is for your own safety. You just go to your tent, and I'll get this back to you when you're sober. You're lucky. No arrest tonight."

"If you take my bike, what do I get? Got to have something to make sure you give me back my bike. Otherwise no deal, loose wheel."

Salas looked around and pulled out his wallet; he thought against giving her his driver's license or cell phone. He looked at Ronnie. "Here, you can have him. I've got to come back and get him later." He grabbed Ronnie by the elbow and was pushing him toward Crazy Bitch. Salas's grip had Ronnie flinching in pain.

"But Detective, I need to go…Ouch." Ronnie was more than flinching now.

"Deal!" Crazy Bitch held out her hand.

Salas shook it.

She walked away from Salas and her bike, arm in arm with Ronnie. She didn't look back. Ronnie did, his face pale.

Salas lifted the bike off its side and tossed his leg over the saddle, just like he'd watched several hundred bikers do over the past few days. When he hit the ignition button, the bike jerked forward, and his head snapped back.

"Shit, the clutch," he muttered. "Gas, clutch, brake, gear shift." He was squeezing both the clutch and the front brake, both his feet on the ground. When he hit the ignition button again, the engine roared, but the bike didn't move. He released the clutch; the bike jumped forward, the motor died, and his head snapped back again. "Slower on the clutch," he told himself. "It can't be that hard. That crazy bitch was doing it."

Salas was now moving. He slowly rode alongside the bikers who were patiently waiting their turn. The bikers were yelling, voicing their disapproval of Salas's cutting in line: "Asshole." "Great idea. Why didn't anyone else think of that?" "Dick."

First gear was a good speed for Salas. It was slow, and he held both feet out, ready to hit the ground in the event he fell over. He was thinking he needed a helmet and maybe shoulder pads. He made his way through the Chip exit and to the first stoplight. As he pulled up to light, he remembered to engage the clutch and release the throttle and planted his feet firmly on the ground. He felt a degree of accomplishment.

As he was parked under the streetlight, a Harley pulled up next to him on his right side. The bike had a large front fairing, a windshield, saddlebags, and a rear seat with a lady sitting in it. Salas had none of those extras.

The woman in the passenger seat looked at Salas and said. "Nice bike."

"Thanks," Salas replied.

The light turned green, and the couple sped off. The lady yelled, "Crazy bitch!"

Salas was focusing on his clutch and throttle. Slow on releasing the clutch and slow on the gas, and he was moving forward. The bike was roaring, the engine groaning in pain as Salas was now in full-throttle mode.

A biker pulled up at his left shoulder. "Shift that bitch, crazy bitch!" The biker was shifting his own bike, gassing the throttle, and leaving Salas in fumes.

Salas forgot he had more gears. He put in the clutch, shifted to second, and slowly released the clutch. The bike whined in appreciation, and he went faster.

He was thankful for a green light at Highway 79. He had to use the clutch again at the Full Throttle Saloon and the gas station exit. Stopping at the light, he placed both feet solidly on the ground, thankful to be upright. He was sweating. A biker pulled up, again on his left. The bike was similar to the one at the last light. Fairing, saddlebags, rear seat with a lady perched on it, her hands on the shoulders of her man. "Nice bike, crazy bitch," the lady proclaimed with a smile, nodding at the gas tank of Salas's bike.

Confused, Salas looked down at the side of his tank; it was painted pink, with bold black letters proclaiming, "Crazy Bitch." Salas lowered his head and groaned. The light turned green. The couple sped off, leaving Salas repeating to himself, "Slow on the clutch." The bike barely moved as he gave it more fuel.

Bike after bike passed Salas on his left. A biker pulled up to pass, slowed, looked over, and yelled, "Downshift, crazy bitch" over the roar off the exhausts. Salas was getting free riding lessons.

When he downshifted, the bike talked back loudly and again roared its approval. Salas then shifted to second gear and was able to get into third before attempting the stopping technique at the traffic light next to Jack's Campers. Salas engaged the clutch, downshifted, road for a while, engaged the clutch and downshifted to first gear, then squeezed the clutch as he came to a stop. Taking off was easier now, especially with no comments about his bike, just some awkward looks.

He used his blinker for the first time, turning left on 10th Street and arriving at the Sturgis Police Department. There was ample parking at two in the morning. Salas had to look at his feet to find the kickstand; he tried flipping it with his boot, gave up, then flipped it down with his left hand.

He took three steps to the police station, stopped, turned, and looked at the bike again. "Crazy Bitch," he said under his breath. "You've got to be shitting me." He shook his head as he opened the door to the Sturgis Police Department.

Chief Brannigan saw Salas enter and waved him through. Salas paused as the door to the hallway was hanging off the top hinges, the door unable to fully open or close. Brannigan approached. "Damn drunk biker slammed the door. He is in lock-up. Maintenance should be getting it fixed soon."

"You got the late shift Chief?" Salas asked.

"Midnight to 3 in the morning is the worst." Was Brannigan's reply.

They had Albert Christianson in a holding cell. The entrance to the cell was a metal door with a lone window. Salas had to bend down to look through the thick clear plastic.

Albert was sitting alone at a metal table that was screwed to the floor. He was wearing a leather jacket and had a white bandage taped to the back of his head; a pink stain peeked through the gauze. His hands were cuffed in plastic ties, his feet cuffed to the legs of the table. Brannigan gave Salas the lowdown on the arrest and on Kevin Buckles.

"How long has he been sitting there? Did you question him?" Salas asked.

"He's been in there over an hour," Brannigan said. "We read him his rights. He nodded that he understood them. Doesn't want an attorney. We asked him what happened, why he tried to kill the guy. Did he know who the guy was? Where did he get the ice pick? The only words he's spoken have been—and I quote— "Father didn't beat me."" The chief shrugged. "Don't know what he meant by that."

Salas said, "Go in there. Give him a prison jumpsuit. Tell him to change into it. And make sure you show him you're putting his clothes into an evidence bag."

Brannigan did as told. A few minutes later, he and two additional officers entered the cell, un-cuffed Albert, and took his clothes into evidence. After he put on a jumpsuit, they re-cuffed his hands in front and his feet to the table legs. Chief Brannigan was last one out of the holding cell; he shut the door then stood by Salas. "Now what?"

"We wait an hour. Let him think about his clothes. Did he have anything besides the pick and wallet on him?"

"Yeah, a cell phone. Here." Brannigan handed the cell to Salas. "What should we do with the clothes?"

"Send them to the lab for testing. They'll probably find blood in the lining and zippers of his jacket and on his boots. The blood will match the DBs in Sioux Falls and Fort Wayne. And have 'em test the pick too."

Salas turned on Albert's cell phone. Less than 20% charge was left. He clicked on contacts, only 14 names and numbers. Recent activity showed no calls over the past three weeks. He clicked on gallery. Several pictures popped up all arranged by month and year. August 2015 a picture of a lake. August 2015 a dark picture taken at night of a camper. August 2015 another picture taken at night but with a flash outlining 5 out houses. Salas recognized the scene. July 2015 some selfies of Albert posing, a biceps shot, pictures of him in a mirror. A picture of Albert's mother laying on the bed, it was another scene Salas had just witnessed. More selfies. August 2014 a shower facility looked like a campground as RVs were in the background. Salas quickly swiped the pictures to the preceding year. August 2013 a red tent in some trees on a grassy field. August 2012 a black Ford pick-up with a camper in a parking lot then a picture of a white bridge, in need of more paint, over a small stream. Albert had taken a few souvenirs, picture reminders of his trips to Sturgis.

At 4:05 a.m., Salas entered the holding cell. Albert was still sitting there. He was staring at his hands, which were resting on the table.

"Albert, how did you let Father kick your ass tonight?" Salas said it loudly, nearly yelling.

Albert flinched but didn't speak.

"Gave you a butt kicking, boy. Bet that made you piss your pants, didn't it?" Salas was just as loud with the second question.

"F-f-father didn't beat me! S-s-someone hit me from b-b-behind," Albert stuttered as he screamed at Salas, slamming his palms on the table.

"You had your chance, Albert, and once again Father outsmarted you. He beat you again."

"No!" He said very clearly, no stuttering.

"Yeah, the pick, Albert. We got blood samples from your pick, your leather jacket, and your boots. Seems you've been busy. In Fort Wayne. That was a good one. You picked Father there. Oh, and your pants tested positive for urine. Did you piss your pants, boy?"

Groaning, Albert struggled, trying to stand, his feet cuffed to the legs of the table.

"And then in Sioux Falls, you picked Father again, stuffed him under the camper. Let's see…you got Father in Valentine, Nebraska too. But Alliance, Nebraska, now there he got you."

"N-n-n-no, he didn't!" The stuttering was back.

"Why did you pick your mother, Albert?" Salas changed the pace.

Albert, his face softening, looked at Salas. "I didn't pick Mother. I came home from work and she was asleep." His face went pale as he spoke about his mother; his voice was quiet.

"Did you pick Father in Auburn, in the big Dodge pickup? You remember him, right? The asshole?"

"No. No."

"Why Father in Fort Wayne, at the campground? He seemed like he was different. Seemed like Father was getting better. Didn't you think Father was getting better?

Albert shook his head. "No. No."

"Where did you put Father in Fort Wayne? I can't recall. Under the camper?"

"No. No." Albert grinned at Salas

"Albert, I've met your father, Ted. You're right—he is an ass. I spoke with him Monday."

"No. No." Albert sat up straight and was looking Salas, making eye contact for the first time.

"Yes, I can see why you wanted to pick him. I agree with you, Albert. I wanted to pick him too." Salas let that sit for a few seconds. "You can tell me, Albert. How many times have you picked Father? How many?"

Albert didn't hesitate "No." He let out a sigh. "I want to sleep now."

Salas stood and placed his hand on Albert's shoulder then left the holding cell. Outside the cell Salas had to step by the maintenance man fixing the opposite door of the hallway. "Stan" was embroidered on his shirt above the left pec. Stan held a screw driver and was lifting the pin from the hinge of the metal door.

"Not too talkative." Salas looked at Chief Brannigan. "If you look at his cell phone, he has pictures of several of the crime scenes. That with the blood from the clothes and ice pick we should be able to tie him to at least two of the murders."

"Yeah, and we can hold him here on assault while you get the case together. That's one crazy son of a bitch there, Salas."

"Yeah, you got that right. He's a crazy bitch."

"All these guys look like his dad?" the chief asked.

"Yeah, all short, loud, maybe mouthy."

"Ha! Got it. I met the vic." Brannigan got the inside joke. "Man, you are one lucky son of a bitch Salas. How you could find one guy in this million-biker mess is like getting hit by lightning." Chief Brannigan slapped Salas on the back.

"I'd rather be lucky than good." Salas said. "I've gotta get some sleep. I'll be back later. We need him extradited to the state with the highest death-penalty rate."

"That'd be Nebraska, Detective. Here, sign this paperwork for me please while I have you in front of me."

Branningan turned to Officer Dinkle. "Dinkle, take Mr. Christensen," Brannigan pointed across the hall "to lock up. Put him in a cell by himself."

Officer Dinkle stepped past Stan as he laid his tools on the window sill and lifted the door from the hinges. Dinkle entered the room with Albert. Salas heard Dinkle say loudly "Well! Al. Bert, off your ass and on your feet. Looks like you are in a world of hurt son. Hope you like shitty food, a lumpy bed and being somebody's bitch. They are going to like a boy like you in the state pen." He grabbed Albert by the upper arm and pushed him into the hallway.

As if in slow motion, Salas watched Albert come through the door. Salas stood frozen as Albert quickly grabbed the screw driver from the window sill turned and thrust the screw driver upward under Dinkle's chin. With both hands on the screw driver Albert lifted Dinkel off the ground. Albert let out a warrior's cry as Dinkle's hands went to his chin, his feet dangling in the air.

Boom! Boom! Two shots rang out. Salas turned towards the noise and saw the smoke rolling out of the barrel of Brannigan's 357 Smith and Wesson.

The impact pushed Albert into Dinkle. Two direct hits between the shoulder blades. His spine crushed, his heart torn apart. Albert crumbled to the ground, the weight of Dinkle forcing Albert to his back. Dinkle rolled to his side. Both men dead.

Salas was first to speak. "You've gotta be shitting me."

"Damnit!", from Brannigan.

Stan, the maintenance man, covered his mouth and threw up in his hands.

Salas stood atop Albert. Blood was running out of the sides of Albert's mouth down to both ears. He looked as if he was smiling, the smile from the Joker in Batman.

Salas walked out of the station as the sun was hinting at rising in the east. His own crazy bitch was sitting there waiting for him. Mentally he reviewed his riding rules: clutch, throttle, shifter, downshift, upshift. Salas straddled the bike, backed into the street, squeezed the clutch, pushed the ignition button. The bike roared to life and he rode down Main Street.

He leaned into the left turn, then a smooth right in first gear, onto Highway 34/Lazelle Street, to the Chip.

Cruising in third gear in the crisp morning air, he passed the tall pines of the city park, a pond, and a fountain; Salas was enjoying the ride. To his left a bike pulled up; the tank had a Honda Goldwing chrome logo. Salas looked at the biker as the biker looked at Salas.

"Want to stop at the high school for breakfast?" Honda asked.

"No, thanks, bro. Gotta get the bike back to my wife," Salas said.

"Too bad." Honda sped off, turning left at Sturgis High School. A large sign read, HOME OF THE SCOOPERS.

Salas was forced to stop at the Chip security station to show his wristband. He didn't want to take a hand off the handlebars while the bike was in motion. Squeezing the clutch, he put the bike in first and showed the guard his wristband. Gently releasing the clutch—he didn't want to kill the motor—he rode into the Chip. He was in first gear the rest of the way.

He found the rental car. Stoner was in his familiar place, in the folding chair next to the tent. He had his sunglasses on and was smoking a hand-rolled joint. Salas parked the bike by the rental car, tried to sweep the kickstand with his foot, again gave up, and used his hand.

"Nice bike, bro. Nice bike." Stoner was smiling, the joint bobbing between his lips as he spoke.

"Thanks. Seen Ronnie?" Salas was still sitting on the bike.

"Crazy night, bro. Crazy night. He's in there." Stoner nodded to his tent.

Salas lifted his right leg over the back of the bike, straightened his jeans, and untucked his T-shirt. "In your tent?"

"The more unintelligent a man is, the less mysterious existence seems to him. Somebody—"

"Yeah, yeah, I know. Somebody famous said that once," Salas interrupted. He stood next to Stoner, bent at the waist, and peered inside the tent.

On the air mattress was Stoner's wife, topless, bottomless, and on her back. She was a hairy lady, old school. Her mouth wide open, she was snoring loudly. Next to her was Crazy Bitch, topless and bottomless, on her stomach, her back slowly and gently moving up and down. Her left hand was on Ronnie's belly. Ronnie's back was against the wall of the tent, his eyes closed. He was in his tighty whities. Salas couldn't tell if that was hair on Ronnie's chest or dirt.

"What the hell?" was all Salas could utter. He stood and looked at Stoner.

"Doris was on a mission, bro. Poor kid didn't stand a chance, not a chance."

"Doris? Is Doris your wife?"

"No, Ronnie brought Doris. Wendy's my wife. Like Peter Pan's Wendy."

"So, I don't...Ya know, I don't want to know." Salas turned and walked to the rental car.

"My Wendy, she likes a lady every once in a while, just every once in a while. And Ronnie, well, Doris was quite complimentary of the young man. Quite. Let's just say he gave Doris a happy day, a very happy day. Yes, Doris Day." Stoner laughed at that one.

Salas opened the rear door of the rental, lay on his back, and put his arm over his eyes. The last thing he heard was Stoner laughing

KEVIN

It was still dark when the cop dropped Kevin off in front of his RV. "Nice rig," the Officer said.

"Yeah, thanks for the ride." Even though he was almost murdered that night, Kevin was still miffed over the eighty-five bucks. He shut the door to the patrol car and watched the taillights turn the corner and disappear.

Kevin pulled out his cell phone, hit the flashlight app, and walked over to the Sons' campsite. It was empty. Tent gone, bikes gone, RJ and Deuce gone. To the right was the guy's tent, the guy who had tried to kill him. No motorcycle, just a tent.

Kevin pulled the beer cooler out from under the RV, grabbed two beers, and plopped down hard on the wooden bench of the picnic table. He downed the first one in three quick gulps, the beer dripping down the front of his shirt, then he opened the second can.

The outdoor RV lights popped on, making the campsite and parts of the road visible. Matt came out in boxers and a sweatshirt that read, "St. Cloud State Wrestling" across the chest.

"Where've you been?" he said, sitting down across from Kevin. "It's four in the morning."

Kevin was quiet then finally said, "You know that little guy who was in that tent?" He pointed across the road. His voice was much slower than usual, his volume nearly a whisper.

"No, what little guy?"

"The little guy on the bus who had the coughing fit."

Matt yawned a "Nope," then added, "I got nothing." He was stretching his arms, arching his back.

"Well, the little shit tried to kill me tonight."

"What do you mean *kill you?*"

"He had an ice pick and tried to stab me with it. Downtown Sturgis. RJ was there and knocked him out before he got me."

"RJ?"

"Yeah, RJ. He said the guy had been following me all week," Kevin continued, he walked Matt through the open container violation, the Oasis, the urinal, RJ, the police station, the ride back.

"Wow. Damn. Sorry, Uncle Kev. I should have been there. You okay?"

"Got to tell you, it's messing with my head." Kevin grabbed another beer and one for Matt. "And want more? Gloria is fucking my best friend."

"Skip?"

"Yup."

"Damn, bad day Kev."

The two men sat at the table, watching the sun rise, Kevin talking his way through the events of the evening, trying to put meaning to the whys. They had another beer.

The sun was above the horizon when they climbed the steps to the RV, leaving the empty beer cans on the table. Kevin glanced back at where RJ and Deuce's tent had been.

Matt whispered, "Try to get some sleep, Kev." He lifted the sheet and climbed into bed next to a sleeping Jessica.

Kevin, back in his room, sat on his bed, lay back, closed his eyes, and was asleep in seconds.

THURSDAY

At noon, Jerico opened the door to the RV, surprised everyone was still asleep. "What the hell, boys! You missed the entire morning." Jerico turned on the radio; Five Finger Death Punch's "Bad Company" was playing.

Matt untangled from Jessica and stood next to Jerico, sporting morning wood.

Jerico backed up a few steps. "Put that thing to sleep, Matt! We aren't that good of friends."

"You won't believe what happened last night." Matt opened the door to the RV and led Jerico outside. "Let Kevin and Jess sleep."

"I had a great night, thank you. A two-fer." Jerico followed Matt outside. He was using the Purell. "Remember those two ladies at Wall Drug?"

"Jerico, Kevin was almost murdered last night in Sturgis." That stopped Jerico's story.

The two men sat outside under the awning as Matt told Jerico what he knew.

"Holy shit," Jerico said.

A few minutes later, a Ford sedan, STURGIS PD on the door, parked next to the trailer. Three men got out. Chief Brannigan, in uniform, introduced himself. The officer looked tired. Matt recognized the other two, stood and extended his hand to the bald guy.

"We met at the bar the other night. I'm Matt." Matt shook his hand.

"Detective Mike Salas, Fort Wayne, Indiana, PD. Good to see you again, Matt." They shook hands. "This is Detective Higginbotham… Ronnie." Ronnie and Matt shook hands.

"Hey, Ronnie, last I saw you, you were feeling no pain." Matt chuckled. "This is Jerico." Jerico exchanged head nods but didn't stand or offer a hand.

"Please sit. I'll make some coffee." Matt pointed to the picnic table. Chief sat next to Jerico, their backs to the RV. Ronnie and Salas sat opposite them.

"Is Mr. Buckles here?" Brannigan asked Matt. "Detective Salas here needs a few words with him."

"Yeah," Matt said." He's sleeping. I'll get him."

The door to the RV opened. Jessica stepped out as Matt stepped in. Salas and Ronnie looked up. Jessica did her morning stretch on the top step. Arms above her head, T-shirt rising above her waist.

Salas whispered, "Damn."

Ronnie's mouth was wide open; he wasn't blinking.

"Oh, didn't know we had company." Jessica came down the steps and sat next to Ronnie. "I saw you at the bar, sweetie. Did you ever get that mojito?"

Ronnie's mouth was still open, but he didn't answer.

Kevin joined them while Matt poured coffee.

Salas introduced himself then gave Kevin the background about Albert, his father, his mother, and then told them of the shooting. The death of Albert and Officer Dinkle Everyone at the table listened in amazement.

After coffee, there were more questions about the profile and how Kevin fit the mold. Kevin showed the officers where the attacker had been camping. They gathered all of the belongings, leaving the tent up, and roped it off with yellow police tape. The three police officers left the RV for the drive back to the Sturgis police station, with Salas giving Kevin the green light to go back home to Minnesota. Albert was dead, it was over.

Jessica went back to work at three. Kevin, Matt, and Jerico opted to stay at the RV for their last night at Sturgis. Each wanted a quiet night—no partying, no people. Matt went to the main-stage bar at 1:00 a.m. and brought Jessica back while Jerico stayed at the RV with Kevin. Jerico was ignoring texts from Ann, the two Wall Drug girls, the masseuse, Julia, Sarah, and his regular girlfriends. He was tired and needed some sleep, but that wasn't going to happen.

Jessica changed into more appropriate clothes and joined Kevin, Matt, and Jerico at the picnic table. Kevin brought out a bottle of

Jameson and some shot glasses. They sat under the awning, listening to FM 98.6, classic rock, sipping the whiskey. The outdoor mood lights were on, they sat under a clear sky and a full moon.

Kevin drank to much to fast. Matt carried him inside the RV and put him to sleep.

It was just after one in the morning when head lights lit up the camp site. The car had Nebraska plates that Jerico recognized.

"Oh shit." Jerico said to Kevin.

"Hi Jerry! Thought I would surprise you for your last night in Sturgis." It was Whitney, Jerico's O'Neill, Nebraska girlfriend.

"Yeah you surprised me." Jerico responded.

"The security guy, Jake he knew exactly where your RV was." Whitney said.

Whitney joined Matt, Jerico and Jessica at the picnic table. At two in the morning Jerico and Whitney went inside the RV

At 2:30 Ann walked up to Jessica and gave her a hug as Jerico stepped out of the RV and sat at the table. Ann took a seat on Jerico's lap, kissing him on the neck, cheeks, and lips. She smelled of vanilla. Jerico shut his phone off, sanitized his hands and was looking at the door of the RV while trying to get Ann to stop.

Matt, Jessica, Jerico and Ann sat at the wooden table. They could see one lone figure walking along the dirt road.

"Hey! Is this where Jerico is staying?" It was a female voice. "The security guard said the RV was this way."

"That's me." Jerico responded as Sarah, with an H came into view. "Oh no." Jerico whispered.

"Thought I would never find you. Want to finish that conversation?" Sarah said, now seeing Ann, Matt and Jessica in the moon light.

"Who is this Jerry?" Ann said loudly.

It was at this time the door of the RV opened with Whitney taking the three steps to the ground. "You going to come back to bed Jerry?"

Jerico's response was cut short by more headlights from an approaching car. The high beams blinded the six people sitting and standing by the picnic table. The car stopped. Two people exited the automobile.

"Jerico is that you? Jake at Security told us how to find your camping spot! Feel like another threesome?" It was the two girls from Wall Drug.

Jerico lowered his head and said "Shit. I'm going to kill Jake."

"You asshole!" Ann yelled and slapped Jerico on the cheek then marched away.

'What a dick." Sarah said. "Wait up." She ran towards Ann.

"Jerry, you've never stopped have you!" Whitney said as she went back into the RV.

"We wanted a threesome not a six-some. Jerk-co." The two from Wall got back in their car and drove away.

Whitney slammed the door of the camper, stood in front of RV, stopped by Jerico and slapped him harder than Ann did. She went to her car and drove out of the camp area.

Matt looked at Jerry and said, "You've been busy."

That was their last night at Sturgis.

FRIDAY

"Kev, I'm staying with Jessica. She wants to ride through the hills for a day. Then I thought I'd give her a ride back to St. Louis. That okay?" Matt told Kevin while they finished loading the RV and trailer.

Kevin didn't hesitate. "Absolutely," he said slowly. "You only live once, Matty."

"Thanks, Kevin. You're the best."

"Could be a little awkward, though. Doesn't she have a guy in St. Louis?"

"Yeah. Might be a little awkward…. For him."

"Here, take your time. Be back in a week or two." Kevin had his wallet out and handed Matt a wad of bills.

Matt wrapped his arms around his uncle. "Love you, Uncle Kev," he said.

Jessica was standing in front of the RV talking to Shelly and Summer. Ann refused to come say good bye as long as Jerico was there.

"Thought you said No relationships Jessica?" Summer said giving Jess a hug.

"I also said I wanted someone to take care of me, Matt wants to do that." Jessica responded. "And neither of you paid attention to my order either."

Both girls laughed, said their good byes and left.

Jessica climbed aboard the Harley, her duffel bag bungee corded to the motorcycle. Matt knifed his leg between her body and the gas tank, started the motor and they were off. Jessica waved, blowing a kiss to Kevin.

Jerico gave Kevin a hug as well. He saddled the Big Dog riding down the same lane before Matt and Jessica were out of sight, leaving Kevin alone.

Kevin checked the trailer hitch, rechecked the straps and tie-downs on his Harley and golf cart, then raised the ramp and locked it. Once he was in the RV, he let the diesel motor idle for a bit then turned the wheel sharply and drove forward. The RV's front wheels flattened the area where RJ and Deuce's tent had been staked down. Kevin said "What the hell" as ran over the tent next to it, yellow tape and all.

After following the familiar path through Sturgis, Kevin took the left at I-90 then traveled up the south ramp and headed due east. Traffic was clear, with Kevin staying in the right line. Fifteen miles out of Sturgis, he saw two bikes approaching fast in his side mirror. The bikes were moving in unison, in and out of traffic, zigging and zagging as if one bike. They rode to the left of the RV. As he looked out the driver's-side window, one bike slowed, while the other sped past. Kevin looked down. RJ looked up at Kevin, nodded, and saluted him, two fingers to his forehead. Kevin smiled and saluted back. RJ hit the throttle and shot forward. By the time he drove past Rapid City, the two bikes were out of sight. Kevin doubted he would ever see them again.

Kevin thought of the short guy that tried to kill him, of RJ watching over him and saving his life. He thought of Matt and Jessica, hoping she was the girl he had been looking for. His thoughts went to Gloria and Skip. He knew Gloria was not his soul mate but maybe she was Skip's. He decided to break up with her when he got home. He wanted Skip and Gloria to work. And he decided, he was going to raise their rent.

Jerico got fuel in Rapid City following Highway 44 to Interior, South Dakota. He parked his bike under the big red-and-white tent and cleaned his hands. Inside the bar, he found Julia, who had a tray balanced on her palm. Jerico went up to her, placed both hands on her hips, and whispered in her ear, "Couldn't wait to see you. I missed your smile."

Julia kissed his cheek. "Oh, Big Rig. You just took my breath away."

"Life isn't about the number of breaths you take, Julia. It's about the moments that take your breath away."

"That line work?" she asked.

Jerico smiled. "You tell me."

"Yeah, I suppose it does." She kissed him again, this time on the lips, and went back to work.

Jerico took a stool at the end of the bar.

Ronnie called several hotels and found a vacancy. He and Salas spent Thursday night at the Hotel Alex Johnson in downtown Rapid City. Each had his own room, his own bed, his own air conditioner, and his own shower. Salas was thankful to sleep in anything other than a car.

Before their early-morning flight out of the Rapid City Regional Airport, they met in the hotel restaurant for breakfast. Salas was still finishing paper work—papers for the Sturgis PD and the state and federal government. Ronnie was finishing an omelet. Salas was deep in thought when a familiar voice grabbed his attention from the lobby. "Just a receipt, miss. Just a receipt. My thanks for your service. The best way to find yourself is to lose yourself in the service of others. Somebody famous said that once."

Salas stood and turned, looking for the voice. He saw the back of the man in a charcoal-gray Harris Tweed suit. He was walking out of the hotel, a woman at his side, they were holding hands. Salas watched as the couple turned left out of the hotel. They strolled in front of the restaurant window. Stoner looked in and smiled at Salas. He had bright-blue eyes, hair that matched the color of his three-piece suit, and a yellow bow tie that matched the kerchief in his breast pocket. Salas noted that he wore expensive shoes that shone in the morning sun. His wife's dress matched the tie and kerchief. Salas realized it was the first time he had seen Stoner's wife awake and with her clothes on.

Salas and Ronnie took the flight from Rapid City to Denver. After an hour layover, another two-and-a-half-hour flight they were back at the station in Fort Wayne by 3:00 p.m.

Salas sitting at his desk asked, "Ronnie, any plans for the weekend?"

"Actually, Detective Salas, I've planned a date for Saturday night in Indianapolis."

"A date? Indy? Who do you know there?"

"I'm seeing Doris, Detective Salas. She lives in Indianapolis."

"You're shitting me. That's great, Ronnie." Salas patted him on the back.

"Salas, Ronnie, in my office," Captain Green yelled from his desk. Ronnie waited for Salas to lead and followed him in.

"Salas, you are one lucky cop. Davis's wife convinced him to drop all charges. But listen to me smart ass you defined my orders. You didn't return when commanded." Green was yelling.

"I called you back, I left you a voice mail. Cell service was for shit. Couldn't load any emails. I tried Tom. It is in my report. And there were no charges to drop. I didn't do anything." Salas said.

"Whatever." Green waved him off. "Ronnie, where are my notes?" Green demanded turning his attention away from Salas.

"No notes, Tom," Ronnie said. "There won't be any notes."

"What the hell, Ronnie? You know the deal. And it's 'Captain Green' to you, young man," Green barked.

"Partners don't take notes on each other, Tom."

"Listen, you little sh—"

"Hey Captain. Let's focus on the results here. We nabbed a five-state serial killer, Tom." Salas interrupted. "And we don't even get a congrats? No press? Figured you'd want some press time on this. He's a murderer no one else could figure out. We got him, Ronnie did great work. Get off his ass." Salas was standing now, leaning against Captain Green's desk. His arms were extended, triceps flexed. "He's a good detective, Tom. Be proud of him."

Green was quiet as he looked Ronnie over. Ronnie's hair was combed back—no more bangs in his eyes. He was in blue jeans, black lace-up leather boots, and a black long-sleeve T-shirt with "FTS" on the chest.

"What happened in Sturgis, Ronnie?" Green asked.

"What happens in Sturgis stays in Sturgis. Right, Ronnie?"

"That's right, Detect…That's right, Salas."

Acknowledgments

Thank you to my loving wife and children for their enduring love, loyalty, encouragement and unwavering support.

I would also like to acknowledge The Buffalo Chip, The Broken Spoke Campground, The Full Throttle, and The Oasis for years of fun and memories.

The Black Hills are a hidden gem of Middle America with Spearfish Canyon Road my favorite ride.

A special thank you to my crew, they know who they are, and especially to my best friend and son who has made every ride to Sturgis a special memory and a great adventure.

About the Author

JJ Spain

JJ Spain is a 25-year veteran of the Sturgis Rally, bringing the Black Hills ride and the Sturgis experience to your fingertips.
Take the ride. Enjoy the rally.

Thank you for buying my book, I hope you enjoyed the ride!

Please take a minute and sign up at my website. I won't spam you, but will alert you when new books are released and when I am offering specials.

Visit MikeSalasNovels.com for the latest updates and a chance to win autographed books.

You can also follow me on Instagram MJ Spain
And Facebook
I look forward to seeing you there.

ALL BOOKS IN THE MIKE SALAS SERIES

IF YOU ENJOYED THIS BOOK OR FOUND IT USEFUL I'D BE VERY GRATEFUL IF YOU'D POST A SHORT REVIEW ON AMAZON. YOUR SUPPORT REALLY DOES MAKE A DIFFERENCE AND I READ ALL THE REVIEWS PERSONALLY, SO I CAN GET YOUR FEEDBACK.

THANKS AGAIN FOR YOUR SUPPORT!

9 798987 273302